Axiom: Collision
of Realms
Monica Red

MR

ISBN: 978-1-962293-01-3

Editing by First Editing

Cover Design: 100 Covers

Map Illustrator: Monica Red

Library of Congress

TO MY WHOLE WORLD, JOSEPHINE

Axiom Sea Periphery

188A25 Year Week 15,
Seventh day, Night

Tom counted to five before turning the corner of the stairs and shooting down. In response, a set of gunshots aimed toward him reverberated against the laminated walls. He pushed his back against the cold metal, holding his gun close to his chest. The lights on the staircase flickered red, reminding him of his horrible time in the Square. Water from the storm flowed through the building as the staircase door opened above him. For a second, he pointed his gun upward, but upon realizing it was Coba, he aimed downward once more, guarding his friend's entrance.

In a few seconds, Coba and another three Corrupts stood by him.

"The airship is circulating, Boss," Coba said into his ear. "We just need to find her."

Tom followed the metal railing with his eyes until it got lost in the darkness of the lower levels. Despite residing there for what seemed like forever, he rarely visited that section. He had no clue where to begin searching for Jess.

"Are you positive there is nothing on the other side?" Tom asked, trying to suppress the trembling in his hands as his imagination placed Jess in one of the isolation cells he'd had the pleasure of sleeping in a few times.

A series of shots interrupted them, causing them to retreat on the staircase.

"We blew up the other side when we got you out, Boss," Coba said, reloading his gun. "Only this photonic side remains, and I don't know for how long."

Tom looked at the inner deck. The steel wire that held the hanging prisoner cages rebounded with the wind, striking the once-electrified metal net that contained them. On the building across the middle opening, he could see the steel rods inside the concrete columns and beams of the few that remained standing, and a jumble of debris and metal formed piles of ruins.

"Let's move them," he said.

Tom opened fire downward while Coba and the other three descended until they got to the next landing. Tom rushed down while they covered him. A few shots crossed too close to him, deafening him for a moment. They reached the sixth level, their actual entry point.

It had taken almost three weeks, but according to Heli-3's research, that neutron's place showed only one weak point—the roof. From there, Tom made a rough plan. His people would conquer the seventh level by air, then descend to the lower levels. The group of five would expedite their descent for a rescue operation.

Tom couldn't risk losing that attack, and although Jess's life was his priority, he was well aware of the risk being taken by his people—and what it would mean to him if he were to lose against his half brother, Randall. With Marshall still out, the Corrupts' loyalty would lead them to choose the winning side.

Tom placed an explosive near the locked door, then hid with his men. In less than three seconds, a loud explosion rumbled through the staircase. Many ceiling pieces fell alongside broken railing sections. Tom looked up, shivering at the sight of the bent steel rods. He understood how weak the structure was, and how easily it would collapse.

Without waiting for the smoke to clear and with his gun ready, he walked to the inside perimeter of the Square. He inhaled, prepared for the repulsive odor of waste and heat that had made a home in his mind. But that night, what welcomed Tom was the smell of gunpowder and oils.

A shot hushed by his ear. He stepped back, leaning on the wall, and the extended view of the Square unfolded before him.

Throughout his months of imprisonment, he'd believed the bright light illuminating the buildings was a form of torture. Seeing the place in complete darkness made him realize the annoying light was for the guards—to give them hope.

Coba was right. Something had caused the collapse of the other two buildings. Amidst the fury of the sea below, the waves crashed into the lower floors, impacting the cells now missing their metal bars. Tom felt an icy shiver as he imagined the current state of the lower level where he used to reside.

The rain kept the hallways wet, reflecting the alarm's red lights—the only sign that something still worked in there.

As soon as Coba signaled him, Tom rushed to the first door and forced it open. He entered, gun in hand, but found an empty storage room. Coba followed a couple of seconds later, with the other three men behind.

"Photons!" Tom shouted.

There were too many doors and not much time. Outside, he could hear men running up. Despite their efforts, the rest of his Corrupts were still fighting to take over. Five men weren't enough to cover the entire Square, even if just one building remained standing.

"We have to split," he said to Coba. "If anyone finds her, get out with her. Start a fire as you exit. Understood?"

Coba's jaw set, but he nodded. Tom was their boss, and they wouldn't argue with him. Not in that moment, when he needed to find Jess before it was too late.

Chaos Realm

188Ch25 Year Week 13,
First day, Afternoon

"It's been almost three years, Yttri." Marshall sighed and sat down in his recliner, staring at the sky outside his window. "Nothing looks the same, and at the same time, nothing has changed."

Yttri shifted his weight to his other foot without taking his eyes off Marshall.

"Fine." Marshall waved his hand dismissively. "Things have changed, but not enough. I fear we'll lose this."

Yttri crossed his arms and took a step forward. "I understand..."

Marshall stared at him, his eyes mirroring the weight he felt on his shoulders. "The recent developments may jeopardize everything in Chaos, and well... we need to act now."

After a silly tune played by knocking on the door of his office, it opened, and a half-drunk Tom made his way in, laughing.

Tom was still younger than their father had been when Marshall first started remembering him—a tall, strong figure who had once made the world feel safe. Now, each time he saw his older brother, that resemblance cut deep, stirring the ache of everything he'd lost.

"Marshall!" Tom's joyful tone, along with his clumsy steps, made Yttri groan and move to the corner of the room. "Did you hear what we did this time? It was epic."

Tom let himself down on the leather couch, crossed his arms behind his head, and rested on them.

"Epic?" Marshall said as he leaned toward Tom. "That's a word you don't use often, and I have done a lot of things in my life."

Tom's laugh filled the office, free and rich, making Marshall hesitate to share his news first. It seemed appropriate to let Tom enjoy the day a little longer. "So," Marshall added, "are you going to share with us, or do we need to read it in our daily news tomorrow?"

Tom gave one fast look at Marshall and then at Yttri. In less than a second, he sat up, losing his smile, and with a groan, he held his head. "What the hell happened?"

Marshall nodded and signaled Yttri to close the door. He sometimes forgot that Tom wasn't Randall, and he was the most suspicious person he had ever met. Not that he blamed him, considering what he had experienced in recent years. Once a humble contractor with no aspirations, he now stood as a leader among the Corrupts, openly challenging Axiom's government and earning a spot on the Agency's most-wanted list.

As soon as the door was closed and Yttri blocked it, Marshall answered, "Well, the director of the Agency decided to retire and leave his son, Darius Ven-Larve, in charge."

Had this been his younger brother, Marshall would have known what to expect. However, his older brother, despite his limited experience in the family business and being visibly intoxicated, was hard to read—a fact that made Marshall both concerned and proud.

"Did he decide to leave, or was he forced to?" Tom asked, then corrected himself. "Of course he was kicked out. He wouldn't have stopped annoying my life voluntarily."

"Correct," Marshall said, walking to his desk.

"I'm not thinking clearly here," Tom said, holding his head with both hands. "Can we talk about it later? It doesn't seem like something we can change now—or at all."

"Time is imperative here, Tom." Marshall picked up his transmitter and ordered, "I need a very strong coffee and painkillers." He turned his attention back to his brother and exhaled. "This change raises two significant problems, and I'm confident you won't like either of them. And to be clear, I just learned about this issue this morning."

"It's very suspicious when you open with that," Tom said with a smile that almost got Marshall to relax.

He wanted to trust his brother and see him as a true partner. However, even with three years of serenity, healing the wound inflicted by Randall proved challenging.

Yttri greeted the shy waitress, who entered with a tray of medication boxes and a steamy cup, filling the room with a cozy aroma. Marshall pointed at the tray, smiling at Tom. Tom got up with a groan, and after sorting through the medicine boxes a few times, he picked two and swallowed them. Cup in hand, he sat before the desk. No one talked until the girl left and Yttri returned to his guarding position.

"Feeling better?" Marshall sat back but didn't wait for an answer. "This new guy, Darius Ven-Larve, is an authentic piece of art. He grew up with privileges beyond what you can imagine, enjoys suffering, and is not shy about showing it to his personal... umm... how would you call them, Yttri? Assistants? Friends? Family? Rumors say he used to be married, but the bride just vanished. You get the point. He has always worked in his father's shadow in the government, but he has some rational sense. Not dumb, and with an immense desire for power. Get the picture, Tom?"

"Yep." Tom took a sip of his coffee. "So basically, you."

Marshall couldn't avoid laughing as he obtained a glimpse of insight into why he disliked the idea of that new guy in charge. "Pretty much. Less handsome and nowhere near as intelligent as me, but close."

"So, the old director was just an idiot trying to ignore the issues at hand," Tom said. "Now we have a new guy eager to prove himself by hunting us and punishing Chaos? Sounds like a normal day to me."

"There is a minor detail, Tom." Marshall took a second to continue. "Darius has been seen with Bill and Radnar 88 in the past weeks. Your former friend has a tendency to aspire to greatness, just like Darius. Back when I first heard of this, it didn't matter, but now they made an announcement."

"An announcement?" Tom's voice lost the mocking tone. "I just blew up Bill's last political event—the Congress's annual dinner[1]. We blew up the garden, burned food and drinks—well, drank some of those. Then we blocked the main roads and streets for miles! When did he have time to—"

"I'm afraid the event may have been a distraction."

Tom remained quiet, holding the cup in his hands and keeping his eyes down. Once again, Marshall wished he knew him well enough to understand what he could be thinking.

"Distraction or not, they played their cards, Tom. The director and the Agency are long gone."

Tom looked up and stared at him. "What do you mean, the Agency?"

"Darius supposedly intends to unify Axiom. His initial major move involved demolishing the Agency's installations and converting agents into government officers. No more agents, no more research, no more commerce deals with Chaos."

"That's interesting." Tom looked at Yttri for a second. "But there is no way the Agency will allow it."

Marshall shook his head. "The Agency's power has been declining since the [2]Disruption, and after we blew up the Square," he shrugged his shoulders, "they have nothing. None of the other high-ranking agents will be able to fight this decision from their new director."

"All right. So what does this mean for us?"

Marshall sighed and fidgeted with a pen, spinning it among his fingers and avoiding Tom's eyes. His world was changing again, and he needed to gain control of something—anything—to remain sane.

"Well, obviously, two smaller enemies are better than a large one. Furthermore, there are some... umm... things they have kept in their buildings, Tom. We need them back."

"What are you talking about?"

"For years, I have been trying to find our father's belongings. They weren't in the Welder's tower, the mansion, or even in his cabin."

"Our father—Marshall, is this more serious than a bunch of old stuff? What could he possibly have that is so important?"

"It is important enough that the new director of the Agency is destroying their buildings as soon as possible." Marshall gave Yttri a quick look and lowered his voice. "Father figured out how to manipulate the energy wave, Tom. He discovered it years ago, and the only thing I know is that it had to do with the train system."

"I thought he didn't like the train system because of its extension, and possibly the lack of control over it."

"Ha! I see someone talked to you about it." Marshall leaned closer. "That's partially correct, but there is more. We need to recover his stuff before those new idiots in town do it."

Tom nodded and took a sip of his coffee. "Do you want to go full blast into the Agency, then? I kind of like it."

Marshall smiled at the idea. No one would expect it, and it would bring fear into the city. However, big acts like these rarely left permanent results, and he couldn't jeopardize the outcome. Also, he still needed to mention the other important issue.

"Although it sounds tempting, we have to be more precise in this. I don't want them knowing how much power they have in their hands."

"If you want to recover all the items they stole from your—our father, it may be hard to park at the front with a moving crew in secret. You just told me they wiped clean at least three properties from him."

"Well, as much as I would love to get everything back, I'm not that greedy. We just need to recover Father's logbook—and only the one from the 188CH9, right before he closed the tracks."

Yttri crossed his arms and took a small step forward.

"Relax, Yttri, that's where I'm going now. Don't worry, we have no secrets here."

"So there is more?" Tom asked, extending his legs and getting comfortable in the chair. "Of course, there is always more."

MARSHALL PAUSED BRIEFLY TO prepare for the next part of the news.

"I'm sure they don't know about the logbook," he said, "but I'm certain they are trying to find our father's research. They are looking for someone to do it for them."

"Just get to the point, Marshall. My head may be clearer, but it isn't—"

"They are setting a trap for Jess."

This time, Marshall knew exactly what to expect from Tom. He set the cup on the desk as his expression darkened and his tone lowered when he leaned against the desk. "Say that again."

"This is the thing, Tom. The Agency knows how Jess worked for my father and me, and—"

"She didn't work for your father. She was doing an undercover mission to protect your ass."

Marshall sighed and nodded. "Correct, but... the problem is how much she could have learned by doing it. No one has the details of her mission, but they are aware that she had contact with me and my father for over a year. You have to understand that she is the best agent to find anything against us."

"She isn't an agent anymore."

"Right, and as far as I'm aware, no one has seen her for years."

"Two years, eleven months, seventeen days, and..." He looked at the clock on the wall before continuing, "five hours and a half... but who's counting?"

"You need to find her."

"Are you nuts? No! I won't put her life in danger, Marshall." Tom stood up and paced around the room, causing Yttri to step closer to Marshall.

"Her life is in danger now." Marshall inhaled and spun the pen on his desk. "They are the ones looking for her, and their reach is extensive. It's a matter of time before they get her."

"How do you know?" Tom's voice rose as he moved closer to the desk. "I can barely see the relation between the photonic book you want and her. How could you possibly think those two will—"

"Bill made another announcement. It came just half an hour before you arrived and he—believe me—made sure we, the Corrupts, heard it."

Tom crossed his arms and stared at him. His eyes resembled the way his father used to challenge him from time to time when they weren't in full agreement, and it just made Marshall more aware of his coming disclosure.

"Here," he said, glancing at Yttri, who switched on a vintage radio recorder.

The room buzzed with static that soon changed into high pitch and unintelligible voices as he rewound the tape on the top of the wooden box.

"Mr. Hiem-Sagac," the voice of a reporter said, "last night's attack seemed more personal than the previous ones. Would you agree with this?"

"What Tom Umbrar-Ment does mirrors his rotten character," Bill said. "Just like his entire family."

"Is there a counterattack coming?" the reporter asked. "The residents of Main City and Sector 8 are concerned that—"

"There should be no concern," Bill interrupted him. "I'm not at all like Umbrar-Ment. I have principles and ethical standards that prohibit me from..."

Tom groaned loudly, shaking his head and crossing his arms. "What the void, Marshall? He sounds just like any other—"

"Listen, Tom!" Marshall said right before Bill's recording got to the most important part.

"...she came to me, begging for my help. The way she looked mortified me and my wife; scared and sick, and pregnant."

The reporter's voice, filled with alarm, asked, "Are you saying Umbrar-Ment is going to be a father?"

"Yes, exactly that," Bill said. "More importantly, my family and I will make sure his wife and unborn child are safe."

Tom pointed at the radio and yelled, "What the hell is he talking about? If he hurts Jess, I will—"

"Jess is not with him, Tom," Marshall said as he stood up in front of him. "That message is not for you. Think. Who is he really talking to? How could he possibly know about your marriage?"

"How does he—" Tom kept his voice loud as he paced faster toward the door. "I don't care! But whoever told him is dead. Dead, Marshall."

Marshall blocked Tom, and Yttri moved behind him. "It's all right, Yttri. He's just not thinking clearly."

"You can't stop me, Marshall," Tom said. "I will kill him this time. I don't care about your plan. I will kill him."

"Maybe, maybe not, but first you need to help Jess—the one who is being set up here."

"What are you talking—"

"Like I told you, they are looking for her. The trap is for Jess. Think! Bill has no way of knowing about your marriage, but he witnessed how you two feel about each other. You almost killed him because of what he did to her. And Jess? Well, he had years to watch her interact with you. He knows the best way to make her come out of hiding is by breaking her. You could have moved on to a new wife and started a family. I'll bet it was Darius's idea to start with her heart."

"How could you possibly get all of this from that message? Bill said he has my wife. Jess is my wife."

"Your pregnant wife, to be more specific. I'm certain you would know if Jess was expecting your baby. Or did I miss something?"

Tom rolled his eyes. "You know I haven't seen her."

"Then she can't be your pregnant wife. The problem is, Jess has no way of knowing if you are having a child with someone else. He also said she went to him for help."

"Jess would never look for his help." Tom sat down and held his head in his hands. "What if he has Jess? She could have moved on, too."

Marshall sighed and crouched in front of Tom. "That's the thing, Tom. He is bluffing. He doesn't have her."

Tom's expression made Yttri move closer to him, ready to grab Tom if necessary.

"Listen to the message and remember how Bill acts. He would never use your marriage with his sister openly. He would never accept your marriage, and even less if Jess was pregnant. That would destroy the reputation as an upstanding man he has so eagerly created. Plus, his mother would never approve of such a display and scandal—and he still lives with her. Whoever he has is not Jess. I met her. She wouldn't work with her brother... not even before the wedding fiasco!"

Tom's gaze shifted from Yttri to Marshall. "Let's say you are right. How is this a trap for Jess? He's talking about my family."

"Exactly!" Marshall moved back and sat on the couch in front of Tom. "Bill only knows two things about his sister. First, she worked with me and my father, and second, she has feelings for you. You are Jess's weakness. You know it. Isn't this the reason you are the only one who has never tried to find her?"

Tom closed his eyes and slowly shook his head. "Bill needs her to find the stupid things from our father, and he is using me? He is trying to make her look for me?"

"He has a win-win situation." Marshall shifted to get comfortable. "I don't think he believes for a second that Jess is with you. Your behavior has proved that much to him."

Tom stared at Marshall but said nothing. He had warned him before about attacking Bill, but now wasn't the time to mention it.

"Jess knows her brother and how much you two hate each other. There is no way Bill would protect your family. If that baby was yours, I'd be getting the fuzzball from his hands immediately—something I can see Jess doing. Sacrifice and all. Bill is in a great position. He either destroys his sister's heart, or he just confirms she is with you and tries something else."

Tom stood up again, pushing his hair back. "Son of the void."

"See the point now?" Marshall asked. "This isn't Bill's final message, and the next one may not be for us."

Tom crossed his arms and stopped moving. "Although I'm going to kill Bill, this is also very convenient for you."

Marshall moved his head from side to side. "Would it be easier to find the logbook with someone from the Agency who also worked with the person who hid it in the first place? Yes."

"Marshall, I won't put Jess in danger for a—" Tom started, but Marshall didn't let him finish.

"Nevertheless, I like Jess. I even tried to protect her before all this mess started, and I'll do it again. Especially now that I'm aware of how much she means to my brother."

Tom took a step closer to Marshall. "Why do you care about her? And don't pretend it's because of me. We didn't know about our family situation before—"

"Well, I knew who you were, but had instructions to never look for you. I agree, though. I had no idea you were in love with my ex-fiancée, but..."

Marshall looked at Yttri, who sat down and stared into the distance, so he continued. "I'm not in love with Jess, if that's what you're implying."

Marshall felt a familiar hard knot growing in his throat—one he hated so much, one that still hurt. "A long time ago, I was in love with someone. She was..." He had to stop as he swallowed the tears threatening to escape his eyes and smiled at no one. "Well, you understand how that feels. And like my father and you, I tried to leave her to protect her from our lifestyle... or so I thought."

Marshall looked at Yttri, who was avoiding his gaze. "I had problems with her older brother, and we fought a lot until one day she got in the middle and... well, it is hard to deny a last wish to someone you love."

"Yttri?" Tom said so quietly that Marshall doubted the other man in the room heard him, so he just nodded.

"I promised Darmy that I would take care of her siblings, and he promised he would take care of me."

Marshall moved back to his desk and sat down, taking his time to regain his composure and letting his memories submerge themselves again—buried where they should remain. Tom asked nothing, simply waited, which Marshall appreciated more than his brother would ever understand.

"So yes. I want the logbook, but Jess is the priority."

Tom nodded and walked toward the door, where he stopped. "Make sure He-li-3 is ready to meet me in Sector 15."

"Yttri will go with—"

"No," Tom said, opening the door. "I'll work with my people, as usual."

"That is ridiculous. Mer-80 and Coba-27 aren't the best for this mission."

"And the huge guy with tattoos all over his skull is the perfect one to remain unnoticed?" Tom stepped out and, from the hallway, continued, "I'll take my people and keep you posted."

Marshall picked up the pen on his desk and stared at it for a while. He didn't like not having control of the situation, especially one as important as this. He hadn't lied about Jess—she was the priority—but he knew her. Jess's life wasn't as important to her as it was to his brother.

He also avoided mentioning the reason he had kept the logbook out of his reach for years. At any time, he could have infiltrated the Agency and, with the luxury of time on his side, he could have found it. He didn't know Tom that well then.

Now he was certain his brother suffered the same disorder as their father, and he hoped Tom could decode his father's writing. It was a long shot, but having the ability to see with the same dyslexic perspective might be the difference in finally understanding his father's entire plan.

"We need to be ready to act, Yttri."

Yttri stood up.

Marshall looked at the window behind his desk. "Let's ensure we are just a step behind him."

1. **Congress's annual dinner**; the most pivotal event in Axiom due to its gathering of all Congress members. The annual dinner in Axiom brings together all members of the Congress - including activists, reactors, and passives - to showcase their yearly progress and propose initiatives for the upcoming year. Attendance to the event is restricted to prestigious Elite Social families, although a handful of Chaos members have also been graciously included to contribute to the noble cause of fostering harmony in the realms.

2. **Disruption**, tragic incident with the Barrier that occurred on 188A22 Year Week 18, First Day. The automobile accident resulted in a collision between Chaos and Axiom, where sections of the real collapse into each other, causing significant damage in terms of hundreds of injuries, several fatalities, and millions of dollars in economic losses.

3

CHAOS REALM

PETER'S LEG STILL HUNG from the window of Holm's apartment when the old man's shouting filled the house.

"He's in a terrible mood," Phoebe said with a smile that Peter had learned was anything but friendly.

"Any idea of the reason?" he dared to ask as he pulled himself into the small space. Less than a month had passed since his previous visit, and the surroundings had changed. The once-cozy home now looked like an operations center, full of mechanisms and beeping machines, along with boxes and files all over the floor.

"You didn't hear the news in Axiom?" Phoebe pointed at a screen that had a bunch of small lights flashing all over it.

"Get inside here!" Holm yelled again, making Peter roll his eyes but walk toward him.

They weren't fans of each other. The only reason they worked together was what had happened before the Disruption—and Jess. Not for the first time, Peter wondered how different he would be if he had taken a different path that night. If Marshall hadn't gotten to him first and drugged him, forcing him into a relapse and months of therapy afterward.

"What's the deal, Holm?" Peter asked from the office door. "I'm sorry, but I can't come whenever you ask. It's important that we maintain our secrecy here."

"As if I didn't know that, neutron! This is a major issue. What about the director's retirement?"

Peter groaned, taking a seat in the small chair behind the monitors that covered half of Holm's face. "I'm aware of that."

"That's all? What are we going to do about it?"

"What can I do about it, Holm?" Peter tried to remain calm. He hated the new director for personal reasons. Reasons everyone in that house knew, and probably made them more concerned about the future. "It's not like I can make sure he stays working. His son isn't easy to—"

"His son is destroying the Agency, Peter!" Holm stood up so abruptly that two of the monitors fell, and one threatened to follow, shaking in its mountings. "That son of the Maker is taking everything we built—everything we fought for—and tossing it to the stupid government of Axiom. Didn't you hear that part?"

Peter grabbed his hair at the side of his head and rested his forehead on his knees. "Of course I did, but again, what the photons can we do? It's a done deal. They are clearing and evacuating every building as we speak. They already relocated Amy to one station in Sector 8. It's a matter of days until they move me."

"We have to be missing something," Holm said, moving toward the small window in his office. "I just can't figure..." He sighed. "I'm getting old for this."

"You are old," Phoebe said from the doorway. "However, that isn't the problem, right, Holm?"

The old man frowned and turned back to the window.

"So, what is the problem?" Peter asked. The striking absence of joy from her face answered for her. "Is Jess all right?"

Phoebe lifted her shoulders and exhaled. "I don't know, but apparently Tom is doing great."

"What do you mean?" Peter stood up. "What did that son of the void do now?"

He had never trusted Tom, and he disliked him even more after he left them. They had jeopardized everything to save him, and instead of staying with them to fix what he destroyed, he just walked away. Jess was so wrong about him. She swore he had the answers they needed about the Disruption. She believed in him, and because of him, she was nowhere to be found.

"Well, according to Bill, Tom's wife ran away from him and asked Bill to protect her—she and her unborn child."

Peter glanced at Holm, who continued to stare out the window. "That's not Jess," he said to Phoebe as a weight lifted from his shoulders. Now he was certain Jess wasn't with Tom. "She hates her brother. She wouldn't have run to him—"

"Of course not." Phoebe's voice was dry and edgy. "But this will break her heart. Something you know about, right?"

Peter shook his head but didn't argue. Jess had never loved him, even when they went out a few times. She cared for him and made sure he got clean from his addiction while covering the real reason for his absence. Phoebe preferred to believe he broke Jess's heart instead. That way, Tom wouldn't seem so special. Peter knew better. After all, he had tried to start a relationship with her many years ago.

"So, what do we do?" he said to no one in particular.

"Obviously," Holm turned to him, "we find Jess before they do. Who knows what her brother wants from her this time."

Finding Jess was out of the question, but their efforts over the past few years had been unsuccessful. She was an amazing agent and had specialized in undercover jobs. If she didn't want to be found, Peter doubted they could do it.

"You and Millie have to stay in your new positions," Phoebe said. "You'll update us if there's anything new."

Peter nodded but remained quiet. He would follow the instructions but couldn't speak for Millie. Recently, she had started to question their alliance. She was right in her concerns, but she could become a hazard to their mission: restoring the Barrier. He wanted to keep this from Holm and Phoebe. They already had their questions about him, and Millie wasn't someone they had met in the past.

Not for the first time, he wished Jess was around—or that he had a way to find her.

4

Axiom Realm

Tom's pounding headache vanished as they got ready to cross to Axiom, but it didn't bring him much relief. Marshall's warning about Jess haunted his mind. Although Tom hadn't looked for her, Marshall's insinuations were deceptive. There was no secret code between them. Tom just feared that if he didn't find her, it would confirm that she wanted nothing to do with him—and that he would make things worse for her.

"Mer should go first, boss," Coda said at Tom's side while they walked toward the building that would turn into a portal.

"Ladies first?" Tom said. As expected, Mer frowned at him.

Those two were a peculiar pair. Tom ignored the reason they liked to work together, but it wasn't a romantic one. Coda's heart died with his wife when the Chaos government neglect forced him to join the Corrupts, and rumors said Mer had no heart. Tom had accidentally learned the truth about Mer, and he understood her resentment towards relationships.

"I'll say few will expect such a sight in Axiom," Coba said with a wide smile that made his round face look joyful, in contrast to his usual grumpiness.

He was right, though. Mer was as tall and strong as Tom, if not stronger. She kept her hair blazed short, probably to draw more attention to her eyes, which, although pretty, had tattoos on the eyelids.

"Too much talk," she said, taking out a metal sprocket from her pocket and pulling her shotgun over her shoulder. "Let's move."

Tom lifted his shoulders, smiling at Coba, who just shook his head. "Follow close, Coba," he said, taking a pocket watch out of his jacket.

Every time he crossed realms, Jess and their first visit to Chaos came to mind. Unlike the Corrupts, Jess had a special key to open the portals—a chain with a cuckoo clock he had given her as a present when they were younger. He learned she had chosen it because it had a special meaning for her. His wasn't that special.

The Corrupts didn't have a welder to create keys. Instead, they obtained them illegally from agents and used them to infuse other metallic objects. Most lacked power and only lasted a round trip. As chief, he possessed an original one that a questionable agent had sold to the Corrupts years ago.

The now-familiar light illuminated the street, and Mer, with no hesitation, walked through it. Tom held his breath out of habit and crossed soon after.

Axiom's alley was darker than Chaos's streets, as expected for that realm's midnight. Nevertheless, the sound of sirens and cars driving by wasn't the norm, and the loud shouting of someone close by put Tom's nerves on edge.

Although he had visited Axiom yesterday, he had arrived in another sector, several hours north. The last time he stepped into Sector 15 was after he escaped the Square. The reason to travel to that sector was to talk to the Tracker, Heli-3. He might be capable of helping him find Jess.

However, Marshall was right—things were changing, and neither of them liked it. The home realm of his childhood was long gone. In only a few minutes there, Tom confirmed they were running out of time.

Jess's life had been in danger since she joined the Agency many years ago. The biggest difference now was her brother. Bill was an idiot but had become a powerful politician in Axiom, and his new friends shared his narcissism and lack of values. Bill finally had the power to get anything he desired without considering the consequences.

Tom's life wasn't the most honest, but at least people knew who the Corrupts were and their intentions. If you wanted trouble, you joined them. Over the years Tom spent with them, he discovered how much they shared—minus the fear and torture, the ideals for the future of both realms were similar. They also questioned the same principles from Axiom he had been struggling to accept throughout his life.

"He-li-3 should have been here already," Mer-30 said, walking to the far end of the alley.

"Punctuality is not his forte," Coda-27 replied while packing his sack at Tom's side.

Tom walked toward Mer and looked at both sides of the crossing street. A familiar essence flowed in the air, but he couldn't put a name to it.

"It has to be an accident," he said, trying to find a logical reason for the constant shine of patrol lights and what seemed to be a fire glow on the horizon.

"Boss," Coba said, rushing to him. "You need to stay back here. We got this."

Tom waved off his warning, but Mer blocked his way. He knew it was a lost battle. Those two were always overprotective toward him, overreacting to everything. He knew it had to do with the way they lost his father, Lezar Mos-lum 115, the former chief of the Corrupts—the person they used to protect before him.

Once Tom joined forces with Marshall, Mer and Coba volunteered to work with him. According to both, Tom had saved them, and they owed him their lives. He didn't see it that way, but at the beginning, he didn't care about anyone or anything. He just let them do whatever they wanted. His conscience shifted when he started to work on missions, and they became his people. He had grown to appreciate them, despite their strange looks and ways.

"Something is off," Mer said. "I don't know if we should wait for the Tracker here."

"Let me try to reach him," Coba said, taking a transmitter out of his sack.

Tom noticed a car turning into the crossing street ahead of them. "Photons!" he said, pushing Mer back. "Stay hidden."

Her expression was easy to read, but he didn't care. His peculiar eye color was a hazard, but he might have a chance. She would never pass as an Axiom native.

The car stopped in front of the alley, blocking the way out. A guy wearing an official's uniform jumped down from the car and pointed a flashlight at them.

"I can just shoot him," Coba said.

"Officer," Tom said cheerfully, pulling his hat down, pretending the light bothered his eyes. "I'm so glad to see you. We appear to be lost."

The officer stopped near Tom, shining the light in Coba's eyes, then back at Tom, who frowned and covered his face.

"I need to see your face, sir," the officer said to Tom as he moved his other hand to his belt.

"Well, I wish you wouldn't try to blind me with that light," Tom said, maintaining his smile until he heard the second door of the car closing and the footsteps of another person approaching.

"You two are breaking the curfew," the new officer said. Tom could only see his silhouette, but his new lifestyle had taught him how to recognize by the shape and size the gun he was pointing at them.

"A curfew?" Tom asked, moving his hand away from his face. "That's interesting. Since when has there been a curfew here?"

The first officer realized who he was talking to, but it was too late to inform his partner. Mer jumped from the shadows and kicked the gun from the second officer's hand. At the same time, Coba smashed the flashlight from the other officer's hand and tossed him against the wall.

"The chief asked you a question," Coba said in the officer's ear. "I suggest that you answer."

The other officer attempted to approach Mer. She swiftly grabbed his hair and pushed his head against the hard stone of the street, where he remained motionless.

"You can't be here," the officer said, still in Coba's hands.

Tom moved closer and touched Coba's shoulder, who hesitated, then let the guy go. Once he was free, Tom noticed the short height and weak body—just a young boy. Still, the hate in his eyes was undeniable. Something Tom needed to get used to. Most days, he forgot how much the people of Axiom despised Chaos, just because they had learned to blame them for everything. He also kept trying to ignore how Axiom now blamed him for the Disruption and everything that happened after. They loathed him.

"You'll regret this," he said to Tom, but his voice lacked authority.

"I'll regret what?" Tom asked, but he never got an answer.

A speeding car turned into the crossing street, and a second later, Tom's instinct took over before his mind registered the reason. "Get down!" he yelled. A growing whistle filled the alley at the same time Tom pushed the officer down. He lifted his eyes just in time to see the missile hit the car.

A force lifted the vehicle up on two wheels, blocking the alley. It held up for a second before turning into flames, and the explosion that followed propelled Tom backward into the street.

For a moment, he stared at the car burning. The officer who had been at his side a second ago now lay a few meters inside the alley. Tom's ears were buzzing, but still, he recognized the sound of an engine approaching them.

He got up on his knees, retrieving his gun from the carrier as if by second nature—a far cry from how he did it the first time he had tried to draw a gun. He smiled at himself, thankful that neither Mer nor Coba had been there. It was embarrassing enough thinking that Jess had witnessed how much of a neutron-head he had been.

A new vehicle stopped right behind the officer's car, and when the driver's door opened, Tom pointed his gun at it. Mer moved faster and stood up, pointing her shotgun while Coba slid closer to Tom.

"Don't shoot!" A familiar high-pitched voice reached Tom's semi-blocked ears. "It's me. Just me." Heli-3 peeked from the door with his hands up.

"What the photons?" Mer said, putting her gun down. "You want to get killed?"

"No!" Heli-3 yelled. "So we better go now."

He waved his hands, looking back and forth on the street. "This is going down the crack too fast."

Once Tom stood up, Heli-3 jumped back into the driver's seat, his hands shaking. He had always been a nervous guy, but right there, he seemed to be in the middle of a panic attack. Still, without hesitation, they all climbed into the car.

After Tom closed the door, Heli-3 maneuvered around the burning vehicle and accelerated forward at full speed. He didn't care about hitting the side of the car and kept driving, scraping it until Tom reached over and moved the wheel so they stopped, sending sparks all over the street.

"What's going on?" Coda yelled from the back, holding the seat in front of him. "You finally lost it?"

A hysterical laugh escaped Heli-3, who immediately refocused on the road. "This went down today. I couldn't believe it—I tried to tell Marshall to have you cross somewhere else. I was going to meet you there... if I was alive—dear Maker, I don't know if we'll make it out of here."

"What went down?" Tom asked, trying to keep his tone even.

"Everything!" Heli-3 said, turning into a smaller street, the centrifugal force sending Tom, Mer, and Coda sliding to the side of the car.

"Heli!" Mer yelled, hitting the back of his head. "Stop the nonsense! What do you—"

Mer didn't finish. Ahead of them, the street opened, allowing them to see the sector. Tom used to build over there, and although he couldn't remember the entire city's map, he had a good idea of how it was supposed to look. The sector sat on a hill, granting most of the buildings a view of the forest that blocked Sector 13—a less desirable place to live.

But instead of a thick mass of trees, the forest was now an inferno of smoke and flames as people evacuated the buildings. The essence Tom had perceived in the alley became stronger, and now without question, he knew what it was: burning oil and wood.

"In the Maker's name," Coba said, pulling himself forward, "what happened?"

"Are you driving there?" Mer asked. "That is suicide!"

Heli-3 nodded, squeezing his hands on the wheel. "Well, the other way is worse. The government blocked everything—streets, highways, even sewers—all tracked. They are checking everyone. If they lived here before, they let them out. If not, they take them in the wrong direction."

"So you think our chances are better in the fire?" Coba asked. "We can just go back to Chaos."

"No, we can't!" Heli-3 turned to the back passengers without stopping the car. "The fire is sucking the energy wave—like a vacuum! You can't fight against that force. That's how they reached you before me. You opened a portal in the right direction. They noticed the particles crossing over."

"How did they stop the energy wave?" Mer asked, looking out the window.

"Stop," Tom said, and when Heli-3 turned to him, looking confused, he raised his voice. "Stop the car now!"

Heli-3 pushed the brake so hard that Coba's body made Tom's seat bump forward, and he had to use both hands to stop himself from hitting the windshield.

"Sir! We can't stop. I'm sure they are behind us! We need to—"

"We need to go," Tom said, opening his door, "but you are going to kill us before they reach us."

"What? I would never..."

Tom didn't wait and simply walked to the driver's side of the car. "You can't drive like this, Heli," he said, opening the driver's door. "Move over."

Heli-3 briefly looked confused, then slid down, hitting the board on his way, turning off the heater and switching on the radio. "Sorry," he said as he made it to the seat. "I just... sorry, Sir. Can't believe how fast it all came down."

Tom took a second to look ahead of him. It wasn't the first time he'd seen a city in flames, but when it had happened before, it had been his doing. He controlled them and ensured most had an escape, though. He turned around, and the lights of the patrols and streetlamps appeared dim compared to the view ahead.

"Tell me what happened," Tom said as he climbed into the car and started driving.

Heli-3 took a deep breath and explained—as much with his hands as with his words. "The alarms went off this afternoon. The radio said a wildfire was spreading, and we needed to evacuate. At first, people just moved slowly, but then things got nasty." He looked into the distance. "You see, the smoke hit us first. It was so thick it made the day darker, and the smell... it reminds me of my shop in Chaos. People panicked and tried to run away. That's when I got worried. They couldn't just leave the sector. A bunch of officers' cars blocked the roads, and before they allowed anyone out, they checked them. Like asking for papers and all!"

Tom drove in a zigzag, avoiding any cars behind, but had to keep driving toward the fire—not ideal.

"Papers?" he asked. "What papers?"

"Like birthrights. Licenses. Anything that says they belong to Axiom."

"This is a commerce sector," Coba said. "We are allowed here... well, those with a permit, like you, Heli."

Heli-3 shook his head. "They didn't care for that. I saw them putting our people in different vehicles and driving away. Not sure where. Some tried to run, but the fire prevented them from getting far. That's when I tried the portal, but nothing. Then Marshall sent the message of you coming. I thought he meant a whole troop, not just... well, you three, and it was too late when I realized what he meant."

"Heli!" Mer said, hitting the side of his head. "How did you miss this? Were you drunk again or something?"

"Hey! I tried my best, but I wasn't expecting anyone today!"

Tom groaned and clenched the steering wheel. "I guess this new guy isn't fooling around."

"What new guy?" Heli-3 asked, making Tom look at him for a second.

"You didn't hear the announcement about the Agency?"

"The Agency? What about them? These are officers. I thought it was the government, the one—"

"It is, but..." Tom switched directions, making his passengers hold tighter and complain again. "Is the Barrier still standing around here?"

Heli-3's eyes opened wide. "Yes, but... well, no one goes close to it anymore. It has been emptied for a while. The creatures just became nastier. The residents moved back from it years ago."

Tom felt a pinch in his heart. When he worked there, the sector's future seemed promising, particularly near the Barrier. He had built enormous homes with luxurious yards so families could enjoy life away from the city. Now, it was only a dream—for any family and for himself.

"Great! That should clear the path for us," he said, accelerating the car.

"The path?" Heli's voice rose. "There is no path, Sir! The jungle took over everything by the Barrier! And what about the Agency?"

Tom smiled, enjoying the engine at his disposal, the speed of it, and the rough roads that kept challenging him.

5

Axiom Realm

188A25 Year Week 13,
First day, Evening

Bill sat in his wheelchair by the fireplace in his mother's new home. From the next room, he overheard laughter and a chatty conversation that he didn't care to understand. Memories of Tom's destructive actions haunted his thoughts. He only wished he could have seen Tom's face when he heard his announcement.

"For what reason would you hide here instead of celebrating our alliance?" Darius asked as he walked into the room, taking his time.

That man was everything Bill wanted to be. Wealthy, of course, but more importantly, powerful and respected in his position, with a family history that backed up his actions, and capable of moving around on two legs—something Bill would never do again, thanks to his former friend Tom.

"I don't think we should celebrate yet," Bill said, turning his wheelchair toward Darius. "This is just the first step. Until we have Jess, I wouldn't count anything as a win."

His new partner made himself comfortable on the couch in front of the fire. "That's your problem, Bill. You need to learn how to enjoy the little wins in life. This is a new beginning for both of us."

Bill frowned but nodded. Their new alliance had started to change things around Axiom, and it was a matter of time before they could set the second part in motion.

"See, that's better," Darius said, raising a crystal glass to Bill. "Leave the problems for tomorrow. Tonight we can just play with the possibilities in our future."

"Possibilities in our future?" Bill took the cup he had left on a side table beside him. "Our future looks promising, then. We will get rid of the obstacles to take control over Axiom and make sure Chaos's government has no option but to work for—I mean with—us."

Darius smiled, sitting back while crossing his legs. "This craziness in our realms has been around for too long already. My father should have stepped down many years ago. The Disruption shouldn't have been a thing. It's time someone stepped up and ended it."

Bill took a sip of his drink, and the bitter taste left a warming sensation in his throat—sort of like what they were doing. He didn't like Darius, and trusted him even less, but he understood his point of view. Working with him gave Bill the position to change his life for good. Plus, Darius also wanted to get rid of Arlett's father, which Bill couldn't wait to happen.

Up until now, the man had helped Bill secure a privileged position in Axiom, but Bill was aware that it wasn't because of his benevolence. He feared the day Radium Radnar 88 would ask him to reimburse the favors.

"I completely agree," Bill said, letting a smile cross his face.

Darius erased it with his next comment. "And having your sister as my wife will seal this for sure."

It wasn't the first time he had mentioned that, and just like the many times before, blood rushed in Bill's ears as his muscles tensed.

He hadn't come up with that part of the deal. His mom, over dinners and social events, had met Darius and, without knowing their alliance plans, had suggested that he needed to get a wife. Little by little, she planted the seed of this woman being Jess. Of course, his mother wanted to clean his stupid sister's reputation, but Bill knew it was a bad idea.

Darius liked the proposal because it gave Tom a good reason to hate him, though. According to his new partner, making things more personal created a sweeter outcome. Bill disagreed with all of this. Tom had shown himself not to be someone to play with, and although Bill had overlooked it before, Jess was the most important person in Tom's life. This deal put all of Bill's family in danger.

"First, we need to find her," Bill said, controlling his tone.

"Well, your kindness to protect Tom's wife will do just that for us." Darius raised his glass for a second and then took a sip of his drink. "And you are right. We should not get ahead of ourselves on that topic. I'm afraid I cannot listen to your mother talking about weddings anymore today."

Bill pretended to laugh. A few weeks ago, when Darius and he completed the plan, they talked to his mom. Although he was the head of the family, they needed to have Amelia's permission to actually arrange the marriage. There was no doubt that his mom would agree, but Bill hadn't foreseen her excitement and eagerness.

For years, they had lied to their friends about Jess's whereabouts. Amelia decided it was a good idea to pretend she had been so affected by the Disruption that they had admitted her to a hospital to help her deal with the trauma. Not knowing where she was or what she had been doing was killing his mom. Bill attempted to deceive his mom by claiming that his sister had probably run away with Tom, but Amelia didn't trust his words. Darius was the perfect opportunity to bring Jess back and socially clear her name.

For Darius and himself, Jess was the key to controlling the Corrupts.

"It may not be that easy, Darius. Jess is... complicated," he said, but his warning only made Darius chuckle.

"You think she won't find me attractive?"

Bill pretended to evaluate Darius's physical appearance. He couldn't be certain whether his brown hair and dark eyes would attract Jess. He sensed, though, that she wouldn't like his cocky behavior, which other women often found appealing.

"Maybe it's you who won't like her," Bill said. "Do you even know her?"

"Umm... I saw her a few times in the Agency, although we never talked. But that isn't important. I'm a very open guy, and I like challenges."

The tone in his voice left an edgy feeling in Bill's stomach. It wasn't the first time he had negotiated with dangerous men. He had dealt with Marshall and Randall way back. However, Darius was mentally unstable—something that caused Bill to be extra cautious around him.

"There you are!" Arlett said from the doorway, smiling as she walked into the room. "We are about to sit for dessert."

"Dessert sounds perfect," Darius said, standing up.

Arlett grabbed Bill's hand. The love she had for him shone in her—as it did every time she looked at him—although a sad smile shadowed her happiness as she moved behind him to push his wheelchair. He hated that she had to do that, but he pretended to smile back.

Soon Tom would pay for what he did to him. To them.

6

Axiom Realm

188A25 Year Week 13,
First day, Night

After a couple of hours, Tom finally parked the car just south of Sector 9 in one of the Corrupts' safe houses. Heli-3 jumped out of the car and threw up at the side of the road. Coba and Mer exited the vehicle somewhat less dramatically.

"Nice driving," Coba said, making Tom smile.

It wasn't Tom's fault they had to move through roads the jungle had reclaimed or abruptly change directions to avoid being attacked by a pack of takuosums. He couldn't believe what he had witnessed, though. Axiom had always been the perfect realm—the place everyone wanted to live. Even its worst neighborhood was a million times better than the best one in Chaos. What Bill and his new friend had done to his home realm was unforgivable.

"What's your business here?" A short guy holding a shotgun on his shoulder stood by the house's door.

"None of yours," Tom replied, closing the car door and ready to push whoever moved in his way. What he saw made him question his decisions in recent years. He enjoyed annoying Bill but had neglected to observe what was happening in Axiom. The Agency or the government's burning of Sector 15, trapping people inside, was genocide. He understood he was one of the bad guys, and Axiom hated him for the Disruption—but he couldn't let that happen again.

"What did you just—"

"You better watch it, boy," Coba said, standing in front of the guy.

"Such ignorance!" Mer said, grabbing her own gun. "No wonder the poor sector got destroyed like that. This is Umbrar, you idiot."

Just like Phoebe had told him long ago in her kitchen, people from Chaos didn't like his name. Tom was too unimportant to them. This was the reason Marshall introduced him by his last name, Umbrar-Ment, and soon enough, that changed to just the first part of it. He didn't care and had grown to like it.

"I'm so sorry, sir," the guy said in a different tone—one Tom liked more. "I—I wasn't expecting you—or anyone. We heard about Sector 15 and—well, we need to keep this house safe for... I guess for you."

"No problem." Tom pushed him to the side and walked into the house. "I need to talk to Marshall. Where is your transmitter?"

The guy hopped down the steps of the house's entrance to follow Tom into the first room.

"Is Marshall in Axiom?" the guard said. "If not, I'm afraid we only have the light system [1] to—"

"Photons!" Tom stopped, and the poor guy almost bumped into him. "Heli!"

Still clumsy, Heli-3 ran through the door. "Yeah, sir?"

"We have work to do." Tom pointed at Mer, still standing at the entrance. "We need to inform Marshall what happened in Sector 15."

Tom hadn't changed his mind about recovering the logbook, but he needed to help his people too. Marshall was a businessman and wouldn't take action to protect anything in Axiom unless it was necessary. This changed everything. Whoever attacked the people from Chaos would have to answer for their actions. If Bill was looking for a fight, he'd just found it.

"With the light system?" Mer asked.

"No." Tom didn't trust that system. Holm had shown it to him, and he understood why nothing worked between the realms. It was impossible to communicate by voice. The light system was Morse code that a few knew how to send, and even fewer knew how to interpret. "Mer, I need you to go back and personally tell Marshall."

"But sir," Mer stood taller. "It'll take too long, and you can't be alone here. Your head has a price in this realm."

Tom sighed and took a step closer. He understood Mer's need to prove herself, but that wasn't the right time. "I know, and that's the reason Coba and Heli will stay here. You can move faster by yourself and will make sure Marshall acts fast. Tell him he needs to be ready to respond around Main City. I'll update him when I find the stuff. Got it?"

Mer frowned, and Tom was aware that, if he were anyone else, she would have punched him. "I'm fast here too, sir."

Tom nodded. "Yes, but it's difficult for you to go unnoticed, and I need complete discretion this time."

Mer tried to respond, but Tom didn't let her. "If you think I'm doing this out of chivalry, you have no idea who I am. I make decisions based on my assets, and you are the best one to reach my brother. Understood."

"Yes, sir." She didn't seem sure, but he didn't have time.

"Where is the closest portal?" he asked the house's guard, but didn't wait for an answer. "Coba, make sure she gets there."

Coba walked toward Mer, but Tom stopped him. "After, check this place. Security doesn't seem up to scratch."

Coba nodded and walked out with Mer.

As Tom watched them go, he wondered if Marshall would respond to his petition. In previous instances, he had led missions without relying on his brother. He figured it was time to test his family's loyalty.

"That was nice of you," Heli said, smiling at the now-empty space. "I always believed you were a romantic at heart."

Tom just stared at him, and the smile vanished from his face. "Let's find a place to talk." He turned to the house's guard again. "What's your name?"

"Umm... Polo-Ium-84."

"All right, Polo. I need a private place to talk to my people."

"Yes, sir," Polo said and motioned for him to follow.

It wasn't a big house, but it had many rooms. Polo led them upstairs and gestured toward the end of the hallway. "The last door is the attic. It's soundproof, and the only access is that door."

A shiver ran down Tom's spine. He didn't like the idea of rooms with only one entrance and hated the sense of being trapped. After surviving the Square for several months, he hated being in closed spaces—as well as dark and wet places. However, he pretended it wasn't a problem, and despite his racing heart and difficulty breathing, he followed Heli up the narrow stairway.

Once up, he felt thankful for the large round window that allowed the sunlight to illuminate the room. They had set up the space as a bedroom, with a small sitting area—most likely designed for occasions when an important person had to stay there while discussing business. Heli walked around the room, checking everything in it, while Tom just sat in one of the chairs.

"Do you know what I need?" Tom asked.

Heli-3 walked confidently and sat on a chair beside him. "I brought my equipment, sir. I figure we're tracking something here?"

Tom crossed his arms and sat forward. "Not something. Someone."

Heli scratched the side of his head and shifted in his seat. "I guess I can do that too, but—"

"Is there a problem?" Tom liked Heli but enjoyed making him sweat. He still remembered how Randall's team had almost trapped them because of him. And although Heli denied knowing it was Randall, claiming he was trying to reach Marshall, Tom had his doubts. After all, this man was supposed to oversee everything.

"Well, sir, if who you're tracking is who I think it is, then yes! I hope you're aware that I've tried everything to find her. For years! She's just impossible to track!"

"Who?" Tom let himself enjoy the guy's confusion.

"Umm... well, I suppose Jess—I mean, Agent Jessica Hiem-Sagac?"

"Hiem-Sagac?"

Heli's hand trembled as he pushed his hair back, and Tom noticed the sweat on his forehead. "No, no. Sorry, I mean Umbrar... Umbrar-Ment. Jessica Umbrar-Ment. But sir, I've tried and—"

"Don't worry, Heli," Tom said, as calm as he could be when someone talked about Jess. "She isn't the person I need to find."

Heli's color seemed to return as he sighed loudly. "That's great."

"Great?"

"Well, I mean—I'll be able to actually find—"

"Let's get working."

Heli-3 nodded and sat forward but avoided looking at Tom.

"How good are you at tracking people's movements? Like, from three years ago?"

Heli nodded rapidly. "It can be done. It may not be as easy as tracking a proxy, but I can figure out someone's—"

"Great!" Tom leaned forward and waited until Heli looked at him. "We're going to check on Bill's movements, Heli. I want to know everything he's been up to for the last three years."

"What—who?... Sir, haven't you—don't you know what he's been doing?"

"I have a good idea, but this time, Heli, I need a more detailed approach. Especially after the Square. Can you do it?"

Heli tilted his head and fidgeted with his hands. After a few seconds, he nodded. "I think so. It can be done. I'll need my equipment, and it may take time to—"

"Nope, Heli. I need this information fast. Like, yesterday."

Heli stood up and walked toward the door, but before leaving, he turned to Tom and, with an exaggerated nod, added, "Yes, sir. I'll get to it."

"Excellent! You'll work here. And Heli—" Tom waited for him to meet his gaze. "Not a word to anyone about this. I won't forgive anything from you. Got it?"

The color left Heli's face again, and back to his clumsy ways, he climbed down and left the room.

---

1. **Light System;** a system that serves as the principal mode of communication between realms, utilizing a set of lights that operate on Morse Code, as the transmission of sound through portals is unattainable.

7

Chaos Realm

188Ch25 Year Week 13,
First day, Night

M ILLIE WAS STANDING BY the bed in her room, throwing things into a suitcase. She had been doing it for the last hour, but her mind wasn't on it. It should have been a simple task: pack and move to the government building in Sector 8. Still, she didn't have the heart to do it. Despite being small, her room within the Agency's complex was her home. It had been ever since she finally achieved her dream.

All her life she had wanted to be an active agent, and she had sacrificed plenty to make it happen. The training school wasn't easy for her, and she ended up spending most of her time off and vacations in extra classes, training to improve her career. Her father begged her to just work in security or administration. At some point, he told her she should be content with becoming a government officer. After that, she barely saw her family—even now, when things were so dangerous.

The news of the dismantling of the Agency was devastating, but her reassignment as an officer horrified her. What was the point of all those fights with her family? Missing events like her older sister's wedding or the birth of her four nephews?

"Hey, girl!" Peter said with a soft knock on the door.

Millie sighed and tried to contain her tears as she turned to him. "Did you hear the news?" It was a stupid question, but she wasn't in the mood to pretend.

He stepped into the room—something he rarely did—and when his eyes met hers, Millie's throat closed. After the Disruption, Peter had lived in Chaos for a long time. She believed he was in rehabilitation, but when he returned, he confessed that besides going through recovery, he had been working with Holm and Phoebe on a plan to fix the realms.

Millie had some questions then, but when he asked her to help, she couldn't refuse. It was a task outside their official duties, but it seemed that no one was trying to fix their world anymore. The Agency had found a scapegoat and blamed it all on him—the person who had actually saved her life.

She became an informant, and although the idea never sat well with her beliefs, it made sense. The Agency's erratic behavior needed someone to keep track of it. Years later, she wasn't sure the decision had helped at all, and she kept questioning it.

"Millie," Peter said, grabbing her hand and lowering his voice. "You are more than an agent. You are everything to me. We just need to figure out what's behind this decision."

Although his hand sent the same tingling sensation all over her body, Millie tried to ignore it.

"We? Did they change your title, take your uniform, and give you a position as a guard in a building, too?"

Peter sighed, looking away, so Millie went back to packing. She wanted to believe the last months had turned their relationship into something solid and easy to trust. Nevertheless, most days, even the Agency's movements were easier to read than what he truly felt for her.

"We can't give up now, Millie. This is something we need to fight for."

"Fight?" Millie raised her voice, unsure if her annoyance was at the question or at his priorities. "How are you planning to do that?"

Peter crossed his arms. "This isn't the place to talk."

Millie frowned and looked away from him. "So where, Peter—or when? Oh, wait, it can't be in this realm, and since I don't have a key anymore, well, I'll never know. Right?"

To her surprise, instead of storming away and avoiding the discussion, he stood so close she could see the speckles in his eyes.

"It'll be all right." He grabbed her hand in his and pushed the hair away from her forehead, making the tears she had been fighting roll down her cheeks. "This isn't over, and I won't let them hurt you. You are all I have left, Millie. Please, just hold on a little longer..."

Millie didn't want to talk anymore. She didn't want to listen to how Holm needed her to keep her ears open and keep giving them information from the inside. She didn't need to hear why it was so important to continue fighting, even when nothing was working. What she needed was to forget everything—so she pulled him closer and kissed him, making sure he understood that, in that moment, all she wanted was him.

8

AXIOM REALM

188A25 YEAR WEEK 13,
SECOND DAY, MORNING

TOM WORKED WITH POLO and Coba, trying to prepare the house in case some people from Sector 15 also found their way there. Tom understood they were not supposed to take in victims, but he was certain Marshall would appreciate the exception this time. Just like him, they deserved protection.

After a few hours, he couldn't contain his relief as he finished the despair-inducing task and made his way upstairs to speak with Heli-3. As he moved up, Tom heard the noise of beeping machines and papers rustling before he reached the stairs to the attic. Once he made it up, he laughed at the big change in the room. Instead of a welcoming bedroom, he found himself in a chaotic, improvised office.

"Where did you get all of this?" Tom asked as he pushed stuff around, making his way to the middle, where Heli stood by a large monitor and a board full of lights.

"What do you mean?" Heli briefly looked up from the papers in his hand. "I'm always carrying the essentials. Your family is very demanding."

Tom nodded, giving another look around. "Well, I appreciate the effort."

This time Heli stopped moving and stared at him. "I don't know what to say—I mean, I guess thanks." He put a hand on top of his heart, and for a second Tom saw tears filling his eyes. "No one has ever said anything... I'm sorry. I never—"

"Understood," Tom said, and leaned down to pick up a paper. In moments like that, he regretted having shattered Heli's knife, Silvie. Even when Jess's life had been in danger, he should have behaved differently. However, everything became clearer as he recalled the circumstances of the events and his new position as a Corrupts chief. Heli was a criminal, too. Neither of them deserved redemption.

"So, what have you got?" he asked, staring at the paper in his hand with no intention of reading it.

"Well, Bill is a busy guy," Heli said. "He has been working with plenty of government people. He bought several properties, to the point of looking suspicious."

"Suspicious?" Tom chuckled. "Because our business is spotless and legal."

Heli smiled, shrugging his shoulders. "But we don't pry into our ethics."

"True." Tom crossed his arms. "All must come from his father-in-law. Not that Radium Radnar 88 is good at any business, but he was born into the right family."

"Umm..." Heli looked at the monitor, avoiding Tom's gaze. "The right family... I wasn't part of that deal." Before Tom could say anything, he continued, "Bill's salary is ridiculously high, and his nights seem busy. He is always hosting some kind of event. I don't think Axiom's government is the only benefactor, and well... you know about gray business."

Tom felt a very familiar heat in his stomach, like every time he heard anything about Bill. Despite being as despicable as any of the corrupt individuals, he walked free, and everyone admired him. "I'm sure the collaboration with the Agency brought additional sources of benefactors into his life." Tom tossed the paper in his hand. "But I don't care what he is up to now. What did you find from his past?"

Heli kicked some papers on the floor, as if that was the best way to find anything in a pile of stuff. "Well, right after the Disruption, he wasn't very active. I guess getting paralyzed slowed him down or something."

Tom nodded, trying not to think much about that incident. He was aware that was the moment he stopped caring about others. At least on that topic, he had been honest with Jess. He lived for a year in a horrible prison, thinking he had killed the son of the void, and most nights he still wished he had done it. Both had turned into monsters, and neither seemed to care.

"A few months after, he accepted a job with his father-in-law and moved up from there."

"What did he do back then?" Tom asked, making space for himself in a chair.

"Well, nothing for a while, until he got more... umm... popular."

"Popular?"

"Yes... well, he changed his narrative."

Tom leaned forward.

"You see, at the beginning, he kept trying to attack you." Heli's voice shook, and he fidgeted with the papers in his hands. "I don't... I respect you, sir. So, please... this is what you asked—"

"Just talk, Heli," Tom tried to sound casual, although he was eager to hear the rest. "I know this isn't what you think of me."

"No! Of course not, sir. No..." Heli moved around the room and talked faster. "Before Marshall disclosed how the Agency had messed up the arrest, Bill tried to accuse you of assault. When Marshall introduced you as his half-brother, Bill stopped the suit... or charges."

"I suppose he enjoyed the idea of me being in the Square."

Heli nodded, his hands continuing to shake. "I supposed that too, because when we attacked the Square, Bill lost his mind!"

Tom frowned, but Heli didn't give him time to ask.

"Bill attacked anyone and anything that was related to your past, sir. He bought the buildings you two built and tore them down only weeks after. He purchased an entire neighborhood in Sector 8 for a ridiculous amount of money. First, he fixed some houses, but he stopped after he got approval to demolish several blocks, including your—"

"He demolished my grandfather's house?"

Heli stopped and stared at Tom while he cleared his throat. "Um... well, yes... among others around it..."

Tom stood up, trying to get a grip on his growing desire to throw everything around him. He'd purposely avoided visiting that neighborhood or his grandpa's home. It was the last pure thing he had in his life. Destroying it was the last thing he wanted.

"Um... sir?"

Tom stared at Heli, who stepped back. "That's not all."

Tom closed his eyes and inhaled slowly before he sat back down. "Just keep talking."

"All right, well... ah... he also convinced the sector to redesign the train station and the plaza—he demolished your workshop... sir."

Tom leaned over, resting his head in his hands, pondering why he had requested all that information. "Did he burn the intermediate school, too?"

When Heli didn't reply, Tom looked up at him. His eyes were fixated on the floor.

"All right," Tom said. "He lost it. Got it. Did any of that seem off... well, for this stupid photonic bastard?"

Heli straightened and, almost with a smile, nodded. "Actually, yes. You see, besides buying and destroying, he sued many people. I assumed they were your clients or friends? He claimed that the company you two had—what's the name? Bridge up? Ramp down?"

"TowerUp," Tom said, rubbing his face. "Why would he sue anyone from there?"

"Well, he had an elaborate way to do it, but in short, he stated that anyone working or doing business with you had to be an accomplice and had links with the Corrupts."

"What the photons!" Tom stood up again. "The only one with links was him!"

Heli seemed to have shrunk into the far corner of the room, and his voice became a whisper. "He won a lot of money with this, because most of them settled. No one wants to fight an influencer like him... I suppose."

"Photons!"

"But sir, something changed."

Tom turned back to Heli and crossed his arms. He didn't want to take out his frustrations on that poor guy. "What is it?"

"Well, he was winning a lot of this stuff until he stopped."

"Stopped?"

"Yes. I thought it was odd, since he was doing substantial business out of the—"

Tom groaned, making Heli take another step back. "Sorry, sir, I didn't mean—"

"Finish, Heli!"

"Of course. After a few months, he stopped all of this behavior. The next I found was his current stuff. Working with the government, all political; expensive charity events, pretending to talk about safety and better times, blah blah blah. You know it."

Tom frowned and kept his eyes on the surrounding papers. "That is strange. What was his last suit?"

Heli moved and gave him a piece of paper. "He didn't win it. He tried to sue a guy from your old company for treason against the realm, conspiracy, and fraud."

"What guy?"

"Frank Ge-Arje. It's all in that—"

"Frank," Tom sat down and rubbed his face. "Well, now this is interesting. And Bill lost?"

Heli shook his head. "Not exactly. Bill dropped the suit."

The room's air seemed to clear up, and for the first time, Tom believed he might have a way to find Jess.

"Heli, listen carefully."

Heli moved closer and stared at him. His eyes reminded Tom that the small, fragile-looking man in front of him was a corrupt—a very dangerous one. His mental state wasn't at all right, and he thrived on anticipating danger.

"Stop tracking Bill."

"Really? I thought you might want me to plan a way to break into his house and—"

"I'll keep the offer in mind, but we aren't here for him. We have another priority, remember?"

"Right. So now what, sir?"

"Track Frank."

"What? Who the hell is this guy?"

"That is exactly what I want you to figure out."

9

CHAOS REALM

188CH25 YEAR WEEK 13,
SECOND DAY, AFTERNOON

MARSHALL SMILED TO HIMSELF as he let the pen rest on his desk. Letters were an old-fashioned method of communication, but he found it suitable for the task. He needed to buy Tom time to track Jess, and this was the perfect distraction for Bill and Darius.

"What do you think, Yttri?"

Yttri remained in the corner, observing the world below from the airship window.

"I agree," Marshall smiled. "There is nothing like attacking personal principles and family to get answers from anyone. I'm sure it's time Bill's mother learned a little bit about her daughter."

Yttri groaned as the door of the office opened.

"Sorry, Boss," Nik-el-28, a short, old lady who had been his secretary for as long as Marshall could remember, spoke from behind the door. "Mer says this is important."

"Mer?" Marshall stood up, and a strange feeling of concern filled his mind. "What happened? Where is Tom?"

Mer's expression was unreadable. As usual, she looked mad, and that only reminded him how she was one of his father's people, whom he didn't know well or trust. He still wondered why Tom had such an attachment to them.

"Umbrar sent me back," she said. "We found trouble in Sector 15."

Marshall looked at Nik, and she immediately closed the door behind her. Yttri was now standing by the desk.

"What trouble?"

Mer frowned and took a second to respond, which seemed peculiar to Marshall. It was the most emotional he had seen her in all his life. "Someone set the sector on fire. The government then blocked the roads and highways. People couldn't leave without authorization. Obviously, they weren't selecting anyone from Chaos."

Marshall sat down. He knew the importance of what Mer was saying, but he also understood his job. They were a crime organization. For a price, they provided protection to people. They weren't soldiers trying to save anyone. That didn't take away the trembling in his hands or the desire to make Axiom pay for Mer's news.

"Why did you leave my brother?"

Mer cleared her throat and shifted her weight from one foot to the other. "He is in Sector 9, working on the mission, and wants you close and ready by Main City... He is the one who actually got us out of Sector 15."

"Interesting."

Marshall leaned back and rubbed his face, wondering what his father would do. Not for the first time, he longed for his guidance.

"This changes our plans," Marshall said to no one in particular. "Instead of sending the letter, we will deliver it in person, and I have a strong desire to visit Sector 9. It's time to show how much of that sector belongs to us. Let's make sure anyone from Chaos knows we are there. I'm sure gossip will reach the important people behind this massacre."

Yttri crossed his arms.

"We won't attack, Yttri. We'll be ready to respond to any offense, though. And more importantly, we'll be in the right realm, ready to assist Tom."

He turned to Mer as he stood up and walked toward the door.

"Nik," he yelled, "let's get the ships ready to travel and send a message to our people in Axiom. We are going to visit them."

10

Axiom Sea Periphery

188A25 Year Week 15,
Seventh day, Night

Tom jumped from the broken air duct and hid behind it just in time. Bullets struck the metal on his back, giving him a slight push forward. He charged his gun and waited a couple more seconds before shooting back to cover his men's entry. Coba had taken the other two Corrupts with him to search the sixth level, while Tom moved down to the fifth.

Jess crossed his mind as he sprinted down the hallway, wondering how easy it would be for her to aim at those photonic traitors. He crouched down the second his companion joined him and waited for the shots to stop, thinking about how quickly his life had changed once again.

The threat had come to Chaos just a day ago, but it had been two endless weeks since the last time Tom had had news from Jess. It was a brief message, but enough to make Tom act on it.

"Sir! Sir!" Heli-3 had shouted, running out of Holm's office. "The light board! Sir, we got a message!"

Tom had rushed to the office, his heart in his throat as hope filled his mind. Jess knew how to use that board system.

"We have the wife of the fake Corrupts' chief," Heli read the second he stopped by the door. "Not the pregnant one. More details soon."

Tom's world sank as the message engraved itself in his mind. He could see Heli moving his mouth, but his voice came from a vast distance. Unlike Bill's ridiculous announcement, Tom knew this was real—and Jess's life was in deadly danger.

He let himself drop, and once he felt the ground beneath him, he had to hold his head with both hands as terrifying images flashed through his mind. He prayed she had just been trapped and hadn't endured torture during the many days he hadn't heard from her.

Luckily, he knew the kidnapper, which gave him a good idea of her whereabouts.

Axiom had been under attack a few times, but only one sector had been cleared out. Sector 15 happened to be the last city before the Square—a perfect hideaway that, thanks to its horrifying former use and history, no one wanted to visit. The last place he wanted to go back to, just like the son of the void who took Jess.

As soon as his airship got sight of the Square, Tom heard the alarms going off, confirming his decision. The best part was that he caught them off guard.

The two weeks of waiting to have news from Jess had helped his leg heal, though he still suffered from a cramp in his calf at the end of long days. That night, the pain should have been unbearable—after hours of walking and standing, getting his people ready to attack—but somehow he barely felt it.

His heart was another story, though. As he ran down to reach the next room, a pressure tightened his chest, and it became more difficult to keep his breathing even. He was certain the poison had damaged it, but he wouldn't allow a minor discomfort to stop him.

"There are more sons of the void down here, Boss," his man said, bringing his mind back to their ongoing attack.

Tom shot the handle of the door, which burst open. "Good sign. We must be getting closer."

He let his man check if the room was empty while keeping watch on his pursuers' advance. He saw one of his airships landing on the roof, shooting down toward the sea. It was loud and forced the people chasing him to turn and shoot upward. Blowing up what remained of the Square would have been easier, but he had specifically instructed them not to destroy the building. Jess was somewhere in there, and he wouldn't risk her life.

"Boss, you have to see this."

Tom rushed inside.

They stumbled upon the file room, which had been in full use for quite some time. Photos of the Corrupts, Axiom, and Chaos covered the walls. He recognized Bill and Arlett, and as he moved farther in, he found photos of Amelia and Dan, along with a few of Marshall and himself.

The two tables in the room were covered with documents and photos. He ignored the papers—there wasn't time to read any of them—but paid close attention to the photographs.

There were several of places in Chaos, of Sector 15 before the fire, of the Square cells in their current destroyed form, and of

Axiom's Main City. The photos included the buildings in Main City and Marshall's airship, all in their pre-attack condition. They had been taken within the last three years, and Jess was the only missing person on them. He even found Phoebe, Gall-i, and Holm.

A shiver ran down his spine as he picked up a small metal bar—just like the one he had found in his father's typewriter—inside one of the file cabinet drawers. He opened the next drawer and smiled when, among papers and folders, he found a logbook with a leather spine and the name *L-115* in the lower corner.

"I need you to take these back to our ship," Tom said.

He retrieved the logbook and examined its pages. Handwritten numbers filled them, but there were no letters. A paper fell from the book, and he realized they had been trying to decode his father's logbook. As far as he could see, they hadn't been successful.

An explosion forced him to crouch down and hold on to the cabinet. After things settled, he heard a cracking noise from the other side of the room. He moved closer and discovered a faint glow outlining a slim door in the wall. The wall moved back when Tom pushed it, revealing a new hallway.

"Take everything in that drawer, too."

Without waiting, he exited the room.

The hallway was narrower, but the red light from the alarms illuminated it, letting Tom know the guards used it. After charging his gun, he hurried down the hallway, hoping to get closer to Jess.

Axiom Realm

Tom had barely finished talking to Coba when Heli called him back. This time Tom had to force himself not to run up to the attic. It was a long shot, but no one had ever tried to find Jess through his brother's erratic behavior, and he knew her well. She wouldn't let anyone suffer if she could avoid it. Bill could have easily proven Frank and Tom were good friends. They had even lived together for a while after he left Charlotte and was looking for a new place to live.

Tom's hands were sweating as he walked up the small stairway. Another good reason for Bill to drop the suit was if Frank was dead, and at that point Tom didn't doubt Bill had Frank's blood on his hands.

"Sir!" Heli said, almost bouncing on his heels. "I found him!"

"Alive?"

Heli stopped for a second and then smiled. "Yes, of course!"

The weight of the world lifted from Tom's shoulders. "So?"

"Well, he moved from Sector 15 to Sector 8. That's where Bill sued him. After all charges were dropped, he moved to Main City."

"Really? What is he doing there?"

"He isn't in the city, per se. He has a bar right in the middle of the Rupture, and his reputation is... well, his clients are mainly the Radicals.[1]"

"The Radicals. So he is working for the imbeciles that are disturbing our work."

"Yes, sir. The losses from there jeopardize the supplies from Element 2 to 3 in Chaos."

"Is he one of them?"

Heli fidgeted with the papers again and avoided looking at Tom. "I'm not sure, sir." Heli's voice trembled. "I couldn't find anything that incriminates him, just the business's location."

Tom smiled, which only made Heli take a step back. "Great job, Heli. I guess we are going to visit Main City."

"But sir," Heli shook his head. "We aren't welcome there! It's bad enough in Axiom, but there... Those are murderers, sir. If they find out who you are, they will kill you, or worse, they'll use you against Boss Marshall!"

Tom chuckled. "Let's hope they figure nothing, Heli. Think about it. The last thing they are expecting is a social visit from me."

"But sir—"

"Nonsense. We have a mission, Heli." Tom pretty much jumped down the small stairway, yelling, "Coba! We are leaving now. Get everything ready."

Heli ran after Tom. "Sir, I can't leave everything here. My station is very important. We may—"

"You are right, Heli." Tom turned and grabbed Heli by the shoulders. "We'll need all your stuff. Pack fast. Ten minutes."

Tom left Heli complaining as he climbed back into the attic. He knew it was important to bring the equipment, since he might need Heli's skills again. However, for the first time in nearly three years, he could picture himself conversing with Jess. More importantly, if he found her, Bill wouldn't be far behind—and he was not going to let him hurt her again.

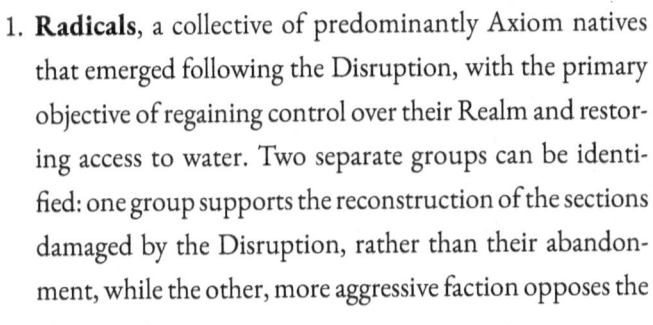

1. **Radicals**, a collective of predominantly Axiom natives that emerged following the Disruption, with the primary objective of regaining control over their Realm and restoring access to water. Two separate groups can be identified: one group supports the reconstruction of the sections damaged by the Disruption, rather than their abandonment, while the other, more aggressive faction opposes the government.

12

AXIOM REALM

188A25 YEAR WEEK 13,
SECOND DAY, NIGHT

GETTING TO MAIN CITY wasn't as difficult as moving around it. Heli wasn't joking about the Radicals. The Agency had left the city and abandoned its residents after the Disruption. Three years later, the Radicals had seized control of the entire east side of the city, including sites near the lost Barrier. Tom understood why anyone would still want to live there. Main City provided all the necessary services for a convenient life. He just wished fewer people were walking those streets that day.

If the insecurity wasn't enough, that section of the city was now extremely unstable. It didn't suffer earthquakes, but in the Rupture's zone, the underground sent constant explosions, probably because of the new instability of the energy wave. That part, Tom felt responsible for.

In just a few hours of driving, he saw burned houses and one park transformed into ashes. A horrible tightness in his chest, along with an uncontrollable rush of memories, kept him disoriented and on edge. Perhaps no one had recognized him as the Barrier crasher, but his mind vividly relived the event.

"I think we are close, boss," Goba said. "You can see up there. More people are gathering outside that place."

Coba was right. As Tom slowed down, he noticed a large gathering in the street ahead. Considering the late hour of the night, it could only mean one thing: a bar.

He pulled to the side and stopped the car. "This is the plan. I'll go in first to check if we have the right place. You two will come at least a quarter of an hour after. Got it?"

"Boss!" Coba said, "that is not safe. I'll go first to make sure all is clear. Then I'll give you the signal—"

"Coba," Tom said, grabbing the door handle. "If you come in and out, that will be more suspicious. And you haven't met Frank. How are you going to find him?"

"But, sir," Heli said in his characteristic high-pitched tone. "They will recognize you! Your eyes are a bad legend here."

Tom had to laugh at that. "That's not what girls have told me about them, Heli."

"Heli is right, boss. They could easily recognize you."

Tom opened the door and smiled at them. "It's late. Most people going in are looking for something, and it isn't me. I bet it's dark and smoky inside." He climbed down, but before closing the door, he looked back at the two of them. "If you hear shots, run inside ready. Otherwise, wait 15 minutes, then come in."

He walked down the street, pulling the collar of his coat up and lowering his hat as much as possible. Heli and Coba were right: his anonymity was in jeopardy, but it was a risk worth taking.

Once he reached the entrance, his concern decreased to a mild awareness of his surroundings. As he had expected, the place was packed with drunk people trying to reach the bar or grab a table. An untalented band played at the far end of the room, and no one seemed to notice the newcomers.

Nostalgia washed over him as he squeezed his way to the bar, longing for the uncomplicated days when a drink brought pure joy. His life was a mess, and going back wasn't an option.

"Sounds good, Jack," a familiar voice from behind the bar reached Tom. "I'll be there on the Fifth. Don't forget the packages!"

A guy left—Jack, Tom assumed—opening the line of sight to Tom's old friend. Frank looked older. He had less hair and looked so skinny Tom wondered if he was sick. However, he had the same joyful smile, and it only grew wider when he saw Tom.

"What in the Maker?" Frank exclaimed, extending his arms to give Tom an awkward hug with the bar in between them. "Never thought I'd see you again!"

"Hope it's nice to see me?"

Frank laughed and hit Tom's shoulder. "Of course it is! Man, you look good, To—" he began, then abruptly stifled his mouth with his hand, which made Tom laugh.

"Sorry!" Frank said, "I shouldn't say—"

"Better keep the name away from other ears."

Frank nodded and stood back, looking at him. "This is great, man. You want a drink, or—?"

"Sure. Do you have time to talk?"

Frank's expression turned serious, but he nodded. "Sure thing. Let me get someone to cover for me here, and I'll meet you at that table. Or you want to go somewhere else?"

"Here is fine."

Tom found a table in a corner, hidden from the band but with a view of the door. Frank hadn't finished pouring their drinks when Coba and Heli walked inside the bar. In just seconds, Coba located Tom and smoothly positioned himself to be able to observe him. Heli was another story. He walked around looking either mesmerized or stupid until he saw Tom, then immediately bounced on his heels. If it wasn't for Coba, Heli would have waved and yelled his name.

"Here," Frank said, sitting in front of Tom and raising his cup.

Tom raised his cup too and took a sip. The glasses made that funny, twinkly noise they did every time two pieces bounced together, waking Tom's nerves in a way that had never happened when he met his friends before. Over the past few years, Tom had learned the significance of a simple toast: it could seal deals involving matters of life and death. For the first time, he wondered about Frank, and hated his own suspicion.

"I see you are doing well?" Tom asked, trying to avoid his own train of thought.

Frank smiled, looking around them. "It isn't fancy, but it's a nice place to forget your day. We kind of need that around here."

Tom nodded and took another sip. "You could improve the music, though."

Frank chuckled, looking at his drink. "Most days are worse. We have karaoke."

Tom laughed, horrified by the idea. He had heard Frank singing, and it wasn't pretty.

"I can't say I'm surprised, but a bar? I'm sure it's different running one than just coming in to drink?"

"Tell me about it! But construction is pretty much dead, unless you're one of the big boys, and well... I'm not."

Tom wanted to learn more about his friend, instead of getting to the point and asking what he needed. Since Bill's wedding disaster, being around people he had met before was a rarity. It was refreshing to go back to a time when his major concerns were finishing projects within deadlines and enjoying sunsets.

He lost track of time, and eventually, the band started to sound better. The drinks were presumably the reason for this, rather than any improvement on the part of the musicians themselves.

"How come this place hasn't blown up?" Tom asked between jokes.

Frank chuckled, and after finishing a bunch of peanuts, answered. "We kind of figure that the more movement around, the fewer chances for the wave to emerge."

"How do you mean?"

"Well, the explosions are the wave pushing whatever it's made of to the surface. We made it worse with our services, like gas lines and combustibles. But when people and vehicles go on with their lives—even animals or stuff—we have fewer incidents."

"So, no one has died around here?"

Frank choked and, clearing his throat, tried to answer. "Well, it isn't proven science. From time to time, some buildings with people..." He sighed. "For the most part, it's getting better. Our biggest problem is the pest around here."

"Pest?"

"Yep. Those killers from Chaos—the takuosums[1] and the hyaerodeas[2]—ended up here, and they're nasty! They don't fool around. So we try to keep lights and movement to scare them, but... it isn't a pretty area of Axiom anymore. Like the Village? That's a dump. That's why the government avoids this place."

Tom decided it was time to push the conversation. "Why did you move here?"

Frank looked at the table, and for the first time that night, he lost his smile. "This is the best place for me. Here, no one bothers me."

Tom's muscles tensed, and without noticing, he tapped the table with his finger. "Was it Bill?"

Frank nodded without looking up.

"What happened?" Tom asked, even though, thanks to Heli, he had a good idea.

Frank sighed, and before answering, took a long sip of his drink. "Things were bad after, you know... the failed wedding and all. Bill stayed in the hospital for a long time. I had no idea where you were, and Bill totally ignored me. Charlotte eventually reached out and told me the company was done and they canceled all our projects."

"I thought you'd been killed during the Disruption and no one wanted to talk about it." Frank met Tom's eyes. "When Marshall made his announcement, I finally understood the silence about you."

Frank shook his head. "Listen, I know you, and I'm sure you had nothing to do with those people... at least not back then. I tried to get to the Square, but I couldn't visit you. The government only allowed family members."

Tom felt a tingle in his chest. It had never crossed his mind that someone—anyone—would have cared where he was.

"I was happy to hear you got out of that hell, but you vanished again and I thought you got killed, man. Then one day, you showed up in the news again." Frank chuckled. "Bill lost it. He attacked everything associated with you. Our constructions, some of our providers, your family's workshop! I mean, he really wanted you to suffer. And then he found me."

The growing heat that flared in Tom's gut when anyone mentioned what Bill had done settled in.

"Did he even dare to talk to you?"

Frank puffed, shaking his head. "Have you met him? He wouldn't lower himself to my level. He sent a bunch of officers and lawyers. I got arrested for..." He pointed at Tom. "Well, for working with you and conspiring with everything you do now."

Tom looked at Coba and Heli, trying not to think too much of Frank's comment. But his friend was right: he was a criminal in both realms. And he was a pretty good one.

"How did you make it out?"

"Tom, I—I'm sorry. I can't tell—I don't... I guess he changed his mind?"

"Are you asking me?"

Frank moved uncomfortably in his seat, to the point of making Coba take a step closer.

"I don't... maybe Bill got busy with something else. How do I know?"

"So, she helped you."

All color drained from Frank's face, and his hands trembled, making him spill some of his drink. "What—who? No, no one helped me. I got very lucky. That's all."

Tom sat forward and rested his hands on the table. "I appreciate more than you can imagine how you are trying to protect her. But here's the thing. Her life is in danger, and unless you can swear in the name of the Maker and your dead family that you will keep her safe, I need to find her before Bill and his new buddy do."

Frank's gaze never left Tom, and the fear in his tone was clear. "How can I be sure you won't—"

"Frank," Tom lowered his voice to almost a whisper, "we talked about our lives plenty of times. Everything may have changed, but not how I feel about her. I consider you my friend. Because of that, I never tried to find you. I didn't want to mix you with my criminal life. It's only because I fear for her life that I'm here, asking for her."

Frank's expression hardened. "For the past few years, she's been fine, Tom. I don't see how—"

"I'm here and asking for her. Did anyone else show up and ask before me? Before today?"

Frank lowered his eyes. "But you know her better than anyone."

"If Bill takes a second to pull his head out of his butt and thinks, he'll figure this out, too. It's a matter of time, and we are short of it. His new mission is to get her."

Frank pushed his hair back and shook his head. "I can't betray her, Tom. She doesn't deserve any of this. She is a wonderful person, and she risked her life to save me. How could I just... I can't..."

Tom's instincts awoke, a hint of jealousy lingering, but now wasn't the time to question Frank about his feelings for Jess or any potential history between them. He needed to find her.

"How did she stop Bill?"

Frank looked heavenward for a second before exhaling. "She paid my bail. The first time I saw her, she was waiting for me outside the police station. I didn't recognize her. I never met her before!"

"Her hair?" Tom recalled an unpleasant memory of a rough conversation with Jess. "Still dark?"

Frank nodded, and Tom recognized the accusation in his friend's expression.

"She is so sweet and kind." Frank shook his head and cleared his throat. "Anyway, she told me she could prove Bill had business with Marshall before the Disruption and that it would be easier to incriminate him for... well, your friendship. After that, it was a simple call to Bill's lawyer, and a few days later he dropped the charges."

Tom felt a slight relief to know Jess didn't have to interact with her brother, but the unpleasant taste of Frank's reference to her lingered in his mouth.

"I have no idea why, but she stuck around, and for a brief time, we worked together."

A wave of cold hit Tom's core. "She worked with you? In what?"

Frank smiled, shrugging a single shoulder. "She wanted to learn how to build stuff. I'm not an expert, but I thought she kind of wanted to learn about you."

"About me?" Tom leaned forward. "Did she ask you—"

"No, no," Frank said quickly, "she barely ever says your name, but the way she tried to learn... I guess I could be wrong."

Tom's heart skipped a beat, not missing the sudden present tense in Frank's answer. "You still see her."

"What?" Frank shifted again in his chair. "No, of course not. I mean—said, not— I haven't seen her for years."

Tom put his hands on the table, and he knew his expression had changed when Coba and Heli moved closer, ready to attack.

"If Bill finds her before me, for the Maker's existence, I will make you pay for it."

Frank's voice trembled when, for the first time, he noticed the other two guys. "Tom, come on, we are on the same side. I don't want anything bad to happen to her, but... she isn't weak. She has defended herself all this time. And I swore to her—I don't want to lose her friendship. You have to understand. Don't you?"

Tom's stomach roiled, knowing how easy it had become for him to make anyone fear him. He questioned whether he had always possessed that ability or if he acquired it in his new life. Still, he hated doing this to a genuine friend. A friend who was also trying to protect Jess. Just as he was about to reply, a fight erupted between two drunk individuals across the bar.

"Sweet neutrons!" Frank stood up and walked toward the conflict. He intervened just as a guy was about to throw a punch at the other one. The second guy attempted to stand but accidentally flipped the table and fell to the floor.

"You two have had enough!" Frank yelled, and the music stopped. "If you want to come back, you better leave. Right now!"

Frank signaled something to the band, who started playing again, and with the help of the other guy behind the bar, he walked the drunk guys outside. Frank's sudden return surprised Tom. If he had wanted to escape, that would have been the moment.

"Sorry, Tom," Frank said. "The fights here are dumb and easy to stop. The cost is sometimes high for this poor establishment, though."

"We got into a couple of fights before, remember?" Tom asked, trying to change the atmosphere between them. "Have you ever called the officers?"

"I don't call them often. I mean, the sheriff is a nice guy, but we are basically family here. He usually detains them, but I hardly ever press charges. Jess is a good friend to him. She is usually helping him to deal with the Radicals and—" Frank hit his face and looked down.

"The Radicals?" Tom's tone dropped. "Is she working for them?"

Frank frowned, but shook his head.

"Of course not," Tom exclaimed, relieved. "She is helping the survivors by the Rupture. I should have figured that."

Tom waved at Heli, and Coba approached the table, which made Frank straighten up and look very concerned.

"Frank, these are Heli-3"—who crossed his arms and tried to look taller, unaware that it was his psychotic look that gave him the edge of danger—"and Coba," who just nodded, aware of his fear-inducing presence. "As you are aware," Tom said to his henchmen, "Frank is my friend and will help. In fact, he just provided some important information."

"Do I need my equipment?" Heli asked, and Frank slid as far away from him as possible.

"Can you track the Radicals?"

Heli whistled and rubbed his head. "Not sure, sir. We still know little about them, and the Maker knows how much Marshall wants to catch their leaders. Maybe I could figure something, but it'll take weeks. Those people aren't exactly organized."

"Coba?" Tom asked, even though he knew the answer.

"The few infiltrations we have in there are too raw." He shrugged his shoulders. "It can be done, but you won't like the timing, Boss."

Tom frowned and looked at Frank. "If I leave a message with you, can you...?"

Frank shook his head. "I don't see her often, Tom. And I promise you, I have no idea where she lives and don't have a way to contact her. I just get little pieces of what she is doing. You had this problem before. I mean, we talked about it many times. She is very secretive."

Tom chuckled and looked at the bar's entrance. "Yes, she is."

It was a good thing she was hard to find, but he ignored how much advantage Bill already had on the search. He needed to figure out a way to warn her of what was happening.

Outside the bar, someone bumped into a few metal cans, and shouting reached them from the street.

"Those two!" Frank exhaled. "I need to make sure they get away from here."

"Wait, Frank." Tom stood up. "I have a crazy idea."

"To get those drunks out of here?" Frank asked.

"No... Well, we could if you want to, but I don't think you'll like our methods."

Frank seemed to shrink in his seat, but Tom ignored it.

"If you don't want to send a message, we can have someone more official sending it."

Frank shook his head, but Tom didn't let him talk.

"You said she knows the sheriff. He must have his ways with the Radicals. Everyone here is like family, right? If Jess is helping people, I'm sure they have a way to reach her."

"We could make the sheriff give us the information, Boss," Coba said, deepening the frown on Frank's face.

"We could, but we don't want to get Bill's attention, and I don't want to waste time. We can trick him into reaching her, though." Tom smiled at Frank. "I only need the name she is using nowadays. That way, she can be my family contact with the sheriff."

"Are you out of your mind?" Frank exclaimed. "You want to get arrested?"

"Yes! I need to get arrested. It's perfect. This way, Jess will decide if she wants to bail me out."

Frank stood up. "If you tell the sheriff who you are, he won't keep you here. He will send you to Main City. And if you use a fake name, how will she know it's you?"

"Like you said before, I know her, and she knows me better than anyone. She'll understand it's me."

Frank threw his hands up. "What if the message doesn't reach her? You'll get arrested, and when no one bails you, the sheriff will send you—"

"To Main City?" Tom asked.

Frank extended his hands forward, palms up, fingers spread, and opened his eyes wide. "Yes! And then what?"

Heli chuckled with a wide smile. "The boss won't get to Main City. We'll get him out before that."

Coba didn't even bother looking up from the chips he was pushing into his mouth.

"And if she doesn't get the message," Tom sighed, "well, then I'll try something else. Right now, I just need the name."

Frank rubbed his face and remained quiet for a moment. "You could torture me to get it, Tom."

"No, I couldn't," Tom said, losing all the humor in his tone. "You are my friend, and I would never hurt my friends."

"Besides," Coba said, "if he learns you can give her away so easily"—Coba moved his finger up and slid it slowly across his neck—"we don't like loose ends."

Frank's face went white, but he spoke up. "I would never give her away."

For a second, Tom feared his friend wasn't going to help, and he hated to think what he would have to do then. Thankfully, Frank leaned toward him and whispered, "Karen Ge-Arje."

Tom frowned. "What?"

"No, no!" Frank said, shaking his hands. "It's not what you think. My last name isn't because—sister. The sheriff—everyone here thinks she is my sister. Just my sister."

Tom laughed, shaking his head. "I didn't even get that part. Karen... did she tell you about that name?"

"She didn't explain... I thought she just liked it. See? I just get little clues about things..." The way Frank lowered his eyes and cleaned the invisible crumbs from the table made Tom feel bad. There he was, ready to give up his life for someone he barely knew. He had been there, and it didn't end well.

"Karen is the person who betrayed the Agency and blew up our apartment building. The one we built years ago, and Charlotte took the penthouse, remember?"

Frank went still, which only made Tom laugh louder.

"It's the perfect name. I would have never linked it to Jess. Smart girl." Tom clapped his hands. "All right, let's get going."

---

1. **Takuosums**; native mammal with extremely strong front limbs and claws, which allow them to burrow quickly with great power. It has a fur coat and a toxic array of spines. Capable of surviving in subterranean areas and a remarkable resilience to high oxygen concentrations but a limited resistance to light. An encounter with these creatures can be deadly due to their behavioral pattern of hunting in large groups, isolating their target and using poison to subdue and finally immobilize it. It is mandatory to report them when found in cities or transportation systems. Aggression level: 4 out 5.

2. **Hyaerodea**, a carnivorous mammal that relies on scavenging carrion, yet is extremely dangerous when it comes to protecting their territory. These creatures are characterized by long skulls, slender jaws, cone-shaped teeth, slim builds, and a plantigrade stance. Posses little to no capability to adjust to any sources of light. They could be located in all parts of Chaos, especially in locations with poor hygiene in cities. Aggression level: 5 out 5.

13

AXIOM REALM

JESS DROVE HER TRUCK up the curve and turned off the engine. It had been an unusually tough week, and she was ready for a break. After the Disruption, Axiom moved the survivors to the section of Main City now known as the Rupture. After that excuse for help, they closed their eyes to those people. For a while, the Corrupts helped both realms, but after the Square, that stopped. Chaos still got their help, and she couldn't blame them. Her realm had never been nice to theirs.

On top of that, the takuosums were all over the place, taking over the water supply for the survivors. The best way to move them was to bring lights and set explosions behind them to scare them away. However, this week, the Corrupts moved their airships, forcing the creatures into the Rupture territory.

Not for the first time, Jess wished she could stop caring, but after a long sigh, she climbed down from her truck to finish the delivery.

Lucille-71, a girl not much younger than she was but with a less rough past, was already waiting for her.

"Hey, KG," she greeted her. "How did it go?"

Even after all those months, that name remained unfamiliar to Jess, and she had to consciously remind herself they were addressing her. She was thankful that, at some point, someone had started a rumor that she might have lost some of her hearing, which explained why people needed to call her more than once.

"Tough one," Jess said. "The Corrupts are up to something, and the takuosums are acting up again."

Jess opened the back gate of the truck and climbed onto it.

"You think the wave is changing course again?" Lucille asked.

"Not sure," Jess said, plugging the hose that Lucille gave her into the first barrel's opening. "I'm hoping it's again about the weather getting colder and nothing else."

"That'll be good," she said with a sigh, making sure the hose was filling their well. "Although luck seems to be scarce here."

"Hey, girls!" Jess turned and rolled her eyes as a guy approached them. "Glad to see you working here."

"Someone has to do it, Eril Ungu-Ter," Lucille said, but her tone was soft and welcoming. "You can help us. KG needs a break."

Eril looked at Jess, and like always, her stomach seemed to revolt.

"Are you tired, beautiful?"

Jess ignored him, but he still jumped on the back of the truck.

"Why don't you let the big guys take over now?"

Jess refrained from punching him, not wanting to draw any attention to herself. "That'll be nice. Too bad I don't see any big guys around. All of them are still driving back. Trying to get food and water to the Village? You remember that, right?"

Eril didn't lose the smile, but the happiness left his eyes. "Those aren't big guys, KG. We are the ones fighting to get our land back, the ones using the guns. We aren't afraid to kill for what is right."

Jess let the hose fall into his hand and jumped down off the truck. No one there knew she had spent years killing people. They also ignored that the fight for the land was just a way for a new group to take over innocents. She hadn't used a gun since the Disruption, and although she wasn't sure if it was fear or pride, in that moment, it didn't matter.

"I'll get back in a few days," Jess said to Lucille.

She hadn't moved more than two steps when Eril interrupted her. "KG, you got a message."

That stopped Jess in her tracks and made her heart beat faster. "What is it?"

Eril smiled as he leaned over the truck. "I didn't know you had two brothers."

Jess frowned, pretending to be annoyed and hiding the sweat in her palms. "So? I don't think I need to give my family history here."

He raised his hands, palms out, in mock surrender, and chuckled. "It's not a biggie. And I don't blame you for hiding the other one. I mean, sweet Frank doesn't want to deal with him? He must be scum."

"What do you mean?"

He shrugged his shoulders, taking his time to relish Jess's annoyance. "Frank doesn't want to pay for your brother Randall's bail. So... the sheriff needs to know if he should send him to Main City or what."

Jess turned around to avoid Eril noticing the trembling in her hands and probably the lack of color on her face, since a sudden cold covered her entire body. Only two people could use that name. Either Randall was alive and got his hands on Frank—which she couldn't ignore—or Tom was looking for her—which she should ignore.

"Eril," Jess said, trying to control her tone. "I need the truck. You think you can finish faster?"

"Sure thing, beautiful." He jumped down and, with a condescending smile, touched Jess's shoulder. "I can go with you, too."

Jess shook her head. "It's just family drama. I got this."

"All right. Give me three, maybe two hours?"

Jess nodded. "Thanks. I'll be getting the report ready."

Jess walked to a small tent that had seen better days. The mud around it had already ripped the bottom of the fabric, and the poles needed to be barricaded to avoid collapsing. Regardless of its condition, they stored research information about weather, animal behavior, and wave changes in there. The Agency's lab where she used to work had no comparison with that rudimentary place and outdated system. Still, she believed one day, with the data they collected, someone would be able to fix the realms. Otherwise, she had no idea what else to do with her life.

Usually, she enjoyed that part of her days. She felt connected to a past life that no longer existed. Nevertheless, after Eril's message, her mind was elsewhere. She wanted Frank to be safe, and she dreaded the idea of facing Randall. Above all, she couldn't deny the growing desire to see Tom again.

14

AXIOM REALM

THE PLAN HAD WORKED so far. Tom had a black eye and a slight cut on his lower lip. He could have avoided them, but the fight needed to look real. He suspected Frank took the liberty of hitting him extra hard, though—something he probably deserved. Not too long after, the sheriff arrived and, almost smiling, arrested him.

The big guy with gray hair and a joyful personality didn't like Tom. That was expected, considering how Frank had pretended not to care about his brother because of his irresponsibility and tendency to get in trouble. Nevertheless, it had been his supposed relationship with Frank that stopped most of the sheriff's suspicions about his eye color.

In the end, Tom wasn't sure if the sheriff was angrier about Frank's secret brother or having to handle his arrest. It was obvious how thrilled he was to have a reason to talk to Jess, even though the sheriff and guards kept scolding Tom and saying Jess didn't deserve any of it.

What Tom didn't consider was the way he would feel. The second the metal touched his wrist, he had to fight the urge to hit the sheriff and run away. It only became worse when an officer walked him down the small corridor and led him into a custody cell.

Tom had to control his breathing and force himself to walk inside. It looked nothing like the Square, but the memory of being trapped threatened to take away his rational mind. Constantly, he had to check his shoes, making sure he wasn't barefoot and that water wasn't running inside the cell.

He knew Coba and Heli were around. They had sneaked in and visited as often as possible. Still, the fear of returning to those days kept his nerves on edge, his hands sweating, and his breathing difficult at times.

"Hey, sir," Heli-3 said from the other side of the bars.

Tom remained seated on the bench, barely glancing up. This time, Heli, wearing a janitor's uniform, swept the floor by the cells.

"Anything happen?"

Heli shook his head. "Nothing, sir. But we are busting you out of here tonight."

Tom groaned.

"I can have Coba working his magic right now!"

"No," Tom rubbed his face, "we agreed to wait until tonight."

"All right, sir. But if you change your mind, we are close by." Heli turned around, but before leaving, he looked back at Tom. "She may show up. I mean, they gave you two days. She may be far away."

Tom rolled his eyes, leaning against the wall, trying not to think about where he was or why Jess hadn't come. The last time they talked, it had also been in a prison, and he had behaved like a jerk.

He sighed and rested his elbows on his knees while he grabbed his head and counted the tiles on the floor once more. That had been the way he spent his days back then: counting and calculating things.

The Square's darkness had a weight on all prisoners and made everything tougher. Tom had no idea if it had been days or weeks before he got a hold of a loose rock by his cell and realized he could write on the concrete walls. The small pebble left greenish marks on his fingers that burned at night, but he didn't mind. It was worth it to make sense of his time.

It was then that he figured out things about the energy wave and the Barrier. He understood how he crashed it and, from the little he heard of the world outside, he also figured out why he destroyed part of both realms. It all sounded perfectly rational until he talked to Holm after they rescued him.

In summary, the old man told him he was bluffing and should move to the void. He left them for that reason and began working with Marshall. Why tolerate pity and being treated like an idiot if Jess wasn't present?

Footsteps echoed in the hallway, but he didn't bother to look up. Heli-3's persistence was too much for Tom after his fifth visit of the day. However, when a shadow covered the tile, and he sensed a presence looking at him, he knew it wasn't Heli.

He lifted his eyes and lost his breath.

Jess stood across the bars, gazing down at him. Her expression was severe, and the dark hair just made her look angrier. He couldn't blame her, though. He deserved her hate and would gladly listen to whatever she had to say to him. At least she would be talking to him again.

He stood up but was afraid to move closer, so he remained farther inside the cell. Time had no effect on her beauty or the way she made his heart race.

"KG," the sheriff said from far away in the hallway. "Let me know if you need anything. I really appreciate you coming down here. You are very busy, and this goofball probably doesn't deserve it."

Tom pushed his mouth closed; he couldn't agree more with the sheriff.

"Thanks, sheriff," Jess's voice eased Tom's nerves, just like it always did. "I just need a word with my brother."

She turned to Tom again. "Right, Randall?"

Tom chuckled, daring to take one step forward. "Of course, Karen."

Jess kept her eyes on the hallway for a few seconds, probably making sure the sheriff left. Then she crossed her arms, staring at Tom for what felt like an eternity.

"Randall? Really?" she finally said, lowering her voice and taking a step closer. "Did you consider how worried I would be if I found out he was looking for me?"

Tom's head flinched back slightly. "He is dead. How could he—" he shook his head and softened his tone. "I'm sorry, but it's not like I can use my name, Karen."

Jess pushed her hair behind her ears and looked away. "Well, I'm here now. What do you want?"

Tom's stomach hardened—not at the question, but at her tone. Cold and without kindness, it forced memories full of regret that confirmed his desire not to lose her again.

He cleared his throat, hoping he could actually have a conversation with her. "I have a question for you."

Jess narrowed her eyes and put her hands on her hips, but her silence prompted Tom to continue.

"Are you pregnant?"

Tom was unsure what he had expected, but when she didn't immediately yell at him and gazed away as if contemplating the possibility, it wasn't his first guess.

"I don't see how that would be any of your business," she said with a blank expression. Tom couldn't stop himself and walked to the bars.

"Well, as my wife, it's kind of my business," he said so low that he wondered if she heard him, but her cheeks turning red answered for her. He grabbed the bars, but she didn't let him talk.

"As if you care about that." She raised a hand in front of her, stopping him from answering the accusation. "And even if you do, obviously it wouldn't be your baby, so still none of your business."

Tom straightened, and his tone became serious. "Although I will hate and probably kill whoever is the father, Jess, I will die protecting your baby. How can I not care for anyone sharing a part of you?"

As Tom said it, Bill's plan to hurt Jess became crystal clear, and a desire to step on Bill's head became one of his priorities.

Jess's eyes shone, so she looked away for a second. "You can be at peace, Tom. I'm not pregnant."

All Tom's muscles relaxed—not only because of her answer, but also because she said his name.

"I'm glad this makes you happy. If that's all, I'm leaving."

Tom stretched his arm out of the cell, barely having time to touch her arm before she was out of his reach. She didn't push his hand away, just froze, giving Tom hope and making the last two days worth it. Despite this, he knew she was about to go, leaving him with no choice but to involve her in Marshall's plan.

"I need your help to find something, but... I can't talk here."

Jess tensed and turned away from him. "I'll get you out."

15

Axiom Realm

188A25 Year Week 13,
Fourth day, Evening

Despite weak legs and trembling hands, Jess made it back to the small police station's desk. Of course, all her feelings for him were still there. She just didn't expect to be afraid of him.

The news of how Tom kept attacking Bill's events, ambushing his plans, and stealing from her brother was the reason she had stopped listening to the news. She had purposely remained oblivious to the happenings in Axiom and Chaos. In the Rupture, things made sense; people needed basic supplies to survive. Period.

She hadn't seen Tom for nearly three years, and her only information about him came from attack reports. Bill could rot for all she cared, but knowing how much Tom had grown to hate him—and how far he was willing to go for revenge—was dreadful. Tom had ended up in the Square because of her. She had basically put him there. What should she expect from him now?

"KG," the sheriff smiled widely as she approached him. "Did you straighten out that brother of yours? I had no idea he existed! Frank was so pissed off—he couldn't wait for me to send him to Main City!"

Jess smiled, but inside she hoped Frank was all right. "Family, what can I say? But I'll get him out of your hands."

"Are you sure?" The sheriff leaned closer and lowered his voice. "I owe you for your help with the water and the pests. Just nod or something, and he's out of your hands."

Jess shook her head. "I'm happy I can help, and I appreciate the offer. But, like I said—family."

The sheriff nodded and gave her some papers to sign. "I'll excuse the bail, though," he said, and before Jess could argue, he lifted a finger. "I owe you at least that much."

"Thank you."

She finished signing, but when she handed the papers back, her hands were still shaking—something the sheriff noticed.

"Are you all right?"

"Yes. It's just... I haven't seen him in a very long time, and..." She sighed. "I wasn't expecting to see him ever again. I guess I need time to... get used to it."

The sheriff nodded and patted her hand. "Say no more. You just do what you need to and get your truck. Take some air and all. We'll get him ready and send him out soon."

Jess wondered if the sheriff would do something to Tom, but she needed to compose herself before talking to him again. "I appreciate it, sheriff. I'll be outside when he's ready."

"Sure thing, KG."

J ESS LEANED ON HER truck, watching the police station across the street. It was odd to see certain parts of Axiom seemingly stuck in a better past. People walked around chatting; cars drove down the streets, and even a few Zeppelins crossed the sky—just like they used to, oblivious to the danger closing in on them.

It took almost twenty minutes for Tom to walk out. Jess could have sworn he was running when he finally appeared at the top of the outdoor stairs. He looked around until his eyes found her and smiled, making her heartbeat quicken.

He climbed down, two steps at a time, and crossed the street to meet her. "I'm glad you didn't leave. The sheriff really is fond of you and Frank. He gave me an endless lecture."

Jess tried to ignore her desire to hug him and instead walked around the truck to the driver's seat.

"Let's go. I don't want to be here at night."

Tom took a step back, giving her truck an appraising look. "You drive this?"

"Why are you surprised?"

Tom climbed into the passenger seat, filling the small space with his familiar scent—old treasures and metal gadgets.

"I don't know. I always took you for a more fashionable girl."

She felt a flash of annoyance, but his teasing smile stopped her from snapping back. Instead, she turned on the engine and drove down the road.

16

Axiom Realm

Millie walked past Peter and entered the small shop in Main City where they had agreed to meet. It was about to close, but the owner knew better than to stop an agent. The new director's announcement hadn't yet sunk into people's minds, and the Agency's uniform still carried weight. She looked down at her regular clothes and missed the familiar dark colors, unconsciously touching her shoulder, longing to feel the embroidery of the Agency's emblem.

Nausea traveled up her throat when she thought of the tan colors of the officer's uniform. After being forced to do what she did, she had thrown the uniform in the garbage and left the unit. She would rather die than wear that thing ever again.

Millie moved between shelves and tables filled with items she could only assume were meant to decorate fancy houses—places she wasn't sure she belonged to. A large grandfather clock caught her attention, and she stopped beside it. The pendulum's echo had a calming effect on her heart—something she desperately needed.

"Millie," Peter said, and she had to fight the urge to hug him. He was wearing his Agency jacket, but it was missing his rank patch.

"Did they take it away?" She pointed at the space by his shoulder. "Are you not a captain now?"

Peter pressed his lips together and ignored the question. "What did you find out? We weren't supposed to meet until the sixth."

Millie took a deep breath and looked around. The shop owner was busy closing the curtains, and the woman at the cash register seemed distracted counting the day's earnings.

"It's Sector 15."

Peter frowned. "Sector 15? Are the Corrupts trying to steal the water over there now?"

"Not the Corrupts."

Millie shook her head, trying to erase the images of people running from the fire while her superiors forced her to stop them from escaping their fate. "They ordered—forced me..." She bit her lip, trying to swallow the knot in her throat. "I won't go back, Peter. They are monsters, and I can't—I won't have any more innocent blood on my hands."

Peter grabbed her arm and guided her farther into the store. "What happened? You were supposed to be in Sector 8."

She closed her eyes for a second. She was a trained agent and hated behaving like a scared girl. Yet her hands had been trembling for days, and the fear of her nightmares made her avoid sleeping.

"Right after I arrived in Sector 8, we got orders to move to Sector 15. I had no idea why the change—until I saw it." She shook her head, staring at the floor. "The sector was on fire."

"On fire? What do you mean? Did the wave break loose again?"

"No, the entire sector was on fire, Peter." She rubbed her face and paced. "The flames looked like they'd been burning for some time. The houses by the Barrier, the forest along the border—everything. Even the entrance to the highway... all destroyed. I thought we were there to help. Like you, I assumed it had been the energy wave, but... I was so wrong."

Peter held her hands. His grip felt strong—safe.

"They ordered us to block the only road left, to stop anyone who couldn't prove they were Axiom natives."

He pulled her close and wrapped his arms around her.

"I had to do it, Peter." This time she couldn't stop her tears, her voice breaking between sobs. "I'm a monster! It's my fault they died. I should have disobeyed, but... they would have killed me."

Peter kissed the side of her head and held her until she stopped crying. Gently, he moved her back and met her eyes. "You are not a monster. And you're right—you cannot go back."

Millie tilted her head. "I'll become a deserter. I have no valid reason to resign, and..." She drew a shaky breath. "The new government said they'll enforce consequences for anyone who abandons their role."

"It's good we know people who can hide you."

"My family?"

Peter shook his head and gripped her shoulders. "We'll make sure they're safe, I promise. But, Millie, we need to get you out of here. Now."

Millie looked down, but Peter lifted her chin.

"This is all wrong, and it isn't your fault. We're trying to fix it, all right?"

She nodded, struggling to keep her voice steady. "Where should I go?"

"We are going, Millie. We." He hesitated for a second, then added quietly, "I never thought I'd say this, but Chaos is safer now. Are you ready to cross over?"

Axiom Realm

188A25 Year Week 13,
Fourth day, Night

Bill pulled his leg down from the wheelchair and rubbed his thigh toward his knee. He longed to stand up and give his hip a break, but that required assistance—and he wasn't in the mood to engage in conversation with Dan. Most people assumed he was paralyzed and felt nothing. Most nights, he wished that were true. In reality, Tom had broken the bones in his hips and the connection to his femur, but not his spinal cord.

He now lived with constant pain. It dictated his mood and decisions as much as his desires and dreams. He had no recollection of what it felt like to have fun or enjoy a day. All he wanted now was to make Tom pay for everything.

"There you are," Arlett said as she walked into their bedroom. "Why didn't you call me, silly? I would've brought a warm compress and a tonic for you."

She knelt beside him and tried to touch his leg, but he pushed her hand away. "I'm fine."

Arlett stood and crossed the room, wearing the tired expression Bill despised. He often wondered how long it would take her to leave him. He was positive that if he hadn't known about her and Karen's relationship, she wouldn't have even stayed long enough to see him leave the hospital.

"I'm just trying to—"

"To help?" Bill shook his head and pulled his leg back onto the chair. "I told you, I'm fine. And I don't want you pretending to be nice to me."

"Pretending to be nice?" Her voice trembled. "I love you, Bill. I'm not pretending anything. What did I do to make you think that?"

Bill groaned and positioned himself by the window. The nights were darker now, with clouds covering Axiom all the time. He could feel the cold through the glass—something he feared, since it only intensified the pain in his bones. He chuckled, thinking how he had become a grouchy old man. Nothing was left of the joyful, carefree man he once was. How could Arlett possibly love him now?

"Did Darius mention anything about Charlotte?" Arlett asked, her voice barely above a whisper.

"Charlotte?" he repeated, not looking away from the scene below. "What does he have to do with her?"

The covers on the bed shifted, and he pictured Arlett getting comfortable beneath them. A distant, rare memory of their happier nights together crossed his mind, bringing a strange numbness to his chest.

"Over dinner, he mentioned something about a baby and..." She stopped, and the sound of her quiet sobs made Bill turn toward her.

She was clutching the comforter so tightly her knuckles had gone white as she tried to control her breathing. Bill shivered.

Darius's reputation was that of a man without sanity—someone who often did stupid, dangerous things.

"Did Darius... did he threaten you or hurt you?"

Arlett looked up, and though her eyes were filled with tears, she shook her head. "No, sorry. He did nothing to me. Bill..." She wiped her face and cleared her throat. "I'm scared he may have hurt Charlotte, though."

Bill rolled his chair forward and stopped in front of her. She was so close—if he wanted, he could have reached for her hands.

"I don't think Darius knows Charlotte. What made you think that?"

Arlett looked at everything but him. "He was talking to your mom about his arranged engagement with Jess, and then he mentioned how he'll make sure Tom's baby grows to become a decent man."

Bill tried to ignore the heat rising in his body at the mention of Tom's name. "You know about the public announcement I made today. And you already knew about my mother's plan with Darius. None of this has anything to do with your friend."

"But it does, Bill," Arlett sighed, reaching for his hands. "Charlotte is pregnant. I just learned this today when she left a message for me. I'm afraid Darius will... that he'll hurt her."

"Is it Tom's baby?" Bill asked, failing to hide his curiosity.

"I guess. I don't know if I should talk to her." Her voice rose as she pushed herself closer. "I don't want him hurting her because she might ruin your plans."

Bill leaned back in his chair, weighing the consequences of the news. He was well aware of how Charlotte loved to lie to make herself seem more important. Part of him wanted to believe she was expecting Tom's baby, but he doubted it.

Years of friendship had taught him a few things about Tom. His former friend wasn't the cheating kind—and Bill's own crippled state was living proof of how far Tom would go for his sister. He also knew Tom had a sick sense of loyalty to his people. If Charlotte was pregnant, it didn't matter whether it was his child or not—knowing she was in trouble would make Tom act on it.

Bill felt his facial muscles relax into a smile as he looked at his wife. He might just have a way to trap Tom and Jess, all while improving his relationship with Darius.

"Let's talk to Charlotte," he said, tightening his grip around Arlett's hands. "I promise you, I won't let Darius hurt her."

Arlett leaned into him, and this time he didn't push her away. Instead, he savored the soft skin of her neck brushing against his jaw and the warmth of her body easing his aching muscles. An overwhelming urge to kiss her forced him to press his lips together—until Arlett responded with the same eagerness and longing.

Perhaps it would be a good night after all.

Axiom Realm

188A25 Year Week 13,
Fourth day, Night

Jess kept checking the mirrors as she drove away from
Main City. Tom had been unusually quiet, which left her
unsure if that was a good or bad sign. Too many thoughts
crossed her mind—questions she wanted to ask but didn't dare.
She was more concerned about being followed and getting
caught. If Tom got arrested for real, she wouldn't be able to help
him without her older contacts.

"If you're tired, I can drive," Tom said, breaking the heavy
silence and making her jump slightly in her seat. "Sorry, I didn't
mean to scare you."

Jess glanced at him, and his smile set all her nerves on fire.
Afraid of how her voice might sound, she cleared her throat and
focused on the road ahead. "I'm fine."

"All right," Tom said, letting the quiet return. But after only
a few seconds, he shifted in his seat, and when he spoke again, his
voice was closer to her ear. "I know you—and you're not fine."

Jess turned, her heartbeat thundering in her ears when she
found him sitting just inches away, his piercing eyes staring back
at her.

"See?" he said, tapping the steering wheel. "Now you're not
even looking at the road."

"Shut up!" Jess pushed his hand away and tightened her grip on the wheel, forcing herself to focus on the traffic and control her racing pulse. "You just want to drive."

"Can you blame me? This is an exceptional truck. Brings back memories."

Jess tried to ignore his comment, uncertain which memories he meant—the countless times he'd driven her home from the train station in intermediate school, or the last time she saw him behind the wheel, crashing into the Barrier.

"Plus, you're driving kind of all over the place," Tom added.

"I am not!" she snapped, glancing at the mirrors, the road, and him. "I don't want to be followed, and you have no idea where we're going."

Tom huffed and slid back to his side, leaving a cold, empty space next to her that she instantly missed. "I may not know your intentions," he said, "but I'm familiar with this city and its shortcuts."

Jess smiled faintly and straightened. "First, I'm not kidnapping you," she said, raising her voice just enough to stop him from interrupting. "And second, we were being followed by your friends back there. That's why I took the circuit again."

Tom turned to check the mirrors. After a moment, he looked back at her. "I'll be damned—you lost them. Coba won't be thrilled with Heli. You may have just put that poor guy's life in danger, Jess."

Jess rolled her eyes but didn't dare look at him. She recognized his teasing tone, and the last thing she needed was more nerves.

"Did you see the two motorcycles a few cars back?" Tom asked.

Jess sighed and nodded. "I was kind of hoping... Are those your people too?"

Tom shook his head, glancing behind them again. "I don't have people in the city."

"For the Maker," Jess muttered as she changed lanes, her heart sinking when both motorcycles mirrored her movements.

"Are those *your* people?" Tom asked, his relaxed expression tightening as he shifted uneasily when Jess didn't answer. "Please tell me you're just being secretive—like usual."

"Like usual?" Jess's voice rose, and she forced a deep breath before continuing. "I had a job that—forget it. I'm not fighting you."

"Fine. I don't want to fight either."

"Great," Jess said, accelerating and weaving between cars. A flicker of pride crossed her face when Tom clutched the seat to keep from sliding. Usually, it was she who was in that position.

"Where did you learn to drive like—" Tom stopped himself, shaking his head. "Never mind. This must be part of the Agency's training."

"Funny you ask," Jess said, squeezing the truck between an old car and a massive city bus. "I learned from you."

Tom half smiled—but before he could reply, Jess swerved again, making him nearly bump his head on the window. "I did not—wait. Where are you going? I thought the third level was government-only these days."

"That's right," Jess said, pressing the pedal to the floor. The tires squealed as she steered onto the semicircular ramp. "But if those two aren't your people, they're Radicals, and we don't want to deal with them."

"I don't run from those neutron idiots, Jess."

She checked the mirror and finally relaxed when she saw the motorcycles continue past, down on the street below. "Well, you are running now," she said.

"I thought you worked with them."

Heat surged through her chest, and she nearly slammed the brakes. "I do not. Why would I join the people destroying our realms?"

"Well, you kind of did once before."

Jess clenched her jaw so hard it hurt, forcing herself to stay focused on the road.

"No fighting, right?" Tom said, his tone showing he was just as upset as she was. But even if she wanted to respond, the government roadblock ahead stopped her.

She slowed down and swore under her breath. Quickly, she inspected the truck's interior. "We need to pretend here," she muttered, grabbing her documentation from the glove compartment. "Just put your hat on and pretend to be sleeping."

"They won't fall for that, Jess."

"Well," she said, pulling to the side where an officer waved them over, "do you have a better plan?"

Before Tom could answer, the officer approached her window.

"Good evening, officer," she said, trying to sound calm despite her nerves. "What's going on?"

The man looked inside with a blank expression—the same kind Jess had once used as an agent.

"This level is closed to public transit," he said. "I need you to step out and—"

"For the Maker," Tom interrupted, making Jess's stomach tighten. "You did it, right? Oh, honey! I told you not to take any ramps."

He placed a hand on his heart, lowering his window to the officer at his side. "Officers, you'll have to excuse my confused and fragile wife," he said, shaking his head. "With all the changes in the city, I had a rough day and foolishly asked her to drive."

Tom patted Jess's arm, giving her a reproachful look that reminded her of all the outdated ideals she despised.

"You have my deepest apologies," he continued smoothly. "I'll be happy to send my positive reference to my good friend Mr. Hiem-Sagac. It's not often I do this, but I can see you're doing an amazing job."

The officer at Jess's window cleared his throat. "Well, sir, this is a misdemeanor. The third level has been closed for—"

"For ages!" Tom cut in, leaning forward to see him better. Jess noticed his hand moving beneath his coat, and she knew he was holding a gun. "But, officer, what can we expect from a woman beyond being pretty?"

The officer gave Jess a look that made her want to break his nose, but Tom touched her hand, and she forced a smile. Their goal was to get away—no matter the cost.

"I suppose we can let this pass," the officer near Tom said quietly. "But she can't keep driving."

"Of course." Tom opened his door, then turned to Jess. "Just slide over, honey. Let's not burden these fine officers any further."

Jess frowned as Tom stepped out, shutting the door behind him. He shook both officers' hands, all charm and false warmth, while she stayed alert—ready to act if needed.

"I'll make sure not to miss the next exit," Tom said, climbing back in and starting the engine. "And officers, thanks again for your much-appreciated service."

Without waiting for a reply, he drove off at a steady pace, not looking at Jess.

"I suppose you're happy now," she said, crossing her arms.

"That I'm driving and we got away? Yes, but..." He sighed, taking the ramp down. "All that crap about men being smarter disgusts me. I've changed, Jess, but I still despise this realm's ideas about women. I hope you at least believe that much. And for what it's worth, I'm sorry for what happened back there."

Jess studied him. His knuckles were white from gripping the wheel, but his control was steady. She wondered why he'd told her to slide over instead of letting her climb down the truck, but didn't ask.

"I'm glad you kept your hat down," she said softly. "It isn't easy to change your eye color."

"As easy as changing your hair color?"

She looked out the window, brushing her hair back. "Yes."

She heard him shift beside her but wasn't ready to talk about what really lingered between them.

"You need to take the highway northwest, toward the Village," she said instead.

"Frank told me your brother demolished that place a year ago."

"Yes, he did," she said, "but that didn't stop some people from settling by the beach."

"By the—wait." Tom turned to her. "Are you taking me to your house?"

Jess chuckled at his tone of surprise. "Where else did you want to go?"

19

Axiom Sea Periphery

After entering the last room in the hallway, Tom realized he had stumbled upon something significant. Unlike the previous doors he'd checked, a heavily armed man opened fire the instant Tom swung it open. He ducked behind the metal sheet to avoid most of the shots, but one still grazed his arm.

"Son of the void!" he hissed as his forearm burned for a second, followed by a pulsating heat spreading up his shoulder.

He glanced at the wound. Since his shirt wasn't soaked and he could still move his arm and fingers, it couldn't be too bad. From his belt, he pulled out a small explosive—similar to the ones he'd used to blow the door locks—and tossed it into the room. It wasn't meant to cause massive damage, just enough to distract whoever was inside so he could get in.

Tom had taken only two steps when someone lunged at him, slamming him backward into the wall. The smoke from his explosive cleared, revealing his surroundings. He was standing in what looked like a transfer station, where train wagons were unloaded. Unfortunately, he was on the second floor—with only a narrow metal railing keeping him from falling two stories down onto the tracks.

The man struck his side, forcing Tom to crouch, but that gave him the angle to punch back and push off the wall. Heavy chains hung along the railing, used for lifting cargo. Too late, Tom saw his attacker grab one and swing it toward him. He raised his good arm to protect his head, and his gun flew from his hand.

It hit the wall and discharged. The explosion shook the hallway, raining debris and collapsing part of the railing. Tom clutched the wall to steady himself while the other man dropped low.

Seizing the moment, Tom kicked him hard. His boot connected with the man's hand as he tried to block, sending him crashing to the floor. The man threw dust in Tom's face, and a few specks got in his eyes, forcing him to stumble back. He blinked furiously, trying to wipe them out while keeping his distance from the broken edge.

He heard movement—the man was back on his feet.

Still half-blind, Tom stepped back and tripped over one of the dangling chains. He grabbed it instinctively to stop his fall. Pain flared through his injured arm, and his grip slipped. For a second, he dangled over the edge—and then his vision cleared just enough to see why the gunshot had triggered an explosion.

Below, barrels of gunpowder and crates of missile parts filled the lower floor. Even a small spark could level Main City—and High City with it.

A door slammed open behind him. The man recovered his gun and pointed it at Tom's head.

Using the chain, Tom swung himself up and kicked the weapon from the man's hand. The man cursed, clutching his wrist, his face twisting with rage as he reached for something at his belt.

Tom struggled to get his footing on the unstable floor. His boots landed at the platform's edge. To keep from falling, he gripped the chain with one hand and drew his knife with the other.

Behind him, someone rushed toward them just as the armed man charged.

In one swift motion, Tom thrust his knife forward—but instead of hitting his attacker, the blade plunged into the side of the person who had stepped between them. A gunshot echoed, deafening him.

White noise filled his head. The first man's eyes went dark, and he collapsed, tumbling over the railing onto the tracks below. Tom fell to his knees, while the second figure hit the ground in front of him.

His trembling hands loosened the knife as the person on the floor removed their helmet, dark hair spilling over their shoulders.

"Jess," he breathed, scrambling toward her, his heart slamming against his ribs. The feel of the knife, the depth of the strike—it haunted his hands. "No, no... please."

Jess pressed her palms to her side, but blood was already pouring too fast, too much.

"Hey," he said, brushing her hair from her forehead, desperate to see her eyes. "Just look at me... I didn't—please, just—"

Jess looked up, her faint smile blurring through his tears.

"You're going to be fine," he said, voice breaking. "I'll get you out of here."

But even as he said it, his mind was spinning through the blood loss, the wound's depth, and the vanishing time left to save her.

20

Axiom Realm

J ESS OPENED THE DOOR of her house for the first time in weeks. As always, the small space greeted her with a strange mix of damp wood and earth. She assumed it came from the way these homes were built, but she didn't care. It was the only place where she could almost sleep—and leave most of her worries outside.

Tom followed her in, stopping by the glass door that led to the rocky beach. Stars and clouds hung over the dark waters, the night sky stretching endlessly above. He gestured toward the view, and Jess smiled faintly. Seeing his eyes light up at the sight of the ocean was unexpectedly beautiful.

She walked to her old stone stove and placed a wooden log inside to warm up the house. Thankfully, it didn't take long. The place had only two rooms: a small bedroom barely big enough for a bed, and an open space where the stove and pantry took up half the area.

The icy breeze from outside made her shiver when Tom slid the door open and stepped onto the porch. She wondered how nice it must have been to live there before the Disruption—before the collision of the realms changed the weather. She missed the warmth of her home realm as much as she missed her old life.

It didn't matter anymore. There was no way back. What had once been paradise was now an illegal settlement, and she had become an outcast.

"This view is amazing, Jess," Tom said, walking back inside. "I could die watching that..." He smiled and turned to close the door. "I could die watching many things in here."

Jess focused on the stove, pretending her heart didn't exist.

"You don't come here often," he said after a pause.

"Why would you say that?" she asked, her tone flat.

"Well, it's almost empty, and as I recall, your room was always full of stuff." He took off his hat and spun it between his fingers. "Clothes, books, blankets, flowers?"

Jess bit her lip and leaned against the counter. "It's dusty, but you can sit if you want."

Tom smiled, hesitated for a moment, then tossed his hat onto the chair beside him. For a second, Jess thought he might walk all the way over to stand in front of her. The idea of him being that close—like before his grandfather died—made her chest tighten. But instead, Tom pulled out a chair at the end of the table and sat down.

"This feels nice," he said, nodding toward the stove. "I keep forgetting how cold it got here after the..."

Jess poured water into two cups and handed one to him. Then she sat at the opposite end of the table. The distance between them felt enormous, as if the little table could hold an entire world. "Sorry, I don't really store food here."

"What?" Tom raised his voice playfully and tapped the table. "What kind of deal is this?"

"Like you noticed, I don't come often. These aren't times to waste anything."

Tom nodded, looking down at his cup, clearly struggling to find the right words.

"Most of the time I'm living by the Rupture," Jess said. "And before you ask—I told you, I don't work with the Radicals."

Tom nodded slowly, his voice dropping. "What are you doing there, Jess?"

It wasn't an accusation. His tone carried sadness—pain that almost made her cry.

"Well, usually I deal with the pests."

Tom's eyes widened. "The takuosums? The hyaerodeas? The ophidents[1]?"

Jess nodded. "All of those—and a few others. I work with a group trying to find patterns between the energy wave, the explosions, and the creatures' movements."

Tom chuckled softly. "So you're doing research."

"I guess so." She smiled faintly. "It's far from professional, and we lack so much equipment that I doubt it'll ever lead anywhere, but..." She shrugged. "At least I can pretend I'm helping beyond just—"

She stopped when she saw the curiosity in his eyes. She wasn't sure how he'd react to the rest.

"Beyond just what?" he asked.

"I suppose you're not really part of the government in Chaos, so..." She sighed. "I help find clean water and bring it to the Rupture settlements."

Tom opened his mouth, then changed his mind and rubbed the back of his neck. "So you don't work with the Radicals—but you're trafficking our water?"

"Our water?" Jess stared at him. "You really think of yourself as from Chaos now?"

Tom leaned back. "It's not like anyone in Axiom misses me. And I'm working with my family."

"Didn't you hate the remedy^2?" Jess asked, unable to hide the edge in her tone.

Tom chuckled. "How did you put it back then? 'I've got medical bots and gadgets for that', so no need for your glorious remedy." He gave a half-smile. "I guess I'm partly from Chaos. I always have been—even when I didn't know it."

Jess wanted to scream at him, to beg him to stop working with his family. She wished telling him everything she'd seen while living with Marshall could change his mind—but she knew better. He'd likely seen worse himself.

"How's Frank?" she asked, steering the conversation away.

"I guess he's all right." He took off his coat and draped it over the chair. "He's very protective of you. It was tough to convince him to give up any information."

"That's silly."

"How come? He really likes you."

Jess shook her head. "That's even sillier. He's your friend, and he's loyal to you. Plus, I told him that if anyone asked about me, he should tell them where to find me."

"Excuse me?" Tom's voice hardened. "Like you said, he's loyal. How could you tell him to give you away?"

"If someone asked Frank about me, it means they already know too much—about me, about us." Jess lifted her hands. "Just like you did."

Tom stood abruptly. "Your life is in danger, Jess."

"And yours isn't?" she countered, her voice rising. "I don't want anyone else hurt because of me. I can take care of myself. And clearly, you're doing fine."

Tom leaned against the chair. "Fine? I'm a criminal, Jess. You think this is what I wanted to do with my life?"

"Of course not." She crossed her arms, swallowing tears. "I'm so sorry for what I did to you. I just don't want anyone else getting hurt because of me."

She leaned forward and rested her head in her hands. She could hear Tom pacing, but he never came closer—just like that day in the Square when he made sure she knew he blamed her.

"Did you hear the news?" His tone made her want to stay silent, but she forced herself to listen.

"I learned a while ago that I prefer to ignore what's happening."

"That explains a lot."

Jess looked up to find him leaning over the back of the chair, his face closed off. "Your brother has a new agenda. Do you know who Darius Ven-Larve is?"

"The son of the Agency's director?"

"Theodore Ven-Larve retired—well, more like they forced him to leave. His son, Darius, is now in charge—and he's dismantling the Agency."

"What do you mean?" Jess's nerves spiked.

"All agents now serve as government officers. I don't know what kind—police, guards—who knows? But Darius is destroying the Agency. All the buildings, the camps—everything."

She shook her head. "That makes no sense. No sense at all."

"That's not all. Three days ago, when I crossed into Axiom, we reached Sector 15. They burned it down, Jess—and they didn't let anyone from Chaos leave."

Jess clutched her stomach, trying to breathe. "They *what*?"

Tom ran a hand through his hair and rested his elbows on the table. "And there's more. Bill and Darius—they're after you."

"Me?" Jess gasped. She didn't want to imagine the people fleeing a burning city. "Why?"

"Marshall thinks there's something in the Agency they don't want anyone to find—but you might know where it is."

"Marshall's idea..." Jess stepped back, her voice trembling. "You said you needed my help. That's what you need?"

Tom's shoulders sagged. "I need to find it before they do."

Jess covered her mouth, turning away. Her house suddenly felt smaller than ever, the heat from the stove stifling. "You want me to go *into* the Agency?"

Tom looked at her, but she didn't let him speak. "You sat there pretending to care about my safety, and now you want me to what? It's been *years* since I've been there! Everything's changed. It's not what it used to— What exactly do you want from there?"

"Marshall believes his father—our father—found a way to control the energy wave. It's written in this logbook. He thinks Lezar kept it in their cabin, but the Agency took everything after the Disruption."

"A logbook?" Jess laughed bitterly. "Tom, that's just— I get it." She crossed her arms, the tears already spilling down her cheeks. "Is this my repayment for what I did to you?"

"What?" Tom straightened, shaking his head. "Repayment? How can you think—?"

"How can I not? You've made my brother's life miserable—all for a deal with Marshall."

"A *deal* with Marshall?" Tom's voice rose. "Are you serious? Do you care about Bill now?"

"For all I care, Bill can rot in the wave!" she shouted. "But what do you expect me to believe, Tom? Bill had a deal with Marshall that you supposedly knew nothing about." She wiped her tears. "If you nearly killed him for lying to you, what do you think I should expect? I'm the person who you actually blame for everything."

Tom stood still, staring at her. "I don't— I said that, but—" He shook his head, grabbed his coat, and turned toward the door. "Whatever you heard from your brother is a lie. All of it."

Jess closed her eyes, hugging herself. "I'm sure he's a liar, but—"

The cold night air brushed her face as the door opened—and when she looked up, Tom was gone.

Jess sank to the ground, no longer resisting the overwhelming sadness that threatened to consume her.

1. **Ophidents**; poisonous creeping reptiles. It inhabits the wooded regions of the Chaos and Axiom meadows, particularly near the Barrier. Poisoning by this creature ranges from severe to fatal. An annual protective antidote is required for those who work or live in these areas. Aggression level: 5 out 5.

2. **Remedy**, an archaic phrase used in Chaos to describe a concoction of antibiotics, probiotics, and antidotes to increase the tolerance to the high levels of oxygen and other toxins within the domain.

21

CHAOS REALM

"**I**S SHE FEELING BETTER?" Phoebe asked Peter as he stepped out of the room in Holm's apartment.

"She's sleeping." He pushed his hair back and exhaled. "I can't thank you enough for taking her in. You've always helped me and my family—and Millie... she means the world to me."

Phoebe smiled, but the tension in her crossed arms and the furrow in her brow told a different story. Peter's chest tightened in silent agreement with her unspoken worries.

"It won't be easy to help her," Holm said from the kitchen table. "What she's done will take a toll on her soul."

Peter nodded and dropped onto the couch. "I keep trying to make sense of it, but I just can't. What could make them give that kind of order?"

Holm shook his head. "Where did they send you?"

"They fired me." Peter sneered at the memory of the officer who had handed him a paper and pointed to the door without a word. The smug satisfaction on that photonic face had stopped him from asking questions. The police had always envied the Agency—and now, with their newfound authority, they were enjoying it.

"Fired you?" Phoebe murmured. "Who else got dismissed?"

"Most of the high-ranking agents. All the interns. And the entire research department."

Holm rubbed his jaw, staring out the window. "It makes sense. The new government doesn't want anyone questioning their decisions. And I can only assume they already have a plan."

Peter's hands trembled as heat rose along his spine. "I can only imagine what kind of plan that is."

"I can't," Phoebe said, shaking her head. "I understand they want control—but burning? Killing?"

"Fear is a powerful source of control," Holm said, taking her hand. "Axiom has never seen this level of violence. Fear drives people to seek protection. Bill and Darius will offer it—and no one will question them once they define who the enemy is."

A sudden movement by the window caught their attention. Gall-I-31 climbed through and dropped into the room.

Peter jumped up and helped her down, then wrapped her in a warm hug. They didn't see each other often—living in different realms made visits difficult—but when they did, her presence brought him comfort.

"Marshall is gone," she said quietly, standing beside him.

"Gone?" Phoebe asked. "Again? Is he trying to escape—"

"Not like that." Gall-I kept her hand on Peter's arm and her eyes on the floor. "He made it clear where he was heading—and why."

Holm groaned. "Just get on with it."

Peter frowned but didn't argue. For all his dislike of Holm's attitude, he owed the old man—Holm had saved his sister once, and now he was sheltering Millie.

"Marshall moved to Sector 9," Gall-I said. "According to my informant, he sent a message to Bill: he's going to get his family back."

The room turned cold. Silence thickened until it felt heavy enough to breathe.

"You don't think he would..." Phoebe hesitated. "Would he attack Axiom?"

"I don't—" Holm stopped, then walked toward his office. "Did you hear anything about Tom?" he asked over his shoulder.

Gall-I shook her head and sank onto the couch. "Some say he's working in Elemental 6. Others claim he's on a secret mission. Everyone agrees on one thing—he isn't with Marshall."

Phoebe exhaled. "Clearly, they don't know him. He made Jess his priority for years. He must be trying to find her. Tom would do anything for her."

"He left her," Peter cut in. When Phoebe looked at him, he pointed at her. "You were there. You know they're done. He's had three years to rebuild his life—and from what I've heard, he fully embraced being a Corrupt."

"So you think he'd attack his home realm?" Phoebe asked, crossing her arms. "Even knowing Jess could be there?"

Peter shrugged as heat surged through his veins. He hated Tom—was certain he'd done something to Jess in the Square, something that made her leave them. The idea of her being with him again twisted his stomach. He wasn't perfect, but at least he'd changed for the better.

"It doesn't matter where Tom or Jess are," Holm said. "It's bad enough that we don't know his location—but the bigger problem is Marshall, and why he chose Sector 9. This is personal for him, and that never ends well."

"You really think he'll attack?" Peter asked, though Holm didn't need to answer. His silence said enough.

"We're on the verge of a war," Phoebe whispered. "And I'm afraid Chaos will suffer most—when Bill gets his revenge and our government can't protect us."

"Marshall won't let—" Gall-I began.

"Marshall is a criminal, not a savior," Peter snapped. "We're on our own now."

22

AXIOM REALM

188A25 YEAR WEEK 13,
FIFTH DAY, MORNING

WHEN JESS FINALLY FELL asleep, her dreams turned against her. She saw Tom crashing into the Barrier, yelling for her to leave his grandfather's funeral while holding Charlotte close. It had been a long time since those nightmares had haunted her. So when she woke, she decided to call it a night and drive back to the Rupture.

On the way, she turned on the transmitter and listened to the news for the first time in a year.

There was nothing about Sector 15 being blocked and only a brief mention of a wildfire in southern Axiom. Sector 9, however, dominated every headline. Overnight, the Corrupts had moved their airships into Axiom and were flying over that sector. The reporter said the Corrupt leader demanded the Axiom government release his pregnant sister-in-law—or else he'd look for her in Sector 8, where Mr. Hiem-Sagac's family lived. If not, that sector—and all its fancy neighbors—would face the consequences.

Jess's foot pressed harder on the gas. She could picture the panic in Sector 8. Her mother's anxiety. She hadn't spoken to her in years; it was still difficult to forgive the story her mother had spread about her sanity. But she still cared—for her, for

Dan. And after living with Marshall, Jess knew he was capable of following through with his threats.

Of course, Marshall knew her brother didn't have Tom's wife. He was bluffing, just like Bill. The problem was, Jess doubted Darius was smart enough to play that game against someone like Marshall. Darius was a different story altogether.

Rumor had it he'd once handled minor missions within the Agency, though his father had never favored him. Tom probably had no idea that Darius's ex-wife was Gall-I, or that his abuse had driven her to flee into Chaos. Jess had never met him herself, but what he'd done to her friend was enough to make her hate him.

One thing was certain: peace between the realms rested on a thin line—and both sides were about to cross it. She had to stop it.

The drive from her house to the Rupture usually took a couple of hours, longer near the end when she had to abandon the paved roads and follow dirt tracks to reach the makeshift study center—and, to her dismay, the Radicals' hideout. That morning, she arrived earlier than usual.

She didn't waste time. After hearing what Tom said and comparing it with the news, she needed to confirm a suspicion. She went looking for Eril Ungu-Ter.

"KG!" Lucille-71 shouted from the lab's doorway. "Didn't you say you'd be gone a few days?"

"Have you seen Eril?" Jess asked.

Lucille walked toward her, cheeks red, tugging at her sleeves. Jess sighed and rolled her eyes. She liked Lucille—but couldn't understand what the sweet girl saw in that photonic idiot.

"It's not what you think," Lucille blurted out. "We were eating, and he got tired. Poor guy, he'd been out all day... I offered the couch. That's all! Nothing happened, and I'm sure he didn't take anything from the office."

"Are you sure he didn't?"

Lucille looked down, her voice small. "He's still sleeping there."

Jess wanted to hug her for saving her time—but decided against it. She still needed to handle Eril.

"He's trouble, Lucille. You work here to help people. He just takes advantage of them."

Lucille shoved her hands into her pockets. "I get it, but... he's funny. He makes me forget where we are."

Jess bit back her frustration. She wasn't one to talk—she'd fallen for someone dangerous too. If Lucille ever learned that Jess had been in love with one of the Corrupts' chiefs, she'd have every right to call her a hypocrite.

"You deserve more," Jess said finally, heading for the office with Lucille close behind.

The lab was dark, the shades drawn. The low hum of machines blended with loud snoring.

Just as Lucille said, Eril was stretched across the couch, his legs up on the armrest, shoes off, reeking of sweat and mud. Jess grimaced. She didn't want to imagine how long it had been since he'd properly cleaned himself.

Light flooded the room when she yanked the curtains open. Eril groaned and covered his face with one arm.

"Please, sweetie," he mumbled sleepily. "I'm so tired, and the tents aren't good for resting. I thought you liked me?"

Jess huffed. "Hardly. And presumptuous of you to think I could ever like you."

Eril shot upright, eyes wide. "KG! I thought you were gone for—"

"A few days?" Jess closed the office door and crossed her arms. "I can't wait to hear what your boss says when I tell him you're complaining about his tents. Maybe he'll give you better accommodations."

"KG, please!" He scrambled to his feet, snatching a pillow to cover himself when he couldn't find his pants. "You're not mean! He'll kill me if he finds out I slept here."

Jess pulled out a chair and sat across from him. Months with Marshall had taught her how to intimidate someone—though she hated doing it.

"So you're asking me to protect you?" she said, shaking her head. "Why would I do that?"

Eril glanced at Lucille, then back at her. "Lucille's your friend. You wouldn't want her to be sad."

Jess laughed and grabbed the transmitter from the table. When he reached for it, she smacked his hand hard enough to crack his knuckles.

"In the void's name!" he yelped, clutching his hand as tears sprang to his eyes. "Are you insane? That hurts!"

"It'll hurt more when your boss teaches you why you need to stay out of my business."

The color drained from his face. Jess could almost see him calculating what she'd implied—if even his boss was told to stay away from her, he was in serious trouble.

"I'm sorry! It won't happen again, I swear..." He bent to grab his pants, but Jess kicked them aside. "What do you want?"

"Not much," Jess said, smiling thinly. "Just answers."

"I don't know much," he muttered, looking helplessly at Lucille.

"He isn't bad, KG," Lucille said, voice trembling.

A hint of guilt pricked Jess's chest—Lucille had nothing to do with this.

"You know enough," Jess said. "Sector 15. What happened?"

Eril rubbed his head. "I guess it got... uglier to live there?"

Jess leaned forward, eyes sharp. "Do you want to visit the void, Eril? Don't play with me. What did your people do to Sector 15?"

"I don't—"

Jess kicked the table between them and stepped closer. Lucille jumped aside, reaching for the door.

"Lu," Jess said, her tone calm but deadly, "you're my friend, but if you open that door, Eril is dead."

Eril pressed himself against the couch, hands shaking. "Wait—wait! I just overheard the boss say we needed more water and that the photonic creatures were everywhere, so..."

Jess crossed her arms. "The creatures here?"

He shook his head. "No, in Chaos. He's always there, and finding water's getting harder. That son of the Maker—Tom—was getting too close, so the boss came up with a plan." He waved his hands as if tracing the memory. "He figured if the realms are connected above, they must be connected below too. He sent some Radicals to burn the woods near Sector 15, but..." He looked up at Jess. "I wasn't there, KG! I didn't do anything! The fire got out of control. They didn't mean for it to reach the sector. There are hundreds of miles between the woods and the houses—that wasn't the plan, I swear!"

Jess rubbed her eyes, fighting to stay calm. "They just lost control of the fire?"

Eril nodded rapidly.

"Do you understand that your stupidity might cost both realms their peace?" She moved toward the door and paused to look back at them. "People died during the Disruption—but it'll be nothing compared to what happens if the Corrupts and Axiom's government start fighting. And your pitiful Radicals won't be able to stop it."

She stormed out toward her truck, anger burning through her chest. The Radicals were a pack of fools with egos too big for their brains. And now, the whole world was in danger because of them.

"KG!" Lucille shouted, running after her.

Jess sighed and waited by the truck door. She was in a hurry, but she'd lost too many friends by not taking the time to explain things. That was the Agency's way—and she was done with it.

"He's not a bad person," Lucille said between gasps. "He shouldn't have slept there, and I know what they did isn't right, but—"

Jess crossed her arms. Whatever expression she gave was enough to make Lucille stop talking.

"He's not a good person, Lu," Jess said, lowering her voice. "He's manipulative, and he's using you."

"Maybe," Lucille said softly. "But he's all I have. And this—" she gestured around them "—this is all we have. We're just trying to survive."

"It's not *we*, Lu. It's *they*." Jess climbed into her truck. "Survival's only for them. You still have a family outside this place. What happens to them when they have to survive a war?"

Without waiting for an answer, Jess drove away from the camp.

A S JESS LEFT THE Rupture behind, she knew her welcome there had ended. It was time to take a stand again.

Once she was far enough away, she reached for her transmitter and dialed a number she never thought she'd use. Her pulse thudded in her ears. It took only two rings for the other side to answer, and the familiar voice made her heart sink—confirming how desperate she had become.

"Who is this?"

"Do you give this number to many people, Marshall?" she asked, for once relieved to realize he was in the same realm.

A sound like a sharp exhale came through the line. "Of course not, my sweet Jess. But you never know who might've gotten this number from *you*."

"I didn't give—oh. I see." She wasn't sure how she felt about that. "No one forced me to do anything, and I'd never give it away. I gave you my word, remember?"

"True," Marshall said, his tone shifting back to that smooth, casual one—as if nothing was happening. "Still, when I gave it to you, things were different. Now our realms are a mess."

Jess sighed, gripping the wheel tighter. "You can't attack Sector 8. It wasn't Bill who burned it."

Marshall chuckled. "Of course it wasn't. Your brother is still the same coward. His new friend, though—he's capable of that and more."

"Well, I'm telling you, they didn't do it. The Radicals burned the woods, and it got out of control."

"What would motivate the Radicals to go that far—just to burn a section of Axiom?" His voice lost all humor. "Who's with you, Jess?"

"No one, Marshall. I'm driving alone. The only person I spoke to yesterday was Tom."

"Great!" His tone sharpened, the edge she recognized all too well—the one he used right before losing control. "And why isn't he with you? I talked to him too and... well, he's not exactly emotional, but when something's wrong with him, it's usually your fault."

Jess brushed a loose strand of hair behind her ear and cleared her throat. "The Radicals burned Sector 15 by accident. They believed the realms were connected underground through the water system, and they thought fire would shift the flow and drive the creatures away. I'm sure you've heard of more attacks in the north of Chaos lately?"

There was shuffling and faint voices on the other end before Marshall came back, sounding calmer. "I've heard bits of that. But here's the thing, Jess—even if you're right, it wasn't the

Radicals who stopped my people from escaping that fire. That was Axiom's new government. They need a lesson."

"Marshall," Jess said quietly, "you don't care about the people from either realm. Justice isn't what you fight for. You're a businessman."

"Jess, that hurts," he said lightly, his humor returning. Jess let out a slow breath—she needed him in that mood.

"Attacking Sector 8 gives Axiom the perfect excuse to invade Chaos," she said. "Their government can't protect anyone, and I doubt you'll step in. It'll be a massacre."

Marshall chuckled. "You just told me I don't care about people. Why would I care about this?"

"Come on, Marshall. Even from here, I can hear Yttri scolding you."

"What? That is not—fine." He sighed. "If it pleases you, I'll ease your concern. I'm not here to attack Sector 8. But I *am* going to support my brother in his mission—something you didn't do."

A pang shot through Jess's chest, stealing her breath. "Tom and I are done, but... you're right. I should have helped him."

Marshall's tone softened, losing its arrogance. "I doubt you two are done, Jess. One day, you'll have to figure it out."

"Then let me help him," she said, leaning forward. "If you tell me where he is, I'll find whatever you need from the Agency."

Marshall was silent for a long time—rare for him. Jess could almost imagine Yttri beside him, quietly urging restraint.

"I gave you my word before, Marshall, and I never broke it," she said. "You have it again. I'll find what you need from your father. Just tell me—where is Tom?"

"All right," Marshall said finally. "Tom is preparing to attack the Agency in Main City."

"He's *what*?" Jess's body went rigid. "Is he already there?"

"Or at least close enough. I'm here to create a distraction—and, of course, to be nearby in case he needs assistance."

Jess's world seemed to crumble around her. She whispered, "Thanks."

"Jess?" Marshall's voice dropped low. "I'm not exactly a fan of his plan. So if you can persuade him to stop, that'll be a plus."

Then the line went dead.

Jess sat frozen, the weight of his words sinking in. She changed direction and pressed the accelerator, heading straight toward Main City.

23

Axiom Realm

BILL WATCHED ARLETT AS she entered the room, her forced smile failing to hide her nervousness. She'd been like this since early morning. He wanted to believe it was because of the airships flying too close to their home, but he knew better—it was Darius's presence that unsettled her.

Ever since the news about Sector 15, Darius had changed. His demeanor was unnervingly upbeat, almost cheerful—something Arlett clearly noticed. Bill wondered if she understood Darius better now, having survived her mother Karen's attacks and met that lunatic Randall. Strangely, Darius's mood reminded Bill of when he'd first met Marshall's brother in the hospital.

He wished Arlett would just talk to him. But he knew how defensive he'd become about his new alliance, and she hated upsetting him. Some days, he wished she'd confront him anyway—it would mean she still felt something for him beyond pity. Instead, she kept pretending everything was normal, which was ridiculous. Around Darius, her usual warmth vanished, replaced by the rigid, condescending version of herself they both disliked.

"Sorry to interrupt," she said from the doorway. "I thought you'd want to know that Charlotte just arrived."

Bill smiled, but it was Darius who sprang up, clapping his hands as he strode toward her.

"Excellent! I can't wait to meet your dear friend."

"I don't think she's ready to see either of you."

Darius halted and turned toward Bill. The man was not used to being denied, and his expression said as much.

"Arlett," Bill said, rolling his wheelchair closer, "I'm sure Charlotte will love to talk to you all day long. Let's just meet her briefly—and then she'll be yours."

His tone was polite, but it carried the weight of command—one of the few privileges their social status still afforded him. Arlett straightened and avoided his gaze.

"At least let her change her clothes. Her travels were long and exhausting, especially in her condition."

Bill blinked, caught off guard—but pleased. He had half suspected she'd fabricated the pregnancy. This changed everything.

"I suppose we could meet her in an hour on the porch," Darius said, ignoring Arlett and looking straight at Bill. "Women are such fragile creatures. Sometimes better clothing makes them feel empowered."

Arlett left without acknowledging Bill—a small but unexpected act of defiance. Perhaps Charlotte's arrival would be more complicated than he'd thought.

"I'm sure Charlotte will take her time getting ready," Bill said, moving past Darius. "She's never been on time for anything. But that gives us time to talk."

Darius chuckled. "You sound like my mother—'time to talk.' We're *always* talking."

Bill ignored him and rolled onto the porch. It was a pleasant morning, brighter than the dark days before. Finally, the sun had decided to visit. He longed for the warmth of the pre-Disruption era—not just for the relief it brought his aching body, but for the companionship and ease of those lost days. He'd never say it aloud, but he missed his best friend as much as he hated him.

"I don't like the Corrupts being this close," Bill muttered, maneuvering to the far end for a better view of the door. He wanted to see anyone approaching. Darius sat in the nearest chair, his back to the entrance—like always, oblivious to potential danger. It had been three years since Bill had believed he was safe anywhere.

"How come, Bill? I love it!"

Bill frowned, waiting as Darius lit a cigar.

"You see, this is perfect," Darius said. "We're being threatened in our most prosperous sector. People here aren't used to conflict—not like those in Main City or the Rupture. They left that chaos behind and closed their eyes to it."

"Why is it *good* to have an enemy nearby?"

Darius exhaled smoke and smiled with satisfaction. "Because, Bill—this will justify our attack."

Bill's thoughts spun. "Are you insane? We can't attack them! They'll destroy our sector—our homes!"

"Such limited vision." Darius leaned forward, eyes gleaming. "We won't attack them *here*. We'll respond to their assault—with full force—in Chaos."

Before Bill could argue, movement at the doorway drew his attention. Arlett stood there, holding Charlotte's arm.

Charlotte looked... different. It wasn't just the rounded belly half-hidden beneath her loose dress. Her hair was shorter, her curls dull, her complexion pale. Her eyes—once bright and sharp—were empty.

"Bill," she said softly, barely audible from the porch. "I appreciate you taking me in. These aren't safe times—for me, or anyone."

Darius stood and pulled out a chair. "Miss Leph-Anim, please. You must be exhausted."

Charlotte nodded and sat gracefully. "Thank you, Mister...?"

"My apologies." He touched a hand to his chest. "Darius Ven-Larve, at your service."

Bill rolled his eyes, but Arlett cut through the pretense.

"This is the man who wants you to confront Tom."

Darius cleared his throat and backed off, forcing a smile. "Well, I wouldn't ask if we weren't desperate, Miss Leph-Anim."

"Charlotte, please." She tilted her head, mirroring his smooth tone.

There was something in her that Bill almost admired. She didn't play games—she *mastered* them.

"I understand things are complicated," Charlotte said. "But you must realize Tom is dangerous. I'm afraid he might seek revenge on me and my..." She placed a hand on her abdomen and smiled faintly.

If Bill hadn't known her for years, he might have believed the display of tenderness.

"We understand," Darius said, touching her hand. "But the future of your unborn child is already in jeopardy. If we don't stop the Corrupts, this will end badly for everyone—especially us."

Charlotte turned to Bill, trying to read his face. He gave nothing away. Back when Tom shattered his hips, she hadn't cared. She'd even pretended not to know him. When Marshall later revealed Tom's true identity, her testimony could have sealed his fate—made him pay for the Disruption, for everything that ruined Bill's life—but she'd stayed silent.

"I'll do my best," she said at last. "But I don't understand what you expect from me."

Darius leaned closer, his gaze tracing her face. "We just need a picture of you..." He paused, lowering his voice. "In your current condition, of course."

Charlotte's face flushed as she recoiled—a rare sight. "But Tom will know this isn't his baby."

"That's not a problem." Darius placed a hand on her shoulder. "Bill and Arlett explained your history with him. That's what makes you valuable. He won't let harm come to you—and that's when we'll catch him."

Charlotte's expression hardened. She reached up and patted the hand on her shoulder. "Is that so? Or does my presence here simply make your lie about having Tom's wife more believable to Axiom—no matter what Tom says or does?"

Darius's smile faltered, but Charlotte's brightened. She rose and walked toward Arlett.

"Men like you fooled me once. It won't happen again."

For a moment, Bill feared for her—Darius wasn't someone to challenge lightly.

"I'll help, though," she said, stopping by the door. "But in exchange, my future and my baby's must be secured. Can you make that happen?"

Darius smiled, equal parts admiration and menace. "I can make that happen."

"Excellent." She took a few steps before glancing back. "You said you needed a picture of me? Let's get to work, then."

———————◆◇◆———————

A MELIA GAZED OUT THE window, though her mind wasn't on the unusually sunny day. It remained trapped on the letter she'd received that morning.

Darius's recent visit had left her so anxious that she hadn't slept all night. Eventually, she gave up trying, rising before dawn and going for a walk so as not to disturb anyone.

Sector 8 was supposed to be a safe neighborhood—so she was completely unprepared when she encountered that criminal couple.

"Amelia," Dan said suddenly, breaking the silence so abruptly that she jumped, dropping the envelope.

"For the—Dan, please!"

"I'm so sorry, dear," he said, stepping into the room. "I didn't mean to frighten you."

Flustered, Amelia bent down, snatched up the envelope, and clutched it tightly to her chest.

Dan paused, eyeing her trembling hands. "The police officer just left," he said evenly. "No one was found near the house or within a few blocks. Is there anything else you forgot to mention, dear?"

Amelia's throat tightened, her vision blurring. "I don't think so. Those two criminals—they were poorly dressed, probably looking for food or something. They just walked up to me..."

Dan stepped closer, his gentle voice edged with concern. "Amelia, what is that?" He nodded toward her hands. "Why do you have a letter this early? The mail hasn't arrived yet, and you've never cared much for our correspondence."

He extended his hand—not demanding, just patient, as always. If she wanted to keep it to herself, he would accept that. But the weight of the letter was too much to bear alone. Her hands trembled as she handed it over.

"They gave me this," she whispered, her composure crumbling as tears filled her eyes.

Dan unfolded the thick papers and began reading. She had already read them—again and again—especially the parchment she still couldn't believe was real.

"Jess would never do this to me," Amelia said through sobs. "Despite our differences, she would *never* marry the monster who ruined Bill's life."

Dan met her eyes, his voice calm but uncertain. "I don't know, Amelia. It looks very official."

"It has to be fake!" she said sharply, then lowered her voice when she realized how loud she'd been. "Did you see who sent it? He's another monster, Dan. How can I believe anything that man says?"

"This Corrupt leader isn't someone to trust," Dan admitted, studying the parchment. "But... I'm not sure it's possible to forge this kind of document." He traced the seal. "The official mark of Chaos looks genuine."

Amelia pressed a hand to her chest and sank into her chair.

"You can't tell Bill—or—"

She cut him off with a firm whisper. "Of course not! Bill would... I don't even know what he'd do to her."

Dan sighed and knelt in front of her. "Amelia, you're missing the real problem. According to this Marshall's claim, Charlotte may *not* be Tom's wife."

Amelia gasped, her nerves fraying. "But she's expecting that lower-class contractor's baby! Dan, that *proves* the certificate is fake. My Jess didn't marry anyone."

But before that fragile hope could take root, Dan squeezed her hands and continued. "Or Bill is lying. It wouldn't be the first time—and you know it."

She shook her head but said nothing. Deep down, she knew he was right. Lies had always surrounded their family, and Jess had carried the heaviest burden of them all.

"I can't believe she would do that to me," Amelia murmured, leaning into Dan's gentle touch as he cupped her face.

"My dear," he said softly, "I can't imagine how this could be a forgery. Especially because this man asked nothing of us. What would he gain by telling you this?"

Amelia buried her face in her hands, trying to weep quietly. Dan was right again. Bill mustn't know—and she had no idea how to keep it from Darius, who was supposed to marry her daughter.

Dan lifted her chin to meet his eyes. "On the bright side, there *is* good news," he said gently. "His words are written in the present tense. She's alive."

The thought made Amelia's heart leap. She threw her arms around him, her tears now warm with relief. Despite everything—despite the pretense she'd maintained for years—she had never stopped worrying about her daughter. Married or not, all she wanted now was to hold Jess again.

24

Axiom Realm

188A25 Year Week 13, Fifth day, Afternoon

Jess parked her truck on a side street in Main City and hesitated before getting out. Marshall hadn't given her Tom's exact location, and she had no idea what his plans for the Agency were. Because of the street closures, she started walking to get around.

The afternoon rush filled the streets with people oblivious to the danger around them. A quiet resentment stirred in Jess's heart. All she'd ever wanted was a simple life—a normal job, maybe even a family. She had joined the Agency, yes, but becoming an agent had never been her dream. Now, it was far too late to fix her life.

Unconsciously, she quickened her pace, as if she could outrun those foolish dreams, and headed toward her past nightmare.

Although she visited the city from time to time, and she had been there just the day before to bail Tom, she had avoided that section of the town for months.

The Agency building towered over Main City, still the tallest structure in the area. Its slight tilt made it look like it leaned toward the neighboring rooftops, as though bowing under the weight of its own history. The thought of going made her.

stomach twist. It had been years since she'd felt safe within those walls. Even when Karen was alive, doubts had begun to creep in. Once she'd crossed into Chaos, she realized Tom and his grandfather had been right all along—the conspiracies she used to laugh off were probably true.

As she drew closer, the streets emptied. That was unusual. The Agency had once been one of Main City's landmarks. Locals used to have lunch in its gardens; tourists came to take pictures.

Three blocks from the building, she understood why. Signs now lined the streets, warning pedestrians not to go beyond that point. She wondered if those were new signs from the new director and his orders.

Jess turned the next corner casually. The once-bustling district, filled with luxury shops and restaurants, now resembled Chaos: boarded windows, chained doors, and silence. It looked like it had been abandoned for months.

She swallowed hard, trying not to think about all that had been lost.

"Fancy seeing you here," a woman's voice said, just before an arm hooked around Jess's neck and yanked her sideways. "The boss said you were off our radar. I'm guessing that makes you a traitor."

The woman slammed her against the wall, pressing a knife to her throat.

"Mer-80," Jess managed to say, despite the pressure against her neck.

"Excellent memory," Mer said, leaning in close.

"Some faces are hard to forget."

Mer groaned. "You made such a mess with Chief Umbrar and Marshall. If you think I'll let you do the same to—"

"Tom will definitely want to hear about the threats against his wife," Jess interrupted, shoving Mer back. "I need to talk to him."

"Good for you." Mer slid the knife back into its sheath and crossed her arms with a smirk. "Let's see if you can find him."

Jess took a step forward and jabbed a finger into Mer's chest. "You're taking me to him."

Mer laughed and shook her head.

Jess didn't care. "I'm sure Tom will love hearing how you stopped me from reaching him—and Marshall will enjoy learning how you blocked one of his messages."

Mer's nostrils flared as she rolled up her sleeves. "Move fast and stay quiet," she muttered. "It was too easy to find you."

Jess followed, hiding her satisfaction. Being found had been her plan all along. She knew Tom had surveillance nearby. If Mer had been Bill's person instead of Tom's, Jess would've enjoyed the fight—but she'd had enough of those lately. Her years away from the Agency had been anything but restful.

They entered a narrow parlor that opened onto a neglected courtyard. Cracked garden beds and overgrown weeds filled the space between the surrounding buildings. Jess's pulse quickened when Mer pulled down an emergency ladder and began to climb.

Out of all the things she missed from her former life, confronting her fear of heights was not one of them. Her palms were already slick with sweat.

"Hurry up!" Mer yelled from several floors above. "We're too exposed here! You're going to get us caught!"

Jess rolled her eyes. *Yelling isn't exactly helping either,* she thought, focusing on each careful step.

After what felt like forever, she reached the top, where Mer waited near the edge of the tenth floor. Jess didn't doubt the woman would push her if it weren't for Tom.

"Get in shape," Mer said, walking into an office.

Jess's eyes betrayed her; she glanced down. The ground was dizzyingly far away. Tom had once told her that the real fear of heights wasn't the fall itself—it was the strange *urge* to jump. Now, that same call made her breath catch and her heartbeat stutter.

She forced herself to turn away from the edge and count backward under her breath, trying not to think about the drop below—or who might be watching. Her hands instinctively covered her abdomen as she struggled to steady her breathing.

After a few seconds, she took a step forward and entered the room, resisting the overwhelming urge to either kiss the floor or cling to the nearest wall.

"WE DON'T HAVE MUCH intel about the campus," came the familiar high pitch of Heli-3's voice as Jess stepped inside the building.

Following the sound, she reached a front desk where a glass panel offered a view into a meeting room. A large table dominated the space, surrounded by chairs stacked against the walls. Sunlight streamed through a long window overlooking Main City.

Jess entered and immediately recognized the monitors and lights from the tracking setup Heli had once used in Chaos. Blueprints covered part of the table, the rest buried under explosives and mechanical devices.

She moved faster—then froze when she saw Frank seated at the table, his head in his hands. Tom stood opposite him, his back to her.

"Are you certain this is the best position?" Tom asked without looking up.

Mer spun lazily in a nearby chair, her gaze fixed on Jess each time she turned.

Heli pushed his hair back and caught sight of Jess first. His crooked smile appeared instantly. "About fifty-fifty," he said. "But she might know better." He tilted his chin toward the door.

Tom turned.

For one brief second, Jess's breath caught. He looked exactly as he had the first time she'd walked into his grandfather's workshop—focused, strong, alive. Then the expression hardened, and it felt like the sky outside dimmed behind him.

Frank looked up and gave her a small, uncertain smile.

"Mer?" Tom said. "Care to explain?"

Mer stopped spinning and leaned forward. "Found her sneaking around the street, sir."

"Alone?" Tom asked, shaking his head. "Not smart."

Jess bit her lip. "I talked to—"

"Not now," he snapped, turning back to the blueprints and Heli. "Fifty-fifty isn't good enough. If we're blowing this up, we can't risk it."

"Don't you think she could help?" Heli asked, nodding toward Jess.

"She didn't before," Tom said flatly, "and that plan was better. She had no input on this one."

Jess stepped closer to the table. No one stopped her, so she leaned in to study the plans.

The paper showed a rough outline of the Agency campus—main buildings, labs, dormitories, library. But the interiors were blank, the structures unlabeled. Tiny red chips dotted the map; along the gardens, smaller blue ones glowed faintly.

She pointed. "These?"

Heli grinned. "Blasting points and the escape route."

Jess's pulse spiked. "You're really going to blow it up?" She looked at Tom. "You can't be serious. Why would you destroy it?"

Tom crossed his arms, eyes fixed on the map.

"This is madness!" Jess grabbed his arm, forcing him to meet her gaze. "People *live* here. They'll die!"

"And you think I don't know that?" Tom's voice was sharp, the same tone he'd used the day he'd ordered her away from his grandfather's funeral. "I went to you first. You didn't want to help or even be here. You're free to leave. I don't need your help anymore—I have a new plan."

Her knees weakened, but she didn't move. "I'm sorry that—" she tried to keep her tone steady. "that I didn't jump in when you explained your—your insane mission. But I'm here now. I spoke to Marshall. I'll find what he wants. You don't have to hurt anyone."

Tom ran a hand through his hair but said nothing.

Then his eyes widened. Jess barely heard the faint buzzing before he lunged toward her, wrapping his arms around her and forcing her down—

She never hit the floor.

A blinding flash filled the room, followed by a thunderous explosion. Her ears popped as the blast ripped her from Tom's grasp and threw her into the wall. The impact knocked the air from her lungs, and thick smoke made it impossible to breathe.

Debris rained from the ceiling; a heavy chunk struck her leg, tearing skin and sending a stabbing pain up her spine. Warm liquid streamed down her shin. She tried to look, but the smoke was too dense, the ringing in her ears too loud.

Crawling along the wall, she gasped for air. When she finally stood, her leg held. Barely.

"Tom!" she tried to shout, but her voice vanished into the roar.

"Tom!" she screamed again, stumbling forward.

Her foot caught on something, and she fell.

"Jess—" Frank's voice was faint, almost drowned by the ringing. "Jess, what—"

"Dear Maker," she breathed, tears blurring her eyes.

Frank lay sprawled on the ground, blood soaking through his shirt. A deep gash split his forehead.

"Stay still," she said, sliding beside him. "Tell me where it hurts."

He groaned when she pressed his side, just below the ribs. Pulling up his shirt, she found a jagged wound slicing across his torso. She pressed his shirt back down and looked around desperately.

"Here," Tom said, kneeling beside her, handing over a strip of fabric.

She took it, scanning him for injuries.

"I'm fine," he said quickly, standing. "I need to find Coba and Heli. Stay with him—please."

He had barely taken two steps before another explosion rocked the room. Jess threw herself over Frank, bracing for debris that never came.

Instead, Tom's arms shielded her again. When the noise subsided, he pulled her up, his hands still on her face. "Are you all right?"

Jess nodded, unable to speak.

"I found them!" Mer shouted, shoving debris aside as she ran toward them.

Tom released Jess and crouched by Frank. "How about we get the photons out of here?"

Frank tried to respond but only managed a weak smile.

"Coba! Help me out here!" Tom yelled.

A massive man appeared through the smoke. Jess recognized him instantly—the one from the mansion, the man who had realized who Tom's father truly was.

"I told you pouring drinks was safer," Tom said, sliding an arm under Frank's shoulders. With Coba's help, they hoisted him up.

Frank groaned but didn't pass out, though Jess noticed the blood dripping steadily down his pants. Tom noticed, too.

"Mer," Tom said, drawing a gun and handing it to Jess. "You and Jess go ahead. Heli, cover our backs. Shoot anything that moves." Then, lowering his tone when he met Jess's eyes, he added, "We'll head down and away—Marshall won't reach us up here. We need a secure place for him to land safely.

At her side, Mer checked her weapon and strapped a smaller gun to her belt. Jess gripped Tom's gun tightly, praying her hands wouldn't shake.

It was the first time she'd seen this side of Tom—commanding, cold, and utterly fearless. She had always known he was a leader. What terrified her now was knowing she had helped turn him into this.

"I don't think we can get him down the ladder," Mer said.

"We're taking the main stairs," Tom replied. "There's enough chaos below to cover us. We don't need to hide anymore."

25

Axiom Realm

C LIMBING DOWN HAD BEEN the simple part.

Finding the city in ruins brought back memories Jess had buried for years. The gun in her hand didn't help either. She forced herself to focus on one goal—getting out of there. She knew of a plaza nearby, open enough to land an airship or, at worst, use the surrounding rooftops. The problem: it was nearly ten blocks away.

She tried not to look, but it was impossible. People were fleeing from buildings, some carrying buckets or shovels, others dragging loved ones behind them. Though the streets weren't packed, panic made it feel suffocating. Chunks of concrete and clouds of dust fell from the buildings, and Jess couldn't help but wonder if the whole city would soon collapse.

Ironically, the Agency wasn't even close—and from where she stood, that tilted tower still looked intact.

"Stop!" an officer shouted as Jess rounded a corner and collided with him.

Without hesitation, Mer raised her weapon and shot. The woman dropped instantly, her body hitting the wall before sliding to the ground.

"What the—" another officer shouted, rushing into view. Mer turned her gun on him. He froze, but the two behind him raised their shotguns.

Jess lifted her weapon, her hands trembling. She fired. The bullet struck one officer in the knee, sending him crashing into his partner, who lost balance and fired upward. The shot went wild, echoing across the street.

"Void take it!" Mer snarled and fired again, killing the second guard before he recovered. Jess kicked the wounded one hard enough to knock him out, clearing the path for Tom and the others.

Mer's glare was sharp enough to cut glass, but neither woman spoke. They just kept moving.

The deeper they went into the city, the worse the chaos became. Emergency vehicles blocked intersections; others sped past toward the smoke. Jess led them through an old restaurant, slipping past terrified diners and staff who huddled beneath tables.

Through the back door, she guided them down a narrow alley, cutting through several connected buildings until they reached the old medical tower. Despite its maze of hallways, Jess moved without hesitation. She'd been here before—visiting Peter during his rehabilitation. Back then, she'd used this same discreet route to avoid being seen.

When they finally emerged, the plaza opened before them—a wide amphitheater surrounded by manicured gardens and ornamental trees. Miraculously, the destruction hadn't reached it. For the first time that day, Jess almost smiled.

"What the void was that?" Mer shouted, shoving Jess hard enough to make her stumble. "That was a neutron's clean shot! Are you mad—or just trying to get us killed?"

"Enough!" Tom barked, helping Frank lower himself against the wall.

"Sir! We *almost died* because of her!" Mer's voice cracked, raw with adrenaline.

Jess didn't answer. She couldn't. Mer was right.

"We're alive," Tom said, his tone sharp enough to silence her. "And right now, our only priority is getting out."

Still, when he looked at Jess, his expression was a mix of anger and confusion—something between accusation and disbelief. Without another word, he turned away and motioned to Heli.

"We need to contact Marshall."

"Yes, sir," Heli replied, following him toward the far end of the plaza, out of earshot.

Jess stayed where she was, gun hanging loosely in her hand, the weight of everything—smoke, guilt, the past—pressing down harder than the dust-filled air around them.

E VEN THOUGH JESS WANTED to explain to Tom what had happened, she didn't follow him. Instead, she took a deep breath, bit her lip, and knelt beside Frank.

He didn't open his eyes until she pressed on his abdomen. A weak groan escaped his lips before he managed a faint smile. "Are you mad at me?"

Jess focused on his wound, trying to judge its depth. "I should be."

Frank rested his head back against the wall.

From what Jess could see, he was losing a lot of blood. His hands were cold, but sweat glistened on his forehead.

"Your pants... they have blood," he muttered, trying to move but failing. Swearing softly, he shut his eyes. "Are you—did you get hurt?"

Jess looked down at her leg. A dark patch had spread across her pants. The sharp, shattered pain had dulled into a deep burn, but since she could still stand, she refused to check it. Guilt already weighed so heavily on her chest that she preferred physical pain to facing what was in her mind.

"Try not to move," she said gently. "And keep this here." She guided his trembling hand over the wound and pressed it down. "Tight. I'll be right back."

She stood, scanning the area. One of these buildings had to have a first-aid kit—something, *anything* to help him.

"Is he gonna die?" Coba asked, stepping closer.

Jess glanced at Frank, then at Coba. "I hope not."

Coba wasn't someone she liked to cross—and not because of his size. She'd met him years ago as one of Lezar's men, and people like him and Mer were rumored to be even worse than Marshall's crew.

"What do you need?" he asked. When Jess didn't respond, he cleared his throat. "You helped us out of that mansion. I don't forget things like that. Plus, my new boss will kill me if—"

"Coba."

Tom's voice cut through the air as he approached. "Take care of Frank. I need to talk to Jess."

Coba saluted with a mock grin and winked at her before kneeling beside Frank.

"Care to walk with me?" Tom asked, already striding toward a nearby building without waiting for her answer.

Jess's legs wobbled. She wasn't sure if it was from her injury or from Tom's tone—an order disguised as a request. Bill used to talk that way.

Inside, the building opened into a spacious cafeteria. Either it had been evacuated earlier or no one had worked that day—it was spotless.

Tom vaulted over the counter and started rummaging behind it. The clatter of pots and plates echoed across the room.

"What are you—" she began, but he interrupted.

"Got it!" He hopped back over the counter, holding a bundle of white fabric napkins. "Here."

He shoved them into her hands and strode toward the far wall as if he owned the place. The confident rhythm of his steps—so much like the night in the Chaos mansion—made her chest tighten. Involving him back then had been a mistake.

"Found it!" Tom's voice echoed from a small storage room.

He returned carrying a red box in one hand and a white one in the other. Jess immediately recognized the smaller version of the CLEO mechanism—medical tech she'd used on missions before.

"This should help Frank until Marshall gets here."

"So you—" she turned away, trying to steady her voice. "You talked to Marshall?"

"Yes. He told me you two spoke."

Behind her, she heard his footsteps, but he didn't come closer.

"Frank will be fine," Tom said quietly. "Are you this upset because of him?"

Jess's shoulders sank. "Kind of. He has nothing to do with this. But it's not just him. It's everyone. The city. You."

"Me?" Tom asked. "I didn't get hurt."

Jess shook her head, but he continued before she could answer.

"Anyway, Marshall's on his way. He'll take Frank. You should go with them—get your leg checked."

Jess studied his face, trying to read the emotion behind the hard expression. "Are you coming too?"

He shook his head and moved past her. "I need to get my father's things first."

Ignoring the pain in her leg, Jess hurried after him, clutching the napkins tightly. She almost dropped them when she grabbed his arm and forced him to look at her. "You what?"

Tom shrugged. "It's important."

"No," she said, her voice rising.

He gave a humorless chuckle, his anger plain. "No? You're funny."

"I gave Marshall my word. I'll find Lezar's—"

"Great," Tom snapped. "You gave *Marshall* your word. For him, you rushed all the way down from the northern ocean. But when *I* asked for help, you accused me of setting a trap for you?"

"That's not what happened," Jess shot back. "You asked if I knew what Bill was planning, and I didn't—then. You left before finishing the conversation. Afterward, I listened to the news."

"Amazing. So now this is *my* fault?"

"I can't..." Jess shook her head and exhaled heavily. "Haven't you ever made mistakes in your life?"

Tom started to reply, then stopped. After a long pause, he said quietly, "You know I have."

Jess hugged the napkins tighter. "I'm sorry I didn't listen yesterday, but I don't understand how you expected me to—never mind. If you really plan to find whatever it is you're looking for, then I'm coming with you."

"Excuse me? I don't take orders from you."

"Well, I don't take orders from you either." She stepped closer. "You came to me for help. Don't be an idiot now."

"What?" Tom's eyes narrowed, but Jess didn't wait for him to argue. She turned and walked out of the building.

Her priority was Frank. She needed to make sure someone would care for him before Marshall arrived. Tom cared, but his new allies didn't. And Jess doubted any of them knew how to keep a dying man alive.

26

CHAOS REALM

188Ch25 Year Week 13, Fifth day, Night

Phoebe was born in Elemental 6, back when the city was little more than a few houses by the train station. By the time she turned ten, the hot-air balloon line had reached the element, bringing new businesses and prosperity. Back then, things looked promising. People walked the growing streets with smiles, marveling at the bustling traffic.

Until one day, a diplomatic visit from the government brought a foreign asset from Axiom. Phoebe, still young, didn't understand it—but her father did. Their resources were about to be compromised.

Within a year, their water supply was cut in half. The new alliance with Axiom required sending the other half across the realms. Elemental 6 was expendable.

After that, the city began to decay. Dirt roads turned into muddy slicks, and residents barricaded their doors in fear of raids by Corrupts or local criminals—both desperate for water. Phoebe struggled to understand how water could be scarce in a realm where it rained endlessly, until she nearly died from poisoning after drinking it.

Chaos's potable water came from underground, controlled by people like Arlett's father and his government. They didn't

care about their people; they sold the water to the highest bid-
der, as always—for their own benefit.

That night, the air carried a bitter chill that cut straight
through her coat. She was too old for missions like this, but she
had no choice. Holm would rather die than help Tom, but she
still believed in the poor man. On the surface, it looked like Tom
had fallen in with the wrong crowd—but Phoebe knew better.
In all his attacks, whether in Chaos or Axiom, civilian casualties
were minimal. His real goal had always been to sabotage Bill's
work, not to steal from others.

Holm didn't know she'd come back to her birthplace. Desperate times called for desperate choices, and she needed help.

She slowed as she reached Heli-3's workshop and drew her
gun. The light glowing from the doorframe made her stomach
tighten. Nobody left their doors open in Elemental 6.

Her footsteps turned silent as she crept closer, ears tuned to
the muffled sounds inside. Her small frame let her slip through
the narrow gap between the door and its frame. She pressed
against the wall, moving toward the dark side of the room.

The stench hit her immediately. She'd been here before—the
place always reeked of decay—but tonight her focus was sharper. Wood dust coated the floor. Chains and metal hooks hung
from the ceiling, each suspending a carcass waiting to be
butchered.

Phoebe waited for her eyes to adjust, scanning every corner.
When she felt certain she was alone, she moved forward. The
soft layer of sawdust muffled her steps, easing her nerves.

She was halfway across the room when something clattered
at the far end. Voices followed, growing louder. There wasn't

much cover—Heli-3 would never have let himself be ambushed like this.

Phoebe pressed against the wall and crouched, backing into one of the hanging carcasses. Her hand trembled as she brushed its cold flesh. A cloud of flies erupted from a hole in its side, and a thick, whitish liquid dripped to the floor. Her stomach turned.

"That son of the Maker!" a voice shouted, far too close for comfort.

"What did you expect?" another replied. "The coward's probably with Marshall in Axiom."

"He isn't with Marshall," the first man said. "He's working with *the bastard one*."

Something crashed—metal clanging and objects shattering. Phoebe flinched, glad for the corpse shielding her, though her visibility was poor.

"You think the idiots in Axiom already blew him up?" the second man asked.

"Blew the bastard up?" the first scoffed. "I hope not. That would piss off Little Boss, and I'm not dealing with that again."

"You should take over," the second voice teased, now alarmingly close. "Boss Ta-llum 73 has a nice ring to it. Or do you prefer Chief Ta-llum?"

A sharp crack rang out, followed by the clang of a metal pan rolling across the floor and stopping at Phoebe's boots.

"Don't joke about that, Os-mu," Ta-llum said from near the door. "Randall's never been forgiving—and after the Square... he's lost too many screws up there."

"My point exactly," Os-mu replied. The door creaked open, letting in an icy gust that stirred the sawdust at Phoebe's feet. "But I get it. We don't want to mess up the plan. It's kind of genius."

The door slammed shut. Darkness swallowed the room again.

Phoebe stayed still, listening to the ringing in her ears. Her nausea grew—whether from the rotting smell or the words she'd just heard, she couldn't tell.

She slid out from behind the carcass and slumped against the wall. Until this moment, no one had mentioned Randall. Everyone believed he'd died during the attack at the Square. Hearing otherwise—and that he had a *plan*—explained a lot.

Her pulse raced. Randall had always been unpredictable. It had shocked everyone to learn he'd killed his father and betrayed his brother, though in hindsight, it shouldn't have. Even Marshall had admitted as much. Knowing Randall had survived—and was still hungry for retribution—was another matter entirely.

Phoebe didn't understand the full picture, but if these men were planning another explosion, it couldn't mean anything good. The entire balance between realms was collapsing—and now even Bill's life was in danger.

Taking a deep breath, she headed for the door. Holm needed to know. So did Marshall and Tom. And Jess—Jess had to be found.

Phoebe froze. No one had heard from Jess in months. What if Randall already had her? The thought chilled her more than the night air. Maybe, she thought with dread, the worst thing for Jess would be if she *was* still alive.

The wind tore her hood back, biting at her ears and cheeks, but she didn't stop. She ran, trying to outrun the images clawing at her mind.

"There you are," someone said, grabbing her by the waist as a dark cloth dropped over her head. "Told you I sensed something odd back there."

Phoebe recognized Ta-llum's voice an instant before the fabric pressed over her mouth.

"Should we kill her?" Os-mu asked.

"No," Ta-llum said, his breath hot against her ear. "I'm sure Little Boss will *love* to see this one."

Phoebe kicked and thrashed, fighting the arms pinning her, until a sweet scent filled her nostrils. Her muscles went limp, her mind dimmed, and the world vanished.

27

Axiom Realm

Jess stopped at the corner, listening for any approaching footsteps. After ensuring it was safe, she nodded to Tom and moved down the street.

They had waited for the cover of darkness, but with emergency lights flashing and patrols sweeping the streets with flashlights, the city was far from dark. It was bright enough to help those escaping—but not for people like them, trying to sneak *into* the red zone.

"Do you hear that?" Tom asked beside her.

Jess slowed, grateful for the easier pace as her knee finally stopped cracking. She held her breath, straining to listen. In the distance, a faint humming reached her ears. It was familiar, but she couldn't quite place it. She glanced at Tom.

"If I had to bet," he said, "I'd say it's a locomotive."

"A train?" Jess frowned, trying to picture how that could be possible. There were no train tracks anywhere near Main City. The explosion flashed through her mind, and she froze. "Are you telling me part of the realms collapsed again?"

Tom met her gaze. "Would it surprise you?"

Jess closed her eyes for a second, forcing down the panic and the memories. When she started walking again, the pressure on her leg made her wince, but she pushed through. Maybe finding Tom's father's things didn't matter—but at least she was doing something. Neither Tom nor Marshall had caused the explosion, but she couldn't imagine the Radicals having that kind of power. And Bill? He had no reason to.

At the next intersection, she stopped again to check the streets. The Agency's tilted tower still stood, though the surrounding buildings—three full blocks of them—had collapsed. She stared at it for a moment before turning away.

"Where are you going?" Tom asked, pointing at the tower.

"We're looking for the chief's stuff, right?" She bit her lip, hearing the irony in her own voice. "It'll be easier to find whatever we're after if I actually know what it is."

"So you won't go there until I tell you?"

Jess shook her head. "Of course not. I just..." She sighed.

As a former agent, she understood the value of secrets. If this was Tom's turn to keep one, she wouldn't push. And if this was his way of getting even with her, she could live with that too.

"Are you sure the chief's stuff is in the tower?" she asked, though she didn't wait for an answer. "I doubt his belongings are still there."

Tom frowned. "How can you be so sure?"

Jess stopped and leaned against a wall. "Plenty of reasons—years of working there, for one. But the biggest? Karen."

Tom crossed his arms, watching her closely.

"The plan she built took years," Jess continued. "I'm certain she discovered Lezar was the Welder, and she had Randall at her side."

"Randall wasn't that involved in his father's business."

"Yes, that's what Marshall told me when I was undercover. But he also said Randall had no access to most Corrupt information. Still, he was Lezar's son. He might not have known what he was looking for, but he could've figured out *where* to look."

"You think they took our father's belongings before the Disruption?"

Jess shrugged. "It would make sense. I'm not sure what we're looking for, but if Marshall wants it, it's dangerous. Karen worked at the Agency for decades—she wouldn't have left anything important there. Too many eyes crossed those halls every day," she said softly. "She used to say that all the time."

"Marshall said the Agency emptied the cabin—found what they could in the ruins of the mansion and the Welder's tower. How can you be sure it wasn't there?"

Jess brushed her hair back. "I can't. But anything the Agency takes goes through an extreme level of scrutiny. If they'd found something useful, it would've gone straight to higher authorities. Bill's more of a show-off. Could he have hidden something big? Maybe... if you believe he did, then yes—we should go to the tower and forget everything else."

She sighed, as her admiration for Tom deepened—he'd followed her blindly through Chaos years ago.

His expression softened, and for a moment, Jess thought he might reach for her hand. Instead, he nodded. "So, where to now?"

Jess kept walking, refusing to linger on what couldn't be. As they moved farther from the tower and deeper into the trees that bordered the Agency's grounds, the light from the patrols grew faint. No one ventured this way.

"If there's nothing important in the tower," Tom said, "then what's the point of that massive insult to architecture?"

Jess turned to him, brows raised, as he grinned.

"An insult to architecture?" she echoed, struggling to keep a straight face.

"You can't seriously *like* that thing!" He pointed at the slanted structure. "There's nothing good about it."

"What about the inclination?" Jess asked. "Challenging gravity, like the Agency fighting for our security and peace every day?"

Tom burst out laughing, throwing his hands up. "If that's what they tell you!"

"And what's your explanation, then?"

He leaned down to her eye level, a teasing spark in his eyes. "A flashy waste of money—built to show off their arrogance while they pocketed the rest. More realistic, don't you think?"

"What? No!" Jess looked back at the tower. She didn't love the building, but the story behind it had once mattered. It had been part of her purpose. "There has to be *some* philosophy behind it."

"Well, yes," Tom said, chuckling. "Their philosophy of self-importance. Building a massive structure with no real purpose. It wastes space, costs a fortune to tilt like that—and it's ugly."

Jess wanted to defend her former workplace, but she couldn't. After the last few years, she'd learned most of what she'd believed in wasn't real. The conspiracies she used to laugh at were closer to the truth than she wanted to admit.

Tom cleared his throat and stepped back. "Not everyone there is bad, Jess."

She met his eyes. They were softer now—sad.

"You aren't like them," he said quietly. "You never were."

Before she could respond, a loud blast shattered the silence, followed by a bright flash that lit up the sky beside them.

T HE TEMPERATURE SURGED, AND for a brief moment, the blinding light swallowed everything. Jess barely had time to gasp before Tom forced her down, covering her head with his arms. A hot wave pressed against her back, strong but not enough to move them. Then the cold air returned, and distant screams broke through the silence.

"Are you all right?" Tom asked, brushing her hair from her face as he examined her. For the first time, he seemed aware of her injury and gently touched her leg. "Does it hurt more?"

"No. I'm fine, but..." She looked up at him, fear and desperation tightening her voice. "What is going on? Why would anyone attack all those people? What could they possibly gain?"

Tom shook his head and helped her to her feet. "You already know the reason, Jess. You worked for them."

Jess stepped back, wiping her eyes. "You think the Agency did this? Why would they attack their own—"

"The Agency is gone," Tom cut in. "It's been gone for years, and you know it." He paced a few steps. "If you want to keep pretending, fine. But remember—there's a reason you don't work for them anymore, right?"

"That doesn't mean they'd destroy themselves!" Jess snapped. "Or kill innocent people!" She turned to walk past him, but Tom caught her arm.

"Don't do that." His grip was gentle, but his eyes pierced her. "Don't do that again."

"What are you—"

"Running away. Avoiding the truth." He ran a hand through his hair, frustrated. "I'm not a good man, Jess. I've done terrible things these past years. But at least I'm not pretending to be blind to what's happening."

Jess pulled her arm free. "I'm not pretending, Tom. And I didn't run away." She paced, then faced him again. "Do you think I don't understand what's going on?"

"Of course not. You understand better than anyone." He paused, his voice quieter now. "But you can't pretend your brother is innocent... or me. We aren't, Jess. The Agency was never clean, and I'm sure you realized that soon after you joined." He gave a bitter snicker. "Good people wouldn't have forced you to marry someone like Marshall."

She stepped forward, trying to speak, but he kept going.

"Just because it didn't happen doesn't mean it wouldn't have." He kicked the dirt beside them. "You think Karen wouldn't have asked—or forced—you? You already signed the marriage certificate."

Jess bit her lip, the ground beneath her feeling unstable. She didn't trust her voice and had no idea how to answer. Those same doubts had haunted her before—during her time undercover and after discovering the truth about Karen. Instead of replying, she turned and started walking, hoping the research building wasn't far.

Behind her, Tom swore and followed in silence.

Fifteen minutes later, Jess spotted the familiar roof of the building where she'd started her career. Unlike the tower, it still stood—solid, steady, a piece of her past that gave her foolish comfort. She smiled faintly. At least she'd gone back to working for the right reasons. Their resources were limited, and their results barely mattered—but it still gave her purpose.

"That's where we're going," she said.

Tom nodded.

"I don't see any lights," she continued, "but we should circle around. Maybe find a weak spot to break in."

"Sounds good," he said.

Jess stopped and turned to him. "You really think Bill is behind this? That he's bombarding Main City—killing people?"

Tom pushed his hair back but didn't answer. When he tried to walk past her, she blocked his way. "Do you?"

"If not him, then his new best friend," Tom said. "What do you know about Darius?"

"Darius Ven-Larve?" Jess frowned. "Not much. I never worked directly with him, but what I've heard isn't good. I'm not surprised he took over from his father, though. It's like what happened with Marshall and his father."

"My father, Jess," Tom corrected. "Stop pretending I don't belong to that bloodline. And as for taking over—unlike Marshall, Darius forced Theodore Ven-Larve into early retirement, whatever that means. Since nobody's seen him since, I think we can both guess what really happened."

He sighed. "Darius also dismantled the Agency and partnered with the government, remember? Not a good sign. And your brother's standing right beside him. I hope you're not still naive enough to believe Darius was his only deal. Bill surely loves those.

"Love those?" Jess shook her head. "What are you talking about?"

Tom's shoulders sagged. He shoved his hands in his pockets. "I wish I could promise I'd never hurt you—but I already have. More than once. I don't blame you for being afraid of what I might do." He exhaled, looking up at the smoky sky. "Bill had a deal with Randall, Jess. After the one with Marshall fell apart, your brother sold you out—to Karen's partner."

"What?" Jess stepped back, her mind racing to keep up. "That can't be right. Bill never met Randall. How could he—Was it Karen? Did she talk to him?"

Tom shook his head. "No. Karen didn't hate your brother as much as she hated me, but he was still on her list." He gave a hollow laugh. "I can still hear her voice—telling me how much I deserved to die."

Jess reached for him, but he moved back.

"I probably did deserve it," he said quietly. "But someone saved me..." He stared into her eyes. "After I crashed into the

Barrier, Karen got shot a second before she could pulled the trigger of the gun on my neck... I doubt that was a lose bullet."

Jess looked away, trying to erase the images on her mind.

She heard Tom clearing his throat, and when he talked again, his tone was distant.

"Before all of that—when I brought Arlett back—your brother sold you out. Minutes after we arrived, Randall showed up at Bill's hospital room and took the key. Your key—or so he thought." He smiled. "I handed him the cuckoo clock... I'd rather be dead than betray you."

"My relic?" Jess whispered. "Wouldn't Karen's have—"

"He didn't know we'd already found Karen's," Tom said. "He was planning to betray her. He didn't care about me, so he just left. That's when I confronted your brother."

The world seemed to shrink around her. "But... Holm recovered my relic from the hospital. How—"

"Marshall," Tom said, pressing his lips together. "That's when I met him for the first time." He gave a short laugh. "He caught Randall's men as they were leaving the hospital. Your mother and Dan had just shown up in Bill's room. Dan stopped me before I could do something stupid. I ran outside—and Marshall was there. He handed me your supposed key and wished me luck."

Tears streamed down Jess's cheeks, but she ignored them. "You attacked Bill because of what he did to me?" She sighed and closed her eyes. "My mother said you lost your mind. She said you were furious over a contract, and Dan didn't deny it. I thought—"

"You thought I was angry about business?" Tom's voice dropped, heavy with pain.

"Partially." She sat down, shaking. "I thought you were angry because he put my family in danger—and because of what he and Arlett did with Charlotte—but..." She covered her eyes. "I stopped talking to my mother because I thought she was lying. You attacked him because he betrayed me?"

Tom crouched nearby but kept his distance. "The Square changed everything, Jess. Changed *me*. But you never have to be afraid of me. Not you. Never you." He exhaled. "I'm not saying this to excuse what I did. I'm not a good person. But Bill isn't either. He has to be behind all this—and no one will be safe until he and his new ally take control."

Jess wanted to keep asking about their past—to lose herself in it—but she knew better. "Would Marshall let that happen?" she asked softly. "Would either of you let them?"

Tom raised his hands and shrugged. "Marshall doesn't care about defending Axiom. But he won't let anyone take Chaos. We're trying to stop them—but it's not the kind of war you're hoping for."

Jess wiped her eyes and stood. If her home was going to survive, she'd have to fight for it herself. "We need to find the back door," she said. "It should be behind a thick line of bushes. Hopefully, we won't run into any aracnpodas[1] ."

1. **Aracnpoda**, a class of joint-legged invertebrate animals with eight legs, possesses a front pair of legs that have sensory functions. This species does not rely on poison, instead it traps its prey with a sticky thread. It typically resides in humid, dark places and is commonly found as a co-habitant of other species, where it nests beneath its host's skin and nourishes itself with its host's blood. If signs of infection are present, medical attention should be sought out immediately. Aggression level: 2 out 5.

28

Axiom Sea Periphery

188A25 Year Week 15,
Seventh day, Night

Tom set Jess on the floor and helped her rest her back against the wall. His heartbeat pounded in his ears, and the throbbing in his chest made every breath ache. He was certain the bullet wound on his forearm had reopened, and his leg still burned from his last encounter with the hyaerodea. None of it mattered. All he cared about was getting Jess out alive.

He crouched beside her and checked the improvised wrapping. She groaned when he pressed down, and he felt the warmth of her blood soaking through his fingers. He managed to slow the bleeding, but he knew he was running out of time.

He couldn't stop replaying the last fifteen minutes. The moment he realized what had happened, he had torn part of his shirt and pressed it to her side. He refused to look at the wound again—the blood staining her Agency uniform and the memory of his knife pushing into her flesh were enough to haunt him.

He searched the area for anything useful but soon realized it wasn't a room at all—it was a long corridor meant for inspecting chained cargo below. After wasting precious minutes, he found only a small rope and hurried back to Jess.

Gunfire and shouting echoed from the far end of the hallway. It was only a matter of time before someone reached them. Tom picked up Jess's gun, but he needed both hands to carry her, and she couldn't walk—could barely even move.

He blocked the hallway door with heavy chains and three barrels he dragged into place. Then, before lifting Jess again, he crept to the edge and peered down. The lower level was littered with barrels and disassembled missile parts. The tracks below were empty except for a few wagons.

Despite the heavy fortifications, only one guard had been stationed in the hall—the one Jess had killed. The area below looked abandoned, likely due to the surprise attack. That worked in his favor. He just needed to find somewhere safe for her.

Carefully, he wrapped the rope around her waist, making sure a strip of his torn shirt covered her wound. Once everything was secure, he tightened the rope. His stomach twisted when she opened her eyes, shuddering as tears streamed down her face, but he gave the rope another tug and, ignoring her weak protests, lifted her into his arms and carried her down the corridor.

Minutes later, he sat beside her again. The paleness of her face made it even harder to breathe. He rubbed his hands over his face, trying to steady their trembling. He couldn't tell if the pressure in his chest came from the pain—or the fear of losing her.

"Tom," Jess whispered, pausing to catch her breath before continuing. "You have to go."

Tom gave a shaky laugh and shifted closer, trying to keep her still. "As soon as I find our way to the roof, sunshine."

"I won't make it, but you—"

"Stop." He met her eyes. "I'm going to get us out of here or die trying. I'm not leaving you, so save your strength and stop wasting it on photonic ideas." He grunted and ran a hand through his hair. "If you die like this—" His voice cracked, and he couldn't finish.

Jess reached for his hand, forcing him to look at her. Whatever she was about to say, he didn't care. He wouldn't abandon her.

"The guards' elevator," she managed, closing her eyes. Her hand moved instinctively to her wound. "This is the guards' dock. At the end of the building—"

"The dock. Of course. Got it." Tom tightened his grip on her hand and pressed his forehead to hers. "I'll get you out of here. Just hold on, sunshine."

Footsteps echoed from somewhere above them—too close. Tom scooped Jess into his arms again and pressed himself against the wall, moving fast but silent, hoping to reach the far end before anyone found them.

29

CHAOS REALM

188Ch25 Year Week 13,
Fifth day, Late Night

"EXPLAIN AGAIN WHAT IN the void happened!" Marshall's voice thundered through the room, making Heli-3 step back and Yttri fold his arms.

"Right," Marshall said, exhaling sharply as he turned to Yttri, then back to the others. "Why isn't Tom with any of you right now?"

Heli-3 cleared his throat but kept his eyes fixed on the floor. Mer-80 pressed her lips together, silent. She wasn't one to speak out of turn—and in her defense, she had already explained what happened. Marshall simply found her story... unsatisfactory.

"Fine," Coba-27 said, "Tom ordered Heli to help his friend while we waited for you. Mer and I tried to go with him, but he refused. Said it'd be safer if we got back to you and reported what we saw. He didn't want the risk of hiding three people instead of one."

"And you agreed with him?" Marshall asked, struggling to keep his voice level.

"Of course not, but..." Coba scratched the back of his neck. "You know him, sir. Once Tom makes up his mind, there's no changing it. And the agent was with him."

At the mention of Jess, Mer rolled her eyes.

"Is there a problem with that?" Marshall asked her, his tone cool but sharp.

"Leaving our boss with a traitor agent? Why would that be a problem?"

Marshall stepped in front of her and crossed his arms, his gaze drilling into her. "A traitor to the Agency—or to us? Choose your words carefully, Mer. I don't like unfounded accusations."

Mer stared at the floor. For a moment, Marshall thought that was the end of it—but then she exhaled and spoke. "I never betrayed your father, and I never will. Nor will I betray you or Umbrar. But *she* did. She betrayed her people. That alone makes her untrustworthy. What's to stop her from betraying us too?"

Marshall started to shake his head, but Mer wasn't finished. "She conveniently missed a shot at an officer while we were crossing the city."

"She missed?" Marshall turned to Coba, who nodded, then looked at Yttri—whose wide-eyed stare said plenty.

"Yes, sir," Mer said, more confidently now. "We ran into a patrol. I shot one of them. Another turned the corner and stopped right in front of her—she couldn't have missed him. He was close enough to touch. But she shot his leg instead of his head. They could've caught us there."

Marshall paced the length of the airship cabin. He'd lived with Jess—he *knew* what kind of agent she was. She didn't miss. Not like that.

He looked back at Yttri, whose face remained tight with unease.

"Heli," Marshall said, "what did you learn about Jess's whereabouts over the last few years?"

Heli finally raised his head, a faint gleam flickering in his eyes. "She's been pretending to be that guy's sister," he said, nodding toward the small room where a nurse was tending to Frank. "He owns a bar, but she's not really related to him. From what I gathered, she's been working near the Rupture—helping people."

"Helping?" Marshall muttered, tilting his head. "The Rupture's a peculiar place to help people."

Yttri moved toward Frank's door.

"I'm not going in there!" Marshall said quickly. "The man's half-dead. And knowing Jess, he probably doesn't know a thing about her."

He turned back toward the wide window. Even from this distance, he could see the dark smoke rising from Main City, smothering the horizon. He didn't know who had sent the attacks, and he hated it. The obvious suspects were Bill and his new partner, Darius—but Marshall doubted it. Attacking their own city was reckless, even for them. Darius had already announced the Agency's dismantling. Why burn what he was trying to control?

No, this was something else.

"We need to talk to someone," Marshall said quietly, almost to himself. "Someone with another perspective on all this."

He strode down the narrow hall toward the control room. A few seconds later, he heard Yttri's steady footsteps following. Years of partnership had made words unnecessary.

"The Rupture's crawling with Radicals," Marshall said. "Maybe it's time we start taking those idiots seriously." He stopped, lowering his voice. "And Yttri—if Jess really is a traitor..."

He trailed off, shaking his head before continuing down the corridor. He didn't have to say it aloud—Yttri understood.

For the first time in years, Marshall found himself wishing he could still believe in people's character. He wanted to trust the woman who'd once kept him alive—the agent who'd saved his life more times than he could count. Whatever had happened during their escape, there *had* to be a rational explanation.

30

Axiom Realm

188A25 Year Week 13,
Fifth day, Late Night

Tom tore away the rotten wooden board from the second-floor window and tossed it aside. The sensation of aracnpodas crawling across his arms made him shiver. He should have been used to the disgusting things by now. Between construction work and his time in his grandfather's workshop, he'd seen plenty of them—but their swollen black bodies, twisted legs, and twitching antennae still made his skin crawl.

He tugged his sleeve down to cover his hand before gripping the edge of the window frame. The glass had been shattered long ago—likely not by human hands. Ideally, they would have avoided using the window altogether, but the bushes Jess mentioned had grown so thick that reaching the door without machetes was impossible. The same bush had invaded the window, and Tom was using it as an improvised ladder.

"Do you see anything?" Jess called from below.

Tom looked down at her. "Do you happen to have a flashlight?"

"I don't—but you do."

He frowned. "I do?"

"It's in your coat's inside pocket."

Tom reached into his coat, still skeptical, and pulled out a small metallic cylinder. "And how do you know this?"

"Yttri told me."

Tom chuckled, clicking the light on. "Yttri told you? With his *mind*?"

Jess didn't answer. When he looked down again, she was smiling.

"Wait—did he actually talk to you? He doesn't even talk to Marshall. How is that possible? And why would he tell you about *my* coat? Are you joking right now?"

"I'll neither confirm nor deny anything," Jess said, still grinning. "But your clothes look a lot like Marshall's these days. I assume Yttri took the same precautions with you."

Tom groaned. "What else am I wearing?"

Jess shrugged. "Your clothes, your problem. What do you see in there?"

He turned his attention back to the window. The interior was a stark contrast to the Agency tower. According to Jess, this had once been home to the main investigation labs. If that was true, it was a brilliant disguise—no one would ever assume this dump contained anything worth keeping.

Dust blanketed the room, mingling with half-dead vines and stubborn weeds pushing through cracks. A few tables still stood, surrounded by broken stools. When Tom swept the light across the space, something small darted across the floor—a flash of fur followed by the sound of shattering glass.

He shivered. He didn't want to meet any living creatures—especially not humans. After another careful scan, he turned to Jess. "No human movement, but there's definitely *something* in there."

Jess nodded. "I figured. Let me..." She studied the bush for a moment, then started climbing. "I'll be right there."

Tom watched her. If he hadn't known about her fear of heights, he might not have noticed the slight tremor in her hands or the way she avoided looking down. That familiar need to protect her rose again inside him.

He wondered if their earlier conversation had changed anything between them. It shouldn't have. His life had taken a dark turn far from hers, and no matter how much he wanted otherwise, he wouldn't drag her down with him.

He shook the thought off and turned back to the window.

Pulling his sleeve down again, he knocked out the remaining shards of glass and climbed through. Once inside, he reached back to help Jess.

"Here," he said, steadying her as she stepped through. Her hand was warm and soft against his—far too brief a moment of comfort.

"Thank you." She brushed her hair behind her ear. "This looks so different."

"I'm glad," he said. "For a second, I was worried about your job preferences."

Jess gave him a deadpan look, though a spark glimmered in her eyes. "Hilarious."

"Hey, my last two jobs weren't exactly spotless either. The workshop had more dust than any of the construction sites."

She chuckled softly and wandered toward the center of the room, running her fingers along an old counter. "So many memories…"

"Good ones or bad?" he asked before realizing how personal that sounded.

"Here?" Her voice softened into the tone he remembered from years ago. "Mostly good ones."

The warmth in her voice felt like a punch to his chest. Knowing he had no place in that part of her life hurt more than he cared to admit. An irrational urge to destroy everything in the room flashed through him, but instead, he shoved his hair back and crossed to the far side.

"Any chance this place has more flashlights? We'll cover more ground faster if we both have light."

"Ah… yes, of course." Jess opened a cabinet door carefully. "In case something jumps out." She hesitated, just for a second, and Tom's gut tightened.

"Maybe check for batteries in that—" she began, then lit up. "Found it!"

A small light flickered to life in her hand. It was dim, but it worked.

"You take this one," Tom said, handing her his brighter flashlight. "I have no idea where to look, but you do. You'll need it more."

Jess took it, avoiding his eyes. "What happened to your hand?"

He looked down, confused, until he realized she meant the scar. The one from his fight with the mirror—the night after his rescue from the Square. He didn't know how to explain it.

"I'm not sure," he said finally, moving away. "Should we check this room?"

She didn't answer right away. When he looked back, she was still studying him. He forced a faint smile and focused on a nearby drawer. Silence was safer.

"Dr. Falc-Axon's office is on the lower floor," Jess said at last, pushing open the door.

The hallway beyond was darker and even more suffocating. Tom didn't like the look of it.

"Let me go first," he said, stepping ahead of her.

"Didn't you just say you have no idea where to go?"

"Correct. But I still refuse to let you walk into that doom pit before me."

Jess pressed her lips together and let him lead. After a few steps, she asked, "Is it my fault?"

He blinked. "What?"

"Your scar," she clarified. "Is it my fault?"

Tom shoved aside a low branch, harder than necessary. "Is it my fault you missed that shot?"

"No," she said. The certainty in her voice made him stop and turn.

"No?"

Jess lifted her chin, meeting his gaze. "You are right. It wasn't an accident. The last time I fired a gun was when I killed Karen. I haven't held one since—until you handed me yours today."

Tom exhaled sharply. "And that has nothing to do with me?"

"Shockingly, no," Jess said, crossing her arms. "I know what Karen did to everyone, but... she meant a lot to me. Killing her wasn't how I imagined our story ending. I'll always have questions no one can—or will—answer. And no," her voice trembled, "I don't regret doing it. Your life was at stake. But..." She lifted one shoulder. "I miss her."

Tom stepped closer and pulled her into his arms. For a moment, Jess froze, then slowly hugged him back, resting her head against his chest. She didn't cry, and somehow that worried him even more.

"I lost a fight with a mirror," he whispered. "Idiotic and childish, but... I missed you."

Her arms tightened, and for one fragile heartbeat, he wished the world would stop. When it didn't, he kissed her forehead and stepped back. Her eyes avoided his, and guilt twisted inside him. He deserved that distance.

"We should keep looking," he said softly.

Jess nodded.

"Tom," she said after a pause, her voice barely above a whisper. When he turned, she was staring at him. "I miss you too."

He smiled, though his chest ached. Every instinct screamed to hold her again, but the wall between their lives was too high to cross.

"I'm one of your enemies now, Jess."

Jess tilted her head, biting her lip. "You don't have to be."

He shoved his hands into his pockets. "After I lost my grandpa, I thought I was completely alone. Sure, Bill and your family were there, but I always knew they didn't see me as one of them."

"Tom, that's not true."

"So your mom would've accepted me as an appropriate suitor for her daughter?"

Even in the dim light, he saw the blush on Jess's cheeks, and it melted him.

"I didn't think so either." He smirked faintly. "Marshall's a bastard to everyone else—but he's chief for a reason. And even though I'm older, he treats me like a kid brother. He opened his *home* to me, not his business. I like that about him."

Jess lowered her eyes but nodded. "Let's find your stuff, then."

Tom turned to move on, but Jess spoke again.

"Just remember, Tom—I'm not the innocent girl you have in your head. I was a trained agent for a long time. My conscience isn't clean either. I know there's nothing left between us but broken pieces that'll never fit together again. But if you don't want me to think of you as a good man, don't you dare think I'm better than you."

She lifted the flashlight, casting its beam down the next hallway.

"The first level should have more creatures and plants than this one," she said. "Better get ready."

31

Chaos Realm

188Ch25 Year Week 13,
Fifth day, Late Night

Holm paced the length of his office. The place he had always considered safe—his home—suddenly wasn't. It felt hollow now, stripped of warmth, leaving him lost and uncertain where to even begin looking for his wife.

Gall-I's words at the door offered no comfort to his weary heart. She turned to her brother and said softly, "Perhaps she's just delayed. She only missed one contact, Peter... just a delay?"

"No," Peter said. "That's not the case. She left without telling anyone. It's been three hours since her last connection to the main board."

Holm stared at the blinking lights on his desk, deliberately tuning out the rest. It was foolish, but all he wanted was to hear the familiar creak of the ladder outside their window—the sound of Phoebe returning, apologizing for worrying him.

"Holm," Peter said sharply. "I need you to focus. We can find her, but I need your help."

Normally, Holm would have barked something back—dismissed Peter's empty reassurance. But not now. Phoebe was his life, his balance on unsteady ground. Without her, he was nothing but guilt and regret. Part of him wanted to run into the streets screaming her name; another part wanted to collapse and never move again. For the first time, he understood what Tom had felt when Jess disappeared—and the realization made the pain worse.

A pair of hands gripped his shoulders, halting him mid-pace.

"Focus, Holm," Peter repeated, locking eyes with him. "Phoebe's life is in your hands. Help me find her."

Holm's limbs felt heavy, his bones stiff with cold. He knew the odds of finding her alive—and hated himself for even thinking them. "I don't even know where to start."

"I have an idea," came a soft voice.

For an instant, Holm's heart leapt—he thought Jess had returned just when he needed her most. But when the light shifted, it revealed Millie's face. Peter's girlfriend stood in the doorway, determination in her eyes. Holm's shoulders sagged as he sank into his chair.

"I've spent years tracking people," Millie said, crouching in front of him. "Tell me—where was her last signal?"

Holm stared blankly at her. A dark thought crossed his mind—maybe he didn't *want* to find Phoebe. If she stayed lost, she could still be alive somewhere. If he found her body... his life would end with hers.

"I don't know," he whispered. "She left without telling me anything."

"She wouldn't give up on you," Gall-I said. "If she's dead, there's nothing we can do—but if she isn't... Think about that, Holm. You saved me from a monster. What if she's with one now?"

Her words hit him like a bucket of ice water.

"Gall-I!" Peter snapped. "Where's your compassion? He just lost his wife. Let him process."

"He needs to *help*," Gall-I shot back, crossing her arms. "Phoebe has done so much for me. I'm not waiting around for him to *realize* we need to move. We don't have time!"

"Yes, but—" Peter began.

"She's right," Holm said hoarsely. He cleared his throat and steadied his voice. "Phoebe needs us more than I need her."

He turned toward his desk. The board was alive with flickering lights—hundreds of signals in motion. Years ago, he had built the system himself to monitor his agents across Chaos. It also served as their primary line of communication with Axiom—a living map of the realm. Phoebe wasn't hiding from him, so her signal had always been visible. But now her light had gone dark in Elemental 6—and never reconnected. She should have pinged one of the transport lines by now.

"My guess is she went looking for the Tracker," he said, pointing to the lower left section of the board. "This was her last location—Elemental 6, near the main street, close to the boat line."

Millie leaned closer, studying the display. "Could the Tracker have set a trap?"

Holm sighed. "Possible. But I don't see why—unless he's turned on Marshall." He paused, staring out the window. "Since the Square, even when we went separate ways, Marshall's kept a line of communication open. We don't help each other—but we don't interfere either."

"All right," Peter said. "Then we should contact him."

"You can't just grab a transmitter and call the Corrupts' chief," Millie argued.

But it was Gall-I who answered. "Marshall's in Axiom. It won't be easy, but I'll cross over and find him."

Holm nodded.

"Wait—what?" Peter stepped forward. "You can't go back there! Holm, tell her! She's in danger over there—especially now. Her bastard ex-husband isn't just some spoiled heir anymore, he's—"

"I won't cross his path," Gall-I said firmly. "After all these years, I doubt Darius expects to see me."

"Darius?" Millie turned to Peter. "She doesn't mean Darius *Ven-Larve*, does she?"

Peter's jaw tightened. "He's more powerful now, Gall-I. If he finds you—"

"Yes, Millie," Gall-I said, her tone cool. "*That* Darius Ven-Larve. Once, I was young and foolish—and he was every girl's dream."

Millie's expression softened. "Oh, Gall-I..."

"This isn't the time for sympathy," Gall-I said briskly. "I'll find Marshall. You two stay here and track Phoebe."

Peter opened his mouth, but she cut him off. "You and Millie would be in more danger crossing back than I will."

"Let's go," Holm said, moving toward the door.

"Holm," Gall-I said gently. "You don't have to come. What if Phoebe—"

"Checks in? Calls?" He picked up his umbrella and headed out. Behind him, he heard their footsteps following. "If she does, she'll be safe, and this will all seem overprotective and foolish. But we know it won't happen—and two can find Marshall faster."

At the apartment door, he turned back to them. "Our lives are all in danger, but I won't ask you to stay behind. I know what Phoebe means to each of you. Just be careful—and do nothing stupid that'll make me have to track you later."

Peter chuckled. "That's more like it. What do you want me to do?"

"Obviously, help Millie track Phoebe," Holm said. Then, from the hallway, he called back, "And thank you."

32

Axiom Realm

Tom hated having Jess walk in front of him, but at least her limp was almost gone, so the leg had to be improving. He also hated that both of their lights were dying while the noises around them said they weren't alone. A small part of him wished their company belonged to their own species. It didn't. According to Jess, the only reason they hadn't been attacked yet was because the creatures nearby were mainly scavengers.

"Think positive," Jess said, hand on the stairwell door. "At least we don't have takuosums."

"And that is because...?"

Jess eased the door just enough to knife her beam through the gap. "Hyaerodeas are territorial. They won't share the building with anything else."

"Great. They'll be thrilled we're visiting."

Jess rolled her eyes and pushed the door wider. The moment her beam cut across the stairwell, the whole building answered with high, keening screams—like a woman crying for help—only not human. The sound crawled under Tom's skin.

When the screams thinned farther down, Jess slipped inside. Two steps in she stopped and glanced back. "We have to go to the basement."

"Of course we do." Tom swung his light down the stairs.

Ground floor meant the run of steps went both up and down. Either way looked bad: heavy webs sheeted the walls, strands clotted the treads. From the give under his boots, he'd bet the structure wasn't safe for anything that walked.

He aimed his light upward. "Think that photonic tree is still outside, or did it just move in and sign a lease?"

Jess looked at the floor, biting her lip. "It's a shame. I loved this place." She took the first creaking step. "Let's go. Unlike the tree, we're safer inside."

Tom followed, flashlight sweeping their back trail the way Jess had told him. The boards popped under his weight. The railing was a no-go—webs thick as rope, and who knew if ophidents were knitting themselves a nest inside. He hadn't had the anti-venom shots for three years.

Halfway down Jess's light stuttered. A shadow flitted at Tom's side; he swung his gun toward it, but it vanished.

Her beam sputtered again, then steadied to a weak glow— just enough to pick up a pair of eyes watching them.

"I can shoot it," Tom murmured, moving in close.

"We don't know who's outside," Jess said. "Creepy noises are easy to blame on creatures. Gunshots aren't."

"It won't matter if we get hunted in here."

"The file room is the first door," Jess said, stepping lower as her light dimmed further. "If we make it inside, we'll be safe."

"What makes you think they haven't nested there?"

She smacked the flashlight with her palm. It flared a second—enough to show a metal slab door with heavy grates and a big spoke handle.

"It's a safety vault?"

"Kind of," she said. "Opens from both sides. Fireproof and climate-controlled."

Tom frowned, but a growl behind him cut the thought short. The eyes were closer than he'd guessed.

"The dangerous one is on my right," Jess whispered, still watching the door. "They hunt in groups. The second the lights go—"

Tom's light flickered twice and died. For a heartbeat, darkness swallowed them. His eyes adjusted to Jess's failing glow: a hyaerodea crouched by his boots, longer and leaner than he'd hoped, all jaw and claw.

"Jess, we need to move."

"I wish we could." Her back bumped his.

He turned. A larger hyaerodea had planted itself between Jess and the vault, low and growling. Shooting was a losing plan; the chorus of skittering and throat-noise rising around them said they were already outnumbered. Even if he dropped two, he wouldn't have time for the rest.

"We could—" Jess began.

A crack exploded from the upper landing. Another hyaerodea slammed down onto the mid-stair, railing snapping, drywall sloughing in a powdery slide.

Tom shoved his dead flashlight into his pocket and took Jess's hand, keeping his eyes on the dark. "You haven't shot at anyone in years. Can you shoot at something? Not...alive."

Jess pressed her back to his. A growl vibrated behind Tom. "Maybe. I haven't aimed at anything in a long time."

"At least it's not a hard no." He smiled at his own bad idea. "We're close—sort of. I can see the wall pipes from here. One's got to be a gas line. The vault should protect us from a *minor* explosion."

"A minor explosion?" she hissed. "You don't even know there's gas. The place looks abandoned. And what if someone hears us?"

"It's this, or sprint for the door—and from what's breathing down my neck, that's not an option."

She exhaled. "Fine. No promises I'll hit it."

"Good. No promises it'll work." He eased his pistol into her right hand. "Where the railing broke—there's a hole in the wall. Pipes behind it. They bunch together at the top. Aim there."

"You're giving me range directions?"

"Pretty cool, right?" He slid the flashlight from her hand but kept the glow behind him. If something lunged, it would take him first.

Behind his arm, the gun's action clicked. "Then what?" Jess asked. "We run for the door?"

"Hopefully." He drew a breath. "On my count we turn and you—"

Jess reached under his left arm and fired.

Time held its breath. Nothing moved. Nothing happened. Then, a light flared into Tom's eyes; he didn't wait. He flung himself over Jess, driving her flat.

The explosion punched the stairwell. Heat rolled up the walls as a line of flame zipped the ceiling and slammed into the vault door, then vanished as quickly as it came. Tom's instincts screamed louder than the blast.

The creatures panicked, scrabbling away into the dark.

Jess crawled towards the door, but right before she reached it, Tom pushed her hand back. He took his coat off and, using it as protection, he rolled the spoke handle. Underneath the fabric, the heat of the metal seemed to push the wool against his skin, right before a sharp pain ran up his fingers and palm.

"Let me help you," Jess said.

Tom ignored her, and using all his strength, he forced the last turn, releasing all the teeth of the lock. With a groan, he pulled the door.

Stairwell fire washed the threshold with light. Jess had been right: the vault wasn't small; it mirrored the floors above. The cold air coming from it gave a brief respite for his burned hands.

Jess walked inside, and Tom forced the door shut. It was easier from the unheated side, where fire hadn't touched the steel. Darkness swallowed them, broken only by the weak glow in his pocket. He'd forgotten he still had the flashlight; lucky. Without it, they'd be blind.

"There are tall windows in the next sector," Jess said, tugging him along. "Let me check."

She didn't wait. She caught his hands and hissed. "What were you thinking?"

"Getting inside," he said. He tried to pull away, but she held his wrist and searched his face.

"Your coat is *wool*." She leaned in, then kicked the floor in frustration. "We need more light. There's got to be a first-aid kit—or at least wraps."

He bent closer, this time searching her eyes. "You're sure those things won't be in here?"

Jess nodded.

"And we won't run out of air?"

"This vault is massive. Two more levels below. The cold keeps creatures out, and that door is the only way in."

"The windows?" he pressed. "You said—"

"Fireproof. Soundproof. Outside, they're barely above ground. We couldn't use them to break in even if we wanted to. The bushes will have them choked off."

Tom pressed his lips together. He hated the idea of being locked in *anywhere*. Still, not fighting hyaerodeas was a massive improvement—and Jess being with him helped.

"Let's get to the next sector," Jess said. Before she released him, she tugged his hands a little closer. "I'll find wraps. Then I'm cleaning those burns. Understood?"

Tom smiled. When she let go, he gave her a mock salute. "Whatever you say, Boss."

She rolled her eyes, but even in the dark, he saw a smile.

33

Chaos Realm

P ETER CLIMBED INTO THE hot-air balloon right after Millie, who had already jumped into the basket. For the first time in days, a smile lit her face—a sight he'd missed and wished he could bring out more often.

"Sir!" the man holding the tether shouted, snapping Peter out of his thoughts. He stumbled as he landed in the basket with a loud *thump*, right at Millie's feet.

Millie laughed and offered her hand. "Don't do this often, huh?"

"I wasn't paying attention," he said, careful not to singe his hair on the flame above. "Someone really pretty made it look easy on her first try."

Her cheeks flushed, but she shook her head and sat down. "We need to focus. Phoebe needs our help."

Peter nodded, settling beside her. "Right. Last time she checked in, she was near the Tracker's place. We start there and hope for the best."

"You always hope for the best?"

"Not really," he sighed. "But in this case, hope's all I've got."

Millie turned to look over the edge of the basket, and the smile faded. A shadow crossed her face—he felt it too. Everything was unraveling too fast, and control had slipped through their fingers.

The Agency had been home to him—and to so many others. Now, at best, his people were scattered and uncertain. At worst, they were being forced into assignments like Millie's last one. The line between fighting an enemy and murdering innocents had blurred, and the weight of that truth sat heavy in his chest.

"You never told me about your sister," Millie said suddenly, pulling him out of his thoughts.

He blinked. "You mean about Ven-Larve?"

She tilted her head. "That—and that you even *have* a sister. One living in hiding in Chaos."

Peter rubbed the back of his neck. "Now you're one of the few who knows Gall-I's my half-sister."

"Is that supposed to—"

"No," he cut in. "It's not an excuse. But her life's the one in danger. Keeping it secret was the only way to protect her."

Millie squeezed his hand. "I get that. Still... you had to work with that man. That must've been hell."

Memories hit him like static—Gall-I's first visit after he joined the Agency. He'd loved having her there. They'd walked through Main City, explored the restaurants, laughed at the tourists. Back then, she was so full of light. Then everything changed.

"We don't share a last name," he said quietly, "so that bastard never knew how much I hated him." He kissed Millie's hand and let it go. "Gall-I met him waiting for me one day in the gardens. You've seen him—full of charm and empty promises. She fell for it, and he used her innocence to chain her. Married her.

Then buried her under all that photonic high-society etiquette he loves so much."

"How did you find out?"

Peter exhaled hard. "I dropped by unannounced once. She had bruises everywhere—arms, legs, face. Claimed she'd fallen. The next time, I got a call from the hospital."

"Dear Maker," Millie whispered, covering her mouth. "She's so tough now... I can't imagine anyone—"

"She wasn't, back then." He twisted his fingers, staring down. "I got lucky. I'd met Holm and Phoebe a few months earlier, when I first crossed over. I snuck Gall-I out of the hospital and brought her to Chaos. Holm's place was the only portal I knew. I planned to stay, make a life for us both." He smiled faintly. "Holm found us on the street instead—and had a better plan. Phoebe hated men like Darius. They took her in while I kept working for the Agency."

Millie frowned. "Did you ever try filing a report? Something official?"

Peter gave a bitter laugh. "By the time I got back, the hospital had no record she was ever there. When I went to their apartment—nothing. Whole building emptied. 'For Lease' sign on the door."

"The *building*? Not just her apartment?"

He nodded tightly.

"That's horrible!"

"At least she was safe," he said, exhaling. "My mother died when I was born. Two years later, my father married Gall-I's mom. They both died when I was fourteen, and she was ten. She became my responsibility. I failed her." He paused. "Maybe that's what broke me. It's not an excuse, but... that's the truth. Being an agent was all I ever wanted, but working for that bastard—" He looked up at Millie. "After everything, I don't even know if it was worth it. Any of it."

Millie took both his hands, her eyes unwavering. "I remember people thanking us for what we did. We *saved* lives, Peter. The Corrupts aren't saints—they've done terrible things in both realms. Marshall might be helping now, but don't forget who he is. The Agency's flawed, but what we did—the good we did—still matters."

Peter kissed her hands again and nodded. "You're right."

The balloon shuddered, slowing for a moment before dropping faster, then stabilizing again.

"I forgot about this baffling part of the ride," he said, rising to his feet and helping Millie up. "Let's go find Phoebe."

34

Axiom Realm

"This isn't Heli-3," Randall said with a smile, enjoying the sight of his two men shifting uncomfortably, fidgeting, and avoiding his eyes.

Before the Square, people had been cautious around him. After prison, fear replaced caution. The burn scars along his neck, chest, and hands made him unsettling to look at, but it was his erratic moods and sudden bursts of rage that terrified most.

"We tried, Boss," Ta-llum said. "We broke into his place, but there wasn't much there. Then Os-mu caught a scent. We found her sneaking out."

Randall crouched, lifting the woman's aged face. She mumbled and tried to pull away, but the sedative kept her eyes half-closed. Heat rose through him as the memory of their last encounter surfaced.

In the Square, he'd lost track of days and nights. The only proof he was still alive was the burning pain that consumed his body. The cage's rhythmic sway and the grinding of the great gears became his entire world. In time, he grew numb to the stench of decay and his own filth. Even eating inside that space no longer made him retch.

What he dreaded most were the moments when the cage moved, pulling him into the light. If there had ever been a schedule, he never learned it. Each time felt too soon, too cruel.

He came to recognize the shift in the gears' hum—seconds before the cage began its climb, his hands and legs would start to tremble. His eyes stayed shut as the bridge opened before him, but the light still seared through his lids. His heart pounded so violently in his chest that he often thought it would burst.

It never did. Instead, he endured the jeers and taunts of other prisoners, the filth they hurled at him, the cuts and bruises from falling. Worst of all was the return—the long walk back across the bridge and the sight of the cage waiting, that iron promise of more pain to come.

"It's funny how someone so insignificant can become so important," he murmured, running a finger across the old woman's wrinkled cheek. He leaned close, inhaling her scent. Beneath the grime and sweat lingered a faint trace of flowers and rain.

He turned to Ta-llum. "Do you know her?"

Ta-llum shook his head, shoving his hands deep into his pockets.

"I saw her once." Randall tilted the woman's chin higher, pressing his finger harder until her eyes snapped open and she struggled weakly against his grip. "Funny how, even in the worst moments, the mind fixates on the smallest details."

He stood and folded his arms, watching her. This time, she met his stare and didn't look away.

"My cozy home," he said softly. "That metallic cage that burst open when your friends attacked the prison." He looked at

Ta-llum and Os-mu. "You two missed that event—you weren't invited." His voice dropped lower. "Neither was I."

He seized a handful of her white-gray hair and yanked it upward. She gasped and raised her arms, trying to ease the pull.

"I saw you running with photonic Jessica," he said, still holding her. "I don't know your name yet, but we'll get well acquainted during our talks."

He let go. She hit the floor with a dull thud. Randall didn't look back. Instead, he addressed his men.

"Our plan stays the same—unless she gives us something more interesting." He turned to Ta-llum. "Prepare one of the small cells. This guest won't do with Heli-3's accommodations. She'll need special treatment."

35

Axiom Realm

188A25 Year Week 13,
Sixth day, Early Morning

Jess felt the light from the window before she opened her eyes. The night before, she had found a first-aid kit after searching through three more sectors and cleaned Tom's hands. Removing the small wool fibers from his blisters had taken nearly an hour, and Tom hadn't enjoyed a second of it. She didn't care. She took her time to make sure nothing got infected—this place was disgusting, and an open wound here could only mean trouble.

When she finished, their options were limited. The night had turned pitch-black—clouds must have covered the sky, blocking what little light the windows could give, and their flashlight had died completely. She was just thankful it had lasted long enough to get them somewhere relatively safe.

After tending to Tom, Jess had sat on the floor, her back against the wall, and drifted off to sleep. At some point, she felt Tom move closer and drape something—his coat, probably—over her shoulders. Exhausted and half-asleep, she hadn't had the energy to protest. Now, awake, she still marveled at how simply having him near made her feel safe. Despite the cold and discomfort, she'd slept better there than in her new house—or at the Rupture.

Morning light filled the file room, but Jess stayed still. She wanted to enjoy Tom's nearness a little longer, her head resting against his chest, pretending his arm around her could keep her safe forever. But that was a lie. Last night's conversation had made it clear—being together wasn't possible anymore.

She exhaled, then shifted forward.

"Why'd you do that?" Tom mumbled without opening his eyes. "I was finally getting warm."

Jess stood. "I'm sure that's impossible down here. If we hurry, maybe we'll reach sunlight before it disappears."

Tom groaned theatrically and made a show of getting up. "You know I'm not fond of mornings."

"I kind of remember that," she said, crossing to the other side of the room and opening a file cabinet. "Is that why you never drove me to the train station on First Days?"

The words slipped out before she could stop them. She hadn't meant to revisit those memories, but the nostalgia felt oddly comforting.

Tom quietly walked past the cabinets, opening their drawers. When he finally spoke, his tone sounded casual, causing her heart to ache as he disregarded her question. She wondered if that pain would ever go away or if one day she would get used to it.

"That's a lot of reading, Jess." He rubbed his neck and gave a crooked grin. "You don't expect too much of me, do you?"

Jess leaned against the cabinet. "We don't need to read everything. We just need files on Karen—or her husband, Samuel."

"Not that I doubt you," he said, "but why him too?"

"Well," Jess shrugged, "the chief of the—your father's—file would be top secret. Like I said, I think Karen took them."

Tom frowned. "More like stole them. Was her husband involved?"

She shook her head. "Samuel was a scientist. After I kill—after Karen died, I had too many questions, so I kept studying her choices. They only make sense if she'd planned everything years before the Agency ever noticed."

"Years ahead? That's a long time to hide something. Sounds like my father's stuff could be anywhere."

"You're right," she admitted. "But I knew her—or thought I did. And I remember when she changed. It was after Samuel died."

Jess stared at the wall, her mind wandering through memories she'd never stop questioning. Karen had been her mentor, her family. Jess should have seen the signs. She should have been there.

"I'm sure his death triggered her betrayal," Jess said. "And considering who your father was, I wouldn't be surprised if he had killed—"

"Are you implying my father killed Samuel?" Tom's voice hardened. "How would that help the Corrupts?"

"Not the chief of the Corrupts, Tom," she said quietly. "Karen discovered your father was the Welder. Maybe he crossed paths with Samuel, or something in his research clashed with your father's plans. Whatever Karen and Randall did to him—it felt personal. It makes sense if she took everything when they captured your father in his cabin. Or maybe Randall did, even before."

Tom crossed his arms, unreadable. "It's an excellent theory."

"But you don't believe it?"

He laughed. "Didn't say that. It's brilliant. It also puts you in danger."

"Danger? What do you mean?"

He rubbed his jaw, eyes steady on hers. "You know too much. That's never good."

"And you don't? You know all this too."

He shook his head. "Not really. I didn't even know Karen's husband's name until now. And I'd never have broken into this dump looking for anything important."

Jess folded her arms. "I've taken care of myself just fine these past three years."

He raised his bandaged hands. "I know. I just don't like you being in danger, that's all." His voice softened. "And it hasn't been three years yet. But who's counting?"

Jess turned away, opening another drawer. Information defined her life—data, patterns, discoveries. Even when she became an agent, it wasn't so different from research; only the variables had changed. But Tom's imprisonment had transformed her world into a nightmare she still hadn't escaped.

When she didn't find what she needed, she moved to the next room—a smaller office with a desk, two bookshelves, and a standing lamp.

The books caught her attention: scientific journals and historical volumes on Axiom and Chaos. She'd read some before, but most were unfamiliar. For a moment, she longed for a quiet hour to read, uninterrupted by fear.

Behind her came a sharp clack of metal.

"I haven't seen one of these in years," Tom said, pressing random keys on a dusty typewriter.

"I'm sure your light keyboard works better."

"You know me—I like the classics. But something's off with this one." He leaned closer, studying it.

Jess smiled faintly, turning back to the shelves. At least that hadn't changed. Tom still loved mechanisms—always fixing, always tinkering.

Near the bottom shelf, she noticed the edge of a round metal bar barely visible beneath the dust. She crouched, but her light wasn't strong enough to see clearly. If she had to guess, it looked like a sewer cover.

"Check this out," Tom said. "I thought it was jammed, but it's something else."

Jess stood, brushing her hands off as she crossed to him. "If you typed something stupid—"

"What? No! I'm serious." Tom held up a metal bar the size of a pen. "This should hold the ink tape in place, but look—it's hollow."

Jess held it to the light. "Does it have a tape inside?"

"I think so." Tom crossed his arms. "But we shouldn't open it here. Could be something hidden inside."

"Like a code?"

Tom grinned. "Wouldn't surprise me. Especially considering who owned this thing."

Jess raised an eyebrow. "Are you going to make me ask?"

"I should," he said, tapping the bar against his lips, "but I won't make you beg."

"Always a gentleman."

"Of course." He touched his heart in mock sincerity.

For a second, his expression reminded her of Marshall, and a chill ran through her.

Tom lifted the front of the typewriter. "See here? Only four bars are marked—L, M, 1, and 5."

Jess frowned.

"In case you doubt me," he added, "the number one's marked twice."

"You think this belonged to Lezar Mos-Ium-115?"

He nodded. "I'm positive it was my father's."

Jess stepped back. "I don't remember the Welder ever being here, but... And the bar? You think someone was using it to contact him?"

"Maybe. Or he used it to send messages. We'll have to read it somehow."

"How?" Jess's mind raced back to her time in the Square—rooms filled with typewriters just like this.

"I'll have to find—" Tom began, but she interrupted him.

"For the Maker's life! Let me see it."

He handed her the bar, and she studied the outside. At one end was a small manufacturer's seal—not an Agency logo. Two rectangles side by side. If she hadn't spent weeks walking those corridors, she'd never have recognized it.

"They had consoles full of these bars in the Square," she said. "When I asked, a guard told me they were to 'hold up the business.' I thought they meant selling the metal—but what if they meant information? What if they were decoding it?"

Tom rubbed the back of his neck, saying nothing.

"Sorry," she said quickly, handing it back. "I didn't mean to bring up that place. I just—remembered."

"Like I said," he slipped the bar into his pocket, "you know too much, Jess."

She didn't answer. His tone was teasing, but his eyes carried fear—and anger. She'd never truly understood what he'd endured in the Square, and she could never forgive herself for leaving him there.

He changed the subject. "What were you looking at before? Under the shelf?"

Jess blinked and tucked her hair behind her ear. "Oh—right. I think there's a sewer cover down there."

"Another level below us?"

"At least one."

Tom rubbed his hands together and gave her a forced grin. "Then let's figure this out."

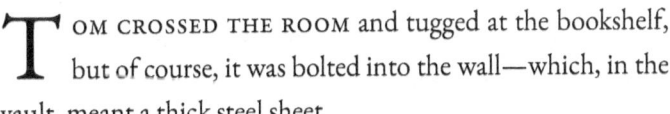

TOM CROSSED THE ROOM and tugged at the bookshelf, but of course, it was bolted into the wall—which, in the vault, meant a thick steel sheet.

"How do you feel about those books?" he asked.

Jess glanced at the shelf. "They seem...interesting?"

When he returned from the previous section, he had a massive steel bar slung over his shoulder and a mischievous grin on his face.

"I asked about the books because it's time for a little demolition."

Jess stepped aside just in time. The crash of splintering wood echoed off the metal walls. The shelf didn't stand a chance; it was lighter than the surrounding structure, and within moments, Tom had cleared it away. Beneath the debris, just as Jess suspected, was a circular metal cover.

Using the same bar, Tom wedged the handle and pried it open.

Jess instinctively held her breath—old habits from her years in Chaos kicking in—but the air that rose wasn't foul. The hole wasn't a sewer line at all. It was a tunnel, wide enough for a person, with a short wall ladder leading down to a concrete floor.

"I'll check if it's safe," Tom said, and jumped.

The sound of his landing made her wince. Though she heard him moving below, the instant she lost sight of him, her heart climbed into her throat.

"It's..." His voice echoed faintly. "I'm not sure. Looks like a tunnel. It's dry—and weirdly clean. My only concern is air. If we shut this lid, we might seal ourselves in. I don't know how far it goes or where it ends."

"It'll be hard to walk in the dark, too," Jess said, peering into the shadows.

"Well," Tom climbed halfway up, "we've got motion sensors down here. Someone's been using this tunnel—not too long ago, either. I just don't know if opening that cover triggered any alarms topside."

Jess bit her lip, uneasy. She hated the idea of stepping into a confined passage with only one visible exit. But if anything of real importance was hidden in these old labs, it would be down there.

"You can wait here," Tom offered. "I'll go first. If there's anything worth seeing, I'll come back for you."

Jess shook her head. "We don't have time to waste. Move over." She tried to push past him, but he didn't budge.

"If we get trapped—"

"We'll get trapped together," she said firmly. "Now move."

Tom groaned but climbed the rest of the way down. When Jess reached the final rung, he turned and caught her hand, guiding her to the tunnel floor.

36

Axiom Realm

The hallway's impeccable condition and radiant brightness were disconcerting, given the deteriorating state of the Agency's research building. Despite having worked in the labs, Jess had never seen this tunnel. Tom's statement was accurate; someone clearly still used it.

After walking for a good fifteen minutes, they found a lobby with three doors. The one ahead continued the hallway, but the other two were locked. With the steel bar in hand, Tom turned to Jess.

"Which one do you like more?"

"Shouldn't we check first?"

Tom rolled his eyes and leaned his ear against one door and then, after a dramatic gesture that made Jess laugh, leaned against the other one.

"Sounds the same to me," he said. "Which door, sunshine?"

Butterflies fluttered in Jess's stomach. She never thought she'd hear it again after the Square. She didn't care about the door, and just chose the one closer to her. "That one."

"Perfect!"

Jess thought Tom would hit the door, but he used the bar as a lever to break the lock instead. The trim by the lock flew back, leaving space for him to reach inside and turn the knob. As soon as he opened it, he looked back at Jess with a gleam in his eyes and a grin of satisfaction.

"For the Maker!" he exclaimed a second later, shaking his head. "I forgot you are great at picking these things."

The last time they walked down an unknown path, she had had to open a lock. One of the many things she learned while training with the Agency.

Jess laughed, and the sensation of lightness it brought her was a welcome one. "It was fun to watch you."

"Impressive, you mean?"

"Sort of," she smiled. "I'll open them whenever we gotta be quiet."

"Fair enough."

They stepped in, but this time, the lights didn't turn on. In the limited illumination from the hallway, Jess realized it was a storage room filled with empty shelves. Tom reached out and pulled the cord hanging from the lightbulb.

"At least we tried it," he said, shrugging when it didn't work.

Jess walked ahead and opened the few drawers in the room, but all were empty.

"Let's check the other door," she said, walking across the hallway.

This time, she used her tools to open it. It took her just a bit longer than Tom, but it was less noisy. From the door, the room looked bigger, filled with file cabinets, each with a set of four drawers.

She tried the light switch, but it didn't work either. Despite that, the lighting was sufficient for her to recognize a photo on a cabinet. Throughout their years of working together, it had been on Samuel's desk.

Jess took her time taking the next five steps, keeping her eyes on the younger Karen, smiling at whoever took the photo while hugging Samuel, who couldn't look happier. She didn't dare to touch it and simply let her hand down on the drawer handle. She had been acquainted with those two people for years, yet never truly knew them.

Tom's steps echoed in the hallway as he walked toward the room, giving Jess the courage to open the drawer. She knew from its weight as she slid it out that it was full, promising answers. She stepped aside, allowing the hallway light to reveal what was inside, and recognized, without a shadow of a doubt, the names of their old studies.

"Did you find something?" Tom asked, sneaking behind her.

"Maybe," she replied, continuing to move the folders. Most were Samuel's studies, either working with other students or by himself. A few were the ones she had helped to create. "These files belong to Karen's husband."

"That's great news," Tom said, opening a different drawer. "Too bad you are on your own reading all of this."

"Tom!" Jess stared at him as he crossed his arms and leaned against the last cabinet.

"I can barely see with this light." He backed away, shaking his head and raising his hands in surrender. "I'm not gonna risk my vision to pretend I can read crap."

Jess shook her head and returned to the files. It wasn't the time to fight such an old issue.

"Can you at least find a flashlight?" she asked without looking at him. "It'll make things easier for me."

Tom clapped his hands. "As you wish," he shouted from the hallway while his footsteps faded into the distance.

Too soon, all was quiet, and Jess's chest tightened. After they finished and Tom left, her life would become an empty silence again. Despite the tight knot in her throat and blurry eyes, she shook her head and continued working on the files. Dwelling on the things she had caused wasn't a smart decision.

Despite the unhelpful light, she managed to check all the drawers and found that everything was about resource studies and demographic research. She started to question her theory. It was possible that Karen didn't take Lezar's belongings, and they should have inspected the tower. With a heavy sigh, she leaned against the last cabinet. Her weight pushed it back until the wall stopped it, almost making her lose her balance.

She had assumed the cabinets rested against the wall, but now she knew there was a gap. She pushed the cabinet to the side, but there wasn't enough space to allow her to see behind it. Against her better judgment, she climbed on top of it. From there, she discovered a set of small security boxes lying on the floor. The cabinet wasn't too tall, but still, she couldn't reach them from up there.

She jumped down and tried pushing another cabinet, but the rest were full, making them extremely heavy. After groaning, she pulled a drawer out and moved it into the hallway. It was heavy but manageable, and although it was a long task, it was her best option. She needed to empty that room.

"What are you—?"

Jess jumped back, startled, losing her grip on the drawer she was pulling. A loud bang echoed in the hallway, and she barely had time to move her foot to avoid getting it smashed by the metal drawer.

"Dear Maker," she said, raising a hand to her heart.

"I'm sorry," Tom said, trying to skip all the obstacles in the hallway. "I thought you heard me."

Jess was still aware of her heartbeat pulsating in her ears.

"I found one," Tom said, waving a flashlight as he managed to get into the storage room.

"Thanks." Jess grabbed it from him. "I found some hidden boxes, but I couldn't reach them, and the cabinets were too heavy."

Tom looked around. "You could have waited for me."

Jess shook her head. "I don't know how much time we have. But I'm glad you are here. After all, I still don't know what I'm looking for."

Tom laughed, crouching down to look at the bottom of the cabinets. "That's a fair point. Also, this won't move, Jess. They are screwed down to the floor."

For the first time, Jess noticed the bracket on the side of the cabinet. A weight seemed to drop on her shoulders. "Well, I can't reach the boxes back there."

"Let me see." Tom jumped on top of the cabinets and tried reaching down. "There should be a way to get them. Can you hand me the steel bar?"

Jess stumbled among the files and empty drawers but managed to hand him the bar.

After hitting and pushing the wall and the cabinets, he finally moved something behind that released the first one. With more room, he reached down and handed Jess the first box. It was surprisingly light, almost giving the impression it had been back there because it was useless and not holding anything important. Jess exhaled and set it to the side to get the other ones from Tom. Hopefully, there was something in any of them.

It didn't take them long to get the four boxes out, and in just a matter of minutes, she picked all the locks. After opening the first box, the day improved.

The first folder in it had the number 115 and Karen's signature. She turned to Tom, but he was concentrating on a file, and she didn't want to interrupt him. Even though he didn't trust her to know what Marshall wanted, she smiled to herself. It was nice to see him reading for a change. She grabbed a few folders and moved to the hallway to get better light.

The thick file contained many documents mentioning the former chief of the Corrupts. However, nothing stood out as important to Jess. Those documents tracked illegal water crossings and marked meeting points that were once under surveillance.

Tom stood by the threshold and leaned on the frame while holding a folder. "We are looking for a logbook."

Jess looked back at him.

"That's what Marshall said," he added with a shrug. "Apparently, at some point in his life, my father worked by the Barrier and discovered important stuff."

"The Barrier?"

Tom nodded. "The Welder, remember? I supposed he figured whoever controls that photonic wall controls the realms."

Jess bit her lip and looked down at the papers in her hand. None were close to a logbook. Now she doubted they'd find one.

"I found something cool," Tom said, waving a leather crossbody bag.

Jess tilted her head but didn't need to ask.

"I figure we need something to bring these papers out of here."

She nodded, but had nothing to say, as all hope of finding what Tom and Marshall needed vanished. Despite this, she returned to the papers, hoping to find a clue leading her to the logbook.

Tom cleared his throat, making her look back up. He was waving a folder in his hand. "Agent Jessica Hiem-Sagac. I like this file the most."

Jess felt her face warming up, so she looked down again, hoping Tom hadn't noticed.

"You don't want to read it?"

She shook her head, taking another file. "Would you like to see what I wrote about you in my diary?"

"Absolutely!" He tapped his fingers on the folder in his hands. "Do you keep a diary?"

Jess threw the folder across the room and went to the next one. "Of course not. But why would you want to know what I write about you? Wouldn't you be scared to figure that out?"

Tom made room to walk back inside the office, and his tone turned serious. "I have a good idea of what you think of me already. Years of silence between us prove it... But it would be fun to see if I got it right."

Jess's throat closed up, so she turned back to the boxes in front of her for distraction. All folders related to Tom's father, but none were relevant until she found Karen's name on a file.

It was only her basic information as an agent—nothing that she didn't know already—but there were notes on the side that showed an evident interest in her life. Especially in her husband.

Jess moved faster, looking among the papers in the folder. Near the file's end, she discovered a slim folder labeled with Samuel's name. The first paper contained his basic information and highlighted nothing, but the second one had the name of his investigation underlined. That project was her first research work when she joined the Agency.

The purpose of the investigation was to figure out how to bring clean water to Axiom without affecting Chaos's supply. Samuel believed life in Axiom required a water supply beyond the meager amount coming from Chaos.

"Something important?" Tom asked while putting down another box by her.

"Maybe," she sighed and closed her eyes, trying to remember what they were doing back then. "This investigation got annulled before I became an active agent. Samuel was quite upset, but we never talked about the reasons they gave him for the cancellation."

"If it's important to you, we should bring those papers."

She glared at him. "We are here because of that logbook. Not me."

"I'm serious, Jess. Don't you want some answers?"

The serious expression on his face prevented Jess from joking.

"I should—I do, but..." She pushed her hair behind her ears. "I'm not sure I want to discover all the secrets of this place."

Tom grabbed the file from her and put it inside the sack he now had hanging across his chest. "Let's do this. I'll bring it with me. If you want it later, just ask for it. If you don't, I'll burn it for you."

She nodded and opened the last box Tom left by her. The color of the files was different, and right away, Jess recognized Karen's handwriting. All the folders lacked names, and to her surprise, her hand trembled as soon as she opened the first one.

A S JESS MADE HER way through the file, she noticed the papers inside weren't typed but handwritten. They were more notes and quotes than actual documents. She turned the pages, finding newspaper clippings, police reports, old photographs from both realms, strange formulas, and symbols. One of them caught her full attention.

"Tom..."

He stopped whatever he was doing and kneeled in front of her. "What's wrong?"

"I don't..." She moved the paper toward Tom but didn't hand it to him. She knew he wouldn't take it and would just get mad at her for trying to make him read. "When we were in the train tunnel—back in Chaos—when you figured out how to escape. Remember?"

His expression tightened, but he didn't move back. "When we crossed to Axiom by my grandpa's house?"

She nodded. "You read a sign on that weird platform. Do you remember—"

"Those papers talk about Parcel 11?"

Jess's muscles tensed. Despite her years as an agent, she had never heard of that parcel. "You know about it?"

Tom rubbed his face, looking lost for words.

"It shouldn't surprise me." Jess pushed the papers into his hands. "Well, that makes these important. I was wrong. I doubt the logbook is here, but if there's any mention of its whereabouts, it should be in those."

Tom slipped the papers into the sack. "What makes you think the location would be in those papers?"

Jess stood and walked back, away from the mess of files and cabinets. "Karen's notes. She wrote things in those."

Tom cleared his throat and, without looking at her, stood up. "It makes sense. I guess eventually she found his office, and after she killed him, she took it over."

"You think this place belonged to your father?"

"Isn't it obvious? We found the typewriter with his initials, and these boxes are all marked with the same letters or numbers. Not to mention you reading about Parcel 11."

Jess took one last chance and asked, "What's so special about Parcel 11?"

Tom pushed his hair back and adjusted the sack on his shoulder.

"Forget it," Jess said. "You don't need to explain anything."

"I want to—and need to—explain it to you," he said, taking a step closer. "But I don't know if you'll like me after, and I don't want you mad at me down here."

Jess crossed her arms. "Why would it matter if I get mad? It didn't stop you before."

Tom chuckled. "I guess I deserve that."

Jess rolled her eyes, but a loud thump interrupted her response.

"And that's why I don't want you mad at me right now," Tom said, offering his hand. "We kind of have to go—and hope there's an exit on this side of the tunnel."

Another loud thump echoed, this time coming from the far end of the hallway—from where they had come.

"What is that?"

"Those hyaerodeas kind of found their way into the vault, and... well, I piled some stuff to block them, but I doubt it'll last long."

"And you're just telling me this now?" Jess crossed the room and grabbed one of their flashlights.

"I was going to tell you, but I found you going through all these things, and this seemed more important."

Jess held the other side of a cabinet and helped Tom block part of the tunnel entrance with it. As soon as they moved farther down the tunnel, the lights flickered on, making her breathe a little easier.

"I didn't close the sewer cover because we need oxygen," Tom said, lowering his voice, "but Jess, the lights won't last long. Those nasty things bit through some pipes up there—they got part of the electrical system. I'm sure eventually it'll affect this place too."

A shiver ran up Jess's spine. If that tunnel led to a dead end, their chances of survival would drop to almost nothing.

37

Axiom Realm

Bill watched Charlotte standing behind Darius, playing the role of the suffering wife perfectly. They had been friends in the past, and for a while, he had liked her fixation on Tom. Granted, he had been jealous when he met her and saw her flirting with his former friend, but it only took a few days to realize the kind of person she was: egocentric and narcissistic—both qualities he found annoying. Nevertheless, she was funny and easygoing, and for all the wrong reasons, she became the best friend of his wife.

Thinking about it pained him, as it had been a trap for Tom and had almost cost him Arlett. Karen, Arlett's mother, had tried to set her up with his former friend just to get to Tom's criminal father. Luckily, Bill met Arlett first, and of course, she fell for him.

"We will handle this attack," Darius stated at the round of microphones in front of him. "The Corrupts will learn not to mess with our citizens. That is a promise. Just like we promised Mrs. Umbrar-Ment to protect her and her unborn child."

The reporters jumped up, shouting questions at him and challenging his decision to put a traitor's life ahead of his people. Bill knew the script and was just glad he wasn't the one giving that press conference. It amazed him how people couldn't see the truth when they didn't want to.

Although they hadn't confirmed the Corrupts were the ones attacking Main City, it had been their orders that blocked the exit to all Chaos's citizens in Sector 15.

"Wouldn't this be in response to your decision to dismantle the Agency?" a reporter yelled from the back.

Darius hadn't rehearsed that point, and the sudden change in his demeanor made it clear he didn't like it. Bill adored it, though. He had been searching for Darius's weak point, and now he had a clear idea of it.

"Are you accusing the Agency of killing people?" Charlotte said, placing a hand on Darius's arm and taking a small step ahead of him.

Bill started to enjoy the conference a little more. He knew Darius hated being interrupted, and Bill was going to enjoy what he'd do to Charlotte later. After the Disruption, when she walked away instead of backing his story, their friendship had vanished. It didn't help Charlotte's case that it had hurt Arlett too.

"I'm just asking if—"

"Are you implying my..." Charlotte placed a hand over her heart and made her voice crack. "My hus—my husband!" She covered her mouth and leaned most of her weight on Darius, who had to reach out to stop her from falling. "Oh, dear Maker. He had control over the Agency too?"

The reporter stepped back, glancing between Charlotte and Darius, whose expression became calm and full of pride.

"We don't know how far his reach is," Darius said, and immediately all the reporters began taking notes. "At the moment, I can't disclose everything we know, but we have a firm belief that Umbrar-Ment's family has been interacting with the Agency for years."

Bill gripped his wheelchair so hard that his palm felt as if it were digging into the handle. That wasn't part of the plan. The Agency shouldn't be connected to any traitorous behavior. If given a reason, those well-trained agents could become dangerous. Dividing their forces and quietly taking them out had been the plan all along.

"Fear not," Darius continued, "Mr. Hiem-Sagac and I will work tirelessly to find everyone who has been involved in this horrible attack. I assure you, justice will prevail."

Bill nodded in response to the reporters' attention but opted not to speak to any of them. Darius was losing his mind, and Bill didn't like that. It was probably time to talk to Arlett's father about it. If he had learned anything in the past years, it was to be clever and learn all the options before taking action.

"This is wrong, Bill," Arlett said as she walked up to him and began to push his wheelchair away from the press.

The second she appeared beside him, people rushed toward them. Reporters loved her polite and beautiful smile and went crazy taking pictures of the two of them. Somehow, Axiom's society looked up to them as a couple. It thrilled his mother, and from time to time, he enjoyed the illusion. He just wished the reason wasn't pity.

"Let's go," he said, touching her hand for the cameras but using a firm tone she understood.

Arlett waved and continued to walk into the Hall—the older building where the government met in Sector 8. She walked to the brass-caged elevator and waited until they were inside and moving up before speaking again.

"You know the baby isn't even Tom's, right?"

Bill rubbed his temples. "Do I look like I care about that bastard's kids?"

Arlett placed a hand on his shoulder. "What about Charlotte? Do you care about her?"

Bill looked back at his wife, and to his surprise, tears filled her eyes. "What's the matter?"

The elevator door opened, and she moved back to push him down the hall. This time, she waited until they were inside his office.

"I talked to Charlotte," she said, kneeling in front of him. "The baby's father is a guy she met a few months ago. I think she fears him, Bill. That's why she came. It may not be Tom's, but I think she's seeking protection from him."

"I love you, Arlett," Bill said, holding her hand and looking straight into her eyes. "That's why I'm saying this politely: your friend is a liar. You can't trust her."

"Yes, but she looked scared when I asked about it. She repeatedly insisted that pretending the baby was Tom's was the safer option. If she is telling the truth about the real father... I don't know, Bill. I saw Tom with Jess... He cares so much for your sister that I can't imagine him lying about his past could be a safe—"

She stopped the second Bill moved his hand away and rolled his wheelchair back.

"I'm sorry," she said. "I didn't mean to bring up Jess or—"

"Did Charlotte say who the father is?"

Arlett sniffed and crossed her arms. "Yes, Ta-llum 73."

"Never heard of him."

"I met him before." Her bottom lip trembled, and her voice dropped to a whisper. "When Tom brought me to the hospital—the guy holding Tom while Randall talked to him. That was Ta-llum 73."

Bill leaned forward. "Are you sure?"

She nodded. "I'm afraid of him—" Her voice broke into sobs, and it took her a moment to compose herself. "He took me from my room at the Village before our wedding. He was with Karen a few times, too."

"I thought all Randall's men got trapped by Marshall outside the hospital." Bill huffed. "The son of the void had the arrogance to leave them outside the police station in Main City. I'm sure they all ended up in the Square before that thing got blown up."

Arlett looked up at him, fear shining in her eyes. "I thought so too, but... nobody knows what really happened that day."

"Right." Bill turned his wheelchair away from her. "This guy could have escaped from Marshall before—or maybe he escaped just like Tom did."

Bill heard Arlett step closer. "I'm afraid he'll come here to get Charlotte. He's dangerous, Bill. He could kill us."

"Don't worry, Ar," he said, half looking back at her. "No one's taking you away from me again. This time we have the means to stop those bastards. And after today, I'm sure Darius won't let anything happen to Charlotte. She's a great tool to trap Tom."

"But Tom won't care about her. He's in love with—"

"Oh, he cares about Charlotte." Bill smiled widely, turning to face her again. "Why do you think we have airships above Sector 8? He's mad, and he's ready to do whatever it takes. I guess you're wrong about my sister's ridiculous romance."

Her eyes widened.

"Don't worry, Ar. This is what we want. We have a plan, and he's falling for it."

Bill stared out the window, ignoring Arlett's complaints and opinions. He found it interesting to learn who, according to Charlotte, was the baby's father. Despite his familiarity with her, he couldn't imagine an arrogant girl like her ending up with a guard. The father had to be more powerful, and the timing suggested the attacks were connected to him. He just needed to decide what would benefit him more: learning the truth or staying back and letting Darius take the heat.

A talk with Arlett's father was indeed in order.

38

Axiom Realm

Tom walked as close to Jess as possible. The lights hadn't flickered yet, but it was only a matter of time, and the tunnel didn't look like it was going to end anytime soon. He had hoped it would lead to the stupid inclined tower. Sneaking into that building had seemed logical, but the tunnel had turned south after fifteen minutes of walking. He only hoped it didn't lead to his father's cabin—that was too far for them to reach under their current circumstances.

It bothered him how clean everything was. He would have expected dense spiderwebs and pests moving along an underground tunnel. The lighting was also unsettling. No one had taken the trouble to preserve the labs, yet someone had made sure this tunnel had perfect illumination.

"I think there's another set of doors," Jess said.

He looked ahead and noticed three doors.

"Great! At least we can shut one to block—"

The lightbulb above them flashed, sparking down the tunnel. The rest of the lights twinkled in response. Instinctively, Tom turned back, and a void opened in his stomach. Not too far behind, the tunnel had gone pitch black.

"Hurry!" he said.

Jess had already opened the first door. "It's just a closet."

It wasn't ideal, but if necessary, they could hide in it. He reached her just as she opened the second door. It was a small storage room full of boxes tagged with the names of various cleaning supplies.

Jess opened the last door, revealing a small room like the one at the opposite end—just as the lights went out. Behind them, the tunnel filled with growling and the sound of heavy footsteps fast approaching.

Jess stepped into the room and turned on her weak flashlight. "There has to be an exit here," she said, moving the beam around the space.

"Check the ceiling!" Tom yelled, throwing boxes. This time, his goal was to block the passage, not inspect their contents.

"I think I found it!" Jess shouted.

For a second, the flashlight illuminated the tunnel, letting Tom see the many pairs of eyes, jaws, and claws running toward them. He shoved another box into the middle of the tunnel and moved back into the room. He was trying to find a heavier one when Jess shouted again.

"I got the ladder down, but—Tom!"

Out of the corner of his eye, Tom saw a claw swipe past his face, and by instinct, he shoved the box in his hands toward it. A high-pitched scream echoed by his ear as he jumped back. The hyaerodea recoiled, rubbing its face, but in its way, a large box from the pile fell, blocking the doorway.

"Son of the void!" Tom yelled, kicking at the box to move it out of the way.

"Watch out!" Jess screamed.

Just in time, he saw another creature leaping toward him. He crouched and used all his strength to pull the door. The few inches it gave blocked most of the attack, but even when the hyaerodea hit the metal surface, it dug its claws into his leg. A sharp pain made him groan, and the heat that followed almost made him lose his grip on the handle as the creature tried to drag him backward.

Tom looked down and used his free foot to kick the animal's jaw. He heard a loud whine and felt a crack through his boot right before the thing dropped dead in the tunnel. He held his breath and dragged himself back into the room.

"I'll move it so we can close the door," Jess said.

"No!" Tom turned to her just in time to stop her from moving. "We need to get out of here."

"I know, but you need help."

Tom used the handle and the doorframe to pull himself up. His leg didn't support him, and for a second, his knee gave out, but he caught himself, leaning most of his weight on the door. When he looked down, he saw his pant leg soaked in blood and the fabric torn open.

The growling in the tunnel grew louder, joined by the sound of falling debris. He gritted his teeth and moved his wounded leg. His skin and muscle seemed to tear from the bone when he kicked the box. The second it shifted, the door swung, pushing him down to his knees, but he kept a firm grip on the handle.

"You have to open it," Jess said.

The door hinges pulled out of the frame, stopping the door a few inches short of closing. "Photons!" Tom swore.

Jess touched his arm. "Get back, Jess. I can't hold it for long."

"Remember the cells in the mansion? I can't break the lock. You need to open it. Your blood's DNA is the key."

Something struck the door, and Tom caught a whiff of a foul, murky scent. "What if you're wrong?"

Staring into his eyes, she answered with a strange calm. "It won't matter."

The weight of the world fell on Tom's shoulders as horrific images of Jess being attacked flooded his mind. She was right, though. Without an escape, they'd both die here. He looked around the room—it was smaller than the one with his father's things, and it was empty except for a desk and a metal ladder leading to the ceiling. A round sewer cover with a single small button marked their only exit.

"All right," he said, staring at her. "But I won't move until you're up there."

"Tom, it's easier if I follow—"

"Go!" He struggled with the door as claws snaked into the room, making Jess jump back.

Without further discussion, Jess climbed the seven-step ladder.

Tom exhaled rapidly, staring at it. Despite being only three steps away, he knew his leg would refuse to cooperate. He took a deep breath, let go of the door, and quickly brushed his hand against his blood-soaked pants.

A fraction of a second later, he lunged toward the ladder. The noise of things falling, growling, and scratching filled the room as Tom jumped, grabbing a metal rung beside Jess.

He pulled himself up, using his body to shield her, and reached for the sewer cover with his stained hand. A clicking mechanism echoed through the room, giving him a momentary breath of relief—until a heavy weight collided with his back, setting his spine ablaze.

A shot fired by his ear, turning everything into a ringing buzz, but the weight vanished.

"Come on!" Jess said, sliding ahead of him and pushing the cover open.

Suddenly, Tom's chest tightened, and his heart seemed to pump bubbles that made breathing difficult. He raised a hand, but the effort made him dizzy.

Jess grabbed it and gently turned his face toward her. Another shot echoed, this time followed by a loud, inhuman scream.

"If you don't come up, I'll jump down," Jess said.

When Tom looked up at her, he realized she'd been shooting down—they were still being attacked. The brief relief of knowing there wasn't another threat above vanished when her threat sank in, forcing him to push himself one step higher.

He wondered if his leg had fallen off, because now his back was the one screaming in pain. He was certain that if it weren't for Jess pulling him up, he would have fallen and died right there. But after what felt like hours, his face finally met the cold concrete surface above.

Jess fired two more shots before the sewer cover clanged shut.

"Tom," Jess's gentle hands brushed his forehead. "We can't stay here. Come on."

She helped him roll over, and he bit back a scream as his back felt like it had been stabbed by a dozen hot needles. A few seconds later, the chill of the concrete numbed everything, and the sharp pain turned into a constant throbbing. Once his eyes adjusted, the night sky of Axiom came into view, startling him.

"Where are we?"

"I don't know, but we need to hide." She slipped an arm under his shoulders. "Let's move by that wall."

Her soft, sad tone made it impossible for Tom to argue. He summoned all his willpower and remaining strength to try walking but ended up sliding along the wall instead. Despite the short distance, it felt endless.

Jess helped him sit against the wall and took the sack from his shoulder. It was ridiculous how, within minutes, a bag filled with papers had become unbearably heavy. He could only imagine the hyaerodea had broken his spine—or punctured a lung.

"I think we're in the Welder's Tower," Jess said. "It makes sense—this was Lezar's office."

"Outside the tower?"

"No." Jess moved something that sent a ripping pain and sudden heat through his leg, letting him know he hadn't lost it. "Sorry. I need to see..."

"If we're inside the tower," he said, trying to distract himself from whatever she was doing—which now had him sweating and trembling—"where are the roof and the other walls?"

"I guess they fell? But I'm positive that's the Barrier, and that spiral stair used to lead up to the Welder's foyer."

Tom looked at the wall nearby and realized she was right, yet something was off. For years, he had worked near the Barrier. The energy behind it always created static and warmth in the air. Now he was freezing, and besides the air growing thin, there was nothing else.

"We need help," Jess said, pulling his focus back to her. "I'm going up there to find a transmitter or something." She brushed his forehead. "Try not to move much, all right? Just rest here."

She kissed his head and walked toward the stairs. He wanted to go with her—to protect her—but even thinking had become difficult, and he had no strength left.

39

Axiom Realm

188A25 Year Week 13,
Sixth day, Night

Jess grabbed the metal railing and shook it before climbing the spiral stairs. If the steps were as ruined as the walls, it would be easier to throw them down than climb up. Much to her surprise, the staircase didn't move, and the central pole remained firmly anchored to the ground. She took a deep breath, gripped the handrail, and began to climb. Her muscles trembled—whether from the height or the exhaustion of helping Tom out of the tunnel, she wasn't sure.

A shiver ran down her spine as her imagination conjured images of what might have happened to him if she hadn't been able to pull him out. For the first time, she was grateful for the years she'd spent at the Rupture, hauling heavy water barrels. A quick glance downward set her head spinning, but seeing Tom steadied her again. Despite his pale face and closed eyes, she could still see his chest rise and fall and hear his faint groaning.

Once she reached the last step, she switched on her flashlight and scanned the area before stepping inside. The hyaerodeas might have stayed underground, but there were other threats here—and not all came from the animal kingdom.

Only a desk, some papers, and a couple of chairs furnished the empty foyer. From there, she could see the edge of the

Barrier. For the first time, she took in the full aftermath of the Disruption. Holding her breath, she forced herself to move closer and look down.

She saw the concrete wall extend along the city and past it. Before the collision, the only thing visible beyond the Barrier had been the top of a jungle. Now, the wall was no longer a division—on both sides, she could see fragments of buildings from Chaos mixed with sections of Axiom that didn't belong there.

From that height, the smoke rising from the Agency's grounds was still visible, and although the main building was still there, the emptiness where the others once stood opened a void in her stomach. The attack wasn't a collision of realms, or a standard explosion like the ones near the Village. Someone bombed the city.

She shook her head and focused on the bottom.

You didn't need to be an expert on the energy wave to know something was wrong. A weak, interrupted stream of reddish liquid flowed along the bottom, exposing the concrete beneath. The Disruption had likely happened nearby, possibly causing the dry channel. But it didn't explain how the energy wave had traveled all across Axiom, triggering explosions. She wondered if the wave had tunneled underground, like it did in Chaos.

Jess shook her head and moved back to the desk. That was something she wouldn't figure out now—and Tom needed help.

The mess was worse than she expected. Piles of folders and binders covered every surface. She pushed papers aside until she uncovered an old radio, but the transmitter was missing. After muttering a curse, she ducked beneath the desk and, to her relief, found a hand transmitter with a wire connection and a light monitor—just like the one Tom used to have.

The last time she'd used one was with her father. He had tried to teach her how to send radio signals across open frequencies. The memory was sweet, one she rarely let herself recall—and now, it nearly brought her to tears. If all went well, she could say her old man had helped save Tom's life.

She pressed the round power button, and the burst of static felt like a relief. Simply calling for help would've been easier, but it wasn't possible. Instead, she plugged the light monitor into the radio. It looked like a miniature version of the one Holm kept in his apartment. After pulling up a chair, she sat down and dialed Holm's station as best she could.

After several failed attempts, she slammed the transmitter on the desk, sending papers flying.

A newspaper clipping slipped out of a folder. The faces of Tom and Marshall caught her eye. She picked it up—but her attention quickly shifted to the photograph underneath. It was of Marshall's family, and her heart skipped a beat as she lifted it. Marshall couldn't have been older than fourteen. His father had an arm around him while Randall stood beside their mother. They were all smiling, huddled together in front of the cabin Jess now knew had belonged to them. A red X marked Lezar's face. Randall and his mother were circled several times. A target covered Marshall's chest.

Jess picked up the newspaper again. The date matched the day Marshall had first introduced Tom as his older brother. She didn't know who had taken the picture—or where—but she hated the arrows drawn toward Tom's head. Turning the clipping over, she found nothing relevant on the back of the article, but written across the back of the photo were the words *Parcel 11 and 15.*

Jess grabbed the transmitter again and adjusted the dial to a frequency she'd learned from Marshall. "Silvie here, over," she said, while tapping out Morse code with the light. "Silvie here, over."

The static cut out, replaced by the high-pitched voice of Heli-3. She had never liked his tone—until now, when it was clear who she was talking to.

"Silvie, this is 3H, over."

Jess exhaled in relief and spoke a string of random phrases, pretending to ask for directions to Sector 6. At the same time, she sent Morse signals requesting immediate medical help for Tom and provided their location.

"You should reach your destination in about ten minutes," Heli said. "Over and out."

She quickly turned the radio dial to erase any trace of the frequency and unplugged everything. At that moment, ten minutes felt like an eternity. She stuffed the photograph and newspaper clipping into her pocket, gave the desk papers one last quick glance, and, finding nothing useful, climbed back down the stairs.

T OM HAD HIS EYES closed when she kneeled at his side. She touched his forehead, uncertain if it was a good sign that his skin felt cold instead of feverish. The Rupture had shown her too many horrors—too many people dying from those attacks.

"Hey, sunshine," he murmured, barely above a whisper.

"Don't talk. You need to rest."

He stared at her and lifted his hand, but it fell halfway. She caught it, and he gripped hers weakly but with intent.

"Help is on the way," she said. "Good thing we saved Heli-3 so many times."

Tom smiled with his eyes closed, and Jess thought he'd fallen asleep. But a moment later, he opened them again, urgency flickering in his gaze.

"I have to tell you about Parcel 11."

Jess shook her head. "Not now. You need to save your energy. We can talk—"

"No." Tom drew a shallow breath. "I can't risk not telling you this."

Jess moved a little closer, her throat tightening at the thought of losing him. When she stayed silent, he took it as permission to go on.

"I talked to Holm," he said, his voice low and breathless. "After all you did to get me out of the Square... I didn't just leave them."

She didn't like where this was heading, but she kept listening.

"While I was down there, trying to stay sane—I thought you were dead. I told you that before...I had nothing left. I kept questioning everything, going over what we learned, what we saw. At first, it was dumb stuff, but then..." He gave a broken laugh. "You know I hate words, but numbers and physics aren't that hard for me. Holm didn't like what I had to say."

He rested his head back, struggling for breath. The effort broke Jess's heart. She glanced over her shoulder, silently praying Marshall would appear soon.

"I tried to prove it—my theory—but he was too arrogant. I gave up on him, not on the idea. I wanted to find you, but I knew that was the last thing you wanted. After I started working with Marshall, I got access to other data—Parcel 11, for instance."

He tightened his grip on her hand.

"When he worked in Parcel 11, he learned about natural portals. That made him wonder. Everyone knows the Barrier, but no one really *thinks* about it. We take it for granted, like it's just there. But building it—that was something else. Conveniently, all the records vanished once it was done. I don't know if he found the documents or figured it out himself, but my father had plans to build a barrier in Chaos. That confirmed what I'd already suspected."

Jess brushed her hair behind her ear. "Did you tell Holm?"

Tom shook his head. "Why bother? He hated my earlier theories. What I told him was that the Barrier is destroying both realms." His grip tightened until it hurt, but Jess didn't pull away. "You'll probably hate this too, but—"

"You think we should destroy the rest of the Barrier, too?"

His eyes widened. "*Too?*"

"Before the Square... Holm didn't like it when I mentioned that. He went on about the massive destruction, the lives that would be lost. I listened then—but after what I've seen at the Rupture, I know he's wrong."

"Marshall doesn't like the idea either."

"Of course not. Control is everything to him."

Tom half-smiled, but Jess didn't have time to answer. Behind her, something cracked through the dry weeds at the far end of the building. She signaled Tom to stay quiet and rose, moving toward the darkest part of the wall.

She drew Tom's gun. This time, her hand didn't tremble. If someone was coming for them, they'd find it difficult. She slipped through the shadows to the opposite side of the wall. When she saw a tall figure approaching Tom's hiding spot, she loaded the chamber and aimed.

Just before she fired, the figure turned toward her, the dim light catching his face. Jess cursed under her breath but exhaled in relief, lowering the weapon.

"You've really embraced the boss role," she said. "Getting sloppy in the field, Marshall."

Marshall rolled his eyes, though his relief was clear. "Maybe I didn't want you to kill me by mistake. Rumor says you can't aim anymore?"

Jess ignored him and moved closer. "Where is—"

Marshall spotted Tom and rushed forward, dropping to a crouch. "Hey, man. The plan wasn't for you to get all busted up."

From where Jess stood, Tom seemed to smile faintly, but she couldn't hear his reply.

"Let's get out of here." Marshall didn't wait for agreement. Yttri appeared beside him, helping Tom to his feet. Marshall started toward what had once been the tower's entrance.

Jess hesitated, glancing back. Nostalgia tugged at her as she looked up the stairwell—but when her eyes reached the top, a wave of dread replaced it. For a split second, she *knew* someone was watching. The feeling clawed through her nerves like static.

40

Axiom Sea Periphery

188A25 Year Week 16,
First day, Hours Before
Dawn

I DEALLY, HE WOULD HAVE ridden the elevator to the roof—or at least the top level. However, he hadn't expected an ancient open-cage elevator with a weak engine. He set Jess down and inspected the machine. Through the shaft, he saw firelight and smoke on the platforms above them. The noise from people shouting and screaming was as loud as the gunfire and explosions. Below, darkness shrouded the scene, and an eerie silence filled the air.

Pressing a button and waiting for the cage to come down felt ridiculous. The slow speed of the thing was even more foolish. All his hopes of riding up while shooting out of the cage vanished. The unusually high ceiling on that level made it possible for everyone to see inside the elevator's cage through the door bars until it reached the next floor. At that speed, their attackers would have enough time to aim at their heads and shoot before the cage moved out of reach. He had no option but to ride *down*, where the cage would at least reach the floor and protect them from an attack.

Behind him, a burst of shots hit the ceiling, sending sparks flying from the metal bars of the elevator shaft. He covered Jess and used her gun to shoot back, though he lacked the aim and proximity to hit anyone. The cage arrived, and Tom didn't hesitate. He ignored Jess's weak protest as he picked her up and leaped into the cage. With a group of guards running toward them, his defense was reduced to pressing the button at least fifty times before the cage finally closed.

By the time the attackers reached the elevator, they had already descended an entire level. As Tom well knew, the outdated brass-and-iron cage was no longer in use because of its weight—but it was excellent for blocking bullets. A loud buzz interrupted his thoughts. He reached down and shielded Jess just as an explosion rumbled around them. The elevator paused briefly, followed by a loud grinding sound as the main pole bent. Two seconds later, the cage dropped.

The crash hurled Jess and Tom upward, and the impact knocked all the air out of Tom's lungs. A burst of pain engulfed his entire body, sending the world spinning. Beside him, he heard Jess groan once before falling eerily silent. The cloud of dust made it impossible to see her face, and the gunfire above drowned out all other sounds.

He pulled Jess as carefully as he could, crawling and sliding out of the now-broken cage. The floor on that level was wet, but it was the smell of salty water that turned his stomach. He tried his best to ignore it and put as much distance between them and the shaft as possible. Tom hadn't gone far when he saw ropes drop into the opening, and the shouting above grew louder. He couldn't let those bastards follow them. The large pieces of metal from the broken cage protected him from the shots while he crawled back and searched through the dust for Jess's gun.

The second his fingers found it, he grabbed it and looked up through the hole above. A few white uniforms were getting ready to jump down. He stood and ran as close as he dared to the elevator's mechanism. He knew such an old piece must have been gathering oil for years, and he hoped the guards had been too lazy to clean it.

Tom fired Jess's gun twice before a small flame ignited in the engine. Then he turned to the control panel and flipped the generator on. He ran back to Jess—but it was the force of the explosion that propelled him forward. Moments later, the elevator shaft became a column of fire.

Tom didn't wait. He picked up Jess and carried her into the cells area, down the dark corridor—the same one he had learned to fear and hate when guards passed on their shifts, mocking the prisoners inside. Though he had kept the attackers away, they were now trapped in the place that haunted his nightmares—the place he had dreaded ever returning to.

41

Chaos Realm

188Ch25 Year Week 13,
Sixth day, Night

J ESS WALKED CLOSE BEHIND Marshall and Yttri through
the hallways of his airship. She had memories of being there,
but it felt like a life from long ago. Nothing had changed,
though—the same blend of luxury and simplicity that had once
surprised her in Marshall's home remained unchanged.

"Where in the void is the doctor?" Marshall shouted as he
kicked open a door. "I said he needed to be—"

"Here, sir." A tall, skinny man in a white robe, with goggle
glasses perched on his head, stepped out of the room. "I brought
all my equipment as you ordered."

Inside, Jess recognized a CLEO machine set up beside a
rolling cabinet full of wraps, bottles, and medicines. Three other people in white robes were there as well.

"Good." Marshall stepped inside and, with Yttri's help, laid
Tom down on a bed.

"What the...?" the doctor muttered as he checked Tom's
pupils.

Jess stood at the threshold. Even from there, she noticed
how Tom's skin had turned ashen, his lips were pale, and he
was barely moving. Only his faint, mumbled complaints let her
know he was still alive.

"I've never seen— I see his leg was attacked, and you mentioned his back, but this is—"

"It's the poison," Jess said, clearing her throat as she stepped inside.

"What poison?" The doctor stared at her; neither his tone nor his expression was kind. "Heli-3 told me hyaerodeas attacked him. There's no poison in those animals. I can't promise I can help him without all the information." His gaze shifted, and fear crossed his face as he looked at Marshall. "Sir, if there's more, then I need to—"

"He was attacked by hyaerodeas," Jess said, forcing herself to move closer despite her trembling legs. "But in the last few years, those creatures have developed a toxin in their fluids. Whatever they're eating in Axiom is triggering it."

The doctor looked back at her. This time, his hands shook as he rubbed his eyes. "I don't know how to treat this new—"

"The toxin slows down the metabolism—like the heart becomes dormant, reducing blood flow. You need to get his heart rate up. We've used nitroglycerin and salicylic acid before."

The doctor glanced from Tom to her. "If I do that, as weak as he is, I could damage his heart. He won't survive it."

Jess nodded and swallowed hard. "If you do nothing, he'll die." She looked at Tom, fighting to keep her voice steady. "It's the only way we've saved a few."

"A few?" Marshall asked, but Jess didn't dare look at him. She could feel his eyes on her.

"I could complain for hours about what's happening by the Rupture and how no one cares or listens—but that won't save Tom. Your medicines are newer, this place is spotless, and your equipment is in perfect condition. He already has better chances than anyone in those woods."

"You heard her," Marshall said. "Let me know the second something happens."

He left the room, and Yttri followed. Jess turned her attention to the bed, but with the doctors moving around, she couldn't see Tom—and she wasn't sure she wanted to.

She stepped out and wandered down the hallway. Eventually, she found a small sitting area meant as a vantage point to admire the view from the airship—something she had no desire to do. Still, she took a quick glance, confirming they were back in Chaos. Almost three years had passed since she'd last visited that part of the realm. Of course, working by the Rupture had brought her into Chaos, but always deep in the woods, far from the cities.

The bright lights of the city stirred memories of a time when she'd found the realm appealing and comforting. She still believed Chaos was nicer, but now neither realm felt like home. Lately, she had grown used to loss and despair, and if she was honest with herself, the only news she expected from the room down the hall would be dreadful.

She sat in a chair away from the windows and rested her head in her hands. All she could do now was wait.

42

Chaos Realm

188Ch25 Year Week 13,
Sixth day, Midnight

"**T**HE DOCTOR WANTS TO see you," Mer-80 said to Marshall from the office door.

It had been almost three hours—probably the longest hours of Marshall's life. In the past few years, his family had changed drastically, and he wasn't ready to lose it again. Sure, when he first met Tom he'd had his questions, but somehow his older brother was everything and nothing like what he had imagined. Even as a child, when his father told him about a brother he wasn't supposed to meet, Marshall had created a fake personality that oddly matched the real one.

As he walked down the hall, he tried not to run. He saw Jess sitting on one of the panoramic foyer couches, curled up with her head resting on the armrest and her eyes closed. Just like when he'd met her, she seemed fragile—fighting a battle far bigger than herself. He knew she wasn't weak, but she was alone. He hoped this time he could change that for good. But that all depended on Tom.

He entered the room without knocking. The best way to face anything was head-on and without hesitation. Yttri was already there; Marshall had asked him to stay with Tom, and with just one glance at his friend, he felt a little easier.

"Sir," the doctor said, stepping away from the bed. For a moment, Marshall caught a glimpse of his brother.

Tom's complexion had regained much of its color, and the CLEO monitor showed that his breathing had stabilized. He didn't like seeing an IV hanging from his arm and a small tube running beneath his nose, but overall, it was a thousand times better than when they had brought him in.

"What's the news, doc?" Marshall asked.

"Well, he's stable." The doctor looked down at his hands and then at Tom. "His leg will take longer to heal—definitely a few weeks. The cuts were deep and damaged part of the muscle, but his bones are fine. The cuts on his back weren't as bad. He'll have a few scars, but nothing serious. I think most of the poison is out of his system, but just in case, we have the IV. The oxygen is to ease his breathing, and so far, his heart is back to normal."

Marshall tilted his head. "So far?"

The doctor crossed his arms, avoiding his gaze. "He may have permanent damage to his heart, sir. The nitroglycerin and salicylic acid seem to have worked, but there's still a chance the poison—or the treatment—could jeopardize his heart's overall health."

Marshall stood by the bed, trying to make sense of the warning. Although not a negative person, he detested the anxiety of uncertainty. "When will you be sure of this?"

"Well... I don't—" Marshall's expression seemed to make the doctor sweat; beads formed on his forehead as he quickly added, "We can run tests and monitor him, but it'll take time." He cleared his throat, aware of how much Marshall hated waiting. "For now, we've sedated him. It'll make rest and healing easier."

Marshall glanced at his brother, amazed by how quickly he'd grown to care for him. He looked at Yttri, who nodded from the corner—of course he would stay and let him know when Tom woke up.

"Thanks, Doc," Marshall said as he walked out of the room. "You'd better make sure his heart ends up in pristine condition."

"But, sir—"

Marshall closed the door. He knew the order was impossible, even ridiculous, but he didn't care. With someone responsible for Tom's recovery, he finally felt a sense of relief—and for now, that was all that mattered.

"No one, scratch," a female voice whispered from around the corner, making Marshall slow down.

"That means nothing."

Marshall recognized Coba's voice, so he stopped to listen.

"Nothing? You saw her." Although the woman's voice was low, her tone carried a sharp accusation. "She purposely missed that stupid officer."

"Mer, just because she missed a shot doesn't make her a traitor. We know how much the boss cares for her. I'm sure he was the one protecting her."

Marshall heard some shuffling before she spoke again. "Don't forget she was Marshall's fiancée first. And see what happened then? The chief got killed, and now—"

"And now what?" Marshall asked, stepping toward them. He'd heard enough.

"Sir, I was just—"

"You were making strong accusations, Mer." Marshall stared at her. "Do you have proof?"

She opened her mouth, but he didn't let her speak.

"Watch your words, because it sounds like you're accusing Jess of my father's death. I won't take that lightly."

Mer lowered her head and fidgeted with her fingers. "Sorry, sir. I didn't... Losing our chief hurt, and watching our boss almost die isn't easy. I just wish I could've been there to protect him, sir."

Marshall stepped closer, standing taller. A voice in the back of his mind warned him that his next words would create allies—or traitors. He didn't need more of the latter. He wondered if Mer had an extra level of care for Tom and made a mental note to discuss it with Yttri later. For now, though, he needed to shut down the gossip.

"If I remember correctly, you were with my father when he got ambushed and killed." Mer's eyes widened, and he could see her throat tighten as she swallowed. "I don't know if being there would've saved my brother from this, but I do know this—talking badly about his wife isn't a smart move."

He glanced at Coba. The man's steady, fearless expression told Marshall he didn't share Mer's opinion.

"If what you want is to protect my brother's well-being, you'll make sure his wife is safe from now on."

Mer's eyes went wide. She glanced at Coba, then back at Marshall. Her hands trembled; she was clearly fighting the urge to shake her head.

"I don't want Jess to come to any harm," Marshall said, leaning closer to meet her eyes. "Especially if she has trouble shooting. Is that clear?"

Mer inhaled deeply and clenched her fists. "Yes, sir."

Marshall straightened. "And in the future, I expect no doubt about your loyalty. No more gossiping in my hallways."

He turned and walked away. Part of him knew it was a difficult order, but the larger part felt deeply satisfied. Jess's life wouldn't necessarily be safer—but Mer would be careful about what she said. His father had died under their protection. It might have been a brutal attack, but unlike his father, they had made it out alive.

MARSHALL FOUND JESS IN the same room. Her eyes were closed, but he doubted she was asleep—or that she was oblivious to the sound of his footsteps approaching. Gently, he touched her shoulder. She looked up at him but didn't move. He pulled the small center table closer and sat on it in front of her.

"Tom is stable, but he'll sleep for a while. The doctor gave him a sedative."

She sat up and stared at him, as if trying to process his words. "Is he going to be all right?" she finally asked.

Marshall leaned back, and Mer's doubts crossed his mind. Jess's serious expression and lack of emotion weren't exactly what he'd expected.

"That's what the doctor said. His leg may take a few weeks to heal, and they need to monitor his heart—but yes, he'll be all right."

Jess closed her eyes and covered her face. When she spoke, her voice was barely a whisper. "It's been so long since I've heard good news... I—I wasn't expecting it."

"So you thought he would die?" he asked, exhaling through a half-huff.

She nodded, and Marshall heard a muffled sob before she sniffed and cleared her throat. "You can't imagine how happy I am to be wrong."

Marshall smiled and hugged her. It was a strange feeling. Years ago, when they were supposed to be together, he had hugged her and held her hand in public—but between them there had always been an invisible wall of personal space. That wall had remained even while they planned Tom's rescue. When she didn't push him away and instead sought comfort in his arms, Marshall realized she was truly part of his family now—which scared him. The thought of losing people he loved was unbearable, and Jess was constantly in harm's way.

"I'm glad he's okay." He glanced around the room. "It might be strange for you to stay in your old bedroom here. There are plenty of other rooms to rest in—or you can stay with Tom. I'm sure he wouldn't mind."

Jess wiped her eyes. "Thanks, but..." She bit her lip, and her expression darkened. "I have to show you something."

She pulled a couple of papers from her pocket and handed them to him.

All his joy vanished, and a heavy weight tightened his chest. Every photo of his parents forced him to wrestle with memories he longed to relive—those moments when his father was invincible, his mother's arm was all the shield he needed, and his younger brother was the sweet child he'd once played with.

Looking at the newspaper clip, his new life flashed before his eyes. It wasn't a bad one, but its existence depended on a very thin line—one that the red markings on both papers now threatened to erase.

"I found them in the tower," Jess said, her tone matching his darkening mood.

Marshall nodded and stood. "Thanks, I suppose."

"Marshall, you can't ignore them."

He walked down the hallway, the papers burning in his hand, trying hard not to hear Jess's footsteps following behind.

43

Chaos Realm

Jess stopped the door of Marshall's office before it closed and stepped inside.

"Clearly, I don't want to talk to you." Marshall crossed the room and sat behind his desk, turning his chair toward the view outside.

Chaos's night sky, with its moons, shone on the other side. She recognized the tall buildings of High City and wondered if that beautiful place would be the next to be attacked—something she didn't want to imagine.

"You can't just ignore it. That won't help."

"Ignore it?" Marshall spun around to face her.

She wasn't afraid of him, but she understood why most people were. There was no discernible kindness in his eyes, his jaw was set in a straight line, and he used his powerful frame perfectly. She was glad Yttri wasn't there; the extra threat wasn't necessary.

"Marshall, those tunnels were spotless." Jess stepped up to his desk. "The labs were destroyed by time and neglect, but everything changed when we found the secret tunnel."

Marshall rested his arms on the desk and smiled faintly. "I don't see the relevance. You said you found these two in the tower, right?"

Jess rolled her eyes. "Yes, but the tunnel led to the tower. Tom has to be right—your father owned that place, and someone's been there recently."

"Do you have someone in mind, or are you just accusing everyone?"

"Did you see the marks on the photo and the newspaper? Someone clearly has a grudge against you two. Someone who knows about the lab, your father, and Karen."

"What does Karen have to do with this?" Marshall's voice rose slightly.

Jess pushed her hair back and took a deep breath. She knew he would hate what came next. "In the last section, we found papers from Karen. There wasn't a logbook, but she had notes. I'm sure if the book still exists, her notes will lead you to it."

"That sounds somewhat good," he said, leaning closer. "Although you promised to find what I wanted if I told you where Tom was. This sounds like a failure, and I'm not fond of failure."

"A failure? That's interesting, considering you're failing to *hear* what I'm telling you."

Marshall slammed his hand on the desk. "I don't fail to see anything here. Do you have any idea how many people hate us? Thousands, if not millions, Jessica. In both realms. I don't run from stupid marks in photographs. I'm used to them. These?" He threw the photo and newspaper clipping on the desk. "These mean nothing to me."

"Maybe millions hate you, Marshall, but only one has access to Karen and your father. Only one betrayed you before."

Marshall shook his head, his hands trembling as he tried to contain himself.

"Randall is behind it," Jess said. "He already got you once—don't let him fool you—"

"Enough!"

Marshall struck the desk with such force this time that everything on it bounced, making Jess take a step back. He shoved the chair out of his way, hitting the window, and for a second Jess feared it might shatter.

"My brother is dead." He advanced toward her. "You were there. You told me he was in a cage hanging over the ocean. Those things fell and drowned. We barely got Tom out alive."

Jess crossed her arms and straightened her back, even as her heartbeat pounded in her ears.

"Yes, that's true. But think about Tom. You know that dead particles exhibit atypical behavior when crossing over, and you're aware that it's not possible to accurately track portals in the ocean. What if there was one underneath the Square—or we accidentally created one? That was the point of the plan: to create a portal into that photonic place. And it worked. We could have made more than one."

"A portal?" Marshall threw his arms up. "Dead particles? What are you talking about? Tom wasn't dead when we got him out of the Square."

"Not in the Square—before that! Tom drove his truck into a concrete wall! You saw his—" Jess's voice cracked as one of the worst moments of her life came rushing back. "Crossing or not, his truck was destroyed, Marshall." She took a deep breath and sat down. "I saw it happen... There's no way he could have survived that impact. If the portals affect dead particles, they might also affect those about to die."

Marshall leaned on the desk, his eyes level with hers. His anger faded, replaced by concern and fear. "Tom also had two powerful keys in his hand."

Jess nodded, but when she tried to speak, he raised a hand to stop her.

"I hear you. Loud and clear. I won't ignore the pictures you found, and I'll consider the possibility that someone is trying to kill Tom and me. If Randall is alive—which I truly doubt—he isn't more dangerous than anyone else who could have access to that tunnel or whatever you and Tom found."

"What if—"

"No." Marshall stopped her again. "No more what-ifs. Right now, you need to rest, clear your head, and see things differently. Nothing will change tonight. I'll have Nik-el-28 prepare a room for you. After all, we're family."

Jess chuckled, shaking her head. "You know better than anyone that isn't true."

Marshall picked up his transmitter and stared at her. "Pardon me? Tom is my brother, and you're his wife. That ties you to my wonderful world. Is that a problem?"

"That's not the problem," she sighed. "You signed that marriage certificate in Tom's name. He was fighting for his life in a hospital room, remember?"

"Tom didn't tell you about this?" He rolled his eyes. "You two are... something. Yes, I signed that paper in his name—and I did an amazing job, by the way. But—" he smiled faintly "—Tom's first request to me was to see the certificate. I won't lie, I feared he'd rip it apart, but instead, he signed it. The overlapping signature might look strange, I'll grant you that, but the document is official."

Jess stayed silent as her heart raced and tears threatened to return.

"See? We're family, Jess." He lifted the transmitter again. "Now, let's get that room."

Marshall was interrupted by a knock on the door, and Nik-el-28 appeared. "Sorry to bother you, sir, but you may want to talk to these people."

T HE DOOR OPENED WIDER, revealing Jess's friend and former captain, Peter, accompanied by his girlfriend, Millie.

"Jess!" he shouted, rushing inside. Jess barely had time to stand before his arms wrapped around her. She hugged him back, though she couldn't miss Millie's stiff expression.

"I'm so glad you're all right. Holm must've been thrilled when he—"

"Holm?" Alarms went off in her mind. "Where is Holm?"

Peter stepped back, his expression the opposite of his earlier excitement. "Isn't he here? He crossed to Axiom, looking for Marshall. He was supposed to—oh no!"

Peter pushed his hair back, panic in his eyes.

"The old man was looking for me?" Marshall asked. "Not sure I like that. We're not exactly friends anymore."

Millie moved beside Peter and touched his shoulder. "Phoebe is missing. Holm was hoping you'd help him find her. She's your friend, right?"

Jess wasn't sure if Millie was speaking to Marshall or her, but the tone was pure accusation.

"Phoebe?" Marshall crossed his arms. "She's a friend. What happened to her?"

Peter shook his head, shrugging helplessly. "We don't know. She left without telling Holm anything. When she didn't show up, we tracked her down. Her last location was at Heli-3's house, but there were no traces of her leaving Elemental 6. Millie and I just came from there. Someone wrecked the place."

"Heli's going to hate this," Marshall said, but Jess barely heard him.

"Phoebe was looking for a tracker?" Jess asked. "Who was she looking for?"

"Can't you guess?" Millie's tone was sharp. "Everyone thought your life was in danger. Who knew you were hiding on this luxury airship? Let me guess—Tom's here too?"

Jess didn't care about the accusation. She and Millie had never been friends. Millie reminded her of Charlotte—but with less hair.

Marshall, on the other hand, had had enough.

"Last time I checked, Agent Gaia-Ico, you were taking orders from the new Agency director and had joined the government. A huge mistake to make in *this* luxury airship."

He stepped forward, prompting Peter to move protectively in front of Millie.

"Do you have any idea how many people died in the Sector 15 fire?" Marshall asked, not waiting for an answer. "In my house, you don't insult my people. And remember—in here, the only traitor is you."

Millie lowered her gaze, and Jess guessed it was more to hide tears than out of fear of Marshall's threat.

"We don't know if she was looking for you," Peter said to Jess. "It's our best guess. But after Marshall threatened Sector 8, we don't—We don't know."

Jess turned to Marshall. "Didn't I tell you, what happened in Sector 15?"

Marshall shrugged. "I was already in Sector 9 and I had to make a point. So, I only casually flew a few airships over Sector 8. It's conveniently close to Main City."

Jess held her breath as she asked, "Did you attack—?"

"Of course not!" Marshall dropped into his chair with a big smile. "I was hoping for a reason to do it. But they turned out to be less stupid than I thought—and attacked Main City instead."

"Main City?" Peter raised his voice. "What happened to the city?"

"Someone fired missiles at it. Near the Agency, but not exactly there." Marshall clapped his hands, a smirk on his face. "For the Maker! You think they're so dumb they just *missed* the tilted tower that many times?"

Jess frowned at him, then turned to Peter. "Why Phoebe and Holm weren't together?"

"Holm and I figured we were on our own once the Agency sent new officers to stop Chaos's people from leaving Sector 15." Peter put his hands on his hips. "You know Holm—too stubborn to ask for help. I guess Phoebe thought differently, and we believe she was looking for you. To warn you about Tom—anyway, she left but sent signals of her whereabouts using the transit sensor system. When she missed her last check-in... Holm went to Sector 8 with Gall-I to find Marshall."

"Gall-I is in Axiom?" Jess raised her voice. "What were you thinking?"

"I tried to stop her, but she wouldn't listen. Phoebe's life was on the line. You know what those two meant to my sister!" He turned toward the door. "I have to find them. Staying here is a waste of time. I need to get to Axiom."

"I'll go with you," Jess said.

"No, you're not," Marshall said, planting his hands on the desk and leaning forward. "Your life isn't safe in Axiom, Jess."

"It's all right," Millie said, moving toward Peter. "We don't need her help."

"And who's going to find Phoebe?" Jess shot back. "You're better at tracking people than I am, and I'm sure Marshall can ask Heli-3 to help you." She turned to Marshall. "Would you leave your family helpless?" She didn't wait for his answer. "You can't stop me. I won't let anything happen to Gall-I."

"I thought this was about finding Holm," Marshall said. "And by the way, he's not worth risking your life for—after how he treated your husband. So no. You're not going."

"Are you taking me prisoner?" Jess smiled faintly. "Because I don't think Tom would appreciate that."

"I'm sure Tom wouldn't like you gone either—especially to Axiom. I can't—I won't— In fact, I'll kill your new friend. What's her name? Lucille-71? If you leave, I'll do it myself. And you know what that means."

Jess crossed her arms. "So you meant Sector 8 was closer to the Rupture, not Main City?"

"It's close to both," he smirked.

She nodded and took a step closer. "Leave Lucille alone. She has nothing to do with any of this. She just works with me in research. And yes, the Radicals burned the woods near Sector 15, but their reason was to redirect clean water to their camps. I'm curious why you took Lucille—but I don't have time to hear it now. Leave her alone. Not everything works with threats, Marshall."

Without looking back, Jess turned toward the door. "Let's go, Peter. I guess it's time to see my family."

"Your family, Jess?" Marshall shouted. "I'm not sure *they'll* be happy to see you after the news. And *we're* your family—which means Tom's going to kill me!"

A pang hit her chest at the mention of Tom's name. She longed to be by his side, to make sure he was okay. But she would never leave Gall-I in the hands of a monster. She couldn't live with that.

"He won't kill you—and you'd better not hurt Lucille!" Jess yelled back as Peter rushed to her side. The little she knew about Darius Ven-Larve from Gall-I's brief talks was enough to make her fear they were already too late.

44

CHAOS REALM

Tom's head hurt before he was even fully awake. For a moment, he hoped it was all a dream and that he'd just had too many drinks with Marshall. Then the pain in his entire body reminded him of reality.

Yttri was seated on the other side of the room, arms crossed, but he didn't look as serious as usual. If that guy ever smiled, that strange line on his face would turn into a wide one.

"You weren't exactly who I'd hoped to see," Tom said, his throat so dry it felt like it was ripping. There was a strange and unpleasant sensation on his face, but when he lifted his hand to check, a small tube blocked his nose. He tried to push it away, but Yttri somehow crossed the entire room and stopped him.

"I can't breathe with this—what's this crap?"

"It's oxygen," a man in a white robe said, walking toward him. "It should help you breathe easier, but we can take it off now, if you want."

Tom frowned and held the tube up. Only then did he notice a small needle in his hand connected to another tube. A large purple and green bruise painted his skin around it, and it tugged at his vein every time he closed his fist.

"I can take that one out too," the man said, now beside the bed. His hands shook so much that Tom feared he'd hurt him more. "It was just a precaution for... How are you feeling?"

"Like crap." Tom watched the man remove the needle from his hand. Unfortunately, the pain just turned sharper around the vein.

The door to his room opened and Marshall came in. He didn't look as confident as usual, which worried Tom, but his attention was fixed on the missing person—the only one he wanted to see.

"Is Jess all right?" he asked as soon as Marshall was close enough to hear. Shouting wasn't an option at the moment.

Marshall nodded with half a smile. "Is he ready to get all those things off?" he asked the man, who Tom assumed was a doctor and who now looked terrified.

"Ah—yes," the doctor said. "We could take it all off since CLEO looks fine."

For a moment, the doctor stood there, silently watching the lights of the CLEO system by Tom's bed. It still shocked Tom how much people feared Marshall. He knew him now, and although he would never take him lightly, he felt safe around him.

"Are you done?" Marshall asked, and that was enough for the poor man to jump and hurriedly remove all the tubes. In less than two minutes, he rushed out of the room.

Marshall pulled up a chair and sat by Tom's bed.

"That's a bad sign," Tom said. "What did I miss?"

"What's with you two and bad news?" Marshall's tone was playful, but his eyes still held a shadow of concern. "Jess almost had a heart attack when I told her you'd be all right."

Tom closed his eyes, grateful to be in a bed, since his muscles seemed to lose all their strength. "She didn't like that I was going to be—"

"Oh no!" Marshall chuckled. "Sorry. She was over the moon to know you'd be fine. She was just expecting the worst... just like you."

The air seemed easier to breathe, and Tom managed a smile. "I suppose we have something in common after all."

Marshall pressed his lips together and shot a quick look at Yttri.

"But there *is* bad news," Tom said, trying to sit up. Of course, Yttri's hand gently pushed him back down.

"She left, Tom," Marshall said, and this time he didn't wait for questions. "Apparently, Phoebe is missing. Holm and Gall-I crossed to Axiom to ask for my help. I didn't see them. I don't know... I guess we missed each other. Jess left with Peter to find their friend, Gall-I. I want to assume they'll also get Holm, but who knows? He didn't sound important during their secretive conversation."

Tom rested his head back on the pillow and counted backward. He wasn't mad at Marshall, but he was getting pissed at his luck.

"Her life is in danger there, Marshall. I have to help her." He tried to sit up again. This time his arm gave out, and he fell back onto the pillow.

Marshall smirked. "That I can't let you do."

"I won't leave her alone!"

"So you're going to drag yourself over to Axiom to make sure she protects you? I'm sure the crutches will do great for your rescue mission. Or should we get you a wheelchair? What do you think, Yttri?"

Tom shook his head, but the movement left him dizzy, so he didn't try again. "Why would I need crutches? I was walking when I got out of that photonic tunnel!"

Marshall laughed. "You weren't walking. Those nasty hyaerodeas tore your leg apart. You're lucky they didn't destroy any bones. Doesn't it hurt?" He looked at Yttri again. "We should check on this sedative. We might have a substantial business under our noses."

Tom groaned, rubbing his face. "I can't leave her alone, Marshall."

"I know." Marshall touched his arm. "Mer is sort of with her."

"Mer?" Tom stared at his brother. "You've lost it. Mer will kill her. Why is she with Jess? And what do you mean by 'sort of'?"

"Well, I got tired of secretive accusations and ridiculous statements. Now it's her job to protect your wife. That way, she'll learn to shut her mouth and be done with the stupid crush she has on you."

Tom glanced from Yttri to Marshall. "A crush on me? You're really off here."

Marshall sighed, leaning back. "She's overprotective of you. I think you're in denial."

"Oh, she has a crush on your brother—but not the one you're looking at. And because of him, she's become overprotective and almost paranoid."

"What are you talking about?"

Tom took his time, smiling to himself. "She was in a relationship with Randall."

Marshall's expression darkened, and his gaze drifted away. "That may explain some things. How did I miss it?"

Tom reached out and patted his leg. "She's good at keeping secrets. Coba mistakenly thought I was drunker than he was one day."

"Is Coba also in love?" Marshall asked, trying to lighten the mood. "I think he's been pretty close to Heli-3 for a while."

Tom laughed, and his muscles reminded him why he was in bed. "Don't make me laugh. It hurts. Besides, I bet he's more into Hafny."

Yttri shifted and crossed his arms, which only made Tom laugh harder for a second before he had to clutch his abdomen and groan.

When Marshall stopped laughing, he turned back to Tom. "Back to your question: Mer is following Jess. Your lovely wife doesn't know it. I'm not that dumb."

Tom's anxiety spiked. Mer following Jess was a good idea, and he was certain no one would stop her from following an assignment. Jess would hate being followed. He just hoped no harm would come if she found out. He sighed and stared at the ceiling, wishing he could be there. It was getting exhausting to keep losing her and, above all, he simply longed to be with her.

"Hey," Marshall patted his shoulder, "there's no point in worrying right now. We'll monitor them. Meanwhile, why don't we learn more about her?"

Tom frowned and looked around the room. "Did she give you the sack with the papers?"

"Not that. We can check those later. Right now I want to talk to someone new. Are you up for a quick walk?"

Yttri cleared his throat.

"Fine!" Marshall said, grabbing the pair of crutches by the wall. "It may be longer than a quick walk."

45

CHAOS REALM

188Ch25 YEAR WEEK 13,
SEVENTH DAY, AFTERNOON

W HEN TOM FINALLY SAT down by a door on the lower level of Marshall's airship, he was surprised he had
made it out of the tunnel. He remembered jumping onto the
ladder but had no idea how he'd climbed up. He only hoped
Jess hadn't been pulling all his weight. If she got hurt because of
him, he'd never forgive himself. And although Marshall swore
she was fine, he doubted Jess would ever complain about anything. He remembered her injured leg, but she was the type to
keep things to herself. Another concern to add to his list.

"Let's go in," Marshall said after opening the door.

"You said you didn't have a dungeon on your ship," Tom
muttered, half using the crutches, half leaning on Marshall to
take the first step.

"It isn't a dungeon. Just the lower level."

"Right."

Tom stepped inside and had to stop to adjust to the lack of
light.

He had never seen an interrogation room before, but the
space matched what he'd imagined: no windows, just a table
and four chairs. His heart raced when he noticed the distant

door—it reminded him too much of the visitation room in the Square.

"Yttri, can you fetch her?" Marshall said, gesturing for Tom to sit.

Tom pretended to be extra tired, taking a few deep breaths before sitting down. Although Marshall offered to take his crutches, he kept them close. He needed something to occupy his hands, as the ghost of the handcuffs he'd worn for months tightened around his wrists.

Marshall took a nearby chair just as the opposite door opened. A short woman struggled against Yttri's grip on her arm. She seemed so fragile that Tom feared Yttri might break her bones. The second Yttri forced her down into the chair across from them, tears rolled down her cheeks, giving her dark eyes a shimmer that matched her caramel wavy hair.

"Thank you, Yttri," Marshall said, keeping his eyes on the folder on the table. "We've got it from here."

Yttri stepped out, closing the door behind him. The air immediately felt heavier. Tom tried to focus on the woman, who fought back tears by constantly wiping her eyes.

"Miss Lucille-71. Or is it Missus?" Marshall lifted his gaze, and for a second, Tom thought he caught a flicker of hesitation in his brother's expression.

She shook her head and looked down, fixing her eyes on the table.

"Miss, then." Marshall glanced at Tom as if to signal it was his turn to speak.

"What are you doing here?" Tom asked, making Marshall roll his eyes and push the papers toward him.

"You don't know her?"

Tom gave her another look, then shook his head. "Never seen her before."

"Interesting." Marshall rubbed his face. "So, when did you become friends with Jessica Hiem-Sagac?"

Tom frowned as the girl cleared her throat.

"I told you." She sniffed. "I don't know Jessica—wait, Hiem-Sagac? The only Hiem-Sagac I've ever heard of is our congressman, Bill Hiem-Sagac, and I've never met him. No Jessica."

"Well, that's strange," Marshall exhaled. "She told me you were friends."

Tom opened the folder. The jumble of symbols and lines made his stomach twist, but he didn't have a choice. He didn't want Marshall finding out about his dyslexia. It was stupid, but he liked that his brother didn't treat him differently because he didn't know.

"Jess told you she was her friend?" Tom asked while moving the papers around, pretending to read even though the few words he recognized didn't make sense together. "Where did you find her?"

"By the Rupture," Marshall said, leaning back and crossing his arms, never taking his eyes off Lucille. "And yes, Jess confirmed it right before she left. They worked together for a couple of years in a clandestine lab. That's why we brought Miss Lucille here."

Lucille covered her mouth, trying to muffle her sobs. "I met no one with that name. I swear it."

Tom set the folder down. "That's because you know her by another name."

Marshall turned to him, raising an eyebrow. "I'd love to hear this."

"Lucille," Tom said, shifting his weight onto one crutch. "Hope it's all right if I call you that. I wonder if you ever met Karen Ge-Arje?"

Her eyes widened for a second. Despite the tears, she hardened her expression and pressed her lips tight. On the table, Tom noticed her fists clench until her knuckles turned white.

"Impressive." Marshall gave Tom a quick glance before turning to Lucille. "I take it you've met her. Which is great—she's a beloved friend of mine. Tom here is her—"

"There is no way she could be your friend."

Tom felt a flicker of pride at her sudden show of bravery—especially for defending Jess.

Marshall seemed to appreciate it too, because he didn't react to the rise in her voice. Instead, he touched his chest and smiled. "I'm hurt. I don't see a reason Jess wouldn't like to be my friend."

"She wouldn't—" Lucille cleared her throat, but her voice shook as she went on. "You kidnapped me. You're one of the Corrupts, and we don't interact with criminals like you. If anything, you probably just..." Her voice broke, and the next words came out between sobs. "You killed her!"

To Tom's surprise, Marshall offered her a handkerchief. "I understand your concern," he said evenly, "but neither Jess's nor your life is in danger here. In fact, it was your radical friend

Eril Ungu-Ter who kindly told me where to find you. You see, they don't share your values. But I treasure loyalty."

Lucille shook her head, staring down at her hands. "He didn't... I'm sure he was just trying to survive. You must have threatened him..."

"Well, that's the problem," Marshall said calmly. "I can guarantee that none of the Corrupts would ever sell someone out to save themselves—especially if they'd given their word. And I promise, nothing bad will happen to you or Jess. We just need some answers."

She dared to meet his gaze for a moment before looking away. "I know nothing about the Radicals. I don't work with them. Please, I'm just—"

"We don't care about them." He leaned forward on the table. "But I would love to hear about your research with Jess. I'm sure she'd want Tom to be aware of it too."

"And why is that?" Lucille pushed her hair back. "She never mentioned any of your names. You're delinquents, and lying is part of your life. She hates people like you; she has told me as much."

Tom shifted in his seat, ready to stop his brother from scaring the poor woman.

"She's sort of right," he said to Marshall. "We haven't proven we're on Jess's side. She's defending her friend—you can't punish her for that."

Marshall frowned. "And what do you propose?"

Tom wanted to ask how Marshall had found Lucille so he might have a better idea of how to help, but suddenly he remembered how he'd first learned Jess was using Karen's name.

"What about Frank?"

"Your friend?" Marshall asked.

The way Lucille straightened up and her skin went pale was enough to make Marshall smile. "I assume you've met Frank?"

She bit her lip, fighting back a fresh wave of tears.

"It's all right," Tom said gently. "Frank's a good friend—and he's here. Maybe if you talk to him, he can explain why you can trust us."

Marshall stood. "Outside. Now."

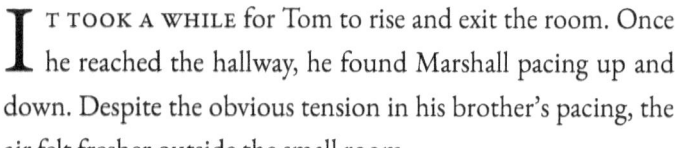

I T TOOK A WHILE for Tom to rise and exit the room. Once he reached the hallway, he found Marshall pacing up and down. Despite the obvious tension in his brother's pacing, the air felt fresher outside the small room.

"You're supposed to be the bad one!" Marshall said. "I'm the nice, polite one—and you're supposed to be angry and eager to get answers about your wife. Not the other way around."

Tom bounced once on his crutches before leaning back against the wall. The effort left him breathless and dizzy. "That's information I'd need *before* you drag me into an interrogation, don't you think?"

"Interrogation? That was a *joke!*"

Yttri found a chair and moved it close to Tom. Any other time he would have refused it, but he was exhausted. He hated feeling so weak, yet there was no way to hide it. Marshall was right—he would have just been a burden to Jess in this condition.

Marshall's expression softened. He leaned closer and placed a hand on Tom's shoulder. "Hey, are you all right? How are you feeling?"

Tom sighed. "I've had better days. Just tired, though."

"Hmm." Marshall glanced at Yttri, who gave a small nod.

"What is it?" Tom's stomach tightened into a knot. "What are you not telling me?"

Marshall tilted his head and rubbed his jaw. "We really don't know. The doctor mentioned the possibility that your heart might have permanent damage from the poison."

"What poison?" Tom asked.

"You missed that much, huh?" His brother exhaled. "Apparently, the hyaerodeas developed some kind of toxin. The doctor said he needs to monitor you for a while. Jess was aware of this change. That's another reason I need answers from Lucille."

Tom's mind slowed as he processed the words *poison* and *heart damage*. He definitely felt breathless and tired, but he had hoped it was just from the attack—or the lack of sleep and food. He wasn't sure how much Lucille knew, but he had no doubts about Jess. A deep concern ran down his spine. Once again, Jess knew more than she should—and more than she admitted.

"It's just a possibility, Tom," Marshall said quietly. "We'll keep you monitored and go from there." He patted Tom's hand. "Your idea of talking to Frank is good. Think he'll get her talking?"

Tom shrugged. "I'm sure he'll tell her the truth. I'm just not sure that'll make her talk."

Marshall nodded. "That's good enough."

46

Axiom Sea Periphery

188A25 Year Week 16,
First day, Hours Before
Dawn

The long corridor, the pulsing red alarm lights, and the splashing under his feet kept Tom's nerves on edge. This time, the pain in his chest and the shortness of breath might have been signs of a heart attack—or an impending panic attack. He clung to Jess as he walked, knowing she was the only thing keeping him sane.

As he passed his old cell, his legs and arms trembled, and he almost lost his balance as he quickened his pace. He didn't want to see the assortment of symbols, numbers, and Jess's name he had carved into the stone walls, nor the small passageways that prisoners had used to navigate between cells, sparking fights and staking territory. Most of all, he didn't want to remember the monster he had become—or the things he had done—just to be left alone.

Before he reached the end of the corridor, he lowered Jess to the ground. He knew she was alive because, even over the pounding of his heart in his ears, he could hear her labored breathing and faint murmurs. She opened her eyes only when he touched her face and smiled faintly at him.

"You're freezing," Tom said, taking off his jacket and placing it over her. "One would think that void uniform would be warmer."

He sat beside her and rubbed his face, trying to ignore the sharp pains and throbbing aches that ran through his body.

"I didn't mean to..." Jess whispered.

Tom looked at her and could almost feel the despair in her eyes.

"Hey, hey," he said, moving closer and brushing her cheek. "Try not to talk. You need to—"

"I swear, Tom," she said, leaning forward and raising her voice. "I would never join— I told Mer when we saw him." She closed her eyes, struggling to breathe.

Tom eased her back into a more comfortable position, but the panic in her voice chilled him.

"Jess, whatever you need to tell me can wait. We'll get out. We'll—"

"I would never betray you," she said, tears brimming in her eyes.

"Betray me?" Tom gave a weak smile. "I never thought..." He cupped her face and leaned closer. "I figured it out the second I recognized you. You're an agent working undercover. I just wish I'd known sooner."

"We saw him with the book." She grabbed his hands and met his gaze. "It was our chance. Mer knew. I told her I would pretend—work undercover, Tom. I didn't mean for you to come like this..."

Tom kissed her forehead, still holding her hands. "Jess, Mer is dead. We were attacked in Chaos—she died when she crossed over."

Jess's lips trembled. "Oh no... She was supposed to tell you. I would've never done it—"

"She told me about Randall. And she saved Gall-I, but... I had no idea where you were, sunshine. And when Randall's message arrived, I couldn't risk your life."

Jess closed her eyes and shook her head. "I'm sorry, Tom."

"You're sorry?" Tom rubbed his face. "It's me who— I can't lose you, Jess. Not like this. Please..."

He sat next to her, wrapping an arm around her shoulders, careful not to disturb her or glance at her side. The pallor of her face, lips, and hands was hard enough to bear, and her trembling voice broke his heart. This was his fault—but if, by some miracle, they made it out, Randall would pay for his lies.

It wouldn't be the first time Tom wanted to kill his little brother. Most of his days in the Square had been filled with ideas of how to make Randall's photonic cage fall. In his mind, he'd often pictured the son of the void screaming as the entity descended, vanishing into the sea—down to the very bottom.

As that image replayed in his mind, another memory surfaced: Jess explaining how portals behaved differently in water. During their search for the relic, they had been forced to jump from Randall's airship and land in an underwater portal—their only escape. Against all reason, Jess had instructed him to swim deeper. Marshall had told him that Randall's cage had dropped into the sea. A cage that heavy should have sunk far beneath the surface.

"Jess," he said, kneeling in front of her. "The portals—when you got me out of here... did you open one in the sea?"

Jess struggled to open her eyes, her focus drifting. "I don't think— I'm not sure."

The weight of the world fell on his shoulders until she continued. "Randall?"

He looked up at her.

"Water portals are different..." she whispered, but her breathing slowed so much that Tom's muscles tensed.

"I'll get you out of here," he whispered, lifting her into his arms and hurrying down the corridor.

He knew this path. For months, he had taken it to reach the other building—the one destroyed during his escape. Now their best way to reach the sea.

"Just hold on a little longer, sunshine. Just a little more."

47

Axiom Realm

188A25 Year Week 13,
Seventh day, Evening

"Explain to me again why we're breaking into your mother's home?" Peter said to Jess. "We don't even know if Darius will be there. Our best bet should be Main City."

After confirming the street was empty, Jess crossed quickly to the other side, Peter close behind. She had already explained briefly but understood his concern. Darius most likely wasn't at her mother's.

"My mother has a great relationship with Bill. She won't hesitate to take me to him, and I'm sure he knows where Darius is." Jess stopped at the next intersection and caught her first glimpse of the small mansion her family lived in now. "It'll save us time to go straight to him instead of trying to find him. Plus, we'll be *inside* instead of breaking in."

Peter scanned the street, then leaned against the wall.

"There are a couple of guards down the block," he whispered. "What you're planning is insane. How would we escape with Gall-I?"

Jess turned to him. "You'll get us out."

"Excuse me?"

She smiled, even though she knew the plan was full of holes.

"You're not coming in with me," she said. "You'll follow me. Once I meet with Darius, then you come in and rescue us."

Peter shook his head and crossed his arms. "I'm not risking your life too, Jess. My sister and Holm are enough to worry about. And you— I don't even want to think about what he'll do to you."

"I have a good idea," Jess said, pulling a pocketknife from her belt and handing it to him. "My mother hasn't exactly been quiet about me. According to her, I'm in a hospital recovering from trauma after the Disruption. She managed to convince Darius to accept me as his fiancée, and together they arranged the marriage."

"How do you know this? I never heard a thing."

Jess lifted her shoulders. "I have a friend who owns a bar. Drunk people talk too much. I asked Frank to keep an eye on my family—especially my mom. When she didn't declare me dead, I figured she had a plan to clean up our family's reputation."

"She clearly doesn't know Darius well."

"He has a clean reputation on paper."

Jess's gaze drifted back to the darkened street, where the elegant new house—its rounded tower and curved windows glowing faintly—stood proudly. Only a few windows were lit, typical for the hour.

"I just wish we had more than just us for this mission," Peter said, checking the bullets in his gun and the extras in his belt.

Jess placed a hand on his arm to get his attention. "We could..."

"What are you thinking?"

She glanced around. The cul-de-sac was dark and quiet, but sirens echoed in the distance. The sector wasn't sleeping—especially after everything that had happened in recent days.

"You can gather us, Peter."

He blinked and shook his head. "Gather *who*?"

"Peter, you're our captain. The agents you work with still respect you. Just like Millie and me, they need a leader. Darius's actions prove he's not the right one. You can—"

"No, Jess." Peter ran a hand through his hair. "First of all, there's no time. Second, they'd never listen to me. I'm an addict. You know that better than anyone."

Jess sighed and looked down. "We all made mistakes."

"Jess," Peter said softly, touching her shoulder. "You didn't do anything wrong."

She gave a small, bitter laugh. "I should've seen it, Peter. I knew Karen was changing." Her voice dropped. "I had a feeling—I just decided to ignore it."

"That was too long ago. You were working on something else. Then that bastard broke your heart and betrayed you. I'd never blame you for any of it."

Heat rushed up Jess's spine. She hated how everyone kept blaming Tom for everything. It wasn't fair—but this wasn't the time to argue.

"Likewise, I don't blame you. And only a few agents know about your addiction. On the other hand, everyone knows the new director's orders—and what he's done to them. You can do this, Peter. We can present a united front instead of looking like two rogues trespassing."

"There's no time, Jess," he repeated. "I won't leave you here."

Jess smiled. "I'm just going to see my mother." Before he could interrupt, she raised her voice. "Besides, our chances of success increase if we have a few more agents with us."

Peter frowned, but she recognized that look—he had made a choice he didn't like. "All right, but I'll wait to see what your mother does before finding our people."

"Our people." Jess took a deep breath. "I like that."

Without waiting for more, she crossed the street, wondering if she still had a place among that group of agents.

For a second, she thought she saw someone else—but the wind only rustled the branches of the tall trees framing the street. Still, the strange feeling in her chest didn't fade.

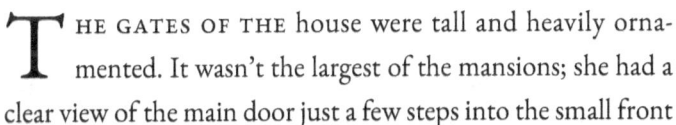

T HE GATES OF THE house were tall and heavily orna-mented. It wasn't the largest of the mansions; she had a clear view of the main door just a few steps into the small front garden. Still, it was a world away from her former home, which didn't need a gate and whose porch welcomed visitors.

"Who is there?" intoned a voice from the main door. She had never met the man, but from his uniform and rigid posture she guessed he was the butler.

"I want to see my mother," Jess said as a few drops of rain fell, making her shiver.

"You must have the wrong house, young lady," the man said. "Please leave before I call the police."

Jess grabbed the gate, forcing the butler out of the doorframe. "My mom will be mad to hear you sent her daughter away."

The man stepped down and opened an umbrella. "The owners of this house won't take kindly to your prank. Their only daughter is hospitalized. Now, get lost."

"You aren't a very dutiful servant. Aren't you supposed to ask for names instead of just kicking people out?"

He scanned Jess from head to toe and smirked. "You clearly have no business being in this neighborhood," the butler said, and made the mistake of unlocking the gate. "I tried to be polite, but you gave me no choice."

Jess smiled and shoved the gate into the man's face. The metal bars struck the side of his nose, sending him stumbling back.

"You photonic woman!" the butler yelled, blood and water muffling his words as it dripped from his hand.

Jess stomped forward, kicked the umbrella from his other hand, flicked it up with her foot to catch it midair, then hooked that same foot behind the butler's knee and jerked. He grabbed at empty air and collapsed to the ground. With a swift turn, she pressed the umbrella's tip to his neck.

"If I wanted you dead, you would be by now."

"Jess!" another voice called.

She turned in time to meet Dan's warm embrace.

"Look at you," he said, holding her face between his hands. Tears mixed with rain ran down his cheeks. "My pretty girl. I missed you so much." He pulled her close and, in a raspy whisper, added, "You shouldn't be here. It's dangerous."

Jess stepped back but had no time to ask questions.

"Jessica Hiem-Sagac," her mother's reproach rang out, probably across the entire alley. "What were you thinking? Dan, help
Mr. Jac-Ocul."

Despite the late hour, her mother looked nothing like someone who'd been tired—her majestic evening gown and styled
hair suggested she was dressed for a grand dinner. Her mother
descended the three steps and wrapped her arms around Jess.
For a second Jess rested her head on those familiar shoulders, but
all too soon her mother pushed her back and stared, analyzing
every inch of her before shaking her head.

"Why must you always be so violent?" she said, then turned
and went back inside. "Better get in before you catch a cold—or
worse. You look awful."

Jess's heart tightened. In a few curt sentences she'd been
slammed back to the reason she'd left as a girl; any softened regret vanished. She glanced once at the street before stepping into
the house, forcing herself to remember why she'd come—and
quietly holding Marshall's words in her chest. She had a family
somewhere else now.

48

Chaos Realm

Tom felt bad for complaining about his condition once he saw Frank lying on the bed. His friend still had several tubes connected to him, and the steady beeping of CLEO made him look worse. Marshall had briefly explained that the doctor's prognosis was promising, but Tom had his doubts. The same doctor hadn't been sure about Tom's recovery—and he was already walking.

"What happened to him?" Lucille asked from the doorway, her trembling hands and pale complexion catching Tom's attention.

"He was helping me when we got attacked in Main City."

Lucille glanced at Tom before turning back to Frank. "You don't think I did this to him," Tom said, sensing the absurdity of the idea. "Do you?"

She shook her head quickly and stepped closer to the bed. "Main City? So you didn't..." She cleared her throat and folded her arms tightly around herself.

Tom pushed his hair back, wondering if bringing her to Frank had been a good idea. He leaned against the wall and exhaled, frustrated by how tired and breathless he felt after just walking up to the first floor of the airship.

"If I wanted to attack Main City, I'd have targeted the main plaza—without a doubt, the Government Hall and the affluent streets," Marshall said as he entered the room. "Wasting missiles for attention serves no purpose. I don't play games like that. If we attack, we kill and destroy."

Lucille lost the last of her color but nodded. "I know the Radicals didn't attack—but I wasn't accusing you. I'm sorry, this is just too—"

"Scary?" Marshall's tone softened. "I'm not a nice man, and I won't lie to you. We could hurt you and make you tell us anything we want, but Jess told me you're her friend—and I care for my family. I won't hurt you, but I need answers."

"Tom?" Frank's raspy, weak voice came from the bed. "Where is..." He stopped and looked around. "Is Jess all right?"

Tom moved toward him, glad for the distraction. "Hey, man. You look awful."

Frank tried to chuckle but ended up grimacing and clutching his abdomen. "You don't look your best either."

Real concern clouded Frank's face as he scanned the room. Although Tom felt a surge of anger, he answered the question Frank didn't need to ask. This wasn't the time to be jealous.

"Jess is helping her old captain find a friend," Tom said. "But I was told she's fine."

Frank exhaled and closed his eyes. "She's always helping someone."

"Frank," Lucille said softly, making him open his eyes again.

He smiled at her before turning his gaze to Tom. This time, his look was hard—accusing—and Tom hated it.

"I see you two met," Tom said. "Marshall and I need answers, and we believe she knows a few. Of course, she doesn't trust us—and she doesn't know who Jess is... or Karen, according to her."

Frank noticed Marshall, and his expression darkened even more.

"What does Lucille have to do with all of this?" he asked.

Marshall took a step forward and crossed his arms. "That's an odd way to thank the people who saved your life."

"I'm just asking—" Frank began, but Tom cut him off.

"We all want the same thing—to help Jess." He looked at Frank, letting the frustration that had been simmering in him show in his tone. "I want you to tell her everything you know about me—about how I feel for Jess—so she can decide if she wants to talk to us. Like Marshall said, we won't hurt her."

Frank's stern look softened into guilt, and somehow Tom liked that even less. He turned and left the room as fast as his crutches allowed, making sure Marshall followed, and shut the door behind them.

"That's it?" Marshall asked, standing beside the door.

"What else do you want to do? I doubt they'll talk openly with both of us here."

Marshall frowned briefly, then shrugged. "Jess told me she knew nothing. The problem is, how can Jess be sure of that?"

Tom nodded but didn't get the chance to answer. The door opened, and Lucille rushed out. Distracted and wiping her eyes, she bumped straight into Marshall. He caught her before she fell.

"I'm sorry," she said, trying to steady herself and wipe her face at the same time, but failing at both.

"What happened?" Marshall asked, crouching slightly to meet her gaze.

"It's all a lie," she said through tears, shaking her head. "I thought she was like me. I believed she only wanted to help our realm, but she... it was all a lie. She was probably setting a trap or something. I just—she was my friend, and—"

"She *is* your friend," Marshall interrupted gently. "Lucille, Jess had to hide her identity. Otherwise, she wouldn't have survived out there."

Lucille looked up at Marshall, then at Tom. "What do you want to know? Everything I believed in is probably another lie. She's just one of you. A corrupt one."

"She isn't a criminal," Tom snapped, his anger breaking through. "She's dedicated her entire life to aiding the realms. Unlike the rest, she didn't join a group of imbeciles once they realized how bad things were. Do you have any idea what she's sacrificed to protect this photonic place—and people like you? You have no right to accuse her."

Lucille stepped back, half-hiding behind Marshall, and Tom drew a deep breath, trying to calm himself. He hadn't meant to frighten her—but he wasn't going to let anyone insult Jess. If people hated him, so be it. But not her. She didn't deserve that.

"Jess wanted to work in research," Tom said, forcing his tone lower. "That was her dream, and she followed it. Life took its course, but her true calling was always research. That's why she joined the Agency."

Marshall moved slightly to shield Lucille, slipping into the "good cop" role he wanted to have. "I understand you're angry and confused. We don't have all the answers yet—but we want the best for our people."

Lucille sniffled and spoke from behind him. "Our research—Karen and… Jess and I—was focused on the water supply and how it's changing. We don't know much yet, but the flow seems to be shifting, affecting species and plants. From what we've seen, it's spreading. If this continues… I don't know. Jess is more optimistic than I am, but I truly think if we can't stop the water from changing paths and crossing over, we'll lose our clean supply soon."

Tom's head spun with questions—about his attack, about his heart, about what Jess had mentioned in the tunnel.

"Let's talk," Marshall said, giving Tom a quick glance before leading Lucille down the hallway.

"I'll be in my office, Tom."

Tom nodded, relieved to be left alone.

He wasn't sure he wanted to hear more anyway. His legs felt like lead, dragging down his mood. He doubted he could stand another accusation about Jess. He also needed to find out what she'd been working on—even if it meant reading, which only made his pounding headache worse.

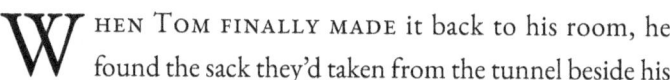

W HEN TOM FINALLY MADE it back to his room, he found the sack they'd taken from the tunnel beside his desk. He picked it up and sat down in the chair. The leather was badly scuffed, evidence of how difficult their escape had been. Jess had mentioned something about a tower, but he couldn't quite remember that part.

He took out several papers but ignored them until he found the folder with Jess's name on it. Just like in the tunnel, seeing her picture brought a sense of peace to his heart.

She had probably just joined the Agency, and her wide smile reflected the innocence of that time. He didn't mind that her hair was dark now, but he missed that peculiar shade that caught and reflected the sunlight. He missed his sunshine in more ways than he could count.

With a deep sigh, he turned the page. The small letters bounced on the white paper, and he groaned but forced himself to focus. Reading wasn't impossible—it just took time and effort. He skimmed the pages, focusing on the titles, and stopped when one long heading caught his eye. It included the word *water*.

Naturally, it had to be the one printed in the tiniest font, with the most forbidding paragraphs. He glanced at the window to clear his mind, wondering how long it would take him to decipher the document. That was when an approaching light caught his attention.

A second later, a low buzzing echoed in the distance—and the airship's alarms began to wail. The crutches slowed him down, and he was only halfway to the door when the first missile hit. The explosion threw him to the floor, sending furniture crashing and sliding. He figured the missile had missed the ship's center—otherwise, it would have gone into a free fall.

People rushed through the hallway, shouting orders and carrying guns. Tom joined them, but his injured leg made it impossible to keep up. The second missile struck just as he reached the stairs leading to the navigation room.

The blast was louder, shaking everything around him and muffling his hearing. He tried to steady himself by grabbing the wall, but the floor gave way as the airship plunged downward. Tom glanced at the men and women nearby. They'd once been criminals, but now—they were his friends. His people.

"Hold on!" he shouted. A heartbeat later, another explosion tore through the wall.

The floor beneath him lurched upward, knocking the air from his lungs. There must have been another missile, but his ears weren't working anymore. He caught a blinding flash of flame racing toward him—then something hard struck his head, and the world vanished.

49

Axiom Realm

188A25 Year Week 13,
Seventh day, Night

The rain continued to hit the car's window, tracing thick paths down the glass as the drops slid away. Jess wished she could just slip away with them—though she was grateful to be out of her mother's house. She had once lived there, but it was clear that house was no longer her home. The social gossip seemed to be the only reason her mother still acknowledged her as a daughter, clinging to the etiquette she both feared and adored.

Beside her, Dan wore a serious expression Jess wasn't used to seeing. He had barely looked at her, but she'd overheard his argument with her mother while she was forced to change into something "more appropriate." Despite the story her mother had crafted for Axiom's society pages, the woman still insisted Jess shouldn't appear like a mental patient. Dan, on the other hand, clearly wanted to show her something—but her mother didn't approve.

Jess tugged at the tight wool dress. It had been years since she'd worn anything like it. Once she joined the Agency, everything had been about uniforms and practicality. Chaos fashion might call for corsets, but not these heavy layers of fabric with metal rings. The high lace collar felt suffocating, and the overly decorated sleeves hanging past her wrists reminded her how hard it would be to fight anyone dressed like this.

"You look good," Dan said, giving her a quick glance. "Though you looked good before, too."

Jess shook her head. "She hasn't changed, at least."

Dan turned slightly in his seat to face her. "She *has* changed, Jess. All of us have."

A knot tightened in Jess's stomach. She had assumed her family was doing fine—Bill in his high-ranking government position, her mother basking in Axiom's elite circles, their new neighborhood as posh as the papers claimed. She had never really pictured Dan in that life. He had always seemed content when her mother was, and she had simply assumed he was fine, too.

"You didn't want me here," Jess said softly, surprised when tears threatened to rise.

Dan took her hands and smiled. "No, no. You're the daughter I never had. I've missed you every day, Jess, but... this man isn't a good one. I couldn't—shouldn't—have let Amelia push this nonsense. I'm not leaving you with him."

Jess tilted her head and smiled faintly. "I'll be fine, Dan. I can tie my own boots."

"Do you know he..." Dan lowered his voice so the chauffeur couldn't hear. "This man has done horrible things. I don't want you to get hurt."

"What horrible things?" Jess whispered. When Dan paled, anger flared in her chest. "Did he hurt you or my—"

Dan shook his head. "He's polite to your mother and tolerates me, but... Arlett's terrified of him. And I have a feeling his father didn't just retire. No one knows where he went, Jess. In my opinion, Bill's keeping the wrong company."

Jess rolled her eyes and looked out the rain-blurred window. Dan had never liked Bill, but she didn't want more conflict between him and her mother. Dan was the only one who had ever truly protected her.

"Jess," he said quietly, "your mother is in denial. She wants you to marry him. Don't do it—not for her, not for anyone. It's a mistake."

She smiled faintly. "I won't be staying that long, Dan."

He exhaled but tightened his grip on her hands. "If you leave again... are you all right, my little girl?"

Jess swallowed hard as her vision blurred, and she could only nod. Dan pulled her into an embrace, and for a moment, she was the young girl he used to drive to the train station on the First—back when life still felt simple.

"I wish things were different," he whispered, then smiled at her again. "You're my eternal concern, Jess—and my greatest failure as a parent."

Jess frowned, but he went on.

"I should have defended you. Shouldn't have let Bill or your mother push you around. I thought you wanted to work in research—not use it as an escape."

"I wasn't escaping," Jess said. "And you've been a great substitute dad."

He nodded. "Still, I should have done more." His voice softened. "Have you seen Tom?"

Jess froze. It was too late to hide the rush of emotion on her face.

"Too bad," Dan said, though his tone told her he'd already understood. "I wanted to talk to him. After the hospital—" He hesitated. "I've thought about it for a long time, and... I'm not sure, Jess. Tom wasn't violent. He was a worker, like me. The only reason I'd attack someone like that is if..." He trailed off, looking away.

Jess's pulse quickened. "What happened, Dan?" she asked, touching his arm. When he didn't answer, she whispered, "Please."

He sighed. "Your mother and I were walking to Bill's room after talking with the hospital staff. We couldn't believe they'd let him be attacked *twice.* I heard screaming down the hall, so I pushed your mom aside and opened the door first. If someone was attacking Bill, I wasn't going to let them near her. But what I saw—" He swallowed hard. "Your mom shoved past me, but I saw Tom. He kicked your brother when he was already down. The sound of it, Jess... I still hear it in my nightmares."

He shook his head. "Thank the Maker, Tom didn't see me coming. I pulled him back. He's stronger than me—and he was furious—but he recognized me when he turned."

Jess listened in silence, her chest tight. Her mother had told versions of this story before, but never one she believed. Hearing it from Dan made it real.

"The doctors' shouting snapped me out of it, and I let Tom go."

"You *let him go?*"

Dan nodded. "If I'd stopped him, they would've blamed him for the other attacks. But he was with you when those happened—in Chaos. How did he come back twice? Where were you? No, it had to be something else."

"Tom told you we were in Chaos?" Jess bit her lip, startled. She hadn't known Tom had spoken to her family after that day.

"After he left, the doctors rushed in and threw us out. Arlett was crying, your mother was hysterical, and there was no sign of you or Tom. I searched the hospital for you." He brushed a tear from his eye and smiled faintly. "When you finally came back late that night... one look at you and I knew something terrible had happened to him."

"By my look?" She tried to laugh. "I thought no one could tell how I felt."

Dan smiled. "Tom showed it more, but yes, I knew. I've known about your feelings for a long time. I hope things are better between you now?"

Jess closed her eyes, unable to answer. Dan hugged her again, and this time, she didn't stop the tears.

"That's not all," he continued. "When I went back to Bill's room, Arlett kept saying he didn't mean it. That she was relieved you'd recover. I asked her to speak up if she knew why Tom attacked Bill, and she asked if I'd talked to him. When I said no... I swear, she looked *relieved*."

Jess felt her blood race as she tried to control her thoughts about Arlett.

"Am I right?" Dan asked. "Tom isn't the monster they say he is. He just acted like I would've—if someone tried to hurt your mother."

Jess leaned back and nodded. "Bill set me up, Dan. He had a deal with the Corrupts, but it fell apart when Arlett was taken. Then he made a new deal with her kidnappers."

"Dear Maker." Dan's gentle features hardened with fury. "What kind of deal?"

"It doesn't matter."

"It does to me."

Jess hesitated, knowing the truth would only deepen his anger. "He promised to hand me over to the ones who broke the Barrier—in exchange for their protection. Tom was helping me find a dangerous artifact, and we ended up saving Arlett too. I wasn't with him when he brought her back—I was shot and stayed behind in Chaos to prevent a bigger disaster. If I'd been there, I'd have been captured and killed. Bill made a deal with the man the police arrested, thinking he was Tom."

Dan's expression darkened. "I wish I'd known, Jess. It's time for me to act."

Jess reached for his hand. "He's made terrible choices, but he was protecting Arlett. You would've done the same."

"No, Jess." Dan met her eyes. "I'd do anything for your mother's safety—but never at the cost of my other loved ones."

"Well," Jess half smiled, "we know he doesn't love me."

Dan shook his head. "You're my little girl, and I love you. Why didn't you tell me?"

"My mom," Jess said quietly. "She's tough, but she needs you. You're the one who keeps her sane."

He laughed softly and kissed her forehead. "Then I'll have to do better."

The car slowed, and for a moment the sound of rain filled the silence. A large mansion loomed ahead. As the chauffeur guided the car through the gate and up the curved drive, Dan squeezed her hand.

"I can still turn the car around," he said. "Despite my age, I can pull a few strings."

Jess leaned in and kissed his cheek. "I'm not alone, Dan," she whispered. "The one who needs rescuing is in that house."

Her door opened. A man in a gray uniform stood waiting with an umbrella. Jess gave Dan a quick smile before stepping out into the rain, letting the cold drops wash the emotion from her face.

Dan followed her inside, where another set of guards was already waiting.

50

Axiom Realm

Peter's muscles tensed when he saw Jess walking up the entrance steps with two guards close behind. She had slipped out of her mother's house earlier and given him the heads-up to head toward Main City. He gripped the steering wheel, forcing himself to wait before breaking in to find his sister and Holm. When Jess's stepfather followed her inside, the doors closed behind them.

He picked up the transmitter from the car's console and dialed his old lieutenant's number. Jess's idea had been a brilliant one—the chances of the two of them rescuing his sister alive were slim, but creating a large enough distraction might just work.

When they'd left Chaos, he hadn't been sure they'd even make it to Sector 8, but now it sounded like the perfect staging ground.

The day Darius had shut down the Agency, he'd sent a squad to that sector. Darius wasn't stupid—he'd mixed the teams so most agents wouldn't know one another, making trust nearly impossible. To tighten control further, he had kept the higher-ranking agents close in Main City.

Peter should have been among those stationed in the capital—and probably dead by now. But Darius didn't know that Peter had already betrayed the Agency long before. The night he'd helped Holm and Jess free Tom, he had become a wild card the new director couldn't account for. A perfect cover.

While Jess was inside her mother's mansion, Peter had stolen a car and driven to the old meeting building where he was supposed to rendezvous with Millie. He'd expected resistance, yet most of the agents were relieved to see him. His explanation was vague, but the mere mention of Bill's connection to the Corrupts had led them to link him to Tom—and to the Disruption. It was a lie, but Peter didn't correct them. Jess would be furious if she knew, but he could live with that. Tom was already branded a traitor; using that image to unite their enemies under one flag was simply strategy.

In the end, the agents were ready. They rallied to his orders, prepared to stand against their new director and defend their realm. They fell into formation behind his stolen car, and one by one, more vehicles joined them as they approached the estate.

"Build the perimeter and get in position," Peter said into the transmitter. He'd carried out plenty of missions before, but never one like this—against his own director, in his own realm. He missed Chaos's constant hum of light and sound, the certainty that the men inside were Corrupts.

Here, the darkness of Axiom's streets felt heavier. The silence, broken only by the pounding rain, set his nerves on edge. Through the downpour, he caught glimpses of his agents moving into place, weapons drawn and ready.

He didn't want to risk exposing their position, so he stayed on the open frequency Holm had taught him to use. Once everyone was in place, he'd switch to the Agency's encrypted signal. The moment he did, Darius would know they were here. Peter would have just one shot to get it right.

Jess had promised to send a sign but hadn't said what it would be. He just hoped he'd recognize it—and reach her in time.

51

Axiom Realm

188A25 Year Week 13,
Seventh day, Night

J ESS KEPT HER EYES open and her nerves alert. The only advantage of her mother's elaborate attire was that it hid a gun easily. Even if someone patted her down, the heavy layers and tiny metal rings would disguise the real danger. She had also tucked a knife into her tall boots—perhaps as a decoy. If Darius didn't find a weapon on her, he'd grow suspicious. And if he decided to search her, he'd face the consequences.

The man leading her stopped in the middle of a large vestibule. A grand staircase curved upward ahead, its landing opening into a second-floor balcony lined with closed doors. On either side of the lobby, three hallways branched off—one likely leading to the parlor, another toward the back and the servants' quarters.

Tom crossed her mind. She wished he were there; he could have easily guided her through the place to find Gall-I and Holm.

Dan stood at her side, his hand steady on her arm. "The elevator is back there," he murmured, nodding toward the hallway. "Bill used it as an excuse to move here a few months ago. Said the old house didn't have one and he couldn't live on the ground floor."

Jess followed his glance to the metallic cage of an antique elevator tucked beside a smaller staircase. Gaudy red-velvet curtains framed its golden doors.

"I can see why he likes it here," she said. "How many rooms are in this place?"

"Well, that depends," replied a man descending the grand staircase. "Do you mean rooms behind doors—or rooms by purpose? Bedrooms, parlors, baths, dining?"

Jess didn't need Dan's tightening grip to know who he was. Darius.

Though younger than she remembered his father, the resemblance was unmistakable. Tall and slender but strong, his muscular frame filled out his crisp white shirt. His hair was perfectly styled, as if ready for an audience. But what caught her attention was the gleam in his eyes—sharp, predatory. The same shimmer she had seen in the *takuosums*.

Just like with those creatures, Jess forced herself to remain calm. Any sign of fear or emotion would be a mistake.

"It shouldn't be any of her concern," came Bill's voice from her left. Jess had to count backward to suppress the heat flooding her veins. "No matter what she's asking about."

Even though she'd expected him, hearing his voice still made her stomach twist.

"I don't know, Bill," Darius said, descending another step. "This will be her home too. She's allowed to ask about it."

Jess didn't look at her brother. She kept her gaze fixed on Darius, who smiled at her—wide and menacing.

"Dan," Darius said. "You're welcome to stay over. It isn't safe to drive in this weather."

"You should have waited until morning," Dan said. "This isn't the time to call on anyone from a decent family."

With a hand pressed to his heart, Darius stopped on the last step, looking down at them like an actor onstage. Jess suddenly understood why Bill insisted on living upstairs; his brother wasn't the type who liked looking up to anyone.

"I apologize for the offense," Darius said smoothly. "After hearing so much about her, I couldn't wait to meet this lovely lady. Besides, we'll soon be a couple. Such an informal meeting won't trouble polite society."

Jess smiled faintly, using the moment to study the room. At least ten guards surrounded them, weapons visible. The only clear exit was behind her—and she didn't need to turn to know it was blocked, inside and out.

"I see this makes you smile," Darius said. "I'm glad you're pleased about our future."

Jess stared straight at him. "You're funny. Last I checked, bigamy isn't legal in Axiom."

"Bigamy?" His tone darkened for a moment. "I'm not married. But you're right—I *was.* My poor wife was ill... I lost her."

"You were married?" Dan asked. "Does Amelia know this? I doubt she'd approve—"

"Being a widower isn't illegal," Darius interrupted. "I'm sure Amelia understands—as Jess will, too. Isn't that right?"

The thinly veiled threat in his voice made Dan step forward, gripping Jess's arm protectively.

Jess forced a small laugh. "I'm not a fan of our society's ridiculous rules—or my mother's opinions. Bill probably told you that already."

"In that case," Darius said, stepping off the last stair but keeping his distance, "I see no problem. I just need to make sure you're... *clean*." He gestured toward a nearby guard. "Search her."

"Search her?" Dan barked, moving in front of Jess. "Are you out of your mind? I won't let you abuse your power. We're leaving."

Darius softened his tone, his expression calm. "Dan, this isn't an abuse of power. Jess is a former agent—one of our best, actually. But according to Amelia, she's been suffering some... mental complications. I can't risk anyone's safety in my home."

"Yes, Dan," Bill added, his voice oily. "Jess is a dangerous maniac."

Dan started forward, but Jess caught his arm. "It's all right, Dan. This is an Agency procedure."

She stepped toward Darius's guard and raised her arms. The man hesitated, glancing at his superior. When Darius waved, he complied.

Jess wasn't exaggerating—it *was* a procedure she'd endured countless times while working with Marshall. Still, she'd never encountered a guard this tentative. His hands trembled slightly as he searched her, and he missed both the knife and the gun.

When he finished, he stepped back. "Agent Hiem-Sagac is clean," he reported, avoiding her eyes. Jess wondered if he had doubts about Darius's new position and hoped many of them did.

"Excellent!" Darius said, finally closing the distance between them. "You're even more beautiful than I was told. I understand why he's so obsessed with you."

"Please," Bill groaned, wheeling his chair toward a side hallway. "Can we get down to business?"

Still watching her, Darius lifted a hand, inviting her to follow. Jess could see how Gall-I might have fallen for him—not for his looks, but for that unnerving focus. It was dangerous, intoxicating.

Dan moved forward, but two guards blocked him.

"I'm sorry, Dan," Bill said. "This is a family matter. It doesn't concern... *additions* like you."

Dan tried to shove past one of the guards, but they pushed him back easily. "I'm not leaving her with you!"

"It won't take long," Darius said. "You can choose a room upstairs. Just stay clear of Arlett's—and her guest's."

"I'm not going to—" Dan began, but Jess stepped closer and touched his arm.

"I'm confident everything will be fine," she said quietly. "But the storm might worsen. You know Mom—she hates bad weather, especially when you're not with her. I'll feel better knowing she's safe, with you, in Sector 8."

"Jess," he whispered. "I don't want to leave you. Not after what you told me about Bill."

She smiled gently. "Please, Dan."

He exhaled and kissed her forehead. "Will you be home soon?"

She bit her lip, pushing a strand of hair behind her ear. "As soon as I can."

Dan nodded, his eyes glistening. Without another word, he turned away. The guards didn't stop him this time. Jess prayed the chauffeur would drive him straight back to Sector 8. The last thing she needed was Dan wandering the streets while Peter prepared his assault. Holm and Gall-I were already enough to worry about.

"Finally!" Bill called, wheeling himself down the corridor.

"After you," Darius said smoothly, motioning for Jess to follow her brother.

52

CHAOS REALM

188Ch25 Year Week 13,
Seventh day, Night

THE NOISE OF PEOPLE shouting grew louder as Tom regained consciousness. He tried to stand, but a sharp pain shot through his leg, reminding him of his injury—and of the attack. He gritted his teeth and pushed himself into a sitting position.

Around him, the once-polished walls were cracked or collapsed. The floor looked like a warped wooden wave, and the hallway tilted unnaturally. Nearby, the staircase had become a pile of debris mixed with shattered chandeliers and broken glass.

The acrid smell of burning wood and metal made him cough. The orange glow ahead wasn't sunlight—it was fire. There were no more rooms, only heaps of drywall and splintered furniture. Beneath him, the ornate floors of the airship had given way to the muddy ground of Chaos.

"Sir!" a voice shouted—not far off.

He turned toward the sound and saw Coba climbing through the wreckage, leaping over beams and debris to reach him.

"Don't move!" Coba yelled. "We'll get you out of there."

Tom tried to rise, but pain flared in his leg again.

"For the Maker," he swore, scanning the area. He needed his crutches. Somewhere nearby, gunfire erupted, making his pulse spike. The battle wasn't over.

"What the photons!" he growled, shoving aside chunks of wood and carpet. He had to be ready to move. Small shards of glass bit into his palms, drawing blood, but he didn't care.

"Let's go, sir!" Coba called, finally reaching him. A shotgun rested on his shoulder as he pulled Tom to his feet.

"I need to find those stupid things—"

Once upright, Tom spotted one broken crutch nearby—but the other was intact, lying a few steps away.

"Forget it, sir. I can help you—"

Another burst of gunfire cut him off, forcing both men to duck.

"We need you shooting, not carrying me," Tom said, his voice tight as he ignored the pain stabbing up his spine while he crawled toward the crutch.

After Coba helped him up, they made their way out. The view outside was far worse. Half the airship was destroyed, its structure twisted and burning. People ran through the wreckage, pulling others free while dodging bullets. A massive fire consumed the parachute valve of the balloon, and the collapsing fabric fell across the deck—right over what had been the navigation room and Marshall's office.

"Where's Marshall?" Tom shouted.

Coba shoved a huge slab of drywall aside. "Not sure, sir! You're the first we've found. Some are fighting the fire—others are holding the line."

Tom followed him through what was left of the main dining area. He recognized it only by the chandelier, still somehow hanging from a steel beam. The fine tablecloths and crimson carpet were gone; shards of glass from the crystal lamps and vases scattered the floor, reflecting the flames in fractured light.

It had never been his favorite room, but seeing that once-grand symbol of power reduced to ashes turned his stomach. A dark realization hit him—it wasn't just an airship that had fallen. It was the end of his family's legacy.

Coba climbed through a broken window and reached back to help Tom down. The cold, damp air of Chaos hit him like a slap, rain mixing with the smoke.

"This way," Coba said, handing him the crutch. "Heli-3 will take you to safety while we finish this fight."

Tom stopped and turned.

The airship lay half-buried in the mud, the balloon deflated and burning, the front section gone entirely. Flames licked upward into the rain, and the entire top deck had collapsed into the lower levels. His stomach dropped. He had no idea how many people had been trapped below.

"Sir, we have to go!" Coba urged.

"We need—" Tom began, but when he looked at Coba, he saw something he never expected: fear.

Straightening as much as his leg allowed, Tom raised his voice. "How many people do we still have?"

Coba hesitated before answering. "Most of our shooters are here, holding off the sons of the void. Heli sent a call for backup to the ships nearby, but they're at least half an hour out."

"Half an hour's too long," Tom said, staring at the wreck. "We need to pull anyone still alive from inside. And we need more weapons. You handle the front lines. Where's Heli?"

Coba pointed toward the woods ahead. "I can go with you."

"No." Tom started toward the trees. "I'm too slow. You take command at the front. I'll send more weapons and ammo as soon as I can."

"Sir, you can't risk your life—you're the last one—"

"I'll find Marshall, Coba."

He didn't look back. Each step was agony, but his mind was clear. He just had to hold out half an hour. Knowing Heli-3, the photonic void would open near those woods.

Relief stirred faintly in his chest. They'd been attacked right before reaching High City—close enough for help, far enough to spare civilians.

"Boss!" Heli-3's voice carried through the rain. The man ran toward him, soaked and breathless. "You're alive!"

Tom managed a weak chuckle at his enthusiasm. He hadn't always been kind to Heli, but the man's loyalty never wavered.

"Heli," he said, gripping his shoulder. "We need to find Marshall."

Heli's expression hardened instantly.

"The last I saw him," he said, "he was headed for his office—with that girl... Lucille."

Tom's heart sank. He thought of Frank in his hospital bed, and dread replaced the ache in his chest. If Frank had survived the fall, escaping the fire was another story.

"I'll get a few men, boss," Heli said firmly, touching Tom's shoulder again. "We'll find them—all of them. You're here now. We have a leader again. We can do this."

With that, Heli ran toward the woods, shouting orders and calling out names.

Tom leaned on his crutch, trying to catch his breath. His lower back burned, and dizziness made his vision swim. The truth was undeniable—the poison had weakened his heart. The question was whether it would stay stable... or worsen.

Jess's words echoed in his mind—about Karen's husband dying of a heart problem—and suddenly, it all made sense. Karen must have blamed his father for that death, and now he understood why. They had been working together in those labs. His father must have known about the toxin—and about the water problem.

He had to find those papers. But as he looked back at the burning wreckage, hope wavered. Maybe Jess's research could help. Maybe she knew where Karen had hidden her work.

Then, despite everything—the pain, the fire, the chaos—he smiled. For once, Jess wasn't the one in danger.

53

Axiom Realm

The house's size surprised her. None of the rooms she passed looked like a dungeon or an entrance to a basement. To find her friends, she would have to rely on Darius taking her there—otherwise, she'd take *him* hostage and use his life as leverage.

Bill rolled into a large room with double-height ceilings and walls lined with bookshelves. An enormous stone fireplace stood in the center, flames roaring inside it. Jess frowned, unsure how the chimney vented through the middle of the room. She smiled faintly to herself—something to ask Tom about someday.

The firelight blocked her view of the opposite side, but she sensed eyes watching her.

"Here we are," Darius said, brushing her shoulder as he passed. She flinched back.

"That won't do, Jess," he said smoothly. "You're supposed to love me unconditionally."

Jess fixed her gaze on him. "Just like you unconditionally loved your wife?"

Darius rolled his eyes and threw up his hands. "That again? Jessica, we were doing *so* well."

"I told you," Bill muttered. "She's a daughter of the void."

For the first time in years, Jess really looked at her brother. The past three years had hardened him—not just because of the wheelchair. His eyes were cold, his face drawn tight. The joyful boy she'd once known was gone, replaced by a man steeped in resentment.

"What a shame," Darius said, settling into a large chair by the fire. "Such a pretty girl, with such a poor attitude."

Jess turned toward the window, ignoring him. The storm outside had worsened, but a shadow crossed the yard, catching her eye. If that was Peter, good—no one else seemed to notice. But she couldn't shake the feeling someone else was out there, too.

"At this point," Darius continued, his voice almost playful, "I have to assume you met my first wife. Your brother just had the pleasure of meeting her. And your *older* friend? What a collection. Your mother's right—you need better company."

Jess kept her expression neutral, though inside her heart leapt. If Bill had just seen Gall-I and Holm, they couldn't be far.

"Speaking of my mother," Jess said evenly, "I can see what she gains from this delusional marriage you think will happen. But what do *you* get? Surely the price is higher on your end—and it can't be my brother's loyalty. That's worthless."

"I know who my friends are," Bill snapped, his voice dripping with contempt. "You're the worthless one. You stole my best friend and turned him against me."

Jess's blood burned, but she forced a mocking laugh, covering her mouth as she turned to Darius. "You didn't actually fall for his ridiculous lies, did you? You can't be *that* stupid."

"Oh, I'm not stupid," Darius said, crossing one leg over the other. "After all, you're standing in my house." He laced his fingers together and smiled. "As for us, we'll have a glorious public engagement—and the wedding of the century. Then who knows? I never planned on children, but you might change my mind. You're certainly prettier than Tom's wife."

A shiver ran down Jess's spine. Tom had warned her this might happen. Still, the words cut deeper than she expected. Darius clearly enjoyed her reaction.

"So you don't know?" He glanced at Bill, who grinned beside him. "I guess you don't watch the news much. No matter. Why don't we introduce the two of you... again?"

A figure rose on the other side of the fire. Through the flames' flicker, Jess recognized the silhouette—the wild curls, the rounded belly.

"Hello, Jessica," Charlotte said, stroking her stomach. The fabric of her dress stretched tight, leaving no doubt the pregnancy was real.

Jess didn't bother to hide her shock. A cold weight sank in her chest, though she quickly understood the brilliance of the ploy. She refused to put an unborn child's life at risk—especially if it was *Tom's*.

She took a step back, shaking her head, reminding herself of what Tom had told her. He wasn't the father. She believed him.

"Oh no," Charlotte said, her tone dripping with mock pity. "You still believed Tom was in love with you?"

Jess forced her mind back to her goal: *Gall-I. Focus on Gall-I.* Not this photonic viper.

Scanning the room, she noted everything—bookshelves, a window facing the gardens, two armchairs with a table between them. On the table sat a glass decanter, a golden paperweight, a box of stationery, and a few crystal cups.

"I stopped wondering about that years ago," she said evenly. "You look better than last time, though."

Charlotte glanced toward Darius, fear flashing in her eyes. "Well, you still look as bad."

"Really?" Jess stepped toward the table. "I'm sure I'm in better shape now. My ribs aren't fractured, and my sweet mother forced me into this absurdly expensive dress."

Darius leaned forward, watching Charlotte closely—but before he could speak, the door swung open.

"Jess!" Arlett cried, gliding into the room in an evening gown. She rushed over and wrapped her arms around her. "I thought I heard your voice—it's so nice to see you!"

Jess didn't return the hug.

"What in the Maker's name are you doing here?" Bill shouted, wheeling himself toward Arlett.

That was all Jess needed.

She snatched the decanter and hurled it at the bookshelves. The bottle shattered, spilling liquor across the books.

"What the—" Darius began, rising to his feet, but Jess flung a cup at him. He ducked, covering his face—just as she grabbed the paperweight and slammed it against the side of his head. He dropped instantly.

Jess didn't hesitate. She lit the stationery set, flames curling up the paper, and tossed it onto the soaked shelves. The fire caught quickly—but when she smashed the nearby window with the table to feed it air, the sudden draft triggered a burst of flame and a small explosion. Arlett and Charlotte dropped to the floor and Bill covered his head.

"That should work as a sign," she muttered, pulling her knife from her boot.

Arlett was struggling to rise when Jess seized her, wrapping an arm around her neck and yanking her upright.

"Let her go!" Bill shouted, pushing his wheelchair closer.

"Where are my friends?" Jess shouted back, tightening her grip. Arlett clawed at her arm, choking.

"Stop, Jessica!" Bill bellowed. "Let her go or—"

"Where are they, Bill? Or I'll kill her."

Bill shook his head, but Jess didn't wait. She pressed the blade against Arlett's throat, just enough to break skin. Warm blood streaked her hand as Arlett screamed.

"No!" Bill shoved his chair forward, but the wheel snagged on a table leg. He toppled sideways with a crash.

Jess didn't flinch. "I'll kill her, Bill," she hissed. "I saved her pathetic life once and lost everything for it. It would *please* me to finish her life—unless you tell me where they are."

"Fine!" he yelled. "I'll take you there."

"No." Through the shattered window, Jess saw figures sprinting through the rain—and heard gunfire. Peter's signal. "Tell *her* where to go. She'll take me. If I don't find them, she dies."

Another volley of shots echoed through the house. Charlotte screamed, curling on the floor and crawling away from the fire.

Bill groaned, rage twisting his face. "The back corridor, behind the service entrance!"

"That's not good enough." Jess pressed the knife again; Arlett shrieked. "This is your last chance. I can find them myself—I'm just saving time. If you don't tell her *exactly* where, she's dead."

"You'll never make it out of this house," Bill spat, a crooked grin spreading. "You think Darius doesn't have an army protecting him?"

Jess met his gaze coldly. "Do you think I came alone?"

Color drained from his face. His hands trembled. "Arlett," he said, his tone suddenly soft—the same voice he used only for his wife. "You followed me there today, Ar. You know where they are."

Arlett tried to nod as her body trembled in Jess's arms.

She dragged Arlett backward toward the door, never loosening her grip. "If you're lying," she warned, "she's gone."

Without another glance at her brother, Jess opened the door and pulled Arlett through.

O N THE OTHER SIDE of the door, Jess didn't find guards trying to stop her—but Mer-80, standing amid the bodies of at least four men.

"Happy to see me?" Mer asked with a grin. "Didn't know you had it in you, but that was a *cool* threat. Guess you're finally learning from the best."

Jess looked around, but the hall was otherwise empty.

"Peter and his new gang are working their magic with the rest outside," Mer said.

Jess opened her mouth to ask something, but a sudden bright light flashed through the window—followed by an explosion that threw her to the floor.

Arlett landed on the far side of the room. Mer crashed into the bottom step of the now half-destroyed staircase. The front doors split in two and collapsed inward, blocking the exit, while the carpet and curtains ignited, filling the lobby with thick smoke.

"In the Maker's name!" Mer coughed, pulling herself up. "What are they thinking? We're still *inside!*"

"I doubt it's Peter," Jess said, pushing to her feet.

To her surprise, Arlett was still on the floor, unmoving.

"If someone kidnaps you and you get free," Jess said, "you should at least *try* to run."

Arlett didn't respond. Her hands trembled at her sides, eyes fixed somewhere distant.

"Are you all right?" Jess asked, hurrying toward her. She'd threatened to kill Arlett but had never intended to do it.

Arlett shook her head and grabbed Jess's hand. "This isn't good."

Mer rolled her eyes. "You don't say."

Jess helped Arlett up, but a cold knot formed in her stomach. The last time Arlett had gone silent like this, she'd known far more than she'd admitted. Jess feared what she knew now.

"I need to find my friends," Jess said, gripping Arlett's shoulders. "And we need to move fast."

"Yes." Arlett nodded quickly, glancing toward the office door before turning away from it. Instead of seeking Bill, she ran toward the back hallway—the one Jess had assumed led to the service area.

"This way," she said breathlessly. "Jess—I didn't know any of this. Not until today. I swear."

Tears streamed down her face, but she never looked back. She never looked for Bill. Jess noticed—and so did Mer.

Both women drew their guns, advancing down the smoke-filled corridor, ready for the next ambush.

54

Axiom Sea Periphery

188A25 Year Week 16,
First day, Hours Before
Dawn

THE WATER WAS COLDER than Tom had expected, and the waves crashing against his back pushed them in every direction. Only a few minutes had passed since he had leapt into the sea with Jess in his arms, but the struggle against the current had already drained his strength.

He knew his best chance of finding the portal was right where Randall's cage had fallen. Half of the crane that had held the prisoners' cages still jutted from the wreckage, and out in the middle of the sea he could see the broken end of the bridge they had crossed—its remnants barely above the water. Tom had to reach it and dive below with Jess.

Every second deepened his conviction that Randall had escaped through a portal beneath the waves. After a year imprisoned in a cage, Randall wouldn't have had the strength to swim across the sea before the Square exploded.

As Tom neared the submerged bridge, the waves grew higher and more violent, throwing him off balance. He tightened his hold on Jess, careful not to slam her—or himself—against the steel and brass structure.

Suddenly, the perimeter net's reflectors flared to life, blinding him. The Square's generator roared on, and the vibrations churned the water even harder. He clutched Jess closer and tried to pull away, but another wave surged, shoving him forward.

A grinding noise overhead snapped his attention upward just in time to see a beam break free and plunge toward them. He twisted, shielding Jess with his body as the metal slammed into his shoulder. Pain shot up his arm and neck. He fought to keep her in his grip, but water flooded his mouth and nose, and she slipped away.

Panic hit him like another wave. He spun around, searching, until a glimmer of light revealed Jess's limp body drifting toward the crane. Swimming with both arms now, he reached for her—but just as his fingers brushed her shoulder, gunfire erupted, bullets slicing into the water around him and deafening his ears.

Looking up, he glimpsed his airship circling overhead. It banked toward the building, its cannon aimed at the structure. Relief flared—Heli-3 must have seen him and was firing at Randall's men—but it didn't matter now. Jess was all that mattered.

With every ounce of strength left, Tom lunged forward, grabbed her, and pushed toward the bridge. He hooked his arm around a bent beam and pulled Jess close. Her lips were blue, her eyes closed—she wasn't breathing.

Frantically, he looked around. The bridge was barely holding together, sections already tearing loose. His chest tightened; he could hardly breathe. Still, he scanned for anything that might keep them afloat—and then saw a chain dangling from a nearby beam.

Sparks burst around him as more bullets struck the steel. He dragged Jess close and used the frame to propel himself toward the chain. The waves fought him, shoving them back, but he pressed on. When his hand finally closed around the cold metal links, a surge of relief steadied him.

The chain was bolted to the crane's frame, but one ring had jammed between two metal plates. Tom looped his arm through it and braced himself. He waited for the next wave, then pulled with everything he had. His muscles screamed. The next wave hit, and he used its force to wrench the chain loose.

It slid free—and instantly yanked them under.

The sea swallowed them whole. All sound vanished. Darkness closed around him.

Tom's lungs burned; he was seconds from gasping when the water suddenly warmed, and a crushing pressure forced the chain from his arm. The current shoved him forward—away from Jess. A brilliant light flared beneath him as a freezing wind slammed into his face and shoulders.

He broke the surface, choking on air. Before he could dive again, he spotted her—Jess—thrashing weakly against the waves.

"Jess!" he shouted, swimming toward her. "Jess, it's all right!"

"Tom..." she gasped, reaching for him. He caught her arms, holding her steady.

"We're safe, sunshine."

He looked up. The sky above them was dark but familiar—their sky. They had crossed over to Chaos. On the horizon, a faint light marked the shore. A city.

Jess smiled faintly, but her strength faltered, and she sank.

"Jess!" He dove beneath the surface, caught her around the waist, and kicked upward. She wasn't bleeding anymore, but her body was limp, her breathing shallow.

Tom carried her through the freezing surf toward land. Each stroke sent fire through his shoulder, but he didn't stop. By the time they reached the shallows, Jess's breathing steadied, faint but alive.

They had made it.

He looked toward the distant city lights, certain his people would find them soon—and praying there was still time to save her.

55

Axiom Realm

J ESS'S ASSUMPTIONS PROVED CORRECT: the house was huge, and it took them a full ten minutes to reach the back section. During the walk, another set of missiles struck the house, making the walls shudder and blowing out one entire side. Jess prayed Peter and the others were okay, and that Dan had been far away when the attack began.

"Here," Arlett said.

She stopped at a white door that smelled faintly of antiseptic and looked more like a surgery-room entrance than anything else.

"Wait," Mer hissed, moving up to press her ear to the door. "We don't know what's inside."

"Is it—" Arlett began, then sobbed and covered her mouth. Tears dampened her fingers. "An interrogation room? Or whatever you call the place where they do those horrible things?"

"Any guards?" Mer asked.

Arlett shook her head. "Darius keeps this room secret. I only saw it because I followed Bill. I wasn't supposed to be here."

Jess took a breath and pushed the door open. A heavy bleach odor stung her eyes and scraped her throat. Dim hallway light spilled into the room and a rat squealed before scurrying into a crack in the far wall.

The space reminded her of Heli-3's little butchery in Elemental 6—only without the carcasses. A metal table sat in the center; implements hung on the walls, their purposes ghastly but easy for her to imagine. The soft, damp mulch underfoot made her stomach churn.

"Jess…" a very weak voice whispered from inside.

She hurried forward, ignoring Mer's string of curses.

Holm slumped against the far wall in the corner. Half his face was burned and cut; his nose was probably broken, and one eye was swollen shut. His arms lay at his sides—either paralyzed or too swollen to move. The swelling in his knees told her he wouldn't be walking anytime soon.

"My girl," he rasped when she knelt beside him. "I thought I'd never see you again."

"Holm," Jess said, voice breaking. "We'll get you out of here. Let me—"

He tried to reply, but blood dripped from the corner of his mouth and a harsh cough cut him short.

"He killed my Phoebe," Holm said, eyes fixed on Jess. Tears welled in hers. "I made a mistake. Marshall left Axiom, and we were about to go, but—he was waiting in the alley, smiling that stupid smile, and he told me what he did to Phoebe. I got Gall-I in trouble. I was so mad I didn't hear her warning. The others trapped us."

Jess swallowed and pushed hair from her face. "I'm getting you two out of here, Holm. Then we'll figure out—"

He shook his head slowly. Jess stopped.

"Save Gall-I," he whispered. "Tell her I'm sorry. I didn't mean—" A coughing fit took him, then his voice returned so faint she had to lean in. "Phoebe loved you as much as I do. You are our girl..." He closed his eyes; his breathing became ragged but he struggled on. "You and Tom were right. I was wrong. My vault, Jess... it's all I know... all I have for you."

He coughed once more. Then his head lolled forward and his chest stilled.

Jess sank to the floor and pressed her hand to her mouth. Another person she loved had died in front of her—and his last words confirmed Phoebe had likely met the same fate.

DESPITE JESS'S DESIRE TO scream or hit something in response to the madness, Mer's touch prompted her to rise and wipe her face. Mer was already holding Gall-I by her shoulder.

"Is she—" Jess tried to ask, but thankfully Mer interrupted her.

"She is alive, but they beat her up pretty badly." She looked toward the door. "The other idiot ran back. You want me to get her?"

Jess shook her head and helped Mer by taking Gall-I's other arm. "Let's get out of here. I don't give a neutron what she does with her life."

"She kind of helped here," Mer said as they walked out of the room. "Maybe she isn't that bad."

"Or she's in denial, and we don't have time to make her figure out who the bad guys are."

Jess didn't want to think about Arlett or her brother and Darius. Otherwise she wouldn't be able to stop herself; risking everything, she'd go back and kill them for what they did to Holm and Phoebe. Instead, she moved on to a different subject. "How did you find me?"

The hallway they came through was on fire, so they had to go around and find another way out. Jess wasn't that worried — that was a service corridor. Residents of those houses preferred not to see their servants performing mundane duties like cleaning and taking out the garbage.

"Marshall ordered me to protect you."

At the corridor's end they found the back door leading to the backyard.

"What?" Jess exclaimed.

Outside, everything was chaos. People ran with no sense of direction, holding guns. Some wore the guards' uniforms, and in others Jess recognized the Agency's research uniforms — the ones used when working by the energy wave: white reflective fabric with helmets and goggles.

Flames engulfed the mansion, blocking the front path despite the pouring rain. The strangest part was the airship flying above. Jess didn't think it belonged to the Corrupts, but it definitely had the older style from Chaos.

She made sure Gall-I was secure in her arm and attempted to walk, but Mer didn't move.

"Come on!" Jess shouted, but when she looked back, Mer's gaze was fixed ahead.

Jess turned her attention in that direction, and a sudden chill ran through her. It confirmed her suspicions and explained so many things, yet it seemed impossible that Randall was walking across the yard, shouting orders. His long hair resembled the last time she saw him — walking in chains from a hanging cage to the Square's bridge. But he'd lost the fear on his face and the weakness in his beaten body. Now he stood tall— probably stronger than when he lived under Marshall and his deceased father's protection.

A researcher handed him a leather sack, too similar to the one Tom had found in the tunnel. Randall stopped and opened it. A wicked smile crossed his face as he pulled out a book with black covers and a brownish spine.

Jess felt queasy when she saw the odd size of the logbook, its covers wider than the spine and definitely bigger than a normal book.

"Make sure she gets out of—" Randall said, and Jess took a step forward to hear better. "Nothing else matters. That cargo is precious to me." He put the logbook back in the sack and kept walking, the researcher following him.

"It can't be..." Mer said, and shockingly Jess saw tears rolling down her cheeks. "He should be dead. No one survived that attack. We— Umbrar barely made it out."

When Mer turned to Jess, the pain and despair in her eyes, along with the anger in her features, told Jess Mer's true feelings about that monster.

"He must have fallen in the sea and somehow crossed over to Chaos," Jess said, trying to focus on the battle outside. She had thought Peter's people were wearing the Agency's old uniform.

Now she realized those were Randall's, and she had no idea where Peter was.

"He shouldn't have that logbook," Jess said, more to herself. "Darius's father must have known about Lezar and Samuel, and..." Her breathing became difficult. "Karen. That's how she concluded the Agency's director betrayed Samuel, too."

"He should have drowned," Mer said through her tears, in a harsh tone.

Jess turned to her. "I don't know, Mer. I'm starting to think the portals or the wave affect particles more than we've assumed."

Mer groaned and pulled Gall-I higher under her arm. "Let's get you two back."

"No," Jess said, looking around. "This is our only chance."

Mer drew a fake smile. "And what do you want to do? Run and kill him? There's no way those photonic guards will let us reach him!"

Jess moved aside, gently placing Gall-I down, and gestured toward a person in a white uniform. "Although that would be ideal, I agree with you. That's why I'm staying here, posing as one of them."

"Did you lose your neutrons?" Mer yelled. "You are clueless and naïve. Do you know what they'll do to you? This is exactly why Marshall sent me."

"This is exactly my job, Mer," Jess said. "I worked undercover for years, and I'm very good at it."

Mer smirked. "You didn't fool me. I always knew you were a problem."

"Did you think I was an agent, though? Or just an opportunist?"

When Mer didn't answer, Jess continued, "Go back. Take Gall-I with you and tell Tom and Marshall what we saw here."

"Tom and Marshall will kill me if I leave you here. I'll stay, and you tell them."

Jess shook her head. "Because it's so easy to hide your tattoos?! They're on your eyelids, for the Maker's sake."

Mer rolled her eyes. "My new boss will torture and kill me if I leave you behind."

"He won't," Jess said, hoping she was right. "Tell Tom that Randall has what he was looking for. Once I find it, I'll look for him. We need information, Mer. If Randall has been the one attacking Axiom, the Maker knows what he would do to Chaos."

She sighed. "Tell Tom about Holm... please."

"Photons, Maker!" Mer shouted, but she pulled Gall-I up. "One week, Jess. Then you get out and find the boss. He doesn't deserve you, or any of this."

"I know."

Jess waited until Mer disappeared from sight. Her pulse pounded in her ears, and with every step her heart ached more, accusing her of leaving Tom alone once more. Blocking it out, she rushed across the field to steal one of those research uniforms. It was time to get answers.

56

Chaos Realm

188Ch25 Year Week 13,
Seventh day, Late Night

Tom stopped to catch his breath as he followed Heli-3 through the line of attack. Even though the shooting was still underway, their reinforcements had arrived, bringing airships, armed motorcycles, and a substantial arsenal that successfully turned the tables and drove their attackers away. Tom didn't care about the number of people they killed. Whoever did it must have known who they were messing with. Retaliation was the Corrupts' second nature.

Over the last few hours they had rescued more people from the airship, and thanks to the arriving cars they transported those who needed medical attention to one of their safe houses. There was no sign of Frank, and it wasn't until the final five minutes, when Heli-3 informed him, that they found Marshall.

"Almost there, boss," Heli shouted to urge him on.

Tom had never been this exhausted before. His leg throbbed and burned and seemed to weigh a ton. The crutch may as well have poked a hole in his armpit, and his palm had become a blister from his weight and the small pieces of glass that by now had probably been forced deep into the flesh. Worst was the pressure in his chest and the constant lack of air that forced him to stop often.

"They finally extinguished the fire, so we made it inside the ship," Heli said once she reached him. "Apparently the boss had a secret shelter by his office or something."

A pungent scent of burning and smoke still filled the air, but the absence of flames made the night darker. The airship had lost its entire front section. The navigation room had shattered, with pieces spread across the ship's first floor.

"Nik-el-28 was the one who found him, boss."

Tom turned and recognized Marshall's assistant — a small woman whose age was impossible to guess. She sat on the ground, staring at nothing in particular. Her usual tight bun was all out of place, and every scrap of her characteristic self-possession seemed concentrated in the tight hold she maintained on the blanket over her shoulders.

"Is she all right?" Tom asked.

Heli nodded but kept walking, paying no attention to the woman. "The doctor is with him, but I didn't hear his prognosis. I ran to catch you."

Tom stopped in his tracks—and not for lack of air.

The doctor who'd treated him was kneeling on the ground, working on Marshall. Tom only knew it was his brother because Yttri stood behind them. The big guy had his eyes fixed on the ground, shoulders slumped and arms folded. He seemed not to care about the blood dripping from his head and the bright red burns on his forearms.

Tom felt the same as he took in Marshall's state. Ashes and wet spots disguised deep burns on his face. Tom appreciated the night for concealing the severe burns that had devoured

Marshall's skin, leaving exposed flesh on his neck, shoulder, arm, and rib cage.

He ignored the sharp pain in his leg and sank down on the ground beside Marshall. The worst became apparent then: his abdomen looked swollen to an unhealthy size, and the doctor kept his attention on it.

"What is it?" he asked.

Only then did the doctor look up at him. "I can't be sure with no equipment, but I fear he has deep internal bleeding, or the crash destroyed his organs."

Tom pushed back his hair and glanced at Yttri. Yttri kept shaking his head and looked on the verge of breaking down.

"He saved me," a weak voice said, and when Tom turned he found Lucille standing on the other side of Marshall. She'd wrapped her arms around herself; her lips quivered, and although her clothes were charred and stained, she appeared otherwise unharmed.

"I was stuck," she said a little louder. "Something fell on my leg and he..." Her voice broke, and although Tom wanted to yell for an explanation, he didn't.

"We need to get him out of here," he said, looking at Heli. "Get a car—"

"Sir!" Coba shouted as he ran toward him. "You need to see this."

"Photons!" Tom swore under his breath. He wanted to stay with Marshall, but now he bore responsibility for all those lives.

"Get him ready to move," he told the doctor, then turned to Yttri. "Stay with Marshall, and make sure Lucille is in your sight. It's her turn to answer all our questions."

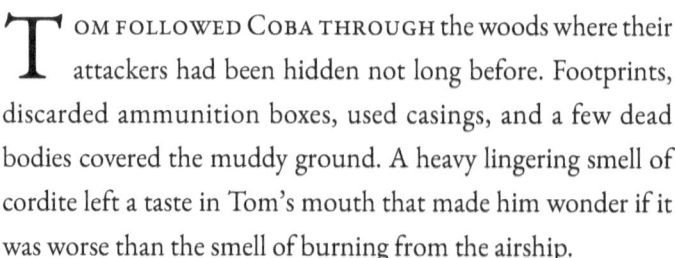

T OM FOLLOWED COBA THROUGH the woods where their attackers had been hidden not long before. Footprints, discarded ammunition boxes, used casings, and a few dead bodies covered the muddy ground. A heavy lingering smell of cordite left a taste in Tom's mouth that made him wonder if it was worse than the smell of burning from the airship.

"Here," Coba said, crouching by a bush. "I found her when we were searching the area. Sir, I believe the attackers made sure there were no survivors."

Tom stopped by Coba and used his crutch to move the branches of the bush. The hundreds of colors of Phoebe's skirt sent a shiver down his spine, but the severe cut in her neck and the wide-open eyes full of fear turned his stomach.

"I don't think they killed her here, sir," Coba said, standing and ignoring Tom's fight to keep his bile down. "She's been dead for a while. My guess is a few days. Is she the one your wife and the other guy were searching for?"

Tom nodded and turned away, failing to expel an image that would haunt him.

"We can't leave her here... like that," he said.

Coba nodded. "I figured as much. I'll make sure we get her body somewhere else. Do you want to keep her, or should we bury her?"

Tom stared at Coba, unsure what the question meant.

"You know..." Coba gestured vaguely, as if that would explain better. "In case the crazy old guy wants to see her?"

"Crazy old—" Tom rubbed his face. "Photons! Holm will lose it."

He didn't like Holm, but the old man loved his wife as much as Tom loved Jess. Tom understood the impact such news would have.

"See if you can keep her." Tom reached down, and although bile rose in his throat, he closed Phoebe's eyes. "I'm sure he'll want to see her."

"All right, sir. I'll make sure it's done."

"Thanks, Coba," Tom said as he turned. "I'll head back to check on Marshall—"

A light opened near the edge of the airship, and two individuals emerged from it. It was a strange sight—portals didn't usually open in the middle of a field—but Tom guessed the one in the airship must have moved with the explosion. The mix of light tones, instead of a single white stream, meant one or both people didn't belong to Chaos.

He pushed the branches out of his way and walked toward the arrivals. The thread of hope of seeing Jess gave him the strength to move faster. The ground cracked behind him, and, not surprisingly, when he turned he found Coba following.

Tom's heartbeat sped up when he realized one of the figures was supporting the other. By the build, he doubted Jess was the one walking, so he hurried, ignoring the pressure growing in his chest and the lack of air.

"I'll bet that's Mer," Coba said not far behind, which only made Tom's concern grow.

A man ran out of the woods, confirming Coba's suspicion. They wanted to leave no one alive. He seemed to be limping as he ran toward the figures. The person stepping from the portal halted and retrieved a shotgun from their back, and the other individual collapsed to the ground.

The man pulling his leg turned back and shouted something, but a set of shots silenced him. At the same time the shotgun holder fired, a new volley came from the woods. Seconds later the shooter fell. Coba ran past Tom, firing into the trees, and everything went quiet after a loud, final scream.

When Tom reached Coba, Coba was cradling Mer's head on his lap, tears running down his face. Not far from them, Gall-I lay unconscious, but her mumbling let them know she was alive. Tom tossed aside his crutch and sank to the ground beside them. Blood coated Mer so heavily it was impossible to find a single wound to staunch the bleeding.

"Sir—boss," she whispered. Tom moved as close as he could.

"Hey, girl," he said. "We'll get you help. The doctor is here and—"

"So sorry. Jess... one week." A cough cut her off and forced more blood from the side of her mouth. Coba sobbed and brushed her face; the touch made her smile. Then she turned back to Tom. "Randall—alive. He has—you wanted..."

Mer exhaled and her body relaxed in Coba's arms. Coba pulled her closer before finally breaking down.

Tom sat back and pushed his hair from his forehead, trying to steady the trembling in his hands. He had to fight the growing urge to cross over right then and find Jess. She had said something about Randall in the tunnel, but he couldn't remember the details. His mind got stuck on Mer's last words.

Randall was alive, and he had something Tom wanted—maybe Jess. If Randall had orchestrated the attacks in Axiom and Chaos, everyone was in greater danger. Tom needed a plan.

He touched Coba's shoulder. "I'll send someone to help you."

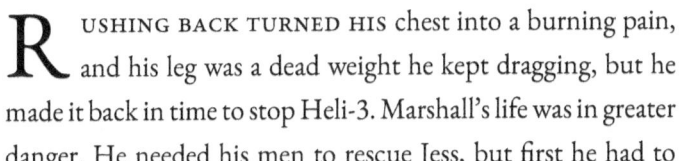

RUSHING BACK TURNED HIS chest into a burning pain, and his leg was a dead weight he kept dragging, but he made it back in time to stop Heli-3. Marshall's life was in greater danger. He needed his men to rescue Jess, but first he had to prioritize protecting his brother. He would kill Randall later. After all, retaliation was in his blood.

"We need a new safe house," he shouted once he was close enough, making everyone there stop. "Marshall can't go to any of ours."

Heli shook her head and stepped forward. "Boss, our houses are fine. The photonic Axiom people don't know about them."

"But Randall does." Tom looked at the group, from Yttri to Heli. "Mer is gone."

Heli crossed her arms close to her chest, unable to hide the sudden tremble. "Sir, if Randall is behind this... I don't know. He was part of the family—the Maker knows what he would do to any of us if he trapped us."

"I'm fully aware of that." Tom paused, thinking, until Heli's warning brought to mind the other person Coba had found in the woods.

"Holm and Phoebe's place!" he said, turning to Heli. "I need a map. I'll show you where to take Marshall. You, Yttri, the doctor here, and that girl," he said, pointing at Lucille. "No one else hears about this. Understood?"

"Yes, sir!" Heli said, running to fetch a map.

If Randall wanted to kill Marshall, he'd have to find him first — and now, he'd also have to worry about Tom hunting him.

57

Axiom Realm

D ESPITE PETER AND HIS agents gaining access to the gardens, the house was still far away and under missile fire. Now he was certain it wasn't the Corrupts. He had just spoken to Marshall and found Jess with them. He also doubted the Radicals had that kind of ammunition. However, his mission wasn't to discover who the attackers were—he needed to rescue his sister, Holm and Jess.

From the corner of his eye, he saw a missile flying toward them and, by instinct, crouched down. The missile missed, landing in the middle of the street. It struck a streetlamp, igniting sparks that started a second fire at the neighboring house.

"Reposition!" Peter shouted into the radio. "The ones in the garden stay with me. Everyone else, help with the second fire."

He didn't know who lived in that house, but he couldn't leave them to die. Helping people was the Agency's mission, and even though sirens were approaching, he knew time was short. Reinforcements were too far away to save the innocent ones in that neighborhood.

He noticed a car stop at an enormous deck on the other side of the house. Armed guards got out and ran up the short stairs.

He signaled to the man beside him to slow down and move in that direction. If the guards could enter, Peter's agents could too.

He was halfway there when two guards emerged, carrying a man between them. A woman followed, struggling to push a wheelchair with a broken wheel, and a second guard came out carrying another man. Peter guessed it was Bill, and the woman who kept glancing back had to be Arlett. A guard at the front shouted something, and the ones carrying Bill hurried, passing Arlett, who had to abandon the wheelchair to follow them down the steps.

Peter signaled to wait. He needed to locate his people, but unless they came out with that group, he preferred to enter only after they left.

As Arlett climbed into the car, an explosion on the second floor shattered the windows. Peter dropped to the ground, and the heat forced him to roll sideways. By the time he regained control, the car had already sped away, shooting its way out of the property.

The deck didn't clear, though. A larger group approached the door. These people wore the Agency's research uniforms—ones Peter only recognized because of Jess.

Although the smoke from the fire blocked part of his view, he could see a few people leaving the house. The uniformed men moved as a tight group, clearly protecting someone. Peter pushed himself up and tried to focus through the smoke and distance.

For a moment, when the group reached the stairs, their formation opened, allowing Peter to see the person in the middle. It didn't matter the distance or poor lighting; she was impossible to forget. After all, Peter had saved her life when Tom pushed her into his arms before the Disruption.

Charlotte had her arm linked with a man—one of the uniformed guards—and right before the group closed up again, Peter noticed her rounded stomach. A rush of anger surged through him, but he forced himself to stay rational. He'd known Tom was a son of the void all along, but now he was working with Marshall. Charlotte wasn't with the Corrupts, but there was no sign she was being coerced either. She couldn't possibly be expecting Tom's baby… and that raised a bigger question: why the heavy protection around her?

"Let's go," Peter ordered the agents beside him and sprinted forward.

Just before reaching the deck, he heard the unmistakable whistle of a missile. A second later, it struck the center of the house, and the explosion threw Peter several meters backward into a tree before he hit the ground.

The impact shattered his teeth and knocked the air from his lungs, but through the smoke and his blurry vision, he thought he saw Mer running from the far end of the garden. Even from that distance, he recognized how she was dragging his sister.

"Gall-I" he tried to yell, but his throat was too dry, and the screams and chaos around him drowned his voice.

He struggled to his knees, but lost sight of them as Mer turned the street corner. A shimmer of light flashed for a second—and just like that, she had crossed over. He tried to stand, but the effort sent the world spinning, and he nearly blacked out.

"Jess," he shouted, though he doubted anyone heard him. Despair welled inside him as he pulled himself up against the tree he'd crashed into, but his legs gave out, and he collapsed again. This time, his mind went dark, and everything fell silent.

58

Chaos Realm

188Ch25 Year Week 14,
First day, Two Hours
Before Dawn

Tom hurried to the airship's far end as the sun rose on the horizon. According to Nik-el-28, they had found a man connected to tubes and wires from a CLEO system. Not knowing what to expect, Tom shouted for a doctor to come with him.

His chest felt as if a pile of rocks had been laid on it, threatening to crush his lungs, but that didn't stop him from dropping to the ground when, without a doubt, he recognized his old friend.

"Frank," he said, out of breath. "Can you hear me?"

A different doctor than the one who left with Marshall kneeled on the other side of Frank and checked his vitals. Frank still had a tube connected to his palm, but with no solution attached. The bleeding and bruising around his hand led Tom to suspect that Frank had either ripped it out or it had broken during the crash. His entire side was wet and darkened again, and his arm showed several burns through the torn sleeve.

"He's alive, however—" the doctor began, but Frank's eyes fluttering open stole his attention.

"Hey, man!" Tom said, sliding closer. "You had me worried here."

Frank's mouth moved, but no sound came out, and his breathing grew erratic.

"I'm going to sedate him," the doctor said and, without waiting for Tom's approval, injected something into Frank's arm. "We must take him to a hospital."

Tom turned to Coba. "How soon can we get him out of here?"

Coba pursed his lips and hesitated—a moment that felt like an eternity to Tom, especially as Frank coughed and blood spilled from his mouth.

"I can call back the car that just left," Coba said. "Ten minutes... maybe more."

"Do it," Tom ordered, then turned to the doctor. "He can't go to a hospital, though. We're not taking this fight to the city."

The doctor frowned and shook his head.

Tom's heart climbed to his throat, and although he feared what he would see, he looked back at Frank. His breathing remained labored, and somehow he had grown paler in just minutes.

"I need to stop the internal bleeding," the doctor said. "I have to evaluate what else is wrong. Our safe houses have equipment, but nothing as advanced as a hospital. I can guarantee he'll need at least one surgery."

Tom groaned and sank to the ground. He wanted to shout at the medic to fix his friend, but scaring him was the last thing he needed. Without Marshall, Tom wasn't confident in the Corrupts' loyalty toward him. He couldn't risk that.

A metal object brushing against his leg reminded him of the fob watch in his pocket. Frank didn't have a price on his head in Axiom. Tom pulled out the watch and stared at it. He could cross over and bring Frank to a hospital.

"Boss?" Coba said as he crouched beside him, his tone heavy with fear and concern.

For the first time, Coba called him *boss*, no sir, and the word landed on Tom's shoulders like the weight of every life under his responsibility.

Tom sighed and turned the watch over. The skyline of Chaos — full of hot-air balloons and strange buildings engraved on the silver — made him smile.

"My airship," he murmured.

"What was that, Boss?"

Tom turned to Coba and gripped his shoulders. "You told me our airship is ready if we need to escape."

Coba's eyes widened. "Yes, but we need it here. If we're attacked again, we need to get you out."

"That's my point!" Tom said, using Coba to pull himself up. "Everyone knows we'd only move that ship in an emergency. Coba, it's perfect."

Once on his feet, he reluctantly grabbed the crutch that had become his nemesis and leaned on it.

"We'll send Frank with this doctor and three—no, two—of our most trustworthy Corrupts."

Coba crossed his arms. "Nik-el-28 is a formidable pilot and would give her life for any of you, and Hafni is helping with the search."

"Yttri's sister?" Tom asked. "I didn't know she was working with Marshall. Can either of them protect—"

"Those two are as good as Mer," Coba interrupted with a faint smile. A moment later, a shadow crossed his expression and his gaze fell.

Tom placed a hand on his shoulder. "Then it's settled."

He turned to the doctor. "My ship has the same equipment Marshall's used to. That'll be enough. You'll leave with them and stay hidden until I say otherwise. Take as many medics as needed, but make sure they all understand my orders. No one leaves until I say so. Understood?"

He didn't consider himself as skilled as Marshall at intimidation, but the doctor's pale face and trembling hands suggested otherwise.

"Get moving!" Tom barked.

The doctor snapped out of his trance and began shouting instructions to nearby nurses.

Satisfied with his decision, Tom stepped away and explained his plan to Coba. "Randall will be looking for Marshall. It's a perfect distraction. If anyone's watching or talking, this will give them something to chase."

Coba nodded, his features relaxing again. "So you're setting a trap? Randall could just blow the airship like he did this one."

"He won't have that chance," Tom said. "Nik will be the only one who knows their destination. They'll stay hidden on the ground but change locations at my command — random days, random places."

"Why only them, Boss? It'd be safer with more of us."

Tom clenched his jaw. "I don't know how many Corrupts will stay loyal to me, Coba. Especially once they realize who's behind the attacks. Randall grew up with them. I didn't."

Coba threw up his hands and huffed. "No way, Boss! That photonic child killed our chief, and now he's trying to murder his brothers. We won't follow that traitor."

Tom gripped his shoulder again. "I know you won't, and neither will many others. But until I prove I can lead, some won't follow me. I can't risk Marshall or Frank's safety on that."

"If you say so, Boss." Coba shrugged and exhaled. "But you underestimate your followers. Still, it's a good plan to protect the chief. Hopefully, it won't get your friend killed."

Tom looked into the distance, avoiding Coba's eyes. He didn't want him to see the guilt eating away at his soul. He could only hope the Maker would have mercy on Frank.

59

Axiom Realm

After Mer left, Jess sneaked back and observed Randall's people before deciding whom to attack. She needed to choose someone insignificant, someone without rank. The last thing she wanted was for Randall to catch her because she couldn't answer a simple question. To avoid being left behind, she had to make herself relevant—and of comparable size.

She hadn't lied to Mer. Marshall's job wasn't her first role, though it had been the longest, and she'd worked undercover for many years. What she hadn't mentioned was the real problem: unlike her previous missions, she had almost no intel on her target, and she rarely had to assume an entirely new identity.

There was no choice, though. Randall needed to be stopped, and ignorance made that almost impossible.

In the end, she incapacitated a small guard responsible for rear surveillance. Strangely, the woman didn't even fight back.

Jess recognized her the moment she removed the helmet. She used to be one of Randall's party girls—one of the daughters of Chaos's elite families, not a Corrupts guard.

Most of the Corrupts had remained loyal to Marshall and his father. Everyone had heard of Randall killing Lezar, and most seemed relieved at the younger son's death. Apparently, society in Chaos had seized the chance to rise against the Corrupts' dictatorship. Once, when Jess first joined the Agency, she would have supported such rebellion—but not with Randall in charge.

Jess stole the uniform, tied and gagged the woman, and after a quick change, returned to the house to destroy the evidence. She made sure her dress, hat, and shoes burned to ash. The fact that the dress had been one of her mother's favorites was just a bitter bonus.

"Back now!" shouted one of Randall's guards, running toward the rear of the house.

Jess took a deep breath and followed them through the streets of Axiom. They ran several blocks before entering an abandoned lot. She expected to find a portal hidden in the yard or the house itself, but they continued into the woods behind it. Then she saw them: a fleet of small hot-air balloons waiting to depart.

Even though they weren't attached to the usual wire routes along the streets, Jess recognized them from Chaos's transportation system. As they boarded, her knees weakened and her breathing quickened. In the past few days, she had flown on Marshall's zeppelin and even climbed a building's emergency ladder—but this was different.

"Keep moving!" a guard yelled, shoving her aside before jumping into the basket.

Jess forced herself to keep walking, focusing on the basket's sturdy wooden floor—on the illusion of safety it promised. She tried to recall what Tom had once explained about her fear of heights, but her mind froze under the growing terror of leaving the ground.

She wasn't the last to climb, and the wait only worsened the trembling in her legs. The instant the basket lifted, Jess bit her lip and silently thanked the Maker for the loud noise and the helmet hiding her expression. She couldn't disguise her fear as the balloon rose above the trees and tilted away from the sector.

Jess knew little about flying—especially in hot-air balloons—but she understood the dangers of altitude. The higher they went, the stronger and more unpredictable the winds became. As the rooftops of Axiom shrank below, her heartbeat pounded so hard it drowned out every other sound, and sweat slicked her palms and brow.

For hours, she flew through Axiom, forcing herself to focus on Randall instead of her fear. She could have sworn he'd hidden in Chaos, yet they kept passing portals that could have taken them deep into its jungles—places no one would ever find.

Only when the balloon tilted downward and a strong scent of smoke and decay filled the air did she realize where they were headed. The truth struck her as the dark ruins of the Square appeared on the horizon. That place—unforgettable to both her and Randall—was the perfect hideout.

The fleet landed on a section of the collapsed bridge, and everyone walked toward the massive fallen doors of the old prison. For the first time in her life, Jess didn't feel safer with her feet on solid ground.

She lingered behind the group and slipped away as soon as they scattered. She wouldn't risk Randall recognizing the "elite girl" she'd knocked out.

As she descended, she noticed guards wearing the original Square uniforms. Upon finding the uniform storage room, she changed once again. Even without a helmet, she could lower the hat to obscure her face. Still, she kept the white helmet, carrying it in a sack over her shoulder—she might need an escape plan.

She took a deep breath and stepped into the hall.

Two men with shotguns slung over their shoulders were walking toward her, so she turned into the nearest corridor to avoid them. Her heart nearly stopped when her mind processed what she saw next.

From the first floor on the guards' side, she had a clear view of the lower level. Once the shipping deck for supplies and food, it was now lined with train wagons stretching as far as she could see. Their cargo made her grip the railing tighter.

Missiles—dozens of them—stacked in neat rows, their circular metal shells gleaming in the dim light. Barrels labeled *explosives* and wooden crates filled with shotguns and ammunition lined the walls, all waiting to be loaded.

Now she understood what Randall had been doing in Parcel 11. It wasn't his father's research—it was his weapons supply keeping him there.

A wave of cold rippled through her.

She had to inform Tom and Marshall—and someone in Axiom. After her last conversation with Marshall, she doubted he'd help her home realm, and she didn't trust Bill.

Jess exhaled slowly. She needed to uncover Randall's plan before she left the Square.

60

Chaos Realm 53

Tom rested his arms on the kitchen table, staring at the flowery tablecloth and his pocket watch. It had been over three days since they'd brought Marshall to Holm's house. The news from Axiom remained elusive, and he had been busy fending off Randall's attacks on Chaos. It was clear his little brother was searching for Marshall, and so far, Frank's decoy had worked. But Randall wasn't the only one hunting—Tom was determined to find him first.

He'd gone back to Parcel 11, certain he might have missed something during his earlier visits with Marshall. After all, that was where he and Jess had been attacked by Randall's people before the Disruption. Yet aside from the illegal cargo and storage train cars, he found nothing.

Randall had three years to erase his tracks—years of planning and waiting. By now, Tom had no idea whether this was still part of Karen's plan or his brother's own brand of revenge.

"Boss, I didn't realize you were back," Hafny said as she stepped out of Marshall's room. "I'll be ready in just a minute."

Ever since Coba changed his title, everyone had started calling him *Boss*. The word carried a weight Tom hadn't expected, and he couldn't help wondering if Marshall had felt the same after their father's death.

"You're staying here today," Tom said, running a hand through his hair.

Hafny nodded, but instead of leaving, she hesitated, then took a step closer.

"Is Marshall all right?" Tom asked, glancing up at her.

"Yes. Well... the same." She stopped beside the kitchen table, gripping the back of the second chair.

Tom leaned back and gestured for her to sit. She wasn't Yttri, but like her brother, she'd known the Corrupts a long time. If there was a problem, he trusted she'd say so. In the past few days, Tom had become painfully aware of his own inexperience.

"Is Frank...?" she began.

Earlier that day, Tom had visited his friend. He should have picked up Hafny and rotated her shift with Heli or Nik, but it was becoming too predictable, and he couldn't risk his routines being tracked.

"The same," Tom said.

So far, Frank had barely opened his eyes between mumbles of pain and delirium. Despite having a team of doctors and multiple surgeries, there'd been no improvement. The thought had begun to torment Tom—perhaps pain relief alone would be the kindest option. If their positions were reversed, he would have chosen that.

But despite the weight on his conscience, Tom had ordered more medicine and additional equipment. The decoy had to continue. The rumors needed to spread—Marshall's survival was essential for morale. So far, the Corrupts had stayed loyal, but if Marshall died, Tom wasn't sure how long that would last. And he still needed them to find Jess.

"I'm sorry, Boss," Hafny said softly. "I understand how hard it is to see the people we care about suffering... dying."

Tom nodded, wishing there was a drink—or several—in front of him.

"Umm... Boss?"

The hesitation in her voice made him tense, but he didn't press her. Instead, he waited.

"It could be nothing, but..." She lowered her gaze, fidgeting with her fingers. "The girl with Marshall. She told me he saved her life. She said she didn't know why, since he didn't really know her."

Tom groaned and rubbed his face. He'd been wondering about that, too. Although she wasn't unattractive, he doubted Marshall's strange behavior had anything to do with her looks. His brother could have any woman he wanted. And Lucille's reaction to Jess's undercover work had made it hard for Tom to feel any sympathy toward her.

"That's what she told me," Tom said. "Though it's not what I'd expect from Marshall."

"It doesn't seem like him," Hafny agreed. "It's just... probably nothing but..."

Tom leaned forward. "Hafny?"

She hesitated, biting her lip as she chose her words. "The day I met you, I thought—well, we all assumed Jess and Marshall—"

"You didn't like me very much," Tom said, half-smiling. "I got your message that day."

"I'm so sorry, Boss." Her face went pale. "I didn't know the truth then, and the chief was the only son—"

Tom patted her hand and smiled faintly. "It's all right, Hafny. If anything, it shows how loyal you are. I just don't see what this has to do with Lucille."

Hafny took a steadying breath. "It might not mean much, but I wanted to remind you—I'm not the best judge of character."

Tom's expression grew serious again.

"She doesn't look much like my Darmy, but..." Hafny exhaled slowly. "I'm not sure if the chief ever told you about my sister. She and Marshall..." Her voice cracked, and she took a moment to wipe her eyes. "She got hurt in a terrible accident and didn't make it. Even though he didn't know she was there during the attack, the chief still blamed himself. Yttri blamed himself for not stopping her. He always took his role as her big brother seriously."

A chill ran down Tom's spine as he wondered where this was heading.

"Darmy mended things between the chief and my brother." Hafny met his gaze. "She made them promise to work together—to protect each other, instead..."

Tom waited a few seconds, then prompted, "Instead of what?"

She shook her head and began fidgeting again. "Instead of killing each other. My brother once fought against the Corrupts with everything he had. You could say he was Marshall's Bill."

Tom shifted in his seat. If Marshall hadn't mentioned Darmy before, he might not have believed it.

"Let's go back to Lucille," Tom said. "You don't think she looks like your sister?"

Hafny gave a small, sad smile. "Not really. Her hair is a little similar, but it's not her looks, Boss. It's the way she talks, the way she acts... her innocence, her ignorance of all this. She reminds me of Darmy. And if what Lucille told us is true, I think Marshall sees that too."

Tom frowned. "You don't think Yttri will approve?"

Hafny sighed and nodded. "I mentioned it to him—the resemblance—and he lost it, Boss." She leaned closer, lowering her voice. "I'm not sure what might happen if Marshall starts something with this girl. In the past, it never mattered. The chief's had plenty of lovers, and Yttri didn't care. But this one... this one's different."

Tom's expression darkened. He could easily picture Yttri becoming a dangerous enemy. "I'll keep an eye on them, Hafny."

"Like I said," she added quickly, "I could be wrong. I'm not saying my brother is—or will be—a threat, but—"

Tom grasped her hand and met her eyes. "I'll watch them closely and tell you if I notice anything. And if I do, I'll keep Yttri with me. I still need to find Jess, and he's one of her biggest supporters. That's a good enough excuse."

Hafny squeezed his hand, then stood and quietly left him alone in the kitchen.

T OM LOOKED AROUND AND smiled as he remembered Jess preparing a horrible potion before sitting at the table in front of him. Too fast, reality hit, and his brief happiness vanished. Time changed things. That kitchen had also witnessed him fighting Holm.

The old man had hated his ideas about the Barrier. Shouting about his experience and knowledge, he'd criticized Tom's immaturity and called him ignorant.

Tom clenched his fist as he recalled the fight. He wasn't a child anymore, and no one was going to make him feel inferior. At some point Phoebe had stepped in front of Holm. When he saw her fearful expression and heard her beg him to stop, Tom made up his mind.

Instead of jumping out the window, he left the house through the door—something only Holm used to do. Tom wanted to show everyone he wasn't afraid of Chaos and that, like Holm, he could defy that realm's rules.

He didn't have a plan, though. He only wanted to disappear. Marshall found him, and with nothing to lose, Tom joined his brother. At the time he had no idea he was about to find a family. After his grandfather died, he'd assumed that part of his life was gone. His grandfather wouldn't have approved of his new life, but Tom learned rules and codes weren't as black-and-white as people thought.

Yttri walked out of the room, bringing Tom's attention back to the present. Just before he asked about Marshall, he heard steel stairs creak as someone climbed. Dragging his recovering leg, he moved to the other side of the window and, right before he drew his gun, a double knock on the ladder followed by a hard hit and a soft tap eased his breathing. They had established that code to prevent accidental deaths from friendly fire.

A few seconds later Millie climbed through the window. He helped her in and gave her a moment to catch her breath. After they'd cleared the crash site and Tom had checked on Marshall, he found Millie with Heli-3. His tracker had explained how she'd been in charge of finding Phoebe while Peter and Jess crossed over to Axiom.

Much to Tom's surprise, she neither resented nor blamed him for the Disruption. In fact, she thanked him for saving her life and agreed to help gather news from the other realm. She was looking for Peter, who'd been with Jess.

"No good news, Tom," Millie said, taking a seat on the couch. "Darius is still in the hospital, and no one's talking. Bill's been working with Arlett's father to contain the panic. He's redirecting all blame for Darius's decision to close the Agency. So far, they blame the Corrupts for the air attack and the fire in Sector 15. They're saying the attacks in Main City and Sector 8 were the result of Darius's irrational decisions, his ties to illegal business, and the Agency's retaliation. Lots of people talk about attacking Chaos, but I guess they'll keep blaming Darius so Axiom can avoid war."

"There's no way Bill can afford a war!" Tom crossed his arms and frowned. "Do you think Bill will continue Darius's plans for the Agency?"

"Doubt it," Millie said, resting her elbows on her knees. "Apparently, during the attack at Darius's house, agents in white uniforms were reported shooting Darius's guards. I don't think

Bill will test the loyalty of the former agents, but I haven't heard anything about the Agency being reinstated."

"Typical Bill," Tom said. "He's happy to give the Agency someone to blame so his hands stay clean. Do you think the Agency will rise against Axiom's government?"

Millie sighed. "Hard to tell. All the reports say the agents attacking Darius's guards wore white uniforms with helmets and goggles. Only Research wears white, Tom—and only for studies around the wave."

"Research?" Tom murmured, glancing at Yttri. "Randall had access to the research building through that tunnel. I bet those were his men attacking Darius."

Yttri pulled a pocketknife from his back pocket and tested the blade.

"We'll get him," Tom said, surprised at how simply the plan had formed. "Anything else, Millie?"

She shook her head and leaned back on the couch. He had countless questions, but Peter was missing too, and if anyone could understand Millie's despair, it was Tom.

He touched her shoulder, but a tiny squeak at the window caught his attention. A second later, someone climbed the ladder's last step.

Tom reached out and grabbed the newcomer by the hair. As he pulled back, he realized it was a man. He seized him by the shoulder, dragged him into the room, and pinned him against the wall with his forearm at the man's neck.

"Stop!" Millie cried as the apartment light fell on Peter's face.

Tom didn't release his hold. The effort left him breathless, but he used his weight against Peter. The former agent looked pale; blood rimmed his eyes. Though Peter's hands pressed against Tom's arm, he wasn't strong enough to push him off—despite Tom's injured leg.

"Tom, please!" Millie pleaded. Her voice made him take a step back, but he didn't let go of Peter.

"How the hell did you find us?" Tom demanded.

Peter cleared his throat and tried to control his ragged breathing. "I didn't know you were here... I came back to Holm's house. I didn't know you were here."

Peter nearly collapsed when Tom released him. Millie didn't hesitate and rushed to embrace him.

"Where is Jess?" Tom's chest tightened and his fists clenched at his sides.

"Jess..." Peter's voice caught; he clung to Millie as his vision blurred. "I lost her."

Tom stepped forward, ready to kill him if he had to, but Yttri grabbed his shoulder and pulled him back slightly.

"This son of the void took her with him," Tom shouted at Yttri. "You can expect me to leave—"

"She was in Darius's house when..." Peter began, and this time Millie stepped back. "We had a plan," he said, looking at her. "I gathered a few agents and we waited for her signal. A window blew out and I knew it was her. But when we moved in, a missile hit the property edge, and I'm not sure what happened. There was a car. They took Bill and Darius—also Arlett. A missile hit them as they escaped, and another car arrived." He turned to Tom. "I recognized her even from a distance. Those other people took Charlotte—she's pregnant. The second they were out, a missile destroyed the house."

"I don't give a photon about Charlotte or her life," Tom said. Lowering his voice, he asked, "What about Jess?"

Peter looked at the floor and went silent. Tom had expected to beat or shoot Peter for abandoning Jess again—treat him like he'd treated Bill in the hospital. Unlike Dan, Yttri would not intervene. Rage tightened Tom's muscles and the authority he held as leader made his threat real.

"You'll pay for abandoning her again."

Yttri stepped toward Peter, who shoved Millie behind him. "I saw Mer. She took Gall-I out of the mansion and crossed over. I know she did. I saw the light from the portal. She has to know what happened to Jess...and Gall-I. You took my sister. Where is she?"

"I should kill her," Tom said. "After taking my time to make sure her screams are engraved in your memory, of course."

"Tom," Millie said, moving to the side. "We'll find Jess."

"Where is Mer?" Peter demanded. "She must know—"

"Mer is dead," Gall-I answered in a weak voice as she emerged from Holm's office. Dark circles shadowed her eyes and bruises marked her face. Leaning on the wall for support, she approached, clutching her side. Tom knew the pain: in the Square he'd had ribs broken more than once.

"And Phoebe too," she whispered.

Peter rushed to her and brushed her cheek before pulling her into an embrace.

Tom only needed to give one word, and Yttri would have taken Gall-I away and killed her. He wanted to make the coward suffer, but he knew Jess wouldn't forgive him—and neither Gall-I nor Millie deserved that. Before doing anything he might regret, he grabbed a cane from the wall and walked out onto the roof.

He climbed to the top and let the cold air clear his head. In the last few days Randall had attacked Chaos multiple times. The horizon was now a permanent blur of smoke and fire. The government had neither the power nor the authority to protect its people. The bustling, vibrant cities had become somber, quiet places, bracing for the worst.

"Boss?" Heli called, catching Tom's attention. "Sorry to interrupt, but you may want to hear the rest of what that traitor said."

Tom sighed and said nothing; Heli continued. "The guy got the official report from Bill's office. Apparently they named him the pro-temp Agency director." Heli frowned. "He just told us it was Jess's idea to gather the former agents, but he got a title and everything."

Tom's jaw tightened; Heli hurried on. "Anyway, the officers found only one body in Darius's house. Yeah, totally believable. How stupid are those Axiom people?"

"Heli," Tom said in a controlled voice.

"Sorry, boss! Sorry. The body was an older male with no identification. The official report identifies him as a Chaos invader. Peter believes they'll use him to claim he planted bombs and blew up the two houses."

"A Chaos invader?" Tom scoffed. "The lies Bill fabricates are beyond—"

"Boss, the point is they found no females. Jess must be alive."

Tom's heartbeat quickened as he stared at the city burning on the horizon. "If we can believe their words." He shook his head. "If she is alive, Heli…"

"We'll find her, boss. We will."

61

Axiom Sea Periphery

188Ch25 Year Week 17,
Third day, Night

Jess's heart climbed into her throat, and for the first time in her life, it had nothing to do with the height as the airship descended toward the rooftop. Her hands trembled and her knees shook, but she doubted it was because of the cold air hitting her face. She had to thank that cold for keeping her eyes dry.

Less than a week ago, she had woken in a room warmed by sunlight. As her eyes adjusted, she picked up on a steady beeping beside her and a faint rocking motion in the bed. The scent of old metal and hard work reached her before she saw Tom sitting next to her.

His severe gaze reminded her of everything that had happened, and the sharp pain in her side confirmed it hadn't been a dream.

The blade pushing into her abdomen was a sensation she would never forget. The metal had created a gentle pressure that made her look down, where she'd seen the knife's handle—but not the blade. Before her knees gave out, she'd understood the damage. A second later, her insides felt as if they were being ripped apart. She remembered being so cold in the water, but at least that cold had numbed her.

"Tom," she said.

Saying his name dried her throat and stole what little breath she had. As his grip tightened, she realized the warmth in her hand was his.

"You need to rest," he said. It sounded like an order, stripped of kindness.

Jess cleared her throat, but Tom shook his head.

"Don't, Jess."

He let go of her hand. The sudden cold made her shiver and brought tears to her eyes.

"No, you can't—" he said. "I get that you were undercover and it was the only choice, and Mer was supposed to tell me..." He sighed. "Do you have any idea? Of course not. You can't understand what it would have done to me, you dying like this." He pushed his hair back and rubbed his face, and after a few seconds of fidgeting with his hands, he just crossed his arms. "What were you thinking, Jessica? You had to know I was trying to kill that son of the void. Why would you jump—"

"Stop," Jess said, trying to contain her tears and control her breathing. "Please, Tom."

He went quiet, staring at her. His expression reminded Jess of the time they'd talked in the Square. The CLEO machine beeped faster and a few lights flared, responding to her racing heart.

Tom started to stand, but Jess's hand brushed his, and he looked back at her.

"I couldn't stand by and let him take your life," she said, relief washing over her when he sat down again. "He was going to kill you. I had to do something."

"Do you remember that silly children's legend about our world being founded in magic, and that knife story?"

"A children's legend... You mean a saber?"

"Same thing..." He shook his head. "I wouldn't have done it."

"What do you mean?"

He held her gaze for a moment. "If I'd been that soldier, I would have fled with the witch and let the world burn."

"The wizard? You mean the girl—"

"You know who I mean." He looked down at the bed. "I never thought much about it before. Silly legend. Overdramatic story. But now... now I get it. There's no way in this realm or the other that I could do that. I'd never forget the sensation of my knife and... when I saw you..."

He took her hand again but avoided her eyes.

"It was my fault, Tom. I was the one who put myself between you and the knife."

He pulled his chair closer and leaned toward her. Now she noticed the dark circles under his eyes, the beard that had become more than just stubble, and a deep sadness that seemed to keep him from ever smiling.

"I wasn't going to let him kill me," he said, trying to joke, but when Jess didn't smile, he brushed the hair off her forehead. "You told me you talked to Mer?"

Jess nodded. "I had to follow Randall, Tom. He had the logbook, and he killed—" Her voice broke as the memory of Holm surfaced. "He killed Holm and Phoebe, and he targeted you in Main City, and he had an arsenal in the Square. I don't know where he—"

"Shh..." Tom touched her cheek. "I'm sorry about Holm. We weren't sure about him, but Coba found Phoebe. I'm so sorry about her, too."

Jess tried to dry her eyes, but a tube connected to the vein in her arm blocked the movement.

Tom kissed her other hand, but when she looked at him, he was staring past her, and the cruelty in his eyes sent a shiver down her spine.

"I got this, sunshine. I'm going to stop him and make him pay for everything."

The tone in his voice planted a deep fear in Jess's soul. Not fear of him—but fear of losing him.

"Tom, he isn't worth—"

"He attacked my people." Tom leaned back and focused on her again. "He destroyed Marshall's airship and has been attacking our cities. Chaos isn't what it used to be, thanks to that man. He's been killing everyone in his way, and he dared to lie—said he had you and was going to teach me not to mess with his family. My family, Jess. And you, the most important one. I won't tolerate anyone endangering my people. Especially you."

"But he didn't have me." Jess tried to sit up, but her head spun and forced her back down. For a moment she had to close her eyes to ease the wave of nausea. When she opened them, Tom was right at her side again.

"I would have left the Square if I'd known he said that to you," she said. "I first heard your name when you attacked the Square. How did you find him?"

Tom smiled. "Randall isn't very creative. The fire in Sector 15 made little sense until Mer told me he was alive. Then I knew he wanted to clear the Square's surroundings. The place was a nightmare, but we learned a lot."

"I figured a few things about his plan..." she began, but stopped when Tom pressed his lips together. "I can help you," she whispered.

"I need you safe, sunshine."

Jess's muscles tensed, and CLEO's beeps sped up again.

He cupped her cheek. "Jess, my world isn't the same. The Corrupts have faced weeks of attacks. There's no safe place for us, and I won't risk having you here."

Jess shook her head, but Tom didn't let her speak.

"If my people were safe, or if you didn't need to recover, I wouldn't leave you. But Jess, even though you're better, you're still in danger." He brushed her hair back, avoiding her eyes for a second. "Remember what you told me about crossing over? You're right. I must have died, or come very close, when I crashed into the Barrier. And if Randall escaped through an underwater portal, he went through something similar. But Jess, I spent almost a month in the hospital and another two weeks in the Containment Clinic before they sent me to the Square."

"I'm fine, Tom."

He leaned back and rubbed his neck. "No, Jess, you aren't. The only reason you survived is because we crossed over. And I need you to recover somewhere I know you'll be safe—which is away from here. For now."

Tom had then explained his plan. How he had to reach out to Dan, because it was the safest place for her now.

Apparently, the Axiom government had accused Darius of the attacks in Main City and Sector 15. Some agents had rebelled against him and accused him of genocide after revealing his order to stop any Chaos native from escaping the fire. Peter, the new director of the re-instituted Agency, was among them.

Arlett's father needed to protect his investments and was working to salvage Bill's reputation and distance him from the attacks. That made Tom's offer impossible to resist.

In exchange for leaving Jess alone, Tom had taken full responsibility for the attacks on Main City and Sector 8. He declared that he had done it because Bill took his wife and needed to learn a lesson. It diverted attention from Bill and elevated him to the status of savior. Once again, Tom claimed the position of Axiom's most wanted man.

Rumor now said that Tom's pregnant wife had gone missing during the attack on Darius's house and hadn't been seen since. Of course, Tom had no comments about that.

Now, four days after that conversation, Tom's airship landed on the rooftop.

Jess felt Tom's hand tighten around hers as he approached. "You could have waited inside," he said.

She couldn't bring herself to meet his eyes. Instead, she held on to his hand as they walked toward the step ladder one of Tom's men was setting up.

Time seemed to move faster, as if she were leaping between seconds. Once she stepped onto the roof, she heard her mom rushing toward her and, without caring, she hugged her.

"I thought you were dead," her mother said through tears.

"Amelia," Dan said, pulling her back. "Jess is injured. You need to—"

"Of course!" Her mom wiped her eyes and stepped away. "I'm sorry, sweetie. I have everything ready for you."

Jess took a deep breath, but her feet refused to move. Behind her, the airship's engine powered up and the wind picked up, but she didn't turn around. Not until Tom gently pulled her arm, forcing her to face him.

He brushed her cheek and brought her hand toward him.

"Here," he said, placing a silver pocket watch in her palm. "This is my key. If you're in danger, use it. I'll know—and I'll find you."

He glanced at her mom and Dan, and his voice darkened.

"Just remember, this is temporary. As soon as I can, I'll be back to pick up my wife."

"Your wife?" Amelia harrumphed. "How dare you? Just because of a piece of paper you had no right to—You're a monster I should never have invited into—"

"Enough," Dan said, mimicking Tom's tone and startling Jess. "We talked about this. Tom is helping your family, Amelia. You might as well be grateful."

"But she isn't married to this—" Amelia covered her face, shaking her head. "She can't..."

"It is a promise, Jess." Tom ignored her mother, closing Jess's fingers around the watch and pulling her closer. "I wouldn't leave you if I had another option. Please understand that, sunshine."

Jess exhaled, knowing he was right, but she felt more exhausted than ever. The prospect of living with her mom, and without Tom again, left her with very little will to keep going.

Tom kissed her forehead and walked back to the airship. Behind her, she felt Dan's arm wrap around her, and as the ship ascended, her world fell apart.

62

EPILOGUE

TOM KEPT STARING INTO the distance from the navigation room's window. It didn't matter that they were already back in Chaos and that Sector 8 was impossible to spot under the realm's hazy horizon. He knew Jess wasn't happy with his decision—and he hated it too—but it was the only way to keep her safe. After what he had just done in the Square, he had discovered his real fear. His life in that prison couldn't compare to what he'd gone through in the last few days.

"Are you sure about this?" Marshall asked, sitting in the far corner with a serious expression.

Tom hoped his bad mood had more to do with the smaller, less luxurious room—very different from what Marshall was used to traveling in—than with his poor health or his growing desire for revenge.

"It took her five days to wake up, Marshall," Tom said. "I almost killed her. Amelia is right—I'm a monster, and she should've never let me into their home."

Marshall shifted in his seat, brushing Yttri away when he tried to help him get comfortable. "You also saved her life. More than once."

Tom rolled his eyes but didn't argue. Marshall wasn't in much better shape than Jess. The only difference was that Tom couldn't leave his brother anywhere. They had too many enemies and too many potential traitors, and Randall's actions had already sown doubts among some of their allies.

His brother was alive only because Tom had taken him along to attack the prison. He had wanted Marshall to get Randall—and accidentally, he'd saved his life. Holm's apartment had been attacked right after they left for the Square.

"Boss," Heli-3 said from the doorway. "We're getting a transmission. There's movement in the woods near Elemental 6."

Tom glanced at Marshall. The fresh scar cutting from his forehead down his cheek, along with the burn marks scattered across his face, made his expression seem even harsher—though his tone stayed calm.

"I suppose it's time to find some answers." Marshall rested his elbow on the arm of his chair and leaned into it, frowning. Tom couldn't tell if it was the sickly color in his brother's face or the absence of his usual confidence that made it so uncomfortable to watch him now.

According to the doctor, it was uncertain whether Marshall's leg would ever heal completely. He might walk again, but it would be painful, and recovery would take a long time—especially since he wasn't taking rest seriously and never did his exercises.

"We could keep working on the logbook," Tom said, leaning against his desk and crossing his arms. "All those papers must be hiding something."

Tom's own health wasn't much better. His heart condition had worsened after rescuing Jess, and the doctor had warned him about the permanent damage and the danger of any strenuous activity.

"Are you telling me you want to read?" Marshall smiled, teasing him about his dyslexia. The jab didn't bother Tom. Marshall's confession—that he'd always known about it and had hoped Tom could decode their father's notes—was probably the only positive thing he'd taken from all of this. He actually felt comfortable talking about it with him, just as he once had with his grandfather and Jess.

Tom looked up as the office door opened. Lucille peeked inside, and Hafny's warning made sense the moment Yttri took a step back and his expression hardened. If Marshall noticed, he showed no sign of it—he just smiled at her.

Tom still had questions about the woman. Beyond her awkward explanation that Marshall had saved her from the explosion in the airship, she had said nothing significant. Still, she'd taken it upon herself to care for him.

Marshall had offered no explanations, and Tom hadn't had the chance to ask. But every time Lucille was in the room, Marshall smiled. To prevent any further issues, Tom had requested Yttri's presence more often.

"Sorry," Lucille said, and when Tom didn't stop her, she stepped inside. "I thought you'd want to know that Gall-I just arrived."

Tom nodded and turned back to his pilot, Coba. "Set the course for High City."

"High City?" Marshall asked, accepting Lucille's help to stand. "Elemental 6 sounds more productive."

"It does," Tom said. "But we need more equipment, information, and people. We lost too many during the last trip to the Square. My bet."

Marshall paused, and with Lucille's help, turned to face him. "You had to save her," he said. "Whether she needed it or not doesn't matter. If you'd abandoned her, more of our people would've turned against you. You are your word, and your family. We don't betray either."

Tom understood, but the guilt of losing so many people on what now felt like a reckless rescue weighed heavily on him.

"Tom," Marshall continued, "those who died did so for what they believed in. The traitors have no place among the Corrupts. I'd rather know who's with me—then I can make sure the rest will learn from their mistakes."

Tom rubbed his face as he watched his brother leave the room.

"He's right, Boss," Coba said. "We lost a few good friends, but we cleared out all the whiners. We'll gather better people now—like your friend Frank. He's improving, and like him, we're all ready to get even."

Coba's smile was both encouraging and unsettling. Tom patted his shoulder.

"Even isn't what I'm after, Coba." Tom turned back to the view outside, where towers of smoke and distant fires marred his adopted realm. "I want revenge. Bloody, painful revenge."

Book 3 EXCERPT:

J ESS REMAINED SEATED IN the study chair, staring at Peter, trying to make sense of his offer. Trust had become a rare commodity for her—especially when things sounded too good.

"You want me to lead your research team?" she repeated, watching his hands fidget with the back of the chair while his eyes stayed fixed on the intricate engraving of the carpet.

"Well, you're my best option." He stepped back and looked out the window. "Our realm has to return to normality, but we need to address many issues first. Starting with research just makes sense."

Jess chuckled, leaning back against the couch when he looked at her.

"You want to fix many issues? Peter, for years you heard me talk to Holm about my beliefs. Not once did you seem to care. And—" she lifted a finger, raising her voice—"since you became the Agency's director, you haven't mentioned the need for a research team. And you've been very busy. Moving the Agency quarters here. Turning the main building into a prison. Just to name a few." She narrowed her eyes. "What are you up to, Peter?"

Peter's shoulders slumped. He shook his head. "I told your mother this wouldn't work out."

That wasn't what Jess had expected.

"My mother?" Her tone rose despite herself.

"Yes, your mother." Peter moved closer and sat across from her. "And to be honest—after listening to her and..." he gestured toward Jess, "...seeing you—I'm worried too. This isn't you."

Jess stiffened.

"I've never seen you wearing so many layers," he went on. "You look good, don't get me wrong. But you're... guarded. Polite."

"Polite?" Jess echoed flatly. "I didn't realize I was rude."

"Jess." Peter ran a hand through his hair. "This socially acceptable version of you isn't you. You belong in the Agency. Fighting for what you believe in. Don't let that photonic Corrupt change who you are."

Anger sparked—sharp and immediate.

"No one is changing me," she said, locking eyes with him. "For years I fought for a cause that was a lie. When everything fell apart, I kept helping while the rest of you pretended nothing was wrong. Including you."

Peter's voice softened. "I'm worried about you."

"And as long as your concern works for your agenda," Jess shot back, "why not."

"I don't have—" Peter stopped, hesitated, then shook his head. His tone lowered. "There are... other things going on," he said carefully. "Things I don't like."

Jess's gaze sharpened. "Such as?"

Peter lowered his voice. "Darius."

Jess didn't blink. "What about him?"

"He's had visitors," Peter said. "Someone with special clearance. Not staff. Not legal counsel. A woman."

Find Here

I N CASE YOU HAVEN'T read it yet, you can discover how everything started with a special bonus chapter and an exclusive Secret Dossier—waiting for you here.

63

GLOSARY

Disruption, tragic incident with the Barrier that occurred on 188A22 Year Week 18, First Day. The automobile accident resulted in a collision between Chaos and Axiom, where sections of the real collapse into each other, causing significant damage in terms of hundreds of injuries, several fatalities, and millions of dollars in economic losses.

Congress's annual dinner, the most pivotal event in Axiom due to its gathering of all Congress members. The annual dinner in Axiom brings together all members of the Congress - including activists, reactors, and passives - to showcase their yearly progress and propose initiatives for the upcoming year. Attendance to the event is restricted to prestigious Elite Social families, although a handful of Chaos members have also been graciously included to contribute to the noble cause of fostering harmony in the realms.

Light System; a system that serves as the principal mode of communication between realms, utilizing a set of lights that operate on Morse Code, as the transmission of sound through portals is unattainable.

Radicals, a collective of predominantly Axiom natives that emerged following the Disruption, with the primary objective of regaining control over their Realm and restoring access to water. Two separate groups can be identified: one group supports the reconstruction of the sections damaged by the Disruption, rather than their abandonment, while the other, more aggressive faction opposes the government.

Takuosums; native mammal with extremely strong front limbs and claws, which allow them to burrow quickly with great power. It has a fur coat and a toxic array of spines. Capable of surviving in subterranean areas and a remarkable resilience to high oxygen concentrations but a limited resistance to light. An encounter with these creatures can be deadly due to their behavioral pattern of hunting in large groups, isolating their target and using poison to subdue and finally immobilize it. It is mandatory to report them when found in cities or transportation systems. Aggression level: 4 out 5.

Hyaerodea, a carnivorous mammal that relies on scavenging carrion, yet is extremely dangerous when it comes to protecting their territory. These creatures are characterized by long skulls, slender jaws, cone-shaped teeth, slim builds, and a plantigrade stance. Posses little to no capability to adjust to any sources of light. They could be located in all parts of Chaos, especially in locations with poor hygiene in cities. Aggression level: 5 out 5.

Remedy, an archaic phrase used in Chaos to describe a concoction of antibiotics, probiotics, and antidotes to increase the tolerance to the high levels of oxygen and other toxins within the domain.

CLEO, centralized panel utilized to guide the mechanical bugs in employing supplemental drugs, medications and electrical treatments to those in critical condition.

Aracnpoda, a class of joint-legged invertebrate animals with eight legs, possesses a front pair of legs that have sensory functions. This species does not rely on poison, instead it traps its prey with a sticky thread. It typically resides in humid, dark places and is commonly found as a co-habitant of other species, where it nests beneath its host's skin and nourishes itself with its host's blood. If signs of infection are present, medical attention should be sought out immediately. Aggression level: 2 out 5.

Ophidents; poisonous creeping reptiles. It inhabits the wooded regions of the Chaos and Axiom meadows, particularly near the Barrier. Poisoning by this creature ranges from severe to fatal. An annual protective antidote is required for those who work or live in these areas. Aggression level: 5 out 5.

Figure 1. Marshall's Airship

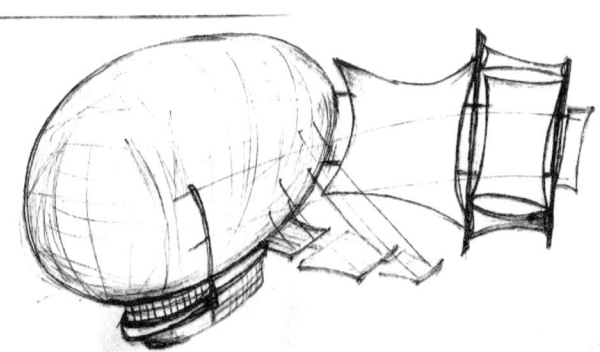

Figure 2. Tom's Airship

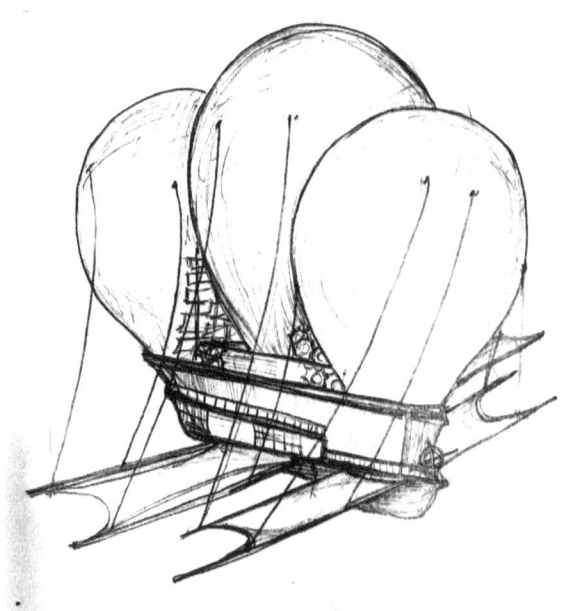

It takes a village to raise a child... and to write a book.

First and foremost, I want to express my gratitude to you, dear reader, for being a part of this journey. Thanks for coming back and sticking with me in this series. I hope you have as much fun reading it as I do writing it.

Over the years, I've had the privilege of meeting incredible individuals who provided guidance in writing, editing, and publishing, but their support and encouragement meant the most. Hayley Millman because of her amazing writing lessons and how the concept of this series came to life during one of her writing exercises. Bryan Cohen and the Ad School crew, for their amazing commitment to help authors like me to succeed. My editor from First Editing, Michael, and my cover designers from 100 Covers, especially Jaime. Teddy, for all the random interruptions and Josephine for the fantastic ideas, countless visits to bookstores and libraries, and our conversations which kept this book going.

And of course, You up there...